BLACK MEDEA

Black Medea

Adaptations for Modern Plays

EDITED BY

KEVIN J. WETMORE, Jr.

Cambria Contemporary
Global Performing Arts Series
(General Editor: John M. Clum)

CAMBRIA
PRESS

Amherst, New York

Requests for permission should be directed to:
permissions@cambriapress.com, or mailed to:
Cambria Press
University Corporate Centre, 100 Corporate Parkway, Suite 128
Amherst, NY 14226

Library of Congress Cataloging-in-Publication Data

Black Medeas / edited by Kevin J. Wetmore, Jr.
p. cm. (Cambria studies in contemporary global performing arts series)
Includes bibliographical references and index.
ISBN 978-1-60497-865-0 (alk. paper)
1. Medea (Greek mythology)--Drama. [1. Euripides. Medea.--
Adaptations.] I. Wetmore, Kevin J., 1969- editor of compilation.

PA3973.M4W48 2013
882'.01--dc23

2013037561

To Kiki Gounaridou and Joel Tansey,
with admiration and friendship

TABLE OF CONTENTS

Acknowledgments.. ix

Introduction: Medea the Outsider/ Medea as a Woman of
    Color.. 1

Chapter 1: *African Medea*.. 15

Play 1: *African Medea*.. 19

Interview 1: An Interview with Jim Magnuson.......................... 67

Chapter 2: *Black Medea*... 71

Play 2: *Black Medea*.. 75

Interview 2: An Interview with Father Ernest Ferlita, SJ.............. 123

Chapter 3: *Pecong*.. 127

Play 3: *Pecong*... 131

Interview 3: An Interview with Steve Carter........................... 219

Chapter 4: *There Are Women Waiting The Tragedy of Medea*
    Jackson... 223

Play 4: *There Are Women Waiting The Tragedy of Medea*
    Jackson... 227

Chapter 5: *American Medea*... 241

Play 5: *American Medea*... 245

Interview 4: An Interview with Silas Jones............................ 289

Chapter 6: *Medea, Queen of Colchester*................................ 293

Play 6: *Medea, Queen of Colchester*.................................. 297

Interview 5: An Interview with Marianne McDonald.................. 335

Bibliography.. 339

Index.. 341

ACKNOWLEDGMENTS

An anthology is always the work of many hands, but this volume would have been impossible without the contributions and support of a large number of individuals and institutions, to which I am truly grateful.

Thanks to the playwrights for their generosity with material, time and insights: Father Ernest Ferlita, S.J., Steve Carter, Jim Magnuson, Marianne McDonald, Silas Jones, and Edris Cooper. Thanks as well to Rhodessa Jones, Paul Kuritz, and Kiki Gounaridou for their instruction, inspiration and work. Thanks to Daniel Banks for the same.

Thanks to John Clum, Toni Tan, and the good folks at Cambria Press. Thanks as well to the anonymous readers for the suggestions to improve the volume. Thanks to Ed Krieger for the use of the cover photo.

Thanks to my assistant Brianna Berlen, who aided greatly in putting together the play texts. Thanks to Loyola Marymount University, William H. Hannon Library, College of Communication and Fine Arts, the Department of Theatre Arts and Dance, my colleagues, especially Katharine Free, Anna-Krajewska-Wieczorek, Matthew Dillon, and Kelly Younger.

Thanks to the Comparative Drama Conference–affiliated classical scholars for their inspiration, scholarship, influence and friendship: Karelisa Hartigan, Helen Moritz, Mary Kay Gamel, Gonda van Steen, Stratos Constantinidis, Michael Ewans, J. Michael Walton, Helene Foley, and Liz Scharffenberger. Thanks to the University of Pittsburgh, where I first began my studies of Afrocentric Greek tragedy and to Buck Favorini and Dennis Brutus.

Thanks to my family: Kevin Sr., Eleanor, Nemo, Lisa, John, Sean, Tom, Eileen and Toni.

As always, eternal gratitude for love and support goes to Lacy Wetmore, without whom none of this would have been possible.

BLACK MEDEA

MEDEA THE OUTSIDER/ MEDEA AS A WOMAN OF COLOR

In 431 B.C.E., Euripides's *Medea*, along with the rest of the tetralogy that did not survive—*Philoctetes, Dictys,* and the satyr play *Reapers*—won third prize behind plays by Sophocles and Euphorion (Aeschylus's nephew). In other words, it came in last. Almost a century later, Aristotle, in *Poetics* singles out the scene in which Medea secures sanctuary in Athens in exchange for curing Aegeus's childlessness as unsatisfactory and an example of inferior playwriting.[1] It was an inauspicious beginning for a drama that has become one of the most popular Greek tragedies in the last hundred years.[2]

Euripides's play is a rather straightforward example of Greek tragedy in its dramaturgy: stage time equals real time and employs a single location. Before the introduction of her character, the audience learns of Medea and her fate as handed down by Creon, king of Corinth. The play depicts the final two hours of her life in that city. Jason and Medea have been living in exile in Corinth when Creon decides to have Jason marry his daughter. In order to do so, he must divorce Medea and send her away, which he readily agrees to do. Medea, who by Greek law would go back to her father's house in the event of a divorce, may not do so, not only because of the distance involved but because she killed and dismembered her brother the crown prince in order to aid Jason's escape with the Golden Fleece. Medea is now without home and without family, city, or any community. She begins the play as a completely disenfranchised being. She thus has multiple motives for her actions: Jason breaks the oath he gave to her when she helped him get the Golden Fleece; he fails to value her contributions to his successes; and even though she has given him two male children (a very important contribution in patriarchal Greece), he is divorcing her so he might marry another and become king of Corinth in time. His arguments to her when she debates these points is that she is a barbarian; that he rescued her from her land and brought her to Greece so she might know true civilization. Medea is angry, wronged in multiple ways, and plans her revenge accordingly.

The nurse presents the background of the story, expressing concern to the tutor in charge of Medea and Jason's two young sons, who appear on stage with the tutor. Offstage, one hears Medea screaming and crying. Medea then enters and gives a remarkable speech in defense of women, analyzing how men oppress them. What makes the speech so remarkable is that a female character, played by a male actor in a play by a male playwright, speaks to a predominantly male audience and clearly demonstrates the inherent oppression of women and inequality of their position in Greek society; men can get divorced, women cannot; men are free to roam the city, women must stay at home; men may take lovers, women may not; and, perhaps most amazingly given that the City Dionysia was also a celebration of Athens' military prowess and featured a presentation of veterans at the beginning of the festival, she argues that childbirth is more dangerous and demanding than going into battle. Women, she proclaims, are braver and stronger than men are because they give birth whereas men must simply "face the spears."

The arrival of Creon interrupts her argument. He insists she leave, but Medea convinces him to grant her twenty-four hours in order to prepare. As soon as Creon exits, she explains she will use the time to kill Creon, his daughter (who is to marry Jason), and Jason. Jason arrives and argues that Medea has received more from him than she ever gave and that his remarriage will benefit their children. Aegeus, the childless king of Athens, then replaces Jason on stage. Aegeus negotiates a deal with Medea: She will be granted sanctuary in Athens if she will use her magic to give him offspring. From this moment on, given that she has an escape route, so to speak, her plan begins to move forward.

Jason reenters and announces that the sons will not follow Medea into exile but stay in Corinth with him instead. Medea then gives the boys a gift for the bride, a robe that has been poisoned. Messengers return and report that the robe has caused the young girl to burn to death and the flames leapt from her to Creon, who also perished. Behind closed doors, Medea then kills her own sons. Their cries, heard through the doors as she stabs them, are chilling. Jason, furious, enters, only to find Medea on the roof with the bodies of her sons in a chariot provided by her grandfather, the sun. She announces that she is leaving for Athens but will bury the boys where Jason cannot find them. In doing so, her revenge is complete, as it is the duty of the living to tend to the tombs of their dead family members, and so she is separating Jason from his sons not only in life but in death as well. The reversal is now complete: At the beginning of the play, Jason had a home, a family, a polis, and a place in the world whereas Medea had nothing; at the end of the play, Medea is the one with a home, a polis, and a place in the world and Jason is now the one with nothing.

Powerful, dangerous, and violent women evoked fear and fascination in the ancient Athenians. The most memorable Greek plays are about such women: Clytemnestra, Elektra, the Suppliants, Antigone, and, of course, Medea. In addition to being a dangerous woman, Medea was a complete outsider to the Greeks. A native of Colchis, in Asia Minor, she was *xenon* (a stranger), *apolis* (without a city or home), *barbaroi* (a non-Greek speaking foreigner), and *agrioi* (a savage). Admittedly, some ancient sources state that Medea was a descendent of the Corinthians (and therefore Greek), whereas most sources, such as Euripides, the *Argonautica* of Apollonius of Rhodes, and Herodotus in Book VII of the *Histories*, view her as Colchian—a barbarian with wooly hair and darker skin.[3] She was a woman out of her element, the opposite of everything by which fifth-century Athenian males defined themselves.

She was also "black" in the sense of having a dark complexion, although the Greeks would not have perceived her as one would today (ancient Greeks had a very different conception of race and ethnicity). Pindar in *Pythian 4* describes the Colchians as "dark-faced" or "swarthy" (212), and Herodotus describes them as "dark-skinned and having wooly hair," having descended from Egyptians (2.104). There is no indication in ancient Athens that Euripides's play featured an actor wearing a black mask or resembling an African, Ethiop, or "dark-faced" Colchian, but the audience would perceive Medea as a dark-skinned foreigner who was savage, mysterious, and different. Medea's stage life likely began as an ethnic outsider and modern adaptations continue to present her as such.

Over the past two decades, Medea has become a popular figure in scholarship. In 1997 Princeton University Press published *Medea* (edited by James J. Clauss and Sarah Iles Johnson), a survey of the representation of Medea in art, literature, myth, and theatre.[4] More recently, *Medea in Performance, 1500–2000* offered a selection of essays exploring the history of Medea on stage.[5] Euripides' original remains one of the top three Greek tragedies read in college classrooms (along with *Antigone* and *Oedipus Rex*). A recent issue of *American Theatre* cited no fewer than a dozen significant productions and/or adaptations of the play within the past two years.[6] Numerous translations of the play have also appeared recently in the United States and Europe.

While Antigone is the most popular Greek figure in Africa, Medea is the most popular figure in the Afro-Greek world (Greek tragedies adapted by artists of the African diaspora or adaptations set in the

African diaspora).[7] Other adaptations of the play have exploded in the twentieth century in a variety of environments and cultural contexts. In the latter half of the twentieth century, the advances of feminism and postcolonialism in theatre and the academic world have rescued Medea from her traditional portrait as a tragic, violent, mad, child-killer by empowering her.

In the original Greek version, Medea is the outsider: a foreign woman, a barbarian who marries a Greek (Jason) and raises their children.[8] She is the non-Westerner who defeats the Westerner. Yet she is also part of the elite: a princess of Colchis, grandchild of the sun, mother of Jason's sons, a divinely descended heroine. Medea and Jason live in Corinth surrounded by servants, comfort, and wealth yet she remains a cultural outsider. As one sees in the play, the men in her life can easily revoke her elite status. While the Renaissance and seventeenth, eighteenth, and nineteenth centuries saw a proliferation of adaptations of Medea, it was not until the twentieth century that Medea comes into her own. This is the period, as Marianne McDonald noted, "When women's rights are taken seriously."[9] From the postwar period to the present Medea is re-presented in dozens of adaptations from Charles Ludlam's camp version to Yukio Ninagawa and Tadashi Suzuki's Japanese adaptations; Robert Wilson's *Deafman Glance* to Heiner Müller's *Medeamaterial*; to Carol Sorgenfrei's *Medea: A Noh Cycle* to Cherrie Morraga's *The Hungry Woman: The Mexican Medea*, to name but a few. In addition to dramatic adaptations, Marianne McDonald identified fifty operas based on or including the Medea myth.[10] Medea, in short, is a powerful, popular figure, frequently adapted and re-created for new contexts.

One of the earliest American conceptions of Medea as a woman of color resulted from the narration through art of the story of Margaret Garner, an escaped slave who killed her own children rather than allowing them to be recaptured and continue to live as slaves in the years before the Civil War and who later served as the inspiration for Toni Morrison's novel *Beloved*. In 1856, Garner, a twenty-two year old

African American slave with four children and pregnant with a fifth, attempted to escape Kentucky by fleeing across the frozen Ohio River. Tracked by her owner to a cabin, she killed her daughter Mary and tried to kill the other three before the men broke into the room. Abolitionists immediately seized the story: A mother would rather have her children die by her own hand than see them returned to slavery. Kentucky painter Thomas Satterwhite Noble painted the scene, titling it *Margaret Garner, or The Modern Medea*. Medea was known as the mother who killed her own children, seeking to take from a man what was rightfully his. The implication was that Garner did the same. Yet Noble's painting also clearly marks Garner as a defiant, tragic figure—an embodiment of tragedy. He framed Garner's story in terms of the Greek narrative, thereby giving Garner a tragic hero identity. Margaret Garner may have been the first representation of a woman of color as Medea, but certainly she was not the last.

Helene Foley wrote in her wonderful *Reimagining Greek Tragedy on the American Stage*:

As a whole, U.S. Medeas tend above all to represent the play's complex and multifaceted heroine as the wronged, if horrific, cultural 'other,' whether that other is black, mulatto, native American, Asian, lesbian, a failed beauty queen, a drag queen or an abused teenage mother.[11]

The specific depiction of Medea as a woman of color in the United States began during the Harlem Renaissance of the 1920s and 1930s. Poet Countee Cullen adapted *Medea* for actress Rose McClendon in 1935 in a play titled *The Medea of Euripides: A New Version*, but McClendon passed away before she could perform the role.[12] Interestingly, even though the part was specifically written for an actress of color, nothing specifies Medea's ethnicity in the script. Cullen reduced the choral odes to brief songs and rendered the dialogue as naturalistic, but nothing in the text clearly states a particular race. In her plaintive cry, "O my native land, where there is peace and quiet, I wish I had never left you!", one might read an idealization of the Motherland common in Harlem Renaissance writing, but that native land is never identified.[13]

Later versions of the script by African American director, poet, and adaptor Owen Dodson introduced a Medea who was much more definitively black. Dodson first directed the play in 1940 at Atlantic University with opera singer Dorothy Ateca in the title role. The year before, Dodson had written an adaptation of *Medea* called *Garden of Time*, set during the post–Civil War Reconstruction, in which John, the son of a while plantation owner, married Miranda, a former slave. This play was first produced in 1945 at the American Negro Theatre in Harlem. After Cullen passed away in 1946, Dodson reworked his *Medea* several times, directing productions in 1959 and 1963 at Howard University and 1971 at the Harlem School of the Arts. Dodson transformed Cullen's nonspecific original into *Medea in Africa*, a critique of colonialism, specifically in South Africa, ending with the death of Jason (an Afrikaner) at the hands of the indigenous.[14]

The plays in this volume reflect recurring themes and approaches to adapting Medea to modern contexts. Numerous modern adaptations see the play as painting a picture of the struggle of the powerless under the powerful, of women against men, of foreigners versus natives. The play has been adapted into colonial and historical contexts to lend its powerful resonances to issues of current import. *African Medea*, for example, sets the play in early nineteenth-century Angola with Medea as an African princess and Jason as a Portuguese soldier. *Black Medea*, set in New Orleans in 1810, posits Medea as a voodoo priestess and Jason as a French colonial aristocrat, much like John LaChiusa's 1999 musical adaptation *Marie Christine* presents Medea as a voodoo queen in 1899 New Orleans. *American Medea* is set on George Washington's estate at Mount Vernon after the American Revolution with Medea as a slave and Jason as a Greek colonist. *Pecong* sets the play in the Caribbean at Carnival time (the period before Lent featuring public celebrations, masquerades, and an overturning of daily life) with a black Jason chasing a black Medea, only to spurn her and then pay the price. As the playwright noted, however, the play also deals with prejudice within the black Caribbean community in which light-skinned individuals are prejudiced against darker-skinned members of the community. *Medea, Queen of Colchester* presents the character as a black drag queen, a young man who is as much an outsider in his society as Medea was in Corinth. *The Tragedy of Medea Jackson* sets the play in contemporary San Francisco. Other versions of *Medea* have presented her as a woman of color, from German Hans Henny Jahnn's 1926 version with Agnes Staub in the title role to South African Guy Butler's *Demea* with Medea as a Xhosa princess and Jason as a nineteenth-century British officer who leaves his native wife for a wealthy Boer family.[15] Medea has thus been frequently presented around the world as a member of a disenfranchised group.

Adaptations of *Medea* also engage the violence of Medea—she kills —and her greatest moral failing (at least in the eyes of contempo-rary ethics), which is infanticide. As Lesley Ferris observed, Medea is "the mythical pariah of womankind" because she killed her children.[16] In *Medea's Daughters: Forming and Performing the Woman Who Kills*, Jennifer Jones identified Medea as "the ur-murderess" and linked her to Lizzie Borden, Ruth Snyder in Sophie Treadwell's *Machinal*, Susan Smith and Andrea Yates (both of whom killed their children), and "many angry, complex and rebellious women."[17] Although it should be noted that Smith and Yates are European American and one could argue that their infamy derives from their ethnicity—they are famous because they are white women who killed their children—it is the act of killing, and especially killing one's own children regardless of motive, that horrifies. Nevertheless, this linkage returns us to Margaret Garner. Euripides's Medea kills out of spite. More recent playwrights have offered other reasons for the killing, including to spare the children pain. Silas Jones even presented a *Medea* in which she does not kill the children, although they die at each other's hands. There are those scholars that argue that Euripides invented the child murder, which was not part of the myth. If this is true then his invention has ensured Medea's infamy and that she would become an archetype.

The violence especially becomes an issue in plays in which Medea is presented as a woman of color. "Black women have historically been represented as hypersexual, ignorant and violent female 'Negro beasts,'" observed Kimberly Wallace-Sanders.[18] One can, however, read the violence of Medea as a Fanonian response to the violence visited upon women. As Nada Elia argued, "Women [are not just] members of a broader oppressed/colonized group, but as an oppressed class by themselves."[19] In other words, even in oppressed cultures, women are more oppressed than men. Jason and Medea are both strangers in a strange land in Corinth, but as a male, Jason has options that Medea does not. Her violence toward Creon, his daughter, and her own children becomes a Fanonian revolution of sorts; her violence toward them is inspired by and in direct response to their oppression and cultural violence toward her.

Medea's violence is also linked to her sexuality. Medea is a sexually available female who gives herself to Jason completely. Her exoticism as a non-Greek becomes a form of eroticism. While her sexuality can be a form of power (and is often represented as such), it is also a means to reduce her to a source of pleasure for men. When men turn Medea's sexuality against her, this fuels her violence and becomes a source of vengeful power.

Lastly, Medea's violence is also linked to her status as "other" and the unwillingness of Greek society (or whatever society for which Corinth serves as metaphor) to accept Medea and allow her a place in that society. As Helene Foley indicated, since the 1970s, audiences were presented with empowered and empowering Medeas but the adaptations all "locate the compelling tragedy of Medea largely in the impossibility of assimilation to a white, male-dominated, unjust and unreliable culture."[20] While this is true of many of the Medeas in this volume, the playwrights who created them would argue assimilation into such a society was never the goal in the first place. Instead, these Medeas confront that society with their very "otherness," a reminder that Corinth is oppressive and corrupt. Modern Medeas, and especially black Medeas, do not seek assimilation; they seek their own dignity, identity, and justice in a society that wants to withhold all three from them.

On the positive side, adaptations of *Medea* frequently present women as keepers of power and knowledge. In *Pecong*, Granny Root tells Mediyah, "Only woman does have power and knowledge of science in this family." In *American Medea*, Medea's sons acknowledge their mother's power and wisdom which is not shared by their father. Medea's power and knowledge is presented as supernatural. Medea, as the grand-daughter of Helios (god of the sun), and niece of Circe (goddess of magic), has powers. She helps Jason win the Golden Fleece. She uses magic to kill Pelias. Medea's magic helps Aegeus have children and it kills Creon and his daughter. She rides in a dragon-pulled chariot to Athens after reversing places with Jason. This magic manifests in adaptations in different forms: Medea as voodoo princess, as isangoma, as witch. Medea has knowledge and powers that others do not. In short, black Medea is an outsider to dominant (often-white) society defined by her power, her outsider status, her knowledge, her sexuality, and her violence, especially toward her own children. While Euripides's play is remarkable in its sympathetic portrait of its eponymous character, modern adaptations recapture her even further.

Perhaps the latest manifestation of black Medea is Mabel "Madea" Simmons, the creation of Tyler Perry. He has performed Madea in films and on stage in such plays as *I Can Do Bad All By Myself* and its sequel, *Diary of a Mad Black Woman*. Madea, whose name differs from her Greek counterpart only by a single vowel, is also vindictive, overreactive, and violent toward her family members. While one cannot make the argu-ment Madea's character is based on *Medea*, there are enough similarities between the two women of color that one can see the echoes of the latter in the presentation of the former—Madea is a vengeful, loud, woman of color, played for comedy.

The purpose in compiling this volume is twofold. The first is to bring these plays (some which have never been published) to a larger audience in the hopes of seeing more productions of them, especially because they offer strong roles for women of color. Having spent years researching adaptations of Greek tragedy from the African diaspora, I have found much of interest in these plays. Many of them also offer gifts from the playwrights to actors, opportunities to play wonderful roles with moments of sheer playability and character depth that challenge both performers and audiences The second reason is to place these plays side-by-side in order to juxtapose the variable representations of Medea. Even with similar elements, the diversity of Medeas of color is remarkable. Simply by taking these six plays together, one begins to sense both the infinite possibilities of the story and the character as well as the mani-fest variations which a single Greek tragedy can inspire. It is also fasci-nating that Medea has proven such a strong inspiration in the form of a woman of color in a manner that Clytemnestra, Elektra, and others have not (with the notable exception of Antigone, Medea's only competition in terms of adaptation).

This volume contains six plays by two women and four men (that statistic alone is quite interesting; even after Euripides, Medea remains a mouthpiece for men); three European American playwrights and three African American. Three of these plays (*African Medea, Pecong,* and *There Are Women Waiting*) have previously been published, whereas the other three (*Black Medea, American Medea,* and *Medea, Queen of Colch-ester*) appear for the first time ever here. The plays span a gap from 1968 to 2003 and span a range of settings from nineteenth-century Africa to contemporary Las Vegas. All of them create new historical contexts linking the present to the ancient Greek narrative and also find contem-porary meaning through variations in the story. All have been performed multiple times and have demonstrated their power on stage. It is my hope that many more productions of each will follow.

A note on the texts: Each play is in its original formatting of each play, honoring the playwright's preferences for structure. While it makes the scripts in this volume inconsistent, it shows authorial intent and allows the plays to be presented as each individual intended.

NOTES

1. Aristotle. *Poetics.* Trans. Kenneth McLeish (New York: Theatre Communications Group, 1999). See Book XV.
2. For information on the Athenian original, the reader is directed to J. Michael Walton's *Living Greek Theatre* (Westport, CT: Greenwood Press, 1987), still one of the best introductory guides to the dramas of Athens; the introduction and translation of the play by Ruby Blondell in *Women on the Edge: Four Plays* (New York: Routledge, 1998), or the University of Chicago series translation by Rex Warner, found in Euripides I, edited by David Grene and Richmond Lattimore (Chicago: University of Chicago Press, 1955). For a general introduction to Greek tragedy that also includes modern adaptations, the reader is directed to Marianne McDonald's *The Living Art of Greek Tragedy* (Bloomington and Indianapolis: Indiana University Press, 2003).
3. Apollonius Rhodius. *Argonautica.* Trans. William H. Race. (Cambridge: Harvard University Press, 2008); Herodotus. *The Histories.* Trans. Robin Waterfield. Ed. Caroline Dewald. (Oxford: Oxford University Press, 2008.)
4. James L. Clauss and Sarah Iles Johnson, eds. *Medea* (Princeton: Princeton University Press, 1997).
5. Edith Hall, Oliver Taplin, and Fiona Macintosh, eds. *Medea in Performance, 1500–2000* (Oxford : Legenda/European Humanities Research Centre, University of Oxford, 2000).
6. Celia Wren. "In Medea Res." *American Theatre* 19.4 (April 2002): 22–25,60–61.
7. See "Chapter Four: Black Medea" in Kevin J. Wetmore, Jr.., *Black Dionysus: Greek Tragedy and African-American Theatre* (Jefferson, NC: McFarland and Company, 2003), 132–204.
8. For a full analysis of the play, see William Allan, *Euripides: Medea* (London: Duckworth, 2002).
9. Marianne McDonald, *The Living Art of Greek Tragedy* (Bloomington and Indianapolis: Indiana University Press, 2003), 145.
10. McDonald, *The Living Art of Greek Tragedy,* 144.
11. Helene Foley, *Reimagining Greek Tragedy on the American Stage* (Berkeley, University of California Press, 2012), 192.

12. See the script in Countee Cullen, *The Medea and Some Poems* (New York: Harper and Brothers, 1935).

13. Cullen, 15.

14. Foley, 201.

15. Guy Butler, *Demea* (Capetown: David Philip, 1990). For analysis of this play see Kevin J. Wetmore, Jr., *The Athenian Sun in an African Sky* (Jefferson, NC: McFarland and Company, 2002), 130–141.

16. Lesley Ferris, *Acting Women: Images of Women in Theatre* (New York: New York University Press, 1989), 125.

17. Jennifer Jones, *Medea's Daughters* (Columbus: Ohio University Press, 2003), xi, xii, 88.

18. Kimberly Wallace-Sanders, "Introduction" in *Skin Deep, Spirit Strong: The Black Female Body in American Culture*, Ed. Kimberly Wallace-Sanders (Ann Arbor: University of Michigan Press, 2002), 3.

19. Nada Elia, "Violent Women: Surging into Forbidden Quarters" in *Fanon: A Critical Reader* Eds. Lewis R. Gordon, T. Denean Sharpley-Whiting, and Renée T. White (Cambridge: Blackwell, 1996), 103.

20. Foley, 125.

CHAPTER 1

AFRICAN MEDEA

INTRODUCTION

Since 1985 Jim Magnuson has been a professor of creative writing at the James A. Michener Center for Writers at the University of Texas, Austin. More recently, he was appointed director of the center. He has authored more than a dozen plays and eight novels, and he has written for television. He was a playwright-in-residence at Princeton University for four years. In the late 1960s, he worked as a playwright in New York City, having recently graduated from the University of Wisconsin. His play, *No Snakes in this Grass* (a one act about the Garden of Eden with a white Adam and a black Eve), was produced in Harlem. Subsequently, Mikal Whitaker, director of the East River Players (who had been in a production of Euripides's play at Howard University), suggested that Magnuson adapt *Medea* with a colonial-African concept.

African Medea is set in a Portuguese colonial city in nineteenth-century Angola at the time of the country's war to gain independence. Magnuson also chose to set the play in Angola because it was one of the last places in Africa from which slaves were sent on the Middle Passage. Medea is presented as a powerful African princess whose marriage to slave trader Jason is dissolved by the colony's governor. Her revenge against Jason is carried out against a backdrop of revolution against the colonial overlords. In the end, she eventually escapes to the newly established United States.

Magnuson followed Euripides's plot closely but uses the narrative to comment on the independent struggles in Africa at the time as well as the Civil Rights Movement of the 1960s in the United States, linking the two struggles for dignity, freedom, independence, and self-determination. Race is at the heart of this version of *Medea*. The explosive racial climate in which Dr. Martin Luther King, Jr. was assassinated in April 1968, followed by the riots in almost every major American city shaped the play. The play's violence echoes the violence of America's streets.

The play presents the New World ironically. Adago tells Medea that across the sea is "a land of hope where you could be safe and free." At the time, audiences could smile at the irony of escaping colonialism by coming to a land where people of color were enslaved. In this version, one reason Medea offers for the murder of her children is that they are part white—an inversion of the American idea of tainted blood—that one drop of African blood makes an individual less than white, regardless of appearance. Medea finds the idea of Portuguese blood in her offspring unacceptable. This is but one of several ironic racial reversals in the play.

Jason wants his sons to study in Lisbon, speak only Portuguese, and become fully assimilated. Under Portuguese colonial law, indigenous Africans who learned to speak Portuguese, converted to and actively practiced Roman Catholicism, and pledged sole allegiance to Portugal were granted the status of *assimilado*, achieving greater standing than Africans who did not (although attaining *assimilado*, however, still did not mean being equal to Europeans in actual practice).[1] Jason knows that if they do not become full citizens under the law they will most likely become soldiers, laborers, or slaves.

African Medea is thus a play of revolutionary change, of resisting assimilation, of solidarity between Africans and African Americans. The play was first presented by the East River Players in 1968 and was revived in Harlem a year later. In both productions critics and audiences alike embraced and acknowledged the revolutionary spirit of the play. More recently, in September 2001, the San Diego Black Ensemble Theatre Company revived the show in California. This time, critics did not acknowledge the play's revolutionary content. Instead, the work was seen as one of profound feminism—a woman who struck back against her oppressors, thereby showing that even adaptations of classical plays often transform through time depending on context.

NOTES

1.   F. Jeffress Ramsay, *Africa.* 6th ed. (Guilford: Dushkin, 1995), 145, 165.

Play 1

African Medea

Jim Magnuson

Characters

CHORUS

BEGGAR

NURSE

JASON

MEDEA

BARRETTO Governor

TUTOR

CHILDREN

ADAGO

SOLDIER

ACT ONE

A large African city on the West Coast The early part of the nineteenth century. A large European house, columns and steps. In the background, harbor and hills.

Late Afternoon. The CHORUS *is huddled before the house, poorly dressed African women. A group of* DANCERS *and* MUSICIANS *enter, dressed in bright holiday finery. The* BEGGAR *hobbles in their midst. He is blind, dressed in tatters, and has only one arm.*

BEGGAR Alms, masters, alms. Coins for a poor blind beggar.

(*The celebrants laugh and dance out of his way.*)

All I ask is the scraps of your blessings... If there is celebration, let me join... I will celebrate too...

(*He fumbles among them. They dance out of his way and he falls to the ground. They exit.* BEGGAR *picks himself up.*)

Celebrate with curses! We shall see how long your music lasts!

CHORUS Be still! You are before the house of Jason. Show respect!

BEGGAR Before the house of the new groom? I will be still for no one.

CHORUS Shame on your insolence.

BEGGAR Don't misunderstand me, women. I am full of respect. I praise our mighty Portuguese masters. Their many kindnesses weigh on our hearts like stone.

CHORUS Quiet! Shh!

BEGGAR I won't be still any longer. Why should we be silent? Because our masters sleep? Slumber on soft pillows, behind those white walls, dreaming that they are in Lisbon. Awake, masters, for you are in Africa!

CHORUS Stop your rant, beggar. You will get no coins for this kind of talk.

BEGGAR Your many kindnesses to us—slavery, death, disease, are soon to be repaid. The time is near.

CHORUS You are too poor a man to risk such prophecy. Hush! You are too full of hate and bitterness. Jesus tells us to love our enemies.

BEGGAR Women, you listen too much to those white priests! Their white gods they use to bless and sanctify our chains.

CHORUS We must forgive, beggar.

BEGGAR Forgive? (*He laughs.*) I forgive? At birth the gods take the sight from my eyes, leaving me no way to live but by begging and picking up what I could. And then...and then...this! (*He waves the stump of his arm.*) This the white masters gave me to add to Nature's insult. A lesson to the others, they said...for taking food from the kitchen. Two of their slaves held my arm to the block. A third raised the meat cleaver. My brothers! I could not see the blade descend. I could only hear it whistle as it cut through the air... No! I cannot forgive this!

CHORUS Hate will not give you your arm back.

BEGGAR No, but it could take others. Their time is coming. It is near.

CHORUS Do not speak of things you cannot know.

BEGGAR I have heard the hushed, fevered words of many men. I have heard the drums singing out at night.

CHORUS We are awakened from sleep by the screaming of monkeys and the and the crying of birds. We lie still, sweating in the darkness, afraid. Every morning the sun rises, glaring with an angry, remorseless blaze. The sun punishes us all. We do not know why. We are only slaves. Dust hangs in the air, poised for some coming event. Though we tread the flat familiar stones to the well each day our jars remain empty. The parched throats of the slaves are silent. The air smells scorched, like a fire far off, a fire that will rage till it meets the sea. The eyes of the slaves search the sky for a sign of rain, and stare silently at the wine bottles on the tables of our masters.

BEGGAR We stand before the house of Jason, slave-trader, dealer in ivory. He will be among the first.

CHORUS We know that he has left his wife Medea. What sickness hides behind those white columns?

BEGGAR We shall soon bring it all down. The drums are beating...soon... soon...soon.

(*The* NURSE *enters from the house. She is an old slave woman. She is indignant at seeing the* BEGGAR *on the steps.*)

NURSE Go! Shoo! Away from here! How brave you beggars have become, sunning yourselves on the steps of respectable people.

BEGGAR Alms, alms, my mistress. A small coin to buy bread.

NURSE (*gives him a coin*) Don't think I didn't hear your crazy talk, beggar. All you ever do is talk and drink. Your Portuguese masters laugh over teacups about such as you. (BEGGAR *exits.*) Oh, I wish the long slave ships had never passed down the Congo.

CHORUS The trees that made her mast and oars would still wave in the jungle and the baboon and the birds still live in their branches.

NURSE I wish that these powerful white traders and adventurers had never traveled to the heart of Africa. We would all be happier now.

CHORUS We would still be free.

NURSE Medea would never had seen Jason, never loved him, never murdered...

CHORUS We would still be free.

NURSE Never fled with him to this Christian city, this slave port.

CHORUS At first it all went well. The whites were kind to her, so pleased and curious about African nobility. Jason loved her much then, he was almost proud of her. This was a happy home.

NURSE Now all is changed. Hatred hangs in the air like the mist over the jungle in the morning, silent and penetrating.

CHORUS Jason has abandoned her; not a Christian marriage, he says.

NURSE He cast her out like an old rag, spit her out, and married the blonde daughter of Barretto, the governor of the city.

CHORUS He is ambitious and needs a proper wife, they say.

NURSE For his ambition he is willing to betray the vows they made to one another, betray the children she has borne him.

CHORUS He is ambitious. We fear the offspring of such ambition.

NURSE Medea lies within the house, neither eating nor drinking, feeding on tears. She speaks to no one, remembering her father's home and her native land.

CHORUS Which she betrayed for this man Jason.

NURSE In the night she cries out to the gods of the Bono to come and rescue her. I try in my humble way to comfort her, but she only stares at me like a stranger...me, who has been her nurse since she was a small child.

CHORUS No one is a comfort to her now. Though she would scorn our prayers, we pray for her...and for ourselves.

NURSE I fear she hates even her own children.

CHORUS Poor Medea, she is learning what it means to have lost one's people, to live as an outcast.

NURSE But she will never learn to be humble, to bow her head, to taste scorn as daily bread.

CHORUS There is too much violence in her.

NURSE Don't speak of violence! I am in terror of that.

CHORUS She killed for Jason's love before. She knows the sight of blood on the dagger.

NURSE No! Not again! Not again...

CHORUS Stealing into the house, searching her way to the marriage bed...

NURSE There are terrors greater that she alone can imagine.

CHORUS She is a strange and dangerous woman.

NURSE I knew this from her childhood. How little Jason understands! To turn her passion to vengeance... But here the children come. How happy they look...no thought of their mother's grief, or of grief to come.

(The CHORUS *moves off.* TUTOR *enters with the children, two young* BOYS. *The* TUTOR *is an old black man, dressed in a worn suit.)*

TUTOR Seven times three, let's have an answer.

FIRST BOY We are tired of sums, teacher. We want stories. About the sparrow and how he set the crocodile against the elephant.

TUTOR Seven times three. You be careful or your little brother will have the answer first.

SECOND BOY The crocodile and the elephant!

TUTOR No stories until I have my answer. Seven times three!

SECOND BOY Just the crocodile?

TUTOR Seven times three?!

BOYS Twenty-one!

TUTOR All right, then. Now about the clever Mr. Sparrow...

NURSE Ndala, when will you stop telling the children your foolish tales?

TUTOR Don't scoff at me, nurse. You're too old for that.

NURSE I thought you were employed to teach.

TUTOR And I do.

NURSE Then why these silly tales? Even I heard them as a child...far from here.

TUTOR And they are now children. African children. As you were.

NURSE You get so heated, teacher.

TUTOR Yes, but they will not be pale Portuguese gentlemen with bows on their shoes if I can help it.

NURSE There is small chance of that. You wish to forget that they are half-Portuguese?

TUTOR And which half is that? No, they are whole children. Let them grow up as children.

NURSE If only they could.

TUTOR Nurse, why do you stand out here moaning? Has Medea turned you out? Surely she must need you?

NURSE The help she needs is greater than any that I can give. She stares without seeing, not even knowing what to call me. Her grief has torn my own heart so I had to come out to speak my troubles to the trees and the sky.

TUTOR Medea has not stopped her crying?

NURSE Stopped? Her rage has just begun. Once fanned it will race like the wind- whipped blaze across the plain.

TUTOR This is unfortunate. How aware is she of the trouble ahead?

NURSE What? What are you saying?

TUTOR Nothing! I said nothing!

NURSE Out with it, old fool!

TUTOR There is nothing to tell. It was simply a remark...

NURSE Curses be on you if you hold this from me.

TUTOR It will not be hidden long.

NURSE Don't speak riddles to me. I am no pupil of yours. Out with it. I will keep your secret. We servants are good at that.

TUTOR Quiet, then. This morning I was down at the docks, where they load the ivory ships and all the scoundrels and freebooters sun themselves. I overheard them speaking... Nurse, it may only be rumor.

NURSE No! It can't be true.

TUTOR Pray that it can't be true, nurse.

NURSE Jason wouldn't allow it! Even if he hates Medea, these are his sons...

TUTOR Jason is no friend of this house. He has other things to concern him now. The wedding is this evening...

NURSE This evening!

TUTOR Whether the rumors are true that it is to avoid scandal or simply to...I don't know. The streets are jammed with the carriage of distinguished guests...

NURSE How can he spit in her face this way?

TUTOR Who has time to think of a black woman with a mind full of Portuguese dignitaries, new honors, and future wealth? He does not think of this house now.

NURSE Is there no hope for us? Tutor, we must flee this place if we want to live!

TUTOR No, nurse. My place is with the children. I am their teacher.

NURSE And sometimes, you think, their father.

TUTOR They need protection from the storm around them. Learning is slow. It takes years to turn a boy into a man. And only a second, a single stroke of steel, to destroy him.

NURSE You see what a father you have, children?

TUTOR Quiet! Do you wish to poison the children with your own bitterness?

MEDEA (*within*) Death! Lost in suffering, I wish that I might die!

CHORUS (*soft*) Ai!

NURSE Quickly! Take the children! Keep them from her. I have seen her stare at them... Don't let her... Run, children, hurry away. It's nothing... nothing. Run!

(*Exit* CHILDREN, TUTOR.)

MEDEA (*within*) Ai! Burning, searing... Let it rain destruction, let it rain curses, crushing hateful mother, children, father, all... Ai! Let it crash! Let it crash!

CHORUS (*softly*) Ai!

NURSE Medea, no, how can your children share in their father's wickedness? Don't blame them. Children, I fear for you.

(*The* CHORUS *moves forward, drawn by* MEDEA's *cries.*)

MEDEA (*within*) Only death can ease this pain! Life only feeds the terrible flames! Ai!

CHORUS What are those terrible cries? The sound of grief draws us near.

NURSE Women, you will never again dream of being high-born. To be like this one, so proud and noble. She was mighty among her people, a great sorceress in our tribe, master of many spells and curer of ills. Now she is stricken and has no one to turn to. Greatness has no profit in it. The anger of the gods strikes first at those who stand tall.

CHORUS When a black woman grieves, it hurts us also. What happened to this great home?

NURSE There is no home here. Jason holds fast to his new bonds. We are left with the grief and rage.

CHORUS But Medea was like a queen to us. She was the only nobility some of us had.

MEDEA (*within*) Nyame, Nyame, giver of life and of death, let me die. Take all breath from me, all life, let it end now! Find a grave for me, give me release from my wounds!

CHORUS Lord, do not listen to the poor woman's prayer. Turn away from her. Unhappy Medea, never pray for death. Death is too close already. He lurks in every shadow, in every slave-trader's smile, walks every morning to the well of the poor, stand silently waiting in the mirrored hallways of the rich. The door shuts and does not open again. Never pray for death. The answer to that prayer awaits us all.

MEDEA (*within*) Nyame, let me die, but let my pain live, let it find a new home with my hated husband and his new bride, let it grow like a great hard tusk, till it tears out heart, entrails, all!

CHORUS She prays to gods we do not know, or have forgotten, yet we fear their power.

MEDEA (*within*) Oh, my father, my people. I left you in dishonor, steeling the holy Fleece, killing my own brother for the love of a traitorous man. Where are you now, father? Where? Is there no river to carry me home? No path? The deeds of the past grow up like a tangled vine? I cannot see...

CHORUS She comes from far away, from a savage tribe far beyond the Congo. She dares to boast of it. How different from us.

MEDEA Again the knife glides easily in my hand like a snake across dark water...

CHORUS How can we stand to witness such suffering? Nurse, go to your lady and bring her out to us... Solitude is a cave full of unseen dangers. Let her speak to her friends.

NURSE I don't know if I can. Anyone who comes near is frightened off with a fierce Look.

MEDEA (*within*) Ai!

(NURSE *runs into the house.*)

CHORUS Her shrieks drive us numb. We hear cries of pain that echo the cries we have always been afraid to utter. Shh! Look...she comes out.

(MEDEA *enters, helped by the* NURSE.)

CHORUS She looks but does not see us! Eyes like whirlpools, filled with visions not human. It is true what they say. She is a witch. No human could have eyes like that. but how can she be evil? We have heard many tales of her curing the sick; we know that she made Jason's father young again. Her people are savage, yet filled with a wisdom we do not have.

MEDEA The sun burns my eyes. Is it day? How could the sun rise on this...

NURSE Medea, my child...

MEDEA (*to* NURSE) You have asked someone here? Visitors? Witnesses? The women of the city... Why have you come? To stare at pain?

CHORUS We come from sympathy, Medea.

MEDEA Sympathy. What strange word is that? You can't leave pain alone? All right, then. What is it that you want to hear? A story that you all know. Don't you ever tire of standing transfixed, listening to a tale told and told again, ending each time the same way, litany of agony. My husband Jason has left me to marry again... But how well you know that, women! A golden-haired Portuguese girl, child of the governor. How Jason loves gold! Gold hair, gold skin, golden future... The Fleece was golden once too, bright as the sun... And you know what I did for this gold lover, this dealer in slaves and ivory, sacker of villages. You all gossip about it in the market.

CHORUS No, no, no!

MEDEA My father, I betrayed. The Fleece, most sacred object of my people, Jason and I together tore from its holy place. Blasphemy! Isn't that the word the missionaries have taught you? Blasphemy... My brother, dear brother, I can see the blade still... Must you hear more? I wanted Jason so much then... We fled down the river... I clung to him like a golden blade, sailing into the future, into the poisoned stream...

CHORUS Don't you think that you are alone, Medea. We are black women too.

MEDEA Black women! You have had all pride and honor pounded out of you by whips, praying to the crosses your masters have nailed you to. You bow and scrape before your masters. Don't tell me... There is no one here for me to turn to...no father, no brother, no mother.

CHORUS You could go back to them.

MEDEA Go back? Do you know what they do to traitors in our village? They drag them by the heels through the village until they are dead.

They burn the traitor's hut and all his belongings, scatter them to the winds until no trace remains. You...you are lucky, slaves, for you have a country. I am a refugee, hated in my land, deserted by my husband.

CHORUS (*moving towards* MEDEA) Come to us, Medea, let us comfort you.

MEDEA No, I want no one near me. I ask only one thing of you.

CHORUS Yes, Medea.

MEDEA If I can devise a revenge, I only ask you to be silent.

CHORUS We know how to be silent. Shh! Someone is coming. The governor. We must don our humility... Governor Barretto! Welcome.

(*They bow as the* GOVERNOR *enters.*)

GOVERNOR You needn't pretend to be so servile. I know a sham as well as you. Medea doesn't bow. (*No response.*) Your gaze is insolent, Medea. It's you I've come about. I've come to a decision. It's been a hard thing for me, Medea...

MEDEA Speak, Barretto.

GOVERNOR I'm banishing you from my city. You must leave at once.

CHORUS Ohh, my lord!

GOVERNOR You may take the children with you.

MEDEA "May," my lord?

GOVERNOR You must.

MEDEA This is exile, then.

GOVERNOR You may go wherever you wish; we will not follow or persecute you. But go.

MEDEA Exile; is that such a hard word for you to pronounce, Governor?

GOVERNOR We cannot have you here any longer.

MEDEA Why?

GOVERNOR I won't lie, Medea. I'm afraid of you. I think you are dangerous. I fear for my daughter.

MEDEA Why should you fear me? Look at you. You have soldiers to protect you and your family, thick walls to sleep behind at night. I have no one.

GOVERNOR Your reputation is well known. Your occult knowledge is feared by the ignorant and even those not so ignorant; sorcery, magic, spells. My servants believe that you can cause animals to talk, and make the sun come up in the west.

MEDEA But didn't your Jesus do magic?

GOVERNOR Don't be blasphemous!

MEDEA He could make bread and fishes multiply, and walk on water. Things I could never do. And promise never to try.

GOVERNOR You threaten my daughter. You must go!

MEDEA I wish your daughter all happiness, my lord.

GOVERNOR You are a witch. It's well known.

MEDEA I cure the sick and make the old young. Is that to be feared? You are an enlightened man, Governor, you should not fear knowledge.

GOVERNOR My mind is set.

MEDEA I wish your daughter no harm; I confess that I hate my husband. But I hope that the marriage will be a happy one. Only let me stay.

GOVERNOR I cannot.

MEDEA Why?

GOVERNOR Many reasons, Medea.

MEDEA Which?

GOVERNOR Pride, for one. You know of the recent trouble here. This city is not what it was. When I first came here it was a delight, a small European city—the finest in Africa. Stately houses in the best Portuguese style. Clean broad boulevards.

NURSE So we have heard, my lord.

GOVERNOR But now—the paint is cracked on all the fine houses and the cattle are sheltered in the Jesuit college. The streets are filled with drifters and ex-convicts from all over Africa. Slave-trading is more brutal than ever. I am not an inhumane man. Some of these people are barbarous in the way they treat the slaves. Violence and murder are everywhere. It is not safe to walk the streets at night. Talk of revolt sings in the air. In the last few nights, drums have interrupted my sleep.

NURSE You must sleep, Governor.

GOVERNOR Don't be insolent! Unexplained fires erupt in abandoned buildings. trouble is close. The fire of revolt could only be fanned by a woman as proud as you.

MEDEA I have had nothing to do with the disturbances.

GOVERNOR Not directly, perhaps. I believe you. But the black people all over the city know of you. Their black princess, they say. How proud she is. Look how tall she stands up against our masters. As if she were almost more noble than they. It gives the poor people ideas. One cannot even be sure of one's own troops. No, you are dangerous, Medea. I know it.

MEDEA You will not listen to my prayers?

GOVERNOR No, for I love my family more than you.

MEDEA Do you know what it means to send children into exile, Governor? I ask Nothing for myself, but the children...

GOVERNOR Stop your pleading, Medea...

MEDEA You remember who is the cause of this.

GOVERNOR It is no use, Medea. Let go of my hand.

MEDEA It was Jason, my lord.

GOVERNOR Quickly. Gather your things and go.

MEDEA Have mercy on my sons.

GOVERNOR It is decided. Go!

MEDEA If you have decided, then let this go no further.

(MEDEA *falls to her knees.*)

GOVERNOR Medea, what are you doing? Stand up! Stand up!

MEDEA Kill me now.

GOVERNOR Medea, I am not asking for your death.

MEDEA I am asking, my lord. You say that you are merciful; then kill. The future holds only pain and hunger and dark memory... Put an end to time now!

GOVERNOR I will not have blood on my hands.

MEDEA The blood will only be bright for a second; then there will be nothing but darkness, restful darkness. Take the knife in your hand, Governor! Quickly, quickly!

GOVERNOR No, no!

MEDEA Have you ever held a knife in your hand, Governor? It is easy, so very easy. I am jason's woman. If I am a threat to you now I will always be a threat to you. I remain faithful to the vows I take. I cannot forget, my lord. Only the sword can sever my memory. You have no choice.

Remove this dark blot from your future... kill! Death is close enough to touch... I can feel it's dark robes...

GOVERNOR Stand, Medea. I am not a violent man. Stand!

(GOVERNOR *grabs* MEDEA *and pulls her to her feet.*)

MEDEA Your heart is a great, soft stone. Very well. I will go.

GOVERNOR Good.

MEDEA You will hear no more begging from me. I ask only one thing, lord. Allow me to stay for just one day. I must make arrangements for the support of my children, as the father chooses to do nothing.

GOVERNOR No! Today. This hour, Medea.

MEDEA You cannot kill; surely this smaller gift you can give.

GOVERNOR Not time, Medea. No, it is impossible.

MEDEA I ask no pity for myself. Only for the children. You are a father yourself. Is there no mercy anywhere within you? Search your heart, Barretto. I must have some time to gather my things; to prepare the children for their new life... Time to sell my treasures for milk and cheese... Time, Barretto, I beseech you, give me an inch of time. I will go then; you will be rid of me. What is a single day?

GOVERNOR I am not a tyrant. I am not inhumane, though there were times it might have been profitable to be otherwise. We Portuguese are not cruel and barbaric with the blacks like the English. I should perhaps be more ruthless. I am not. I give you one day. But if you are seen here tomorrow at sunset, you die. I give you your request. One day is yours.

MEDEA Thank you, Governor. (*Exit* BARRETTO.) You will not forget this day.

CHORUS Unhappy Medea, where can you go? West, into the ocean? East, into the jungle to wander homeless and lost? Or north, into the desert where the sun scorches flesh from bone? All men's hands are raised against the exile. The world is cruel and you are only a woman. We know. We bow low and wait. We know.

MEDEA You know nothing! That is the last you will see of Medea's bowed head. the governor has given me my day. A wedding gift. The governor will learn not to be so generous with beggars. In this day I will make dead bodies of my enemies—the father, the daughter, and my husband. The fool has given me all that I needed. He would not kill; merciful Barretto. He brought me up from my own death. It will be a bloody resurrection. I see the red light shining in the cave...I feel my feet beneath me...now only to go forward to the dreadful act.

(MEDEA *spins away and goes to the door, brooding. The* BEGGAR *enters, sings mockingly.*)

BEGGAR Bow down, my friends, bow and scrape and scratch your heads before one of the true wonders of Nature, an honorable black man, chief of the Mbamba, the singular Adago. He and his warriors arrived in their boats last night. He stays at the governor's house, the only black among the many distinguished guests.

NURSE Did you say the governor's house?

BEGGAR I was there to witness it...though I do admit we entered by different doors. The word of the celebration has escaped and the beggars mass at the kitchen door like flies on fresh meat, fighting for scraps of food. The preparations are lavish enough that even the poor may glut themselves...cakes and breads, fruit heaped in great baskets, red meat lying on silver trays, all just beyond our fingertips...

NURSE Shh!

BEGGAR The cooks entertain themselves by tossing us the leavings and watching us scramble. Someone whispered to me, Adago stood at an upper window, a piece of ebony framed in that great white house. He stared at us, rabble, our hands extended, begging, fighting for bits of food and cursing one another. He seemed ashamed.

NURSE Adago may be our salvation, Medea!

MEDEA My mind is buzzing with too many things. Be still.

NURSE Medea, Adago is here. He may be able to save you.

MEDEA I don't want to be saved. I only want the death of three people.

NURSE Forgive me, then, Medea, for wanting you to live...

MEDEA My mind turns away from hope. Only death waits for Medea now...and I will stride on it like a leopard and die with my teeth at its throat.

(*A trumpet.* JASON *enters.*)

JASON I want to see Medea.

NURSE She is here.

JASON Yes, Medea. I hear you have once again insulted the governor. You see what your temper brings. You've brought the exile on yourself. You are lucky to escape with as little as that.

MEDEA How much had you hoped for, Jason?

JASON I tried to calm his anger...

MEDEA Fool!

JASON I know that you hate me. But I cannot hate you, Medea. I've come to help. To make arrangements for you and the children.

MEDEA You dare to cry out for the children.

JASON I love my sons. I always have. If you hadn't caused this disaster by your anger, I could have kept the children with me. After a few years, when I became governor, they could have lived nearly as royalty and received the finest European educations. They could have enjoyed every advantage. Every advantage. That is what I wanted for them. But it is not longer possible.

MEDEA Are you finished, now that you have convinced these poor people that you are blameless? Such a confident face, without shame, without a line of doubt... Can that be the face that I...yes, that I loved once? Can you remember, Jason, what it was like? The day we escaped, a bright, clear day, Jason. I saved your life. Do your soldiers know that? Cheated my father, my brother stabbed...so that we could escape. I cured you of fever and led you through jungle trails that no European could ever know. Our love danced in the air for an hour...we carried the future with us, soft and golden, in our arms, a sun that shone through long nights and dark forests. And now you repay that hour; you marry the governor's daughter, the lovely Cecilia. Now...there is nothing to be built on the ruins of that love. Now what do you advise me to do? Return to my father's home? In our tribe there is the custom that when a child dies they mutilate the body before throwing it into the evil Forest, so that the spirit will be ashamed to return to haunt the village. You have done worse, Jason. You have mutilated my spirit. I cannot go home!

NURSE (*to one of the* CHORUS) Quickly! Run to Adago! Tell him to come. He is our only hope.

JASON Your tongue is bitter. You failed, Medea, by believing in love. You should learn never to trust passion.

MEDEA Then why do you abandon me for the young, soft Cecilia?

JASON Oh, not for love, Medea. Do you think me a child? For advantage, for power, and all that power can bring. But I am not an evil man. I would have used that power for you and the children if you hadn't disrupted things. I had been beset by difficulties on all sides, Medea, though you never concerned yourself with such matters. People after me to pay debts, enemies on all sides. The opportunity to marry the governor's daughter was too great. It meant a chance to be free. And that freedom is more sacred than even love.

MEDEA More sacred than the Fleece you defiled?

JASON We did it together, Medea! Remember that! Now it seems as if it never could have happened at all. The Fleece...I can remember only that it seemed to shine...with a terrible light. It was, then, the one thing I had to possess. It seemed purer and more holy than anything I had known before, a heart of golden light. If I risked my soul for it, and yours too, it didn't matter, I had to have it!

MEDEA You fouled it, Jason, you desecrated it...

JASON No. All I did was bring it back. That was all. A simple thing, but terrible, because imperceptibly it began to change, like the sun fading in the late afternoon. I tried to explain what it was that I had found, but couldn't, and began to doubt that I had found anything at all. To go back to capture it again would have been impossible. So I rose again the next morning and the morning after that and the faces were all different...the faces that were you and me. We'll talk no more of it. It serves no purpose. I have to move on. There is too much waiting for me in my future.

MEDEA And so you have denied me my future. And my past.

JASON Why do you revile me so? You forget what I've done for you. Anxious enough to leave, Medea, ready to embrace order, to live by law instead of the sweet will of force. Because of me you gave discovered European culture and refinement. And been appreciated in return. I gave you a new world to live in, Medea. You never thanked me for any of this.

MEDEA I never asked for any of this. I only asked for your love.

JASON I would like to see my sons.

MEDEA No.

JASON Medea, my sons.

MEDEA You fill me with loathing. Go.

JASON Later, you will be sorry for this.

(*He exits.*)

MEDEA Go to your virgin, then, Jason, go to your new bride. As you came to me once, new... My flesh that I gave to him I hate—this body that made his child is hate—the body remembers...

CHORUS The iron chains of memory hold her slave, cutting into bleeding flesh. Lord, waken us from this dream of terror, this dream, fathered by hate, mothered by despair, growing wild and strong in the mind's cradle. We struggle, Lord, struggle to shut our eyes, struggle to awaken, watching the wounded lioness turn on the hunter, hearing the roar, deep as a dream, deep as death. Look at her, her eyes filled with the dream of nothing, and of dark night. Love and hate here struggle and grow together like an evil vine.

MEDEA I feel the knife in my hand, and fire. But I am a sorceress. My craft will serve me well.

(*Enter* ADAGO.)

ADAGO Medea, greetings. From a friend, greetings.

MEDEA Greetings, old friend.

ADAGO You speak as if from a grave, Medea.

MEDEA From a grave? Yes, perhaps.

ADAGO You alarm me, Medea.

MEDEA Tell me why you are here, Adago.

ADAGO Oh, foolishness! I came to see the priests.

MEDEA The priests? Did they make you a convert, old man?

ADAGO No, no, no.

MEDEA Did they answer your questions, then?

ADAGO Not in a way to make me glad. You know my sorrow. Everyone seems to know it. I am unable to make children. It has been the same for many years.

MEDEA And they had good advice?

ADAGO The priest muttered something about how I am not to loosen the hanging foot of the wineskin...

MEDEA You don't take his advice?

ADAGO I have been told that before. So I came to see you. I have heard that you are skilled in mysteries.

MEDEA You have come to me to speak of children?

ADAGO Yes, I want a child more than anything I now possess.

MEDEA There can be much bitterness in having children, Adago.

ADAGO You needn't caution me, Medea. I am old. Death is not far away. A child to carry my name after me would ease my pain.

MEDEA I suppose it is important. Do all men feel this, Adago?

ADAGO All men that I know.

MEDEA Then to hurt a man get to him through the children.

ADAGO It would destroy him.

MEDEA Yes, destroy, crush all life from him.

ADAGO Medea, your eyes are lit with a terrible fire. What has happened to you?

MEDEA My husband, Adago.

ADAGO Come, speak clearly. Jason has hurt you?

MEDEA Hurt? He has betrayed me.

ADAGO What? How?

MEDEA Don't lie to me! No pretense, Adago. I can't bear it. Why have you come? Not just for the doctors, old man. You come for the wedding... Jason's wedding. (ADAGO *does not reply.*) And you also know that Barretto is driving me into exile. ADAGO And Jason consents?

MEDEA Approves.

ADAGO I cannot understand. I was told nothing at the governor's house.

MEDEA That is strange, Adago.

ADAGO What can be done, Medea? If I can be of help...

MEDEA What if I asked you to speak to your friend the governor?

ADAGO Medea, I don't know that my word...

MEDEA Don't be alarmed, Adago. I wouldn't ask more than can be given.

ADAGO I offer you my hands, Medea.

MEDEA Look at me, Adago. We do not fool one another. I know you. And of your great standing among these black people. I will not betray your reputation, Adago...as long as my demands are met.

ADAGO Poor Medea...

(*He goes to her. She shies away.*)

MEDEA No! Stay away. No one touches me. I am asking for no pity. Just one thing I ask, Adago. Do not let me go into exile without hope. Receive me in your land. Just accept me there, protect me from my enemies, and I will cure your trouble. Then you will have your children, Adago.

ADAGO You could cure me?

MEDEA I know the spells.

ADAGO Children. I could have children of my own. Yes, Medea, you can come. I will find a haven for you. I make only one condition. That you must reach our tribe by yourself. I can't guarantee passage. Things are uneasy enough between the Portuguese and my people the way it is... Even a chief must be cautious. If I were to be found transporting exiles we would risk waking up one morning with a forest of guns in our faces.

MEDEA But once there you can guarantee safety, Adago?

ADAGO Nowhere in Africa is safe, Medea. Death and treachery shadow every man. The black man fears the dark, the white man fears the sun. What I offer you is passage to the land beyond our own. A ship leaves at the beginning of each month. with a word from me, you could be assured passage and be transported far from this diseased place.

MEDEA Where, Adago?

ADAGO Far from here. Across the sea. A land of hope where you could be safe and free.

MEDEA You promise safety?

ADAGO Of course.

MEDEA Will you pledge it?

ADAGO We can trust one another, Medea.

MEDEA I want a pledge.

ADAGO Medea, you know me. And you know that vows can be broken.

MEDEA Yes, I above all know that. Still, I want the pledge. They hate me here. They might try to drag me from your land and make me a slave. A pledge. Your cure depends on it.

ADAGO I pledge your protection.

MEDEA You break it, Adago...what will happen to you?

ADAGO What happens to those who have no regard for heaven.

MEDEA Priest's heaven, Adago?

ADAGO There are other gods, Medea. We will not speak of them here.

MEDEA You are a good man, Adago. I will bless you with many children.

ADAGO When can we expect you?

MEDEA Expect me? Soon, Adago, soon. Or not at all.

ADAGO Come quickly, Medea. A day is not a long time. It disappears in a breath.

MEDEA You know about the day, Adago? The day that I have been given?

ADAGO Yes. Yes, I must have overheard one of your women...

MEDEA You are wise, Adago. Where have you found your wisdom? I shall come. But I have many things to do first.

NURSE No, Medea. Our salvation is assured. Do not be rash.

MEDEA Some things must be done first! So that my memory will be assured here. Farewell, Adago.

ADAGO Farewell, Medea. Night comes on, we must hurry. The night is safe for no one.

(*He exits.* CHORUS *moves forward.*)

CHORUS Good fortune go with you, Adago. May you have all that you wish for, old man.

MEDEA Yes, Adago, the night comes on, striding like a panther, carrying my triumph in its mantle...it is near...Adago will be my escape.

CHORUS Your safety is assured. Adago is an honest and a good man. He offers you a land you can call your own. We have heard of that land of light and sweet breezes, a fertile, rich land, a land of gentleness and hope where your children can walk the streets under a midday sun and not be spit upon, where the air you breathe is free is free and you need fear no one, a land where men have died to win their liberty, and freedom stretches as far as the mountain's horizon. We remain behind in the darkness. We have no hope for ourselves, Medea, but your salvation is at hand. Rest for you at last. How can you be sad, Medea? A new world is yours. The sun is rising on your freedom.

MEDEA The light fades and my mind turns to the dark deeds of night.

CHORUS What else, Medea? Vipers lurk in your mind. Safety can be yours. Do not let the viper destroy you.

MEDEA You all speak wisely. I have too much pride, you are right. Why end my time here in bitterness and hatred? Rather let me go with love in my heart, and sending gifts. I will show my love and forgiveness to them. Love and forgiveness.

CHORUS That is as it should be.

MEDEA I have some gifts to please them. Gold. They always love gold. I have some African treasures that no Portuguese jeweler could ever reproduce. A gift from my people. They would not refuse it. How dark it becomes. Nurse, have the lights turned on in the house. How good it is in the blackness. My gifts will shine all the brighter. Where is the tutor? Tutor!

(TUTOR *enters.*)

TUTOR The children are hungry, my lady.

MEDEA Their hunger will end shortly. I have an errand. Run to Jason. Tell him I want peace. Tell him I have precious gifts for his bride, the pale, blonde Cecilia. Tell him to come and get them. And to say farewell to his children. Hurry! Run!

(*The* TUTOR *runs out.*)

NURSE My hands shake and sweat. I don't know why. (*To* CHORUS.) Pray, all of us, pray that we may come safely down.

(*Sounds of distant drums.*)

CHORUS The drums will beat again tonight. There will be trouble certainly. Pity the poor African tonight! There will be trouble certainly. It would be better to be a frog or jackal and go unnoticed. The winds are up. The fires will be fanned by them tonight. Who will ever know when that fire will die?

MEDEA Run, tutor, run! Hurry, old man, time is so precious to us now!

Act Two

That night. The sound of drums. The DANCERS *and* MUSICIANS *enter. They seem unaware of the drums and they dance before the house, singing a wedding song.*

MEDEA *enters silently from the house, unseen. She carries a gold dress and a golden coronet in her arms. She watches the dancers. They exit.*

MEDEA There is a wedding. There is dancing. I rememeber once dancing... laughing... My feet have forgotten all music but one, single... But there is no time...not to dance, to sing, only time to make preparations for a final ceremony.

(NURSE *enters.*)

NURSE You surprise me, Medea. I haven't seen you go out...

MEDEA The children are sleeping?

NURSE Yes, but not well. They toss about, excited because you told them they would have a special task tonight.

MEDEA The gifts, nurse, what do you think?

NURSE Oh, they are not for me. Fine, I suppose...for a fine lady.

MEDEA For a very fine lady. For Jason's bride. The golden dress and the gold wreath for her hair.

NURSE You think she will accept them?

MEDEA This is from African nobility. Of course she will. Look how the gold glitters in the light. How beautiful she will be in it.

NURSE You speak in riddles, Medea. I don't understand them.

MEDEA Where is the tutor? I sent him for Jason.

NURSE The old man is not as swift as he once was.

MEDEA Tonight he must be swift. Go. Bring the children out. Prepare them to say goodbye to their father.

(NURSE *goes to the house.* MEDEA *lifts the dress and coronet in her arms.*)

Nyame, sun god, ever ready shooter of life-giving rays, transform your power into destructive fire. The soft and golden folds that were the holy Fleece, healer of the innocent, pure as the dawn, have been torn from your people and are defiled... Fill now this golden gown, this wedding dress, with that defiled power, let the light of vengeance ripple and snake through the golden mesh, transformed by the rising suns of hate and betrayal. Invest these garments with thy burning waters. Soak them in your poison till they drip with fire that scorches flesh, that burns with the flame that licks without pity, that licks with death-hunger, the garments with thy power, Nyame, and take thy vengeance! Let me be thy instrument. Only vengeance can slake my thirst, only vengeance can bring me rest. Only vengeance promises peace. Let thy enemies be consumed by thy power, Nyame, let the fire dance across their flesh, let your poison claw at their proud faces, let your poison wed them to pain, let pain be faithful as a vow, let your poisin reign. Let her be defiled so all will say Nyame has defiled her. For these few hours, Nyame, let your fire rule the night, let there be no power greater, no sovereign mightier, let your poison rain down from the sky!

(*A moment of silence. Enter* JASON *and the* TUTOR. JASON *and* MEDEA *regard each*

other without a word. The NURSE *enters with the* CHILDREN.)

JASON I came back, Medea. Only because the tutor says you have come to your senses. I will have to see for myself.

MEDEA Be still, Jason. Let your anger be over. We will be friends. (*To* CHILDREN.) Come, boys, greet your father.

(*The* CHILDREN *hang back, look to the* TUTOR.)

TUTOR Speak to your father, boys. He has come to see you.

MEDEA You see, Jason, that the tutor has served well in your absence.

JASON Boys? Come on. Say hello to your father. Why so shy?

TUTOR It's been a long time, sir.

JASON Yes, tutor. Come, boys. Surely you remember.

MEDEA Smile for your father.

JASON You're growing, both of you. It won't be long before you're both men. Then you can be ivory traders too, eh? How would you like that?

TUTOR I don't think they're interested.

JASON Is that so, tutor? What, then? Soldiers? Sailors? They must want adventure. All boys want that. Well, tutor?

TUTOR I suppose all boys do.

JASON Maybe they want...what? An education.

TUTOR I educate them here.

JASON Surely. But every teacher must give up his pupils eventually. Allow them to learn elsewhere, to travel, to see new worlds... They can go study in Lisbon or Paris...

TUTOR Pardon, master, but they are, excuse me, mulatto. I don't think your European professors...

JASON They are my sons!

MEDEA Remember, Jason, that you are sending them into exile.

JASON I will look after them.

MEDEA How can you keep that kind of promise? Once beyond this city, how can you help? The jungle is deep, a fathomless night for the outsider. No one knows the name of Jason there. What if—what if they were killed, Jason, and their blood ran on the jungle floor?

JASON Don't be barbarous, Medea.

MEDEA What would you do?

JASON I would... God, Medea, be silent! Not in front of the children.

MEDEA I'm sorry. I forget. It must be hidden from the children.

JASON Boys, here. I have gifts for you.

(*He takes the two aside and hands them gifts.*)

TUTOR Medea, he must not have the children.

MEDEA No one will have the children.

TUTOR You must take them away. This is no place for a child. Look, fires light up the night. It will explode soon.

MEDEA I will find them a darker refuge. Where no one will harm them anymore... The three of them, linked hand in hand, father and sons. How thick can blood run? To get at one must three...

(MEDEA *begins to cry.*)

JASON What is wrong, Medea? I see tears...

MEDEA It is nothing. I was thinking of the children. Forgive me. A woman is frail, and prone to crying. Just leave me. Take them to the governor's daughter, let them see your new bride. Have them kneel and ask her to intercede with her father to let them stay here. If she agrees, it cannot be refused. It cannot. Yes, and I have gifts. Gifts she will not refuse.

JASON She doesn't need gifts, Medea.

MEDEA These she will accept. Gifts to melt her heart and pity the poor children. (*To* TUTOR.) Bring the gifts. Children, here. I want you to go to Cecilia and ask her if she will let you stay.

BOY Mother, you are crying.

MEDEA Shh! Don't bother about me. Just listen. You go and ask the girl if you can stay. Take these presents and give them to her. Don't let anyone else touch them. Put them into her hands from yours.

(TUTOR *and* NURSE *take gifts and hand them to* CHILDREN.)

JASON You shouldn't be so foolish, Medea. She has plenty...

MEDEA This once, Jason, I am to have my way. How can she turn down the children if they bring gifts as fine as these? They are lovely. See how they shine, like fires in the sky.

JASON I will bring them.

MEDEA Good-bye, children. Go quickly so that you can return with good news.

(JASON *exits with the* CHILDREN *and* NURSE.)

How frail they seem...my sons...small flowers to be bent by a great wind. There is no hope left now, not even for the innocent. When the slender young bride dons the dress, how she will cry out... Poison will eat at the young white flesh. When she places the gold wreath on her golden hair, how she will cry out. The wreath will be her crown of death...shared by princes...

CHORUS Medea, stop! Let this vengeance slake your thirst... You can go no further. How can you send your trusting children walking to murder?

MEDEA But how will the girl's death be enough?

CHORUS No, Medea, leave it! Have you let your heart turn to steel? There are some things no woman can do, no human can do... Let it go, Medea!

MEDEA But how will the girl's death be enough?

CHORUS Save yourself, Medea, save us! The children are your own, you have loved them, raised them. You can't destroy what you have given life to... You can't drive spears through your own womb! Rage cloaks your heart, Medea, no!

MEDEA But how will the girl's death be enough?

CHORUS Medea's heart sinks like a stone, plummeting to its rest through a pool of blood. Terror makes me sick. Let us run from here. But where? Fire lights the sky everywhere. The city is torn in half. Danger surrounds us. Where can we escape?

MEDEA I will go to my house and await the news.

(MEDEA *enters the house.*)

CHORUS We are alone. No one to turn to. Hearing the drum makes us remember. We were taken from the heart of Africa, like Medea, but we were slaves and have no pretensions to greatness or nobility. We only ask to live, to bear children, to have a faithful man. Now the city has exploded and men fight. It is a revolt. Against what we hardly understand. To be free, an old man said, to be free we will slay our masters.

But sitting here, alone in the dark, hearing Death so close, we feel not very free. Not very free.

(*Shouts offstage. Enter the* BEGGAR. *He is wearing a plumed hat, yet his clothes are ripped and he is sweating profusely.*)

TUTOR Beggar, you run as if you were fleeing spirits.

BEGGAR Worse, worse! From people more monstrous than spirits. The city has gone mad! There are flames higher than a house, racing fire, the stench of burning flesh...great men of iron, marching, marching...the flashing of steel. I have heard cries...terror's triumph...I have seen it all!

CHORUS God, God, no!

TUTOR Women, do you believe what a blind man has seen?

CHORUS On a night as dark as this his word is as good as any other. Tell us, Beggar, what you know.

BEGGAR There is fighting throughout the city; black against white, black against black, white against white. The police have been ordered out, but many have mutinied.

CHORUS There is no hope for any of us! It is all too far gone, everything is out of control!

BEGGAR How fainthearted you are! You have been slaves too long. Your big chance comes, at last, after all these years of waiting and you're afraid to take it. The time has come. We can bring our masters down. With these poor eyes, I saw a man run onto one of the ships and tear open the holds with an ax. The slaves poured out, rushed over the dead and dying bodies, rushing to freedom. What timid blacks you are! Let the blood run! We will build our cities on their graves. They've whipped us long enough.

CHORUS You talk so boldly only because you've found that Portuguese hat. Where did you get it? Pluck it off some corpse?

BEGGAR I killed a man for it! Killed a man. I heard steps coming at me, felt him grab for me. We fought. He never spoke a word. A knife fell free. I felt it in my hand. I wish I could have seen his face then! Finally, revenge for this! (*Thrusts forward the stub of his arm.*) He is only the first. I will kill one man for every finger...I will kill...

TUTOR When will you stop?

BEGGAR When? When I make the whole world one-handed.

CHORUS You're a fool! Already you ape the manner of a slave-driver! You wear the hat almost correctly. Given a year, you should be an exact replica.

BEGGAR (*fondling hat*) The beggar has earned this.

CHORUS You sound so bold. Are you ignorant of what is going on? There are things happening here that defy the laws of Nature. There eyes have seen a black panther riding a white stallion down the center of the street, teeth buried in its neck.

TUTOR It is an omen. All month the moon has been robed in blood.

BEGGAR Quiet, old man.

CHORUS And I have seen a boa constrictor come sliding out of the door of one of the greatest mansions. Fires spring up that no man has set.

TUTOR You see? You won't mock me for long. All of this has been foretold, a future of violence lying in the prophet's mind, insistent as a memory...

BEGGAR Old man, don't be foolish. You bore us with your tribal tales.

TUTOR They won't bore you when they come to truth. Even the terror that Medea brings...

BEGGAR Are these riddles, old man?

TUTOR There is a story of a tribe of lions that had fallen on bad times and had no food...

BEGGAR Ahh, go on, teacher!

TUTOR Listen and you will be instructed! Having no food they devised a plan. They took the youngest of the lionesses and trimmed her claws, then cut and trimmed her hair, then gave her a woman's things to wear.

BEGGAR What is the point of this, old man?

TUTOR The young lioness was sent into the village to marry one of the young men there, with the plan being that when they were finally reclined on the wedding couch, she would tear out his heart and bring the meat to the tribe of lions...

BEGGAR Foolishness! There are more important things to be doing on a night like this...

CHORUS You are wise, old teacher, but who will tend to your lessons now?

TUTOR The scales will never be lifted from eyes like these. Before you go, I ask you one question: Has the fighting and trouble reached the governor's house yet?

BEGGAR No. The soldiers of the governor lie in a drunken stupor and look no further than the eye of the bottle before them. The fighting is in the center of the city. The governor's house sits on the hill, safe and snug. Tonight there is no sentinel, no one gazes from the window. Instead they all look inward, dazzled by their own brilliance, by the dancing and the downs and the wine and their own good fortune.

TUTOR So he does not know. He will not suspect anything, or be drawn away.

BEGGAR He sits peacefully now. But before the night is over...

TUTOR Not even you, half-man, can suspect what new terrors the night will bring.

BEGGAR Let the terrors roll down! Let them!

(BEGGAR *runs off.*)

CHORUS We can't just look on! Yet we can't stop anything. Evil has a power all its own. We are not powerful. We do not want war, but war has us in its claws. We fear our lives will be crushed under the heel of the marching soldier. The color of the flag won't matter then. Look! The nurse returns with the children. Their faces are happy, joyous. Was all our fear a dream?

NURSE Medea! Medea! Come out! I am back with the children. We are all safe, praise God! Be glad, Medea, fortune will rescue us yet.

MEDEA You are back. You have news.

NURSE Good news. The princess received your gifts graciously. She welcomed the boys, they will be free from exile.

MEDEA Oh, I am lost!

NURSE I do not understand, Medea. The children may stay. Word spread that there was peace between you and Jason. Everyone was happy throughout the house.

TUTOR How long will they remain happy?

MEDEA What of the gifts?

NURSE She looked at them, admired them, as I said.

MEDEA What did she do with them? Tell me exactly.

NURSE She opened the cases. Looked, then put them by her side.

MEDEA I have been tricked by the gods.

NURSE Did you expect her to wear your dress at her own wedding? It is not reasonable...

BOY Mother, Mother, take us to bed. We are tired.

MEDEA Take them away from me. I cannot bear it.

(*The* NURSE *takes them into the house.*)

So, my children, you have a city, you have a home, and I have none. You can leave your mother behind. Why? Why? Because Jason's blood runs in your veins. Because of that Portuguese blood, you draw justice. I cannot bear it. I want no whiteness, no tenderness, near my heart. I will cut it off like fat from lean meat. There must be more news. It will come soon.

(*A* SOLDIER *approaches.*)

CHORUS Hurry inside, Medea. Even you are not safe on a night like this. It is one of Jason's soldiers.

(SOLDIER *rushes in, has gun and uniform.*)

MEDEA Who are you?

SOLDIER I am one of Jason's men.

MEDEA Why are you here?

SOLDIER To bring you warning.

MEDEA Why would you want to help me? You wear Jason's uniform.

SOLDIER You were kind to me when I was here in this house.

MEDEA But you are still Jason's man. A soldier.

SOLDIER No more. No more. Not after what I have seen!

MEDEA You are one of his killers. One who keeps the slaves in line.

SOLDIER No, Medea. No more killing, I can't. my mouth is too full of blood.

MEDEA A soldier is a soldier.

SOLDIER No. No more. (*He throws down his guns, tears away his shirt, throws it away.*) I am not a soldier. I am a man. A black man. My heart beats loud, like thunder, for fear of what will happen to you.

MEDEA Tell me what happened.

SOLDIER You must flee now. Escape! If you have horses, Medea, ride. Or a boat. I can find you one, sail down the coast away from here.

MEDEA First tell me of the beautiful Cecilia.

SOLDIER Ohh!

MEDEA I must hear it.

SOLDIER Ohh!

MEDEA You are my brother now. Tell me.

SOLDIER My eyes burn with what I have seen, my ears ring with the cries.

MEDEA She put on the garments?

SOLDIER Yes! She put on the garments. Did you do it, Medea?

MEDEA Yes.

SOLDIER Yes.

MEDEA Speak softly. The trees have ears.

SOLDIER You are avenged. Horribly avenged. No one could know, or dream... At first there was only the scent of incense and soft music, bright satin dresses and jewels and Jason, tall and erect, waiting. She walked slowly to the altar, her dress glittering, light flashing even from the soft candles that lit the chapel. All eyes were on her and hers only on Jason, Jason's face full of love and yearning... The priest stood stiffly above them, his great soft white hands floating over the scene like solemn doves. The crowd hushed as the rite began, the familiar murmurings of the Christian vows. And then, Medea...then... The girl suddenly staggered back, her face white, her lips flecked with foam. Hands reached out to help her, but pain moved against the young bride... She screamed, she ran, her hair lit by the wreath of gold, streaming flames. The priest fell back from the flames, drawing his vestments up around him. The fine-woven dress fastened onto her flesh. She ran from the altar screaming, screaming, the crowd echoing her screams with their own. Finally, at the end of the aisle she fell, black, hideous, burning flesh swimming in pools of fire, body quivering and writhing, mounted by pain. Screams rose to the high chapel ceiling like trapped birds.

MEDEA Did any die with her?

SOLDIER Barretto.

MEDEA Ohh!

SOLDIER He ran to her and embraced her, crying out his love of his poor daughter. But his body stuck to the fine dress and, struggling against it, the poison tore and ate him, devouring him too. He ripped at his own flesh with his hands, trying to tear pain from old bones. He died screaming, locked to his daughter on the floor of the church, both screaming, flaming, dying...dying...

MEDEA And did the flames shine as brightly as the sun in Jason's face?

SOLDIER Escape, Medea, while there's still a chance. The city is masterless. All's in confusion, looting and fighting are spreading like fire. They'll avenge him, Medea, Medea!

MEDEA Thank you, soldier.

(*One of the* DANCERS *enters, clothes torn, terror-stricken. He stands before* MEDEA *without saying a word.*)

SOLDIER They come already, Medea, you must hurry.

MEDEA It is another witness. What do you have to say, witness?

(*No response.*) What do you want?

(*No response.*) The singers are mute now. The dancers stumble and fall... Speak!

(*The* DANCER *lets out a scream and runs off.*)

SOLDIER They will kill me if they find me. I'm going, Medea.

(*He exits.*)

CHORUS It is over, Medea. You have had your vengeance. Let is be over.

MEDEA For the dead it is over. Not for me. Not for Jason.

(NURSE *comes out on step.*)

NURSE Medea. My child. I set the boys down. They did not want to sleep. They are too excited about the events of the day, even if they can't understand them. To get them quiet I sang an old lullaby. A lullaby I sang to you when you were a child, Medea. (*She sings an African lullaby.*) Do you remember it, Medea?

MEDEA Yes.

NURSE As I sang, my eyes closed, I imagined myself back in those days of peace. I nearly believed that all that happens now was only a bad nightmare to be chased away by the spirit of the morning.

MEDEA Yes.

NURSE Until I came to the door and heard your voice, Medea, I thought we were free of that terror. Let it end now! Let us go away. You have found enough vengeance.

MEDEA No, not yet. The slave's chains are endless, to be broken and broken again. The children are not sleeping yet?

NURSE No, Medea, I said they were too excited.

MEDEA I want you to bring them out.

NURSE But they were just set down...

MEDEA Bring them out. I want to see Jason's children. I want to instruct them. Tutor, you may listen too. It is not too late for you also to learn.

(NURSE, *in confusion, runs in to get the* CHILDREN.)

CHORUS Lord, Lord save us from this whirlwind. Lord, save us from this dark blade that slashes our hopes like a razor.

MEDEA Silence! The time for missionaries' prayers is past.

(*Enter* NURSE. *She has the two* BOYS.) Oh, my sleepy birds! Are you awake enough to understand? Our enemies, who ruled this city, have fallen, their future curls lie smoke into the night sky and the morning sun will find no trace of it. The future! The future. Do you know where it lies? Listen.

(*She pauses. We hear the drums.*) That is the sound of the future. Our people, black people, have a future. The black man will live freely in Africa one day and posses a future all his own... But you and I...there is no future, no choice...(*Turning away.*) Every way says they must die. To be slain by another hand... No! Let their mother kill them!

CHORUS Jesus, Jesus, Lord, save the children, save the babies, take them into your hands.

MEDEA (*suddenly embraces them*) My own! Let me hold you! Forgive me... Brave young eyes, you look without flinching. Your eyes are like mine. The lips, the fine lips, they are...Jason. The nose, mine, the forehead...Jason. The skin...do they call you mulatto, the other children?

(Gunshots offstage.)

NURSE My lady, they're coming. Take the children and flee. Go to the docks, find a boat. Medea, my child, listen to me. They're coming with guns and death. The city is all in confusion; that may be your chance. But hurry! They will come take their vengeance on you.

MEDEA I will go into the house. I can protect myself. Jason's blood runs in their veins...Jason and I mated in their blood, the past nurtured in their innocent bodies... How much unspeakable pain to tear one's self from the enemy! The final act hangs motionless like a hawk in the noonday sun... Come, children, into the house. It is late. Night is for sleep. You are going to sleep now.

(She rushes them into the house.) Quickly! Afterwards weep—though I kill them, they were dear to me!

(She slams the door shut. NURSE *rushes to door, can't open it.)*

NURSE Medea! No. No, my child!

CHORUS What will happen? Jesus, come quickly, stay her hand. We pray, look down on her... We search the heavens for help, whoever can save her... Nyame! Goddess of the sun, who gave Medea a golden birth, hold back her dark hand, drive back this dawn of blood...

BOY *(shrill cry)* Mother, ai!

CHORUS No, Medea! God, stop her! Open the door!

BOY Mother! Mother! Ai!

CHORUS It is too late.

MEDEA Ahh!

(Crying and lamentation.)

NURSE It is over. Oh, my children!

TUTOR It was fated to happen. It was foretold. It passed before us like a dream and now it is all gone...children, pupils, hope...gone.

(*A trumpet offstage.*)

CHORUS Someone is coming! We will all be killed! Who! The cursed father. He carries a gun.

(*Enter* JASON, *gun in hand.*)

JASON Just one word. Tell me where she is. Just point the way and I'll find the way to her. Answer me! The night has gone mad! All my soldiers have deserted me. You will answer me!

CHORUS She is inside. You are the cause of this, Jason.

JASON Silence!

CHORUS There is horror here. If you ever want to be happy again, leave now, and ask no questions.

JASON Nurse, what of the children? I must protect my boys. The governor's people will want them killed to punish her.

(NURSE *falls wailing to the floor.*) Medea has killed herself. That's why you cry. Fine, fine. She was brave, then. It was a wise thing to do. But the children, where are my boys?

NURSE All my children—al the babies I ever nursed and cared for are gone. I am alone.

JASON What are you saying?

CHORUS Your children are dead, Jason.

JASON (*stunned, he is unwilling to understand*) No. No. It's not true. You trick me. They're inside. It's night. They must be asleep. No, it's not true.

(MEDEA *comes to doorway. Her hands are bloodstained.*)

MEDEA Who is it that disturbs me? Oh, it is Jason, the famous adventurer—and now he should be the governor, as the former governor died suddenly. Governor, you see those fires burning? You should have them put out. They may spread and get out of your control. And silence the drums. You must silence the drums. You must have many new responsibilities. Why should you come to this dark doorstep? I'm honored, Governor. Let me give you my hands in greeting.

(*She thrusts forward her hands. They are covered with blood.*)

JASON What is that stain?

MEDEA You have seen it before, Jason. For you my hands have always shone with...blood of my brother, blood of my sons, most precious wine. Come taste it. Lick it from my hands. The wine is too strong for you, Jason? Let it be your communion this night.

JASON I will kill you, Medea.

MEDEA I am too strong for you, Jason.

JASON Give me my sons, Medea. They must be protected. Give me my sons and I'll go away. I will promise you protection.

MEDEA It is too late for protection, Jason.

JASON I want my sons.

MEDEA Go home to your bride, Jason. She waits for you...

JASON (*draws his gun*) Stop!

MEDEA That is no good, Jason. No good. I am safe this night. For I am a witch and a sorceress, Jason, and even your bullets will do nothing.

JASON I'm coming in.

MEDEA Stay back, Jason. Be careful. Do you see the two snakes? (*Points to the snakes on the steps.*) They are full of poison and ready to strike. Come close and you will join your bride.

JASON I must see my sons. The women said...they said...

MEDEA What did they say? They couldn't begin to tell you what you will now see.

(*She throws open the door, exposing the two* BOYS, *bodies pinned against the Fleece.*)

JASON Only you, Medea. Only you could have done this... This is the work of a monster, not a woman!

MEDEA Call me a monster then, Jason...it was hate of you that fed the monster.

JASON My sons...dead, dead, dead.

MEDEA It was a disease they caught from their father.

JASON But you feel no pain, no sorrow?

MEDEA Yes, but finally my sorrow is one that you cannot mock.

JASON You have no pity!

MEDEA My love was too great for pity, Jason. You betrayed that love. How I was despised because of you, Jason, a lonely, strange, black woman, betrayed in a strange land. Now, Jason, this land of yours is stained with your children's blood.

JASON Only give me the boys, let me bury the bodies.

MEDEA No. There is no grave for them here. No!

JASON Let me touch them.

MEDEA No! They are wholly mine. Go bury your bride.

JASON My own two sons...

MEDEA They follow me. I go with the spirits of the night while my magic still holds. You go down to the ships, Jason, weep your tears by the sides of the rotting hulks that hold the corpses of the slaves you took. Find two small bodies and bury those. Mourn, then, over the bodies of strangers, and remember your sons. I must go now. It is cold. Where are the fires? The rebels have disappeared for the night. No more fires. Only the stars give me light now. And they have no pity.

(MEDEA *goes into house.* JASON *collapses on steps. The* CHORUS *begins a mourning chant.* MEDEA *comes out of the side door bearing the two* BOYS.)

CHORUS It was fated to happen. It was foretold, echoed by a thousand whispered voices. Our prayers fell from the sky like broken doves. We watched helpless as violence raced violence, evil mated evil. Medea leaves us for the promised sanctuary, the promised land, yet we don't feel safe, not for ourselves, not for her. The Golden Fleece is black with blood. The future promises no refuge from our deeds, as we end our prayers and wait for morning. That is all we can do now, huddle together against the rising storm and wait, wait for the morning sun.

End of Play

Interview 1

An Interview with Jim Magnuson

Q: What was the impetus behind the play? Why adapt Medea*?*

JM: Adapting *Medea* was not my idea. In the mid-Sixties I was teaching a playwriting workshop at the James Weldon Johnson Theater Arts Center in East Harlem. My very first produced play *No Snakes In This Grass* had been done in the street theaters of Harlem for a couple of summers, a Garden of Eden comedy in which a white Adam is flummoxed when he encounters a black Eve. It was at the Center that I met Mical Whitaker, the director of the East River Players, which was one of the most significant street theater troupes at the time. It was Mical's idea to do *Medea*. While at Howard University, he had been a student of Owen Dodson's, who had written a Black Medea that had left a deep impression on him. Mical's thought was to do an African Medea that would somehow reflect the struggles of the Sixties, the reality of what was happening on the streets of New York.

Q: Why set the play in a Portuguese colony, rather than British or French?

JM: I set the play in a Portuguese colony in order to make the marriage of a white European to an African woman a bit more credible. So much of the research I did forty years ago has faded in my memory, but I do remember that the British definitely did not take kindly to inter-racial marriage.

Q: What were the biggest challenges in adapting Medea *to an African setting?*

JM: The biggest decision in adapting the play was how realistic and detailed to make it. There are touches here and there that reflect actual African history, but at the same time, the language is fairly elevated and poetic. What it really does reflect, I think, is the anger and frustrations on the streets of black America at that time. I didn't want to make it didactic and ham-handed, but there were some liberties taken. By adding the character of the Beggar, I allowed myself the opportunity to add a very jaundiced and contemporary bite on the original play.

Q: In the play, Adago offers to send Medea to "a land of hope where you could be safe and free." Should this be read ironically, as the ship she will sail on is a slave ship bound for America? In 1968, I assume audiences would have seen this as in direct contradiction to the lived experiences of African Americans.

JM: I think that the audiences on 1968 definitely got the joke.

Q: How much is this play thus a comment on America, rather than Africa?

JM: It seems like a very American play to me, just in the same way that Shakespeare's *Hamlet* is an English play, not a Danish one. One story: the first night of rehearsals, the lead in the play, a wonderful young actress named Detra Lambert, was forty-five minutes late. When she finally arrived, Mical was furious at her. He couldn't imagine what possible excuse she could have. "Haven't you heard?" she said. "Martin Luther King's been shot." The first night of rehearsals was the first night of the Harlem riots. All that summer we put on this play about a black woman abandoned and shamed, avenging herself on her white husband. I have never been in a theater where the atmosphere was more electric.

Q: The 2001 production in San Diego was read by critics as being more about feminisim than postcolonialism. How do you think this play reads in 2013, 45 years after it was written?

JM: This is an interesting question. Two summers ago, *No Snakes In this Grass* was revived and done at the Lincoln Center Summer Festival. When I saw it, I realized that those two plays that I did in Harlem in the Sixties both focus on two strong, and wronged, black women. *African Medea* received a very good production in Savannah, Georgia recently. But it may be hard to re-capture the passion and frustration and thwarted idealism that went into those early productions, and when I say that, I'm talking even more about the director, Mical Whitaker and a group of remarkable actors, than I am about myself. We are now living during the time of the first black president; I don't know that any of us then would have thought this would ever have been possible. Having said that, I think the play still possesses the point to inspire real fear. Euripides was a genius, let's face it, and we did all ride on his brilliance.

CHAPTER 2

BLACK MEDEA

INTRODUCTION

Ernest Ferlita, SJ, is a Jesuit playwright and long-time professor of theatre at Loyola University in New Orleans, a city in which many (although not all) of his plays are set. First written in 1976, *Black Medea* sets the play in 1810 New Orleans immediately following the slave revolution in Haiti. Jerome (Jason) is a former French military officer; Madeleine (Medea) is a voodoo priestess.

Jerome and Madeleine are both refugees in New Orleans, which serves as the play's Corinth. Jason is from Iolcus, Jerome is from France. Medea is from Colchis, her namesake from Dahomey by means of Haiti. They have fled to New Orleans where Jerome is offered the opportunity to marry the daughter of Colonel Croydon. As in the original, when Jerome seeks to divorce Madeleine to marry Croydon's (Creon) daughter, Madeleine uses her supernatural powers for revenge.

Euripides presents Medea as having supernatural powers as evidenced by the reported death of Pelias, the gifts that burn with unquenchable fire, and the dragon-drawn chariot, but it is Seneca who focused on Medea as a witch.[1] Ferlita further transforms her into a voodoo priestess with the play structured as a voodoo ritual, revealing the story through flashbacks. The chorus consists of three women who serve as assistants in the rituals of Madeleine and Tante Emilié, the nurse figure who is also a priestess of Damballah.

Damballah is an *orisha*, a *loa*, a god from Africa. He is intimately associated with historic voodoo queens such as Marie Laveau.[2] Depicted as a serpent and the father of serpents, Damballah is the creator of the world and the protector of children. He shows up again in *Pecong*, figuring prominently in the life of that play's Medea. Damballah is also the principle of cosmic order. When Jerome and Croydon begin working against Madeleine, they are, in fact, acting against order and justice. Madeleine is thus free to (and perhaps even obligated to according to the tenets of voodoo and the play) destroy them with the help of Damballah and the other *loa* invoked in the play—Baron Samedi, Erzuli, and Ogun.

As noted elsewhere, voodoo, or more properly *voudun*, was counter-hegemonic and oppositional to slavery.[3] Voodoo brought with it leadership, a theology of freedom, and organization. African religions were banned in the New World and had to be practiced in secret. They also played a role in many slave uprisings. Therefore, in *Black Medea*, Croydon is right to fear voodoo not because it is heathen but because it has social power to foment revolution against white domination.

Madeleine's use of voodoo then drives the second half of the play. She kills the children "in spirit" first, then destroys the children's bodies and sacrifices them to Damballah. She uses a serpent bracelet fetish (symbolizing Damballah) to kill Croydon's daughter and envenom Croyden. Interestingly, the use of the bracelet to kill is mechanical rather than magical, thereby diminishing Madeleine's supernatural abilities. Unlike the original in which there is a face-to-face confrontation, the play ends with Jerome alone in the home he shared with Madeleine, demanding, "Why?" to an empty room. In this play, Damballah serves to unite Africa and the New World, as well as link the struggles of people of color in Africa, the Caribbean, and the United States.

Ferlita's *Black Medea* is published for the first time in this volume.

NOTES

1. Sarah Iles Johnson, "Introduction" in *Medea.* James L. Clauss and Sarah Iles Johnson, eds. (Princeton: Princeton University Press, 1997), 17.
2. Anthony B. Pinn, *Varieties of African-American Religious Experience* (Minneapolis: Fortress, 1998), 37.
3. Kevin J. Wetmore, Jr., *Black Dionysus: Greek Tragedy and African-American Theatre* (Jefferson, NC: McFarland and Company, 2003), 168-9.

PLAY 2

BLACK MEDEA

ERNEST FERLITA, SJ

CAST OF CHARACTERS

Tante Emilie

Madeleine

Colonel Croydon

Jerome, Comte D'Argonne

Captain Pierre Laguerre

First Woman

Second Woman

Third Woman

The Drummer

Time: 1810

Place: New Orleans

Running Time, without intermission: 90 minutes.

Intermission, if desired, indicated in the text.

SETTING: The stage is bare except, if feasible, for two triangular columns that revolve like periaktoi. One side of each column is black, one side is red, the third side is covered with mirrors of different sizes. The two columns are set downstage on either side. Before the play begins, the black side of each column is facing front. There is a raised platform Upstage with a door at the center. Sloping above the door is a stylized staff representing the serpent god Damballah.

AT RISE: The DRUMMER *sits towards one side of the stage with his two tall drums. His face is made up like a death mask, all white with black slashes under the cheekbones and down the nose. At the sound of the drums* TANTE EMILIE *and the* THREE WOMEN *turn the columns to red. They are dressed all in white, bandana, blouse, and skirt;* TANTE EMILIE, *in addition, wears a loose white baldric. From time to time, other percussive instruments sound with the drums: a rattle, sticks, a flat drum.*

TANTE EMILIE *(Whirling.)* Damballah, m' sé couleve ro!

THREE WOMEN *(Moving their bodies rhythmically to the sound of the drums)* Great serpent, king! I am ready, loyo, but the way is barred.

TANTE EMILIE Damballah, m' sé couleve ro!

THREE WOMEN Great serpent, king! Show me the gate, loyo, and let me pass.

TANTE EMILIE If only the ships had never come, great white whales with empty bellies prowling the coast of Africa to swallow up my people. If only the royal house of Dahomey had not been scattered, its remnants sold in the market-place of Port-au-Prince in Haiti. For she who is my mistress, Madeleine, daughter of a prince, never would have coupled with Jerome, Comte D'Argonne, and fled with him in secret to the city of New Orleans *(Whirling.)* Damballah, m' sé couleve ro!

THREE WOMEN Great serpent, king! I am ready, loyo, but the way is barred.

TANTE EMILIE Damballah, m' sé couleve ro!

THREE WOMEN Great serpent, king! Show me the gate, loyo, and let me pass.

TANTE EMILIE If only the great Toussaint L'Ouverture had not been deceived by lying tongues before Napoleon's war ships had beached upon the island. If only Jerome, Comte D'Argonne, had not come with them to claim his lost inheritance and the heart of my mistress, Madeleine. For she never would have killed her brother in her passion for this brazen man whose father had enslaved her own; she never would have given up the bonds of blood to blind herself in exile to an ingrate *(Whirling.)* Damballah, m' sé couleve ro!

THREE WOMEN Great serpent, king! I am ready, loyo, but the way is barred.

TANTE EMILIE Damballah, m' sé couleve ro!

THREE WOMEN Great serpent, king! Show me the gate, loyo, and let me pass.

TANTE EMILIE Where is her passion now? Still there, in the depths of her heart, but coiling with a new and deadly aim. Now it will strike from her eyes and lips and all her senses with a venomous hate. Jerome, the man for whom she gave up everything, has left her for another woman, not a woman even, but a girl. She hates him, hates the sons she bore him. Poor Placide, poor Moise! I begin to fear for them. I dread the unexpected, and yet I know that it must come. Prepare the way! *(Moving Upstage.)* Madeleine! Li le li temps, oh!

THREE WOMEN Now is the hour, the time!

TANTE EMILIE Damballah goes before you.

THREE WOMEN Great serpent, king!

TANTE EMILIE He will show you the gate and let you pass. Madeleine!
Li le li temps, oh!

THREE WOMEN Now is the hour, the time!

(MADELEINE *enters through the door. She is dressed in black and gold brocade with a black turban.*)

MADELEINE

Damballah, I am ready! I have watched you come over the dark waters of the spirit, coiling through the branches of the brain. Look how I am wronged to the very roots of me, upturned in the garden I grew with the very juice of my life, outcast, swept aside, thrown into the fire! In spite of the vows that bound him to me, him with whom I entwined my roots to make one tree, with whom and for whom I flowered in my morning and brought forth fruit, Jerome, my husband of seven years, has up and gone from my bed. Not even the sons of our flesh could hold him. I cannot look at them now without wanting to tear from their skin the traces of him whom I hate. I drew upon him the ocean of my spirit, I opened my depths to him, I held him up! Does he think for a single moment that in the babbling brook of a girl he will find a deeper love, an embrace more sustaining than mine? I clung to him between earth and moon in low tides and high; together we steered for the stars. But this girl! May he disappear with her in the sand! May I see him blasted on his brightest day, him and his bride and the home they live in! Damballah, I am ready! I will tell you everything. I will tell you how I came to suffer what I suffer. I will go with you through all that has happened, so that when we come to what has not yet happened but must happen, you will make it happen. And revenge me!

TANTE EMILIE Damballah, make it happen!

THREE WOMEN Make it happen, make it happen!

(The WOMEN *turn the two columns to black and remain dimly visible in attitudes of listening. The drums fall silent.)*

MADELEINE Four days ago a man came to see me.

*(*COLONEL CROYDON *enters Upstage Left.)*

MADELEINE Even before I saw him I felt the city closing in on me, the river rising with all the mud a continent could wish on me. He was the father of the bride. *(Turns and bows deeply as* CROYDON *advances.)*

CROYDON I hardly know how to address you.

MADELEINE I am Madeleine, Comtesse D'Argonne.

CROYDON No! That title was never yours.

MADELEINE The Comte D'Argonne is my husband.

CROYDON He is not your husband. He never *was* your husband. In this country, in this city where blood is the clearest sign of royalty, he never *could* be yours.

MADELEINE We exchanged vows.

CROYDON Where, in Haiti?

MADELEINE Yes.

CROYDON Before a priest?

MADELEINE Before God.

CROYDON God has not informed us. Do you imagine for a single moment that Jerome would have dared to bring you here if there had been a valid marriage? Do you imagine that a man of his lineage would have entrusted to your womb the future of his family's name? He brought you here as his mistress and set you up on Rampart Street in a way that everybody understands. A stranger should conform to city customs. You have shown yourself incapable of that.

MADELEINE I have conformed better than you think. For seven years I let myself age like a sweet wine in this bottle of a city, sitting here to serve my master's pleasure. But I am no man's slave. My father was a prince of the house of Dahomey. It was people like you that enslaved him, shipped him to the island of Saint Domingue—or Haiti, as they call it now. The old Comte D'Argonne bought him with some ten or twenty others, but soon saw he was no ordinary man, and before the year was out had granted him liberté de savane, yes, with a gift of land and seven slaves. My father was a free man even before Toussaint had won freedom for us all. I am as free as you are, sir.

CROYDON Not exactly. In New Orleans you are free and you are not free. I suggest you leave the city and return at once to Haiti to enjoy there whatever freedom you imagine. Let me get to the point: I *order* you to leave the city. I want you gone before sunset tomorrow. And you're to take your children with you.

MADELEINE By what right, by what power—?

CROYDON The power of my wealth. I might as well be brutally clear. My wealth makes my opinions important. The mayor listens to me. As far as you are concerned, it so happens that he shares my opinion. Crime is rampant in New Orleans, and there are two reasons for it. The first is the Louisiana Purchase, but I won't bother you with that. The second is the Haitian revolution, which has visited upon our shores that vicious thing called voodoo. Only last year another two thousand of your people arrived here, restless and unruly. We know your reputation. We suspect your inclination. Jerome has apprised us of both.

MADELEINE What has he said of me?

CROYDON That you are a priestess of the Dahomey cult. Do you deny it?

MADELEINE I am first of all a believer. Voodoo is a way of the unseen, it is a way of God.

CROYDON It is a way to revolution! It was voodoo that stirred up the slaves to revolt in Haiti, it was voodoo that massacred the French. Toussaint used it and then suppressed it. That was very wise of him. He used it to get to the top, and kicked it away as he would a ladder, so that nobody else could climb up after him. Do you think that I or Mayor Mather can be any less cautious? Do you think that any responsible citizen can sit by and allow that tangle of serpents to nest here?

MADELEINE Damballah, hear my cry!

CROYDON You see! I order you to leave!

MADELEINE What are you afraid of, that I'll start a revolution? Do you see an arsenal here? Do I have an army coming up the river? I am a woman. What is it you're afraid of?

CROYDON I am afraid of your frenzy. Yes, let me be blunt with you again. I am afraid of the things you are capable of. You say you believe in God, I thin rather it's the devil you traffic with. I don't know what powers you command, but I fear that in your rage you will do injury to someone—

MADELEINE To whom? To you? I don't hate *you*. I don't blame *you* for what Jerome has done. After all, I can't expect *you* to understand the special bonds that made us two in one flesh. You were only conforming to the customs of the city. You saw in Jerome, Comte D'Argonne, a man of quality and noble bearing still unattached by Louisiana law. The perfect match for your daughter! I bear no grudge against you, you acted reasonably.

CROYDON I do not trust you. I trust you even less than before. I am afraid not so much for myself as for my daughter Corinne, for Jerome. You cannot stay in New Orleans. I repeat: I want you gone before sunset tomorrow. *(Starts out.)*

MADELEINE Wait! I will go. But let my sons stay.

CROYDON Impossible! What are you thinking of? This is some ruse to gain time.

MADELEINE How can I provide for them? Only their father can do that.

CROYDON But they still need a mother. Take them to Haiti with you.

MADELEINE I cannot return to Haiti. At least not to my people.

CROYDON Why not? Enjoy your "liberté de savane". The country's yours. Go back to your people.

MADELEINE I cannot! To bind myself to Jerome, I had to cut myself off from them.

CROYDON Time heals. Go back. We'll all be happier if you do.

MADELEINE If you only knew the price I had to pay, you would not speak to me so glibly.

CROYDON I will not be swayed. You must go immediately, you and your children. I hope you will not so aggravate the situation that we shall have to use force. *(Starts out again.)*

MADELEINE *(Clings to his hand.)* I beg you—have patience with me. Give me a few more days. How can I leave before sunset tomorrow? Can I cram seven years into my pockets? I must make arrangements. I must see about my children. For their sake, give me three more days.

CROYDON *(Shakes himself loose.)* I am a fool to listen to you. An ill-considered mercy is a double crime. I know I'm making a mistake. Still, I will grant you your request. Three days. But you listen to me, woman: If you and your sons are not gone after three days, you'd wish you'd never seen the light of day. (Goes out.)

(The columns are turned to red. The drums start up at MADELEINE's *command.)*

MADELEINE Beat the drum for me!

TANTE EMILIE Mayen ka! Beat the drum.

THREE WOMEN Mayen ka! Mayen ka!

MADELEINE What I tell to Damballah I tell to you. What I tell to you I tell to Damballah.

TANTE EMILIE Damballah, m' sé couleve ro!

THREE WOMEN Great serpent, king!

MADELEINE I am driven again to the sea.

TANTE EMILIE Where are you going?

THREE WOMEN Enhé, la reine, oh Madeleine!

TANTE EMILIE What house will receive you?

THREE WOMEN Enhé, la reine, oh Madeleine!

TANTE EMILIE What city, what land?

THREE WOMEN Enhé, la reine, oh Madeleine!

TANTE EMILIE Will we see you again?

THREE WOMEN Enhé, la reine, oh Madeleine!

MADELEINE I go with the god in my heart.

TANTE EMILIE Damballah, li le li temps, oh!

THREE WOMEN Now is the hour, the time! Cord cuts cord, oh! Beyond the mountain is the mountain.

MADELEINE What is done to me will be done to them.

TANTE EMILIE Damballah, li le li temps, oh!

THREE WOMEN Now is the hour, the time! Cord cuts cord, oh! Beyond the mountain is the mountain.

TANTE EMILIE What you tell to Damballah you tell to us.

THREE WOMEN What you tell to us you tell to Damballah.

MADELEINE I tell you clearly: The day a leaf falls in the river is not the day it sinks to the bottom. Today is the day, if they only knew! Yes, I too am like a leaf torn from the branch, and I am flung into the river. I shall sink to the bottom or be carried to some island in the sea.

TANTE EMILIE Damballah is like a river, woyo.

THREE WOMEN He will carry you on his back, woyo. He will take you to the island in the sea.

MADELEINE But do you see those other leaves? Four days ago they fell into the river, the bride, the bridegroom, and the father of the bride. The day they fell into the river is not the day they sink into the bottom. Today is the day, if they only knew! Do you think I would have gone crawling to Croydon except to win time enough to dance? Look, I am dancing around him!

TANTE EMILIE Comme ça! Comme ça!

THREE WOMEN Enhé, la reine, oh Madeleine!

MADELEINE Loo, I am holding a big white bird in my hands, one hand around his head, the other around his feet, and his great wings flap across my face.

TANTE EMILIE Mayen ka!

THREE WOMEN Beat the drums! Mayen ka! But I will not let go! Ago-hé! Until I twist off his head!

TANTE EMILIE

THREE WOMEN Ago-hé!

MADELEINE Do you understand what I am saying? I am besieged by three sworn enemies, father and daughter and my own husband. Where is my justice? Who will fight my battle for me? The law strips me in the market-place, makes a mockery of my marriage, laughs at my claim to freedom, tries to bury it above ground in a whitewashed mausoleum of words.

TANTE EMILIE Break the no law, li la lo!

THREE WOMEN Damballah, m' sé couleve ro!

MADELEINE Yes, if I wanted justice, I knew I would have to get it myself, with the power of the god in my heart. But how? I thought of a hundred ways. I would go with a torch to the big white house with the candlelight dancing in the cut-glass door and set fire to the drapes in every window. Or I would steal through the house as they lay in their canopied beds and run a sword through their hearts. But one thing made me pause: What if I die in the doing? Or worse yet, am led away in chains to be hanged in the place d'armes with everybody laughing. Never! I must not bring derision on myself in my striving to right my wrongs. I am sprung from the loins of Africa, the daughter of a prince!

TANTE EMILIE Enhé, la reine, oh Madeleine!

THREE WOMEN Enhé, la reine, oh Madeleine!

MADELEINE I had to find some other way, more skillful, more appropriate. Today is the day, if they only knew!

TANTE EMILIE What you tell to Damballah you tell to us.

THREE WOMEN What you tell to us you tell to Damballah.

MADELEINE I will tell you all that has happened so that when we come to what has not yet happened but must happen, Damballah will make it happen.

TANTE EMILIE Damballah, make it happen!

THREE WOMEN Make it happen, make it happen!

(The columns are turned to black. The drums fall silent.)

MADELEINE Later that evening Jerome himself came through the door.

(JEROME enters Upstage Left.)

MADELEINE He stood for a moment where the light almost forgave him everything. Then he turned.

JEROME I expected more sense in a woman used to shaping events to her ends. Before sitting down to your sweet revenge like a field hand to his bread and molasses, you might've looked to your future. It would've been possible to stay here, quietly, in the Quarter, and maintain your household in as good a style as you've always done. In face, I would've seen to its improvement. Instead, you belch a thousand threats without even caring who hears what. I don't mind your railing against *me.* That was to be expected. But why do you have to talk against Croydon, and dip into your old voodoo bag of tricks to garnish everything with the taste of witchery? I thought you'd thrown that bag away. Don't you know the mood of the city? In the eyes of a man like Croydon, voodoo's more than witchery, it's revolution. I've tried to calm him down, tried to make him see you as I do, especially as the mother of my children. But now he's mobilized all his forces, and there's no holding him back. He thinks I'm blind to the danger you represent, and he won't hear another word on the subject. You have to go. And Placide and Moise will have to go with you. I can see his point. I have to admit they're still too young to do without a mother. Thank God he saw fit to grant you three days' grace. So I've come here tonight to see that you and the children are well provided for. What are your plans?

MADELEINE You bastard! Do you call yourself a man? My heart is full so many things I can hardly speak for wanting them all said. What are my plans? Thank you for asking! Now that all your own plans are made, you give me the liberty of making mine. "So your man is getting married." That was how it came to me. Somebody read it in the papers. The whole city of New Orleans knew about it before you did. What *am* I to you?

Did you pick me up at some fancy quadroom ball, after eyeing twenty others cut from the same cloth, with their mamas waiting bird-like for your offer? Did you think you could have me for your pleasure and then walk out on me one sugery day when you were ready to build your own life? I killed my brother for you! I drove a knife in him when he tried to stop me from going away with you. He had taken all your property and he would have taken your life if it hadn't been for me. I helped you recover some of your wealth, I arranged our passage out of Haiti. And now after all I've done for you, you take another woman to your bed. Woman? She's still a child. Corinne! Is that her name? How delicate! and white! Magnolia white! Have you seen the magnolia when it goes to seed? Seeds like drops of blood upon the ground. That's all that will be left of your Corinne.

JEROME Am I to take that as a threat?

MADELEINE Take it whatever way you like. What are my plans? Well, I must go away, you tell me. And I must take the children with me. Where shall I go? Back to Haiti? To my father's house? To all the enemies I made in doing kindnesses for you? What will happen to your children if their mother is shot or arrested or thrown into prison? Or turned away and sent into exile? Or turned away and sent again into exile? What a fine wedding-present for your bride to have your children wandering from port to port with the one who saved your life! Damballah, the eyes that look to you can tell the venomous snake from the other. But men upon their bodies bear no mark by which we can discern their poison.

JEROME Well, it seems I'd better be careful how I speak. I see a hurricane brewing in the gulf of your impossible anger. As for all those "kindnesses" you did for me, I'm willing to bet you did them as much for yourself as for me. No, let me finish. I'd even go so far as to say you did them out of love. Yes, love is to blame. Or to be thanked, if you'll permit me to say so. Because, after all, it's not as if you weren't also helped by our coming to New Orleans. I won't even try to list all the ways, but I'll say this much: there's not a man in the city who doesn't envy me your

worth. I mean it. If we were to elect a queen of Rampart Street, of the
Vieux Carré even, why, you would be the one. I regret very much your
having to go. As for this wedding you reproach me with, it's quite easily
explained. Believe me, I had you and the children very much in mind.
Let's look at the situation.

MADELEINE I *know* the situation.

JEROME *My* situation. You don't act like you know it. Think back a few
years. Still in my teens—

MADELEINE A *few* years, did you say?

JEROME Still in my teens, I go off to school in France. In the meantime, Toussaint turns the peaceful island that I left behind into a raging
volcano, turns the slaves loose, turns the French planters out of their
land, among them my father, Comte D'Argonne. It was *your* father and
then all too soon your spiteful brother that acquired my inheritance.
When I returned with Napoleon's troops it was to get it back again. We
failed. The whole colony was lost to France. What was left to me? My
title. Only my title, Comte D'Argonne. All right, so you saved a little
wealth. Where is it now? Seven years ate it up. But I still have my title, by
God, and that's what Colonel Croydon wants for his daughter. He's one
of the richest men in New Orleans, the richest, I'd say, and he chooses
me! Talk about luck! I, of all people, invited to sit at the best of tables!
Not that yours wasn't good enough—

MADELEINE Wasn't?

JEROME Isn't.

MADELEINE My table?

JEROME Did you think I meant your bed? Is that the thought that rankles
you? I don't *have* to have another woman. What I want is to live well, and
I mean that not only for myself but for you. And for Placide and Moise.
I wanted money enough to send my sons to school in France. In France,

it's blood that counts, not skin, and theirs is like the best of wines. They would've prospered there. No question. Was that so bad a plan?

MADELEINE How clever, how plausible! The man who speaks with cleverness when he is wrong is most to be condemned. Of course, nothing of what you've said could've been said to me before, coward that you are!

JEROME I'm sure if we had sat down and discussed the whole thing over a glass of sweet wine you would've nobly given your consent.

MADELEINE You couldn't see me as your wife, is that it? You might be proud of me as your kept woman, your personal whore, but not as your wife.

JEROME The customs of the city—

MADELEINE To hell with the customs of the city! May they rot in their own mildew! You're like a believer who smiles away his faith in the midst of scoffers!

JEROME I've told you why I wanted this marriage. It would've meant comfort, prosperity even, for you as well as for me. And for Placide and Moise.

MADELEINE Moise and Placide. May they live to thank you! Aren't they good enough for you?

JEROME How can you even ask? I love them. You know I do.

MADELEINE If you love them—

JEROME And *they* love me.

MADELEINE They do, they do!

JEROME And I mean to do well by them.

MADELEINE Even now?

JEROME In spite of you, yes. If I can, if I may—

MADELEINE What would prevent you?

JEROME Madeleine, in this city, in this time and place, I can only do so much and no more. I could wish I were under no such constraint. After all, they *are* my flesh and blood—

MADELEINE But you want other sons to carry on your name.

JEROME Legitimate sons, yes! Is that so hard to understand?

MADELEINE Our love made our sons legitimate! Our passion! The passion of the spirit that was in me.

JEROME Madeleine, I have never understood those voodoo spirits of yours.

MADELEINE And yet it was a spirit that brought us together. When you say it was love itself that made me do what I did for you, you speak more truly than you think. That night when you made love to me in the open fields, the night before you sailed for France, it was a spirit that did it. How else can you explain the rush of love between us when you came back to the island after seven years?

JEROME I don't know. Except that everything but you was crumbling all around me.

MADELEINE I never told you all that happened that night. And in the morning you were gone. When you came back after seven years there was no need to tell you. Now I will.

JEROME Madeleine, what good—?

MADELEINE Listen!

(*As if from far away in the darkness, we hear the beat of drums.*)

MADELEINE Every year in Haiti we used to sacrifice to the spirit of Damballah. That year it was me he chose, a girl of fifteen whom no man had ever known. Tante Emilie brought me to Damballah's house, gave me a drug to drink while I waited in the shadows. Everything began to rise— the voices, the hands, the bodies, the flames that lit the crowded room.

(Voices of WOMEN *coming from a distance; "Damballah is calling.")*

MADELEINE And then the doves. The priest bent over them and traced a cross on their backs with oil. Tante Emilie took them one at a time by their heads and feet and raised them aloft; to the beat of the drums she danced and danced with them around the room, their wings like white fire dancing around her hair. She tore off their heads and caught the blood in a basin. But some of it splattered the room. One drop fell on my dress. I stared at it as if my eyes were seeing for the first time. Then a young goat was led into the room, a white goat with blue eyes great with terror. He bleated, he struggled. The smell of death was in the air. Suddenly he stood still. Tante Emilie took ribbons of red silk and looped them carefully around his horns; his hoofs she anointed with sweet-smelling oils. She knelt beside his trembling body and crooned a lullaby in his ears, and the priest was telling him how Damballah was calling, calling, and how he must pass through the great door, going before us all. And he was not to fear because Damballah would be there to greet him. After that, he traced a cross and a circle on the goat's forehead with the blood of doves.

(The voices of WOMEN, *though still are away, begin to swell: "Damballah is calling, Damballah is calling.")*

Then they brought me to the altar and made me kneel beside the goat. Tante Emilie was weeping. With the blood of the doves the priest traced on my forehead a cross and a circle, and he wound to face with the goat, staring into his eyes. The priest was chanting over and over: "Damballah is calling, Damballah is calling." I kept staring into those ice-blue eyes like deep pools that welled up from another world. I could hear a moaning and bleating in my ears, but I didn't know if the bleating was coming from me, or the moaning from the goat. It grew louder and louder—until it burst into a scream. The scream was mine. It ripped from my throat at the very moment that the priest's knife flashed. A fountain of blood gushed from the goat's throat. I leapt back, shuddered, and fell to the floor.

(The drums stop, as she drops to the floor. JEROME *starts for her, then draws back fascinated but revulsed. The drums begin quietly again and build with the voices to the end of speech.)*

MADELEINE When I came to, I was alone in a little room. My breasts were like points of fire. The spirit! The spirit was still in me, calling, calling. To what? I fled into the night. Everything was changed. The trees were a great sea whipped by the wind, the night was a ship, the road was its foaming wake. Suddenly, a winged serpent sprang up from the dark. *(Falls back and looks up at* JEROME.*)* It was you!

JEROME Yes, it was me, rearing up on my horse. I almost trampled you. I had come out with my horse to see for a last time that piece of earth that was mine. The next morning I would be leaving for France, and God only knew when I would return. I hadn't been able to sleep, so I stole out of the house to ride in the moonlight, to see the shape of the hills and the bend in the road, to smell the earth and hear the wind in the sycamores. And then I saw you. You had fallen back with a cry when the horse reared up in your path, and I dismounted to see if you were hurt. You were breathing hard, looking up at me. Your breasts, yes, were like points of fire. I bent down and burnt my lips on you. And then I took you there in the road.

MADELEINE The spirit, the spirit that was in me, *he* was the one! He entered you too! Damballah! He held us both!

JEROME I was making love to the earch, that piece of earth that was mine. And I came back to claim it, it was you again that I embraced.

MADELEINE Yes! *(Leaps up.)* Yes, I am the earth, the shape of the hills and the bend in the road. I open the night. I am Africa, I am the New

World. I am the ocean that bursts its bonds to thunder on every shore. I am fire and lightning, the great passion of your youth! I am the way to God for you! And now are you giving me up? For what For custom, for a place at the best of tables, the expected, the comfortable, the acceptable thing!

(JEROME *turns on his heel and starts away.*)

MADELEINE Where are you going?

JEROME Away from you! Because you're afraid of the spirit!

(*The columns are turned to red. The drums start.* TANTE EMILIE *moves Stage Center, as in a trance.*)

MADELEINE The dove sings in the basin of blood:

TANTE EMILIE I am going on a journey, oh.

THREE WOMEN Are you coming back?

TANTE EMILIE I am going on a journey, oh.

THREE WOMEN Are you coming back?

TANTE EMILIE If I do not die, I will tell you everything.

MADELEINE The dove sings in the basin of blood:

TANTE EMILIE I am circling the darkness, oh.

THREE WOMEN What do you see?

TANTE EMILIE If I do not die, I will tell you everything.

MADELEINE The dove sings in the basin of blood:

TANTE EMILIE I am crossing the ocean, oh.

THREE WOMEN Do you see the shore?

TANTE EMILIE I am crossing the ocean, oh.

THREE WOMEN Do you see the shore?

TANTE EMILIE If I do not die, I will tell you everything.

(The drums sound alone for a time, while the WOMEN dance.)

MADELEINE Can you tell me why a man will hear a spirit calling and then choke on his answer? Damballah!

TANTE EMILIE M' Sé couleve ro!

THREE WOMEN Yay yé!

TANTE EMILIE Let him choke!

THREE WOMEN Let him choke!

TANTE EMILIE Let him flee!

THREE WOMEN Let him flee!

TANTE EMILIE Let him sit!

THREE WOMEN Let him sit!

MADELEINE But I must tell you all that I know. I must tell you all that has happened.

TANTE EMILIE What you tell to Damballah you tell to us.

THREE WOMEN What you tell to us you tell to Damballah.

MADELEINE So that when we come to what has not yet happened but must happen, Damballah will make it happen.

TANTE EMILIE Damballah, make it happen!

THREE WOMEN Make it happen, make it happen!

(The columns are turned to black. The drums fall silent.)

MADELEINE Two days ago a god came to visit me. Or so it seemed. That he was sent by a god I have no doubt. Pierre Laguerre, the pirate who had put his ship at our service and brought us safely to this country, Jerome and me and Tante Emilie. Now after seven years he was back!

(PIERRE LAGUERRE, *smiling broadly, bursts into a circle of light.*)

MADELEINE Pierre! Pierre, is that you?

PIERRE *(Singing and dancing with her.)* Congo 'm gros Neg',(Congo, I'm a big man, M'gros Neg' assez!I'm as big as can be. Wa roulé concou moin,Let's give it a whirl, P'r'm, dansé!Come and dance with me!)

(They embrace, laughing with joy.)

MADELEINE Pierre, Pierre! What are *you* doing in New Orleans?

PIERRE Looking for a revolution! *(Laughs loudly.)*

MADELEINE A god sent you!

PIERRE Yay yé!

MADELEINE Tell me truly.

PIERRE What?

MADELEINE Why you're here.

MADELEINE In Haiti?

PIERRE Where else? But now there's two Haitis. In in the South.

MADELEINE Are things quiet over there now?

PIERRE More or less. Christophe rules in the North like a black Napoleon. Petion is president in the South. *(Steps back to look her over.)* How's Jerome?

MADELEINE Are you married?

PIERRE Me? *(Laughs.)* in my pirate days I said, What for? When the revolution started, I didn't even think about it. And now there's Haiti, the first country after this one to win its freedom. But *we* did it all by ourselves! And of course I've always got my ship. *(Laughs.)* I still say it never carried a greater treasure than you. *(Takes her hands between his and kisses them.)*

MADELEINE I owe my life to you.

PIERRE It was worth saving! And for your sake, Jerome's was too. How *is* the bastard?

MADELEINE *(Moves away.)* More so than ever. *(Turns back.)* He did me wrong, but not anything I ever did to him.

PIERRE What's he done?

MADELEINE He's got himself another wife.

PIERRE I knew it.

MADELEINE His *first* wife, according to the code they go by here. What does that make me? Two sons I gave him, two beautiful sons, and he leaves me for—for—

PIERRE A white girl.

MADELEINE Magnolia white. *(Takes out a black lace handkerchief tucked inside her bodice.)* Look, do you see these seeds?

PIERRE Like drops of blood.

MADELEINE Magnolia seeds. That's all that will be left of her

PIERRE What are you up to?

MADELEINE I am driven from the city!

PIERRE What do you mean, driven?

MADELEINE I must leave in two days.

MADELEINE Croydon, the girl's father. He's rich, a man of means, as they say, and he's doing all he can to get rid of me. He's got the mayor behind him, and between the two of them they'll drive me out even if they have to use force.

PIERRE Why? What have you done?

MADELEINE Nothing! What has been done has been done to me! But they're afraid of what I *can* do. They're afraid of the gods. Voodoo, they say, stirred up the slaves in Haiti.

PIERRE They're right.

MADELEINE Now *they* have stirred me up.

PIERRE They're right about you too. But what about Jerome? Does he go along with them?

MADELEINE Of course he goes along with them. That's his trouble. He goes along with everything. He goes to their clubs, he drinks their brandy, he smokes their cigars, he plays their politics, and now he marries one of their daughters. The fool, he *envies* them! Would *you* give up your ocean for a puddle?

PIERRE So what are you going to do?

MADELEINE I can't stay here, that's for sure.

PIERRE Will you go back to Haiti?

MADELEINE Should i?

PIERRE Not the North. That's no place for you. Voodoo is still outlawed there. Christophe wouldn't want you any more than Toussaint did. Like your mayor, they're afraid of another revolution. Anyway, your brother's family are still there, aren't they?

MADELEINE Yes.

PIERRE In the South things are more easy-going. Voodoo everywhere. The only ones that don't like it are the monks that stayed behind and the mulattoes that came from Paris. And there's no need to worry about your children. The president himself had a French father, so nobody would give you any trouble.

MADELEINE *If* I take them with me.

PIERRE You mean you're leaving them with Jerome?

MADELEINE I didn't say that! I have to think about it. *(Turns to face him directly.)* Pierre, will you take me to Haiti?

(PIERRE looks at her, then laughs heartily.)

MADELEINE What are you laughing at?

PIERRE I never thought I'd be loading my ship again with a treasure!

MADELEINE You'll take me?

PIERRE When did you say you had to leave?

MADELEINE Day after tomorrow.

PIERRE Hmm. Maybe I could rush things a bit.

MADELEINE Could you?

PIERRE Yes.

MADELEINE *(Embraces him.)* I told you! A god sent you! *(Pulling back.)* But I most go away in secret. Nobody must see me go aboard. Can you manage that?

PIERRE Why mustn't they see you?

MADELEINE They'll be after me.

PIERRE Who will?

MADELEINE Jerome. Others who may try to stop me.

PIERRE I thought he wanted you away.

MADELEINE He'll want me as far away as the moon...when he sees what I'm going to do.

PIERRE What are you going to do? What are you getting me into, woman? I got no intention of rotting away my life in a New Orleans jail, no!

MADELEINE All I'm asking you to do is help me get out of New Orleans without being seen. You got me out of Haiti, didn't you?

PIERRE The war covered a lot of things then.

MADELEINE Well, start a riot! On the river front they riot over anything.

PIERRE You still haven't told me what you're plotting.

MADELEINE Justice! I'm plotting justice for myself!

PIERRE How?

MADELEINE *(Lays a hand over the seeds.)* Magnolia seeds. That's all that will be left of her.

PIERRE You mean you... *(Takes in what she has said.)* Madeleine, forget her. Forget Jerome. Forget this city. Take your two children and come away with me to Haiti.

MADELEINE No! I will have my justice. The law denies it to me. In Haiti, when the law denied us justice, we started a revolution.

PIERRE But why the girl...?

MADELEINE Of course the girl! Jerome must be made to suffer. Besides, she's as guilty as the rest of them. (PIERRE *turns away.*)

MADELEINE Look at me!

(He turns back to her.)

MADELEINE You have killed for less reason than I.

PIERRE Maybe.

MADELEINE And many times more.

PIERRE True.

MADELEINE Then take me to Haiti!

PIERRE I never said I wouldn't. Let me think about it. I'll get back to you tomorrow. *(Turns to go.)*

MADELEINE Pierre!

(He stops and faces her.)

MADELEINE You won't betray me, will you?

(He looks at her, turns to go.)

MADELEINE Swear it!

(PIERRE stops again, comes up to her and kisses her full on the lips, then turns and goes out.)

(The columns are turned to red. The drums begin.)

MADELEINE Damballah!

TANTE EMILIE M' sé couleve ro!

THREE WOMEN Yay yé!

MADELEINE *(Moving with the* THREE WOMEN *in a serpentine path across the stage.)* Damballah, I see you coming

TANTE EMILIE THREE WOMEN over the dark waters of the spirit;

MADELEINE I see you silently coiling

TANTE EMILIE

THREE WOMEN through the branches of the brain...

MADELEINE You scan all my thoughts,

TANTE EMILIE THREE WOMEN be they deep as the river

MADELEINE or light as the dragon-fly

TANTE EMILIE THREE WOMEN on the sweep of the dragon's back.

MADELEINE *(Whirling.)* Damballah!

TANTE EMILIE M' sé couleve ro!

THREE WOMEN Ya yé!

(The THREE WOMEN *move in a circle around* MADELEINE*)*

MADELEINE You enclose me before and behind,

TANTE EMILIE THREE WOMEN you circle around my brow.

MADELEINE Where can I go to escape you?

TANTE EMILIE THREE WOMEN Where can I flee from your presence?

MADELEINE If I fly to the sun's risinf

TANTE EMILIE THREE WOMEN or go westward across the sea,

MADELEINE swift as a rainbow, loyo,

TANTE EMILIE THREE WOMEN you reach from end to end.

MADELEINE Damballah!

TANTE EMILIE M' sé couleve ro!

THREE WOMEN Ya yé!

MADELEINE Search me and know my heart!

TANTE EMILIE

THREE WOMEN Try me and know my thoughts!

MADELEINE Damballah, shall I not hate

TANTE EMILIE THREE WOMEN the man who hates your spirit?

MADELEINE Shall I not despise in my heart

TANTE EMILIE THREE WOMEN him who rises up against you?

MADELEINE I hate him with a perfect hatred,

TANTE EMILIE THREE WOMEN I count him my enemy!

MADELEINE Damballah!

TANTE EMILIE M' sé couleve ro!

THREE WOMEN Ya yé!

MADELEINE May he stand accused!

TANTE EMILIE THREE WOMEN Ago-hé!

MADELEINE May his own lips condemn him!

TANTE EMILIE THREE WOMEN Ago-hé!

MADELEINE May you find him guilty!

TANTE EMILIE THREE WOMEN Ago-hé!

MADELEINE May he live to suffer!

TANTE EMILIE THREE WOMEN Ago-hé!

MADELEINE May the bride in his arms and the seed in his loins wither and die!

TANTE EMILIE THREE WOMEN Ago-hé!

MADELEINE What I tell to Damballah I tell to you!

MADELEINE I will tell you all that has happened so that when we come to what has not yet happened but must happen, Damballah will make it happen.

TANTE EMILIE Damballah, make it happen!

THREE WOMEN Make it happen, make it happen!

(TANTE EMILIE *sits on a low stoll Downstage*) (*Right.* ONE OF THE WOMEN *brings a low stool for* MADELEINE *Stage Center, but she remains standing until she begins to tell them what she has done. The* THREE WOMEN *sit on the floor around her.*)

MADELEINE The day a leaf falls in the river is not the day it sinks to the bottom. Today is the day, if they only knew. Justice! Where it does not exist for me, I will call it into being. I will give it shape and design, Damballah has set me on my course. When my heart was at its lowest ebb, he sent me help from across the sea, a second time he sent Laguerre!

TANTE EMILIE Damballah is like a river, woyo.

THREE WOMEN He will carry you on his back, woyo. He will take you to the island in the sea.

(MADELEINE *sits.* TANTE EMILIE *motions to the* DRUMMER *to stop.*)

MADELEINE Now I will tell you what I have done. This morning I sent a message to Jerome, I asked to see him one more time. I resolved in my mind to become gain that sweet wine so pleasing to his taste and tell him I approved of all he had proposed. Even of his marriage. Yes! Why not? Passion made me blind, I'd say, but now I see. Nor would I protest my exile. In my heart I have already severed myself from New Orleans, and New Orleans from me. One thing only would I ask of him: that he let my sons remain. But you alone shall know the reason, you and— Damballah!

TANTE EMILIE M' sé couleve ro!

THREE WOMEN Yay yé!

MADELEINE I would use my sons to reach the bride, to pierce the white magnolia flesh and force the bright red see to fall upon the ground before its time. I would send them bearing in their hands a gift, a bracelet made of gold beaten into slender coils, with a clasp like the head of a sleeping serpent. Let me tell you how I got it. When my father was uprooted from Africa, all his possessions fell to the ground like fruit. The slave traders took what they wanted. Forbidden fruit, all of it, the bodies and the gold. In Haiti, old Comte d'Argonne bought my father's body and his gold. When he set his body free he gave him part of the gold, he gave him the bracelet. I stole all the gold I could get my hands on. But I vowed I would never sell the bracelet. One day, in this house, I put it on for the first time. The slender coils caressed my arms. I fingered the clasp, the delicate head of the sleeping serpent. When I pressed down, a scream tore from throat: In the clasp it was a serpent's fang! It was clean then. Now it is filled with a swift poison that waits only for the warmth of flesh to melt into the blood. Justice! *(Signals for the drums to begin again.)* Where it does not exist for me, I will call it into being. I will give it shape and design, fix it to the flesh in the serpent's name.

TANTE EMILIE Damballah! Li le temps, oh!

THREE WOMEN Now is the hour, the time! Cord cuts cord, oh! Beyond the mountain is the mountain.

MADELEINE What is done to me will be done to them.

(The columns are turned to black. The drums fall silent.)

(INTERMISSION, if desired.)

AT RISE: *(JEROME enters Upstage Left, with the two children; he's playing with them and they're hanging on to him and even manage to bring him down to the floor. MADELEINE comes forward into a pool of light.)*

MADELEINE Two hours ago—or was it centuries?— Jerome came in to answer to my summons. I let the children see him first. I could see that in his way he loved them.

JEROME *(Sends the children away and comes forward.)* I thought everything we had to say was said. Why have you called me back? If it's only to tell me more of the same, I will leave immediately.

MADELEINE And no one would blame you. I was beside myself the other day. How could I have been so rash? I'm amazed you let me say as much as you did. Bear with me, Jerome, in these terrible moods of mine. Oh, this bottle of a city! I'm sure it's partly to blame. But remember the love you had for me once and be patient. I've had time to think. Thank God for that! What a fool I am to rail this way against reality, treating everybody as the worst of enemies, looking neither right nor left, and interpreting everything they do for me in the worst possible light! How do I dare set myself against the will of a man like Croydon? Or worse yet, a man like you! Yes, Jerome, I made myself listen to your explanation. "Isn't it just possible," I said, "that he's telling the truth," that his marriage plans were indeed made with me and the children in mind? What better way to secure our future? And since I'll be so well provided for, why do I go on like this? Why can't I cap my foaming rage? "The children," I said, "we must do what is best for them." Thinking such things as these, I realized how foolish I've been, how imprudent, how indulgent, how inexcusably blind. Now I say to you, well done, Jerome.

JEROME Madeleine, I—

MADELEINE Given the customs of the city and the times we live in, you're very wise to find yourself another wife and to beget on her legitimate children, children that will carry on your name. I should've seen that, Jerome, I should've been sympathetic, and helped you further your plans. Instead I acted very much the woman. Don't think evil of me, and certainly don't match my foolish actions with your own. Be always the man you are. The children, the children! Love them, Jerome! Oh, I cringe to think how we've made them suffer! Must they suffer more? If they must, with all my heart I wish them out of this life

JEROME By all means, then, let us end their suffering. Those were splendid words you spoke, Madeleine. I can only praise you for the grace you've shown in speaking them, and I won't hold those other words against you. It's natural for a woman to feel the rage you felt when her man declares himself to be in love with someone else. But now I see your heart is changed for the better; you've schooled your feelings, you've taught them to work for you. We'll all be happier for it. The children especially. I want to be a father to them in every way, respecting, of course, the demands of society and of my new alliance. There will be other sons, I'll see to that; but Placide and Moise have a special place in my heart; they'll grow up into fine men; we'll both be proud of them.

(MADELEINE turns away.)

JEROME Why do you turn away? Are you crying?

MADELEINE Thinking of them makes me weep, that's all.

JEROME Trust me. I promise I'll do well by them. We still have to work out a few details, but I'm sure we can. The greatest obstacle, of course, is Croydon's ultimatum...

MADELEINE That I leave the city? That's no obstacle. I intend to leave, I'll be gone before morning. It's better that way. Both for you and for me.

JEROME Where are you going? What arrangements have you made?

MADELEINE You don't want to know that. Forget me, Jerome. If you can. The financial arrangements you made for me are quite satisfactory. They'll see me through the year. After that, I'm on my own. As for the children, though, they must stay here. Beg Croydon not to banish them with me. How else can you do for them all that you said you'd do? How else an they fulfill your hopes?

JEROME But they're still so young...

MADELEINE Tante Emilie will raise them. You know how she's always mothered them. Knows all their tricks, knows how to keep them good and healthy. And she loves them. Beg Croydon! For their sake.

JEROME I'll try. Whether I succeed or not is another question.

MADELEINE You *must* succeed. You're their father. He'll do as you say. Tell your wife to plead for you; tell her this is the way you want it.

JEROME Well, yes, of course, I suppose I could, but it will not be easy. After all—

MADELEINE I will make it easier for you. I want to send a gift to her, a gift more precious than any other she'll receive. It's a bracelet that only a bride can wear, coils of purest gold, the proudest possession of my family from generation to generation. Your father bought it when he bought his slaves, and then gave it to *my* father when he set them free. Have you ever seen it? I think not. I confess I hid it from you. *(Calling.)* Tante Emilie, bring me the bracelet! Your bride will not despise so rare a gift, especially if she receives it from our children's hands.

JEROME But why deprive yourself of a thing like that? Obviously, it means a lot to you, it's a kind of link with your heritage? Besides, someday you may be glad to have it for the gold.

(Accompanied by the THREE WOMEN, TANTE EMILIE *enters with a small uncovered box. She hands it to* MADELEINE *ceremoniously.)*

MADELEINE *(Lifting out the bracelet.)* Look.

*(*JEROME *reaches for it.)*

MADELEINE No! Don't touch it! Only she may touch it!

JEROME Keep it, Madeleine. Corinne doesn't need it. She has more jewelry than an Egyptian queen.

MADELEINE I want her to have it! For my children's sake. *(Winds it around her arm.)* Tell her to put it on like this. See here, this is the clasp.

Of course, she may not want to put it on right away. I know how women are. She has her pride to think of. It's enough that she accept it; and be swayed as the gods are swayed at the mere sight of a gift. But tell her it's bad luck not to try it on. at all. Believe me, the gods would be angry. *I would give my life to keep my children here; She has only to accept my gift. Will you do this for me? (Returns it to the box.)*

JEROME Madeleine, if I thought--

MADELEINE Please! For the children!

JEROME Well, I *did* say I'd see her tonight at eight. Perhaps then...

MADELEINE Tonight, yes! Come, we must instruct the children.

(MADELEINE *gives him the box. They go out together.*)

(*The columns are turned to red. The drums begin.* MADELEINE *returns.*)

TANTE EMILIE Mayen ka!

THREE WOMEN Mayen ka!

MADELEINE Beat the drum for me!

TANTE EMILIE Mayen ka! Beat the drum!

THREE WOMEN Mayen ka! Mayen ka!

MADELEINE What I tell to Damballah I tell to you.

TANTE EMILIE THREE WOMEN What you tell to us you tell to Damballah.

MADELEINE To Damballah Flangbo!

TANTE EMILIE Flangbo?

MADELEINE Yes, the fiery spirit! I have told you all that has happened. Now that we have come to what has not yet happened but must happen, Damballah will make it happen.

TANTE EMILIE Damballah, make it happen!

THREE WOMEN Make it happen, make it happen!

TANTE EMILIE *(Sounding her ritual rattle.)* I am sounding my rattle to summon Damballah! I am sounding my rattle to summon Damballah! *(Singing an invocation to him.)* Damballah! Damballah!

TANTE EMILIE THREE WOMEN Damballah Flangbo Damballah! Damballah enhé! Damballah, fiery spirit! Damballah!

*(*TANTE EMILIE *gives a glass of water to* MADELEINE, *who is kneeling Downstage facing the hanging staff of the serpent god Damballah. Then she goes around* MADELEINE, *sprinkling her with the sound of the rattle in vigorous strokes. She takes the glass, returns it to its place, and then goes up to the* FIRST WOMAN.*)*

TANTE EMILIE Out of the water into the house, out of the water into the head.

(Her hand presses down on the FIRST WOMAN's *head. Then she dances over to* MADELEINE *and escorts her to the stool Downstage Right. Now she begins the chant, dancing to the beat of the drum and building to a whirling climax.)*

TANTE EMILIE Rosa mystica!

THREE WOMEN Ago-hé!

TANTE EMILIE Turris Davidica!

THREE WOMEN Ago-hé!

TANTE EMILIE Turris eburnea!

THREE WOMEN Ago-hé!

TANTE EMILIE Virgo potens!

THREE WOMEN Ago-hé!

TANTE EMILIE Virgo clemens!

THREE WOMEN Ago-hé!

TANTE EMILIE Virgo fidelis!

THREE WOMEN Ago-hé!

TANTE EMILIE Belecou Gnenou!

THREE WOMEN Ago-hé!

TANTE EMILIE Ogun Badagris!

THREE WOMEN Ago-hé!

TANTE EMILIE Ogun Feraille!

THREE WOMEN Ago-hé!

TANTE EMILIE Erzulie castissima!

THREE WOMEN Ago-hé!

TANTE EMILIE Erzulie inviolata!

THREE WOMEN Ago-hé!

TANTE EMILIE Ossangue Gouegui Malor!

THREE WOMEN Ago-hé!

TANTE EMILIE Simbi en deux Eaux!

THREE WOMEN Ago-hé!

TANTE EMILIE Carrefour!

THREE WOMEN Ago-hé!

TANTE EMILIE Erzulie intemerata!

THREE WOMEN Ago-hé!

TANTE EMILIE Erzulie amabilis!

THREE WOMEN Ago-hé!

TANTE EMILIE Erzulie admirabilis!

THREE WOMEN Ago-hé!

TANTE EMILIE Grand Bois Islet!

THREE WOMEN Ago-hé!

TANTE EMILIE Ibo Lélé!

THREE WOMEN Ago-hé!

TANTE EMILIE Baron Samedi!

THREE WOMEN Ago-hé!

TANTE EMILIE Erzulie Fréda!

THREE WOMEN Ago-hé!

TANTE EMILIE Erzulie Fréda!

THREE WOMEN Ago-hé!

TANTE EMILIE Erzulie Fréda!

THREE WOMEN Ago-hé!

(The THREE WOMEN *collapse on their last cry.)*

TANTE EMILIE Li le temps, oh!

(All is silent for a moment. Then TANTE EMILIE *moves to the* FIRST WOMAN, *takes her hand, and pulls her to her feet with a strong twist of her arm, speaking again the words of possession:)*

TANTE EMILIE Out of the water into the house, out of the water into the head.

(The drums start up again. TANTE EMILIE *takes a replica, smaller in size, of the hanging staff and makes the* FIRST WOMAN *stare at it hypnotically, then draws her with it into a serpentine dance as she moves this way and that.)*

FIRST WOMAN Damballah! Damballah!

TANTE EMILIE SECOND & THIRD WOMEN Damballah Flangbo Damballah! Damballah enhé! Damballah, fiery spirit! Damballah!

(The FIRST WOMAN *lurches violently, striking her head with the palm of her hand, wriggling like a snake and making choked "snake-like" sounds.* TANTE EMILIE *plants the staff Downstage Left, lets the* FIRST WOMAN *fall hypnotized before it, and with one strong jerk brings her to a kneeling position.)*

MADELEINE *(Approaching her.)* Damballah, speak! Speak!

FIRST WOMAN *(Speaking in a husky voice.)* I see...

MADELEINE What do you see? Tell me, tell me!

FIRST WOMAN Candlelight dancing in the cut-glass door.

MADELEINE The house where the Croydons live. Who's there?

FIRST WOMAN I see two children standing in the hall.

MADELEINE Placide and Moise! Are they alone? Tell me, what do you see in their hands?

FIRST WOMAN A box.

MADELEINE Ah!

FIRST WOMAN One of the slaves comes up to them, an old woman. She smiles and smiles, kisses their shining hair.

MADELEINE Where is Jerome?

FIRST WOMAN I see a man.

MADELEINE Is no one with him?

FIRST WOMAN A girl is coming. The light is dancing in her pale blue eyes, in her yellow hair, on her white skin.

MADELEINE Magnolia white.

FIRST WOMAN She throws her arms around him and kisses him.

MADELEINE May she taste the treachery of his heart!

FIRST WOMAN Then she sees the children. She pulls back. The light goes out of her eyes. Her face is twisted with, with...

MADELEINE Disgust, hatred, rage! Forgive me, my children, for sending you to that pale bitch who takes your father from you.

FIRST WOMAN He tries to explain...

MADELEINE Yes, explain to her, Jerome. Tell her that I'm all sweetness now, that I'm leaving the city, that a carriage'll be waiting for me on Esplanade—but you don't know that. Tell her my children have come on a mission, a mission of peace. She needn't even touch them, needn't touch that soft skin made brown by the rush of our blood in my body, needn't ever see them again, once they are given to Tante Emilie's care. Tell her they come bearing a gift, a gift from me, from the gods, to put an end once and for all to our enmity. One thing I ask, one thing only: to plead with her father to let my children stay.

(The FIRST WOMAN *is writhing like a snake and at the same time expressing the resistance of the girl.)*

MADELEINE Damballah, make her take the gift!

TANTE EMILIE Damballah! Damballah!

TANTE EMILIE SECOND & THIRD WOMAN *(An intense but whispered chant.)* Damballah Flangbo Damballah! Damballah enhé! Damballah, fiery spirit! Damballah!

FIRST WOMAN *(Speaking over the chant.)* She takes it!

MADELEINE What?

FIRST WOMAN She takes the box.

MADELEINE *(Whirling.)* Damballah! Damballah! Damballah!

TANTE EMILIE Li le temps, oh!

SECOND & THIRD WOMEN Now is the hour, the time! Cord cuts cord, oh! Beyond the mountain is the mountain!

TANTE EMILIE *(Intense but whispered.)* Damballah, make it happen!

SECOND & THIRD WOMEN *(Intense but whispered.)* Make it happen, make it happen!

FIRST WOMAN *(Speaking over the whispered words.)* She opens it. Her hand flutters like a bird, picks at the paper, lifts out a bracelet.

MADELEINE Only she may touch it. Tell her, Jerome. A gift for the bride. Put it on! No! Don't put it on! But tell her it's bad luck not to try it on at all. The gods will be angry. *You* tell her, Moise, my little Moise, tell her the way I taught you. O God, will I go without knowing? Will I have to leave the city with my rage unsatisfied, my justice unachieved? Damballah, hear my cry!

FIRST WOMAN She bends over the children, touches their hair...

MADELEINE Promises to talk to her father, and then?

MADELEINE Let her go. Let her go now carrying the shape of her doom. Let her climb the serpent stairs and enter alone into the darkness of her mind. Let her wrap herself round with the robes of her confusion and never see the light of day.

SECOND & THIRD WOMEN Ago-hé!

MADELEINE But you, my children, my little princes. How well you have done what I asked you to do. Come home, poor darlings, come home to your mother. No, stay away! O God! Are they coming home? Is Jerome coming with them?

FIRST WOMAN I see her standing alone in a room full of mirrors. She takes the bracelet in her hands, then she sets it down on her bureau. She picks it up, then sets it down again.

MADELEINE She's afraid to put it on, and she's afraid not to. It's bad luck, she thinks, not to try it on at all.

FIRST WOMAN *(Leaps up.)* She tries it on!

MADELEINE Ha!

FIRST WOMAN *(Whirling around the room.)* In a hundred mirrors I see her try it on... I see her turn her hand this way and that...

MADELEINE The clasp, the clasp!

FIRST WOMAN ...in a hundred mirrors...and then... *(Freezes, her right hand poised in the air, palm toward her face, left hand poised lightly around her wrist.)* ...lay her thumb upon the serpent's head...

(The drums stop.)

FIRST WOMAN ...and press *down*!

(MADELEINE and the THREE WOMEN scream. Quickly, TANTE EMILIE uproots the serpent staff, then moves from column to column, turning them to the side covered with mirrors.)

FIRST WOMAN In a hundred mirrors I see her scream...

MADELEINE *(Whirling.)* Mayen ka! Mayen ka!

(The drums grow frenzied.)

FIRST WOMAN ...in a hundred mirrors!

TANTE EMILIE Damballah! Damballah!

TANTE EMILIE SECOND & THIRD WOMEN Damballah! Flangbo Damballah! Damballah enhé! Damballah, fiery spirit! Damballah!

FIRST WOMAN She staggers back, then pounces on the serpent's head, while her screams go flying from mirror to mirror. But the fiery spirit will not let go, his fangs sink deeper into her flesh. The old black woman comes rushing to her side. When she sees the serpent in golden coils around the girl's arm, his head immovable, she cries out in terror, "Damballah! Damballah Flangbo!"

TANTE EMILIE SECOND & THIRD WOMEN Damballah Flangbo Damballah! Damballah enhé! Damballah, fiery spirit! Damballah!

FIRST WOMAN She claws at the clasp. The girl's arm is swelling, the flesh turning brown.

MADELEINE The brown that comes when the blood goes.

FIRST WOMAN A drop of blood, and then another.

FIRST WOMAN Suddenly the father appears. Into the house full of screams he comes, into the room, into a hundred mirrors. He looks with horror at his daughter's bloodless face, the rolled-up pupils of her eyes. At the sight of the coils embedded in flesh no longer white, he pushes the old woman away and tears with frantic fingers at the head intent upon its kill. He pries it loose, twists it off, and with a cry of pain hurls it against a mirror. The mirror cracks in a hundred places. The girl falls like a wounded dove. In a hundred mirrors I see her falling, falling...

TANTE EMILIE Damballah! Damballah!

TANTE EMILIE SECOND & THIRD WOMEN Damballah Flangbo Damballah! Damballah enhé! Damballah, fiery spirit! Damballah!

(TANTE EMILIE *and the* SECOND *and* THIRD WOMEN *kneel and bow as if to the spirit in the* FIRST WOMAN; *then they lift her and carry her out of the room, Downstage Left.*)

MADELEINE *(Moving Downstage Right as the* FIRST WOMAN *is carried off.)* Why do I linger? The carriage is waiting on Esplanade. Pierre himself is sitting in his little boat on the river bank, eyes and ears straining in the night for the first sign of my approach. His men are waiting for his signal to start a riot on the other end. Ten leagues up the river his ship is anchored, waiting to carry me to Haiti. Go now, before the children come and your eyes devour them again and your heart beats wildly with the designs of a fiery spirit.

(TANTE EMILIE, *meanwhile, has turned both columns to black. Now she pauses to look back at* MADELEINE *just before she exits Downstage Left.*)

MADELEINE There *is* a fiery spirit in me. It was a fiery spirit that drove me to kill my brother. Out of love for my husband. That same spirit drove me to kill his bride. Out of hatred for him. Whether I love or hate, I am forced to do evil. Can I carry out the spirit's designs and not do it with his power? What Damballah Flangbo has done he has done through me. What I have done I have done through Damballah Flangbo. How else? And yet I know that the evil is mine because the love was mine. Jerome shall know how great was my love by the evil I have yet to do...

TANTE EMILIE *(Offstage.)* Madeleine! *(Rushing in.)* Madeleine, the children are back!

MADELEINE Is Jerome with them?

TANTE EMILIE No. He started out with them, but the coachman says that after they had gone a mile, another carriage came up from the house and made them stop. Jerome sent the children on their way but *he* got into the other carriage and turned around to go back. You must go, Madeleine. He'll come for you, you can count on that.

MADELEINE Bring me the children.

(MADELEINE moves Downstage Right. TANTE EMILIE, Upstage Left, beckons to the children.)

MADELEINE They must die. Jerome has already killed them in spirit. I will make the murder visible to every eye. I gave them life; I will take it away.

(The CHILDREN *enter and come to* TANTE EMILIE.*)*

MADELEINE No! No! I gave them life: How then, how can I take it away? *(Opening her arms to them.)* O my darlings, my brave little gentlemen! Those eyes, those smiles, precious beyond saying, how could I ever bring myself— No one, never, never, no one must ever touch them, ever do them harm. Shall I, their own mother—O God, cut off my hands before I do such a thing! Flesh of my flesh, sweet flesh, sweet, Sweet... What are you staring at, Placide? What do you see? Don't stare at me so. *(Pulling them to her.)* O God, O God, I cannot bear to look at them! Take them away, ma tante, take them. *(Releasing them to her.)* Steel yourself, my heart. Do not hesitate to do the dreadful thing that must be done. Lay their tiny heads together on the pillow, kiss their sweet lips, their cheeks, their hair, and make them close their shining eyes upon your smile. Then, quick as lightning, take them from Jerome forever. *(Glancing to one side.)* Put the children to bed, ma tante.

TANTE EMILIE But— I thought you said you'd be taking them with you.

MADELEINE I *am* taking them with me. *(A beat.)* Shall I tell you the secret thought that's been burning in my mind?

TANTE EMILIE *(Looks at her, understands.)* No! No, Madeleine! What are you saying? No spirit is asking this of you. No, none! Leave them with me. *I* will take care of them. I'll hide them from their father, I'll take them away. To another city. Somewhere. I will love them, Madeleine.

MADELEINE Will you? Will do this for me? For them?

TANTE EMILIE Yes! With all my heart. I'll spend my whole life for them. They will each of them grow into a prince, another Toussaint to lead the people! Oh, Madeleine, never think your thought again!

MADELEINE Command me, ma tante! Make me obey! *(Embraces her.)* Wait here, while I kiss them goodbye. And then I'll go.

TANTE EMILIE *(Sits down.)* Dear God, how could she even think it? My sweet babies! But how can I do all the things I promised? I must. *(Singing.)* I am going on a journey, oh. Are you coming back? I am going on a journey, oh. Are you coming back? If I do not die, I will tell you everything. I am crossing the ocean, oh. Do you see the shore? I am crossing the ocean, oh. Do you see the shore? If I do not die, I—

*(*JEROME *bursts into the room.* TANTE EMILIE *leaps up, her heart in her throat.)*

JEROME Where is she, that damnable beast of a woman? *(Strides over to the other entrance.)*

TANTE EMILIE *(Quickly, desperately.)* She's gone! Already gone! If she were her, do you think she'd be hiding from *you*? She's gone!

JEROME Did you help her do the things she did? You witch!

TANTE EMILIE The spirits helped her, not I!

JEROME I curse your spirits! I curse your people! They have robbed me of everything I ever loved, my family, my inheritance, my country. They wished on me a devil in the guise of a woman, setting her like a man-eating flower in my path. I curse the day I ever laid eyes on her! I should've known. If she could kill her brother... Witches, all of you! That bracelet! Did you know there was poison in it? She murdered my bride! Made her die a death more terrible than any I could ever imagine. Her father— O God!

TANTE EMILIE What?

JEROME Deathly ill with the same poison. When he wrenched off the head of that hideous serpent, he lanced his finger on the fang. A devil's gift, that's what it was. I left him writhing in his agony, begging God to let him die with his daughter. To think that my sons, in their innocence... Where *are* my sons?

TANTE EMILIE She's taken them with her.

JEROME Where has she gone? Tell me, you bitch!

TANTE EMILIE I don't know—

JEROME *(Raising his hand to strike her.)* Don't you lie to me!

(Offstage, a piercing scream. JEROME *freezes, then whirls around to face the entrance. The* FIRST WOMAN *appears, her eyes wild.)*

FIRST WOMAN They're dead! The children are dead!

*(*JEROME *rushes out the way the* FIRST WOMAN *came, pushing her aside.)*

TANTE EMILIE No! O God, O God! No, Madeleine! Not the children! Placide! Moise! *(Runs to them.)*

FIRST WOMAN *(Holding her head between her hands.)* In a hundred mirrors I see the mother kiss her sons goodbye, in a hundred mirrors. In a hundred mirrors I see them close their eyes, a little smile upon their lips, the curve of their cheeks so perfect on the pillow, in a hundred mirrors. I see the knife flash like lightning across their throats, and in a hundred mirrors the blood, the blood, the blood! I see their eyes wide against the darkness, their mouths fixed in a scream no one hears. In a hundred mirrors, in a hundred mirrors...

*(*JEROME *re-enters. The* FIRST WOMAN *backs away at the sight of him and hurries off behind him.)*

JEROME Madeleine, Madeleine! *(Drops to his knees.)* Out of what hell have you reached into my life to punish me? Was my wrong so great? What *are* you that I should suffer so for spurning your love?

(The drums begin to build. Light builds like fire Upstage. MADELEINE's *face appears (behind a scrim) in the heart of the fire.)*

MADELEINE I am the earth, the shape of the hills and the bend in the road. I open the night. I am Africa, I am the New World. I am the ocean that burst its bonds to thunder on every shore. I am fire and lightning, the great passion of your youth! I am the way to God for you!

(The drums explode in his head. The stage is aflame with light.)

JEROME No. No! NO!

BLACKOUT

THE END.

An Interview with
Father Ernest Ferlita, SJ

Q: What was the impetus behind adapting Medea?

EF: I have always been interested in Greek drama. I have taught it as a part of a drama course almost every other semester here at Loyola University, New Orleans, where I began teaching in 1969. I found Euripides especially fascinating, because a number of his plots and his psychological insights resonate with modern reality. So I have adapted three of his plays: Medea as Black Medea, Hippolytus as *The Twice-Born*, Bacchae as *The Krewe of Dionysus*, all three set in New Orleans.

Q: What about Medea lends itself to adaptation in New Orleans with a woman of African descent?

EF: Medea and Jason were of different nationalities. So in my play Madeleine and Jason had to be of different nationalities. Historically, some of the French and some of the Africans in Haiti came to New Orleans in the early 1800s. And so the two lovers were a Frenchman and a Haitian woman. Gods an goddesses were often addressed by the chorus in Medea; I found it appropriate to have the women in Black Medea call on Damballah (in Louisiana many African rites were fused into one - voodoo, the worship of Damballah). And, of course, race relations in New Orleans intensifies the conflict.

Q: So is race also an issue in your other New Orleans-based Greek adaptations?

EF: *The Twice-Born* is somewhat of a sequel to *Black Medea* in that Jerome is one of its main characters. His wife's nurse is African American. His illegitimate son Hippolyte was born in France of a woman from Martinique, and there was a rumor that she descended on her mother's side from a tribe in Dahomey in Africa. This brings up something of a racial issue because Jerome could not legally recognize Hippolyte as his heir if he was of African descent. Race is not an issue in *The Krewe of Dionysus*. None of the named characters are of African descent.

Q: So you conflate Jason of Medea with Theseus of Hippolytus?

EF: Yes. Jerome is the same character at different points in his life.

Q: The play was originally written to be performed in New Orleans. Has it found a life through production elsewhere?

EF: Oh, yes. It was first performed at Loyola University in New Orleans in April and May of 1976. A year later it was performed at the Dock Street Theatre as part of the first Spoleto Festival USA in Charleston, South Carolina], followed by a performance Off-Off-Broadway at the New Federal Theatre in December of 1978. It was performed again at Loyola, New Orleans in September of 1984 and again Off-Off-Broadway in April and May, 1987 at the Actor's Outlet in a production that was revived for the 15th Annual Black Theatre Festival in October. It won four awards: Dramatic Production of the Year, Best Actress, Best Choreographer and Best Music. Actor's Outlet revived the play again in 1990 Off-Off-Broadway.

CHAPTER 3

PECONG

INTRODUCTION

Like *Black Medea*, Steve Carter's *Pecong* also features Medea (here called Mediyah) as a voodoo priestess. Played out against the backdrop of Carnival on a mythic Caribbean island, Mediyah falls in love with Jason the Ram, who is out to win the pecong, a contest of wit and insult. After Jason wins he abandons his lover for Sweet Bella (the mayor's daughter). Mediyah seeks revenge on the last day of Carnival and then leaves, as the peace of Lent restores the island to tranquility. The play has been produced at the Victory Gardens Theatre in Chicago, the American Theatre Festival in New Jersey, the American Conservatory Theatre in San Francisco, and at the Tricycle Theatre in London. It has also been performed by a student cast at the University of the Virgin Islands.

Steve Carter playfully calls himself "the youngest of America's oldest living playwrights." He began his career at New York's Negro Ensemble Company in the late sixties. In 1981 he became the resident playwright at the Victory Gardens Theatre, where *Pecong* premiered. His other plays include *Eden, Primary Colors, Shoot Me While I'm Happy, Nevis Mountain Dew, House of Shadows, One Last Look,* and *The Inaugural Tea,* which have been produced all over the United States and around the world.

Like other plays in this volume, Carter does not just adapt Euripides's play, he also returns to the myths that shaped the original as well. He blends vulgar wit, clever dialogue, and tragic death, thereby capturing a complexity that reflects both Caribbean life and Medea's own playful revenge against Jason.

Jason here is "Jason Allcock" and "Jason The Ram," defined by his phallic manhood.

When he meets Mediyah he tells her that if he were not dying, his instinct would be to rape her. His description of using his instrument as a weapon also follows a pattern of violence toward females: He fights and kills a female black cat, punching her, and then "slit she open and rip out she gut." Jason uses females to get what he wants regardless of the cost to them. In this he is like Creon Pandit, another man who uses women.

Male power and dominance is a major theme in this work. The pecong itself is a contest in which the contestants sing Calypso and invent rhymes on the spot about his (all the contestants are male) opponent's sexual proclivities, genital size, and ancestry. At the heart of the play, indeed the source of its title, is the contest between Cedric (who stands to win a lifetime of privilege as "Mighty, Royal, Most Perfect, Grand King Calabash" having won four times before) and the upstart Jason. The contest itself is suggestive of rap battles to more contemporary audiences. The 2002 film *8 Mile* is a not-so-distant cousin of *Pecong*.

Another theme related to male dominance is reproduction and legitimacy. Jason has dozens of daughters but no sons and so feels free to continue bedding as many women as he wants, just as Creon Pandit did when he was Jason's age. Jason claims the sons Mediyah bears him saying that, "boys belong with they daddy," implying girls are not particularly valuable except for sexual pleasure and breeding. Mediyah and Cedric are the offspring of Creon Pandit, but the only child he recognizes as legitimate is Sweet Bella the silent.

As in the myth, Mediyah betrays her brother for her love of Jason. The ancient one kills her brother and dismembers him to slow pursuit from Colchis. Mediyah ensures her brother loses Pecong to Jason, thereby killing him socially. In both cases, the actions of Medea/Mediyah guarantee her loss of all family. Her love allows her to give up everything for a faithless man and when he rewards her sacrifices and dedication by choosing another, she seeks revenge.

Pecong is a tale of metarevenge. Mediyah is a puppet manipulated by Granny Root from the beginning. Granny Root arranged for Damballah, the voodoo serpent god, to impregnate Mediyah's mother after Creon Pandit impregnated her with Cedric. Mediyah and Cedric are twins through their mother only. Cedric's father is the island's lothario; Mediyah's is the creator of all life, father of serpents, and ruler of cosmic equilibrium. The revenge of *Pecong* is not merely Mediyah against Jason and Creon but also Granny Root against Creon and his whole line.

Pecong is not a colonialist *Medea* but rather a feminist one. Hate of all men replaces love of one. When Mediyah promises Jason that all she has is his and that she will obey him she loses all of her powers. When she decides he must pay for what he has done and swears she hates all men, her magic powers return, literally with a vengeance. The figures of Persis and Faustina serve as chorus, sometimes with Mediyah, sometimes against her. In the case of the former, it is always in solidarity against the men; in the case of the latter, it is usually out of jealousy of her powers. They serve as comic commentary, but in the end, the solidarity they feel for Mediyah as a fellow woman is trumped by the murder of the children (infants in this version, only recently born) and the slaughter of Creon and Sweet Bella.

Another difference between Carter's play and other adaptations is that *Pecong* is not about black versus white, but rather between dark and light individuals within the black community, as is discussed in the interview following the play. Jason is seen as a superior specimen of manhood because of his light skin. Creon could not marry Cedric's mother because she was too dark.

The play is set in the period right before Carnival, ending on the morning of Ash Wednesday. Carnival comes from the Latin meaning "farewell to meat" and marks a period of inversion and play before the seriousness and somberness of Lent. If Lent is a time of abstinence, then Carnival is a period of indulgence. Mediyah and Jason indulge in pleasures of the flesh. The pecong is a contest of insulting poetic skill that gives the audience pleasure through taunting the members of the community. As in many Caribbean cultures, the Carnival of *Pecong* features masquerade, dress up, and the crowning of a king of sorts. But by the end of the play, as drunken revelers try to keep the party going, Persis and Faustina, (the voice of the chorus and thus the community), tell them to stop. Once Lent arrives, Carnival must end.

Pecong has been published twice before, once as a single volume and in an anthology of plays from the Victory Garden Theatre. This version is newly revised by Steve Carter to be the most complete text available. The following play is the author's preferred, corrected version.

PLAY 3

PECONG

STEVE CARTER

CHARACTERS

(In order of appearance)

MEDIYAH – Obeah Queen

GRANNY ROOT – Her grandmother, also Obeah Queen

CEDRIC – Twin brother to MEDIYAH

PERSIS – An island woman

FAUSTINA – Sister to PERSIS and a minor "prophetess"

CREON PANDIT – The own-all, do-all, and existing Grand King Calabash

SWEET BELLA, THE SILENT – Daughter to CREON

JASON ALLCOCK – A visitor from a neighboring island

DAMBALLAH

PANDIT

OPPIDANS – Townfolk, dancers, musicians, etc. The number of towns-people can vary from theater to theater. It has been done with as few as two and three musicians, but it does tend to make the production look rather spare.

TIME: Well in the past

PLACE: Trankey Island (*Ile Tranquille*) An "island of the mind" in the Caribbean and Miedo Wood Island, a dark, mysterious place.

PROLOGUE

(The wee hours before cockcrow on a lushly verdant Caribbean "island of the mind". On the floor of a hut, MEDIYAH *sleeps on a pallet. Lantern in hand,* GRANNY ROOT *enters, thrice circles the figure of her sleeping granddaughter, utters some "mysterious" words and gestures, symbolically.* MEDIYAH *stirs.)*

MEDIYAH: Is you, Granny?

GRANNY ROOT: Who else?

MEDIYAH: I try to stay up, but you was gone so long, I had was to doze off.

GRANNY ROOT: Plenty to do. Get up from there and wipe the sleep from you eye. We have t'ing and t'ing to do and we ain't have much time.

MEDIYAH: I ain't want this t'ing to happen.

GRANNY ROOT: It have to pass, Darlin'. This old heart done beat long pass she time. These old bone, them tired. Is about time this body get throw in the dirt and cause new tree and food to grow.

MEDIYAH: But, I ain't want you to die.

GRANNY ROOT: Ain't I done told you I ain't like that word? I ain't want you to use it! Ain't I done tell you I goin' alway be with you? Is through you, you old Granny goin' live forever.

MEDIYAH: I know you say this, but how I know it true?

GRANNY ROOT: You callin' Granny "Liar" to she face?

MEDIYAH: I ain't mean it that way. I just want to know if I reach me hand, I could touch you?

GRANNY ROOT: Better than that! Better than anybody "touch"! You goin' feel Granny. Granny goin' be there!

MEDIYAH: I goin' see you?

GRANNY ROOT: Only you, Darlin'. Only you.

MEDIYAH: You make me promise?

GRANNY ROOT: I goin' told you this one last time. You goin' see Granny when you want to see she. Granny goin' let you see she when she want you to see she. And since Granny always goin' want you to see she, you goin' see she. No make me say that again. Now, give me you ear. Time flyin'. Is a lot of thing I never tell you.

MEDIYAH: I all the time know that when you want me to know thing, you goin' tell me and if you ain't want me to know thing, you ain't goin' tell me.

GRANNY ROOT: Well, you Granny goin' meet she maker and still she no say too much, but certain thing you have to do. Certain thing you have to know. Is only one person in this world I ever love like you and that is you mother. I try me best to love you brother, but is you take me heart. You is you mother all repeat. Cedric have too much of he father in he.

MEDIYAH: But, Granny, Cedric and me...twin. We have the same daddy.

GRANNY ROOT: You hear what I say? You is all you mother! Cedric.all he father!

MEDIYAH: Yes. Cedric even look like…

GRANNY ROOT: Hush! Don't even utter that name! We ain't never mention that name. If you have suspicion, keep it in you head and you heart. You ain't need that name in you mouth. Now, we have to go past all that 'cause t'ing already set in motion. I been out doin' and doin'. Come here to me!

(GRANNY ROOT *firmly grasps* MEDIYAH's *arms.*)

GRANNY ROOT: Before, all you did know, for sure, was herb and root and bush to cure a pauper at death door. Now, darlin' granddaughter, you goin' know more Granny leavin' you for your own appliance, all she power and she science.

MEDIYAH: Don't leave me, Granny.

GRANNY ROOT: All is ready. T'ing in motion. You can't stop tide or wave in ocean. Once you was baby then, you wean. So you was Princess, now…you Queen! Stand up tall and wipe you eye. You is Queen and Queen don't cry.

MEDIYAH: What about Cedric?

GRANNY ROOT: Cedric is man! Only woman does have power and knowledge of science in this family. Nothing Granny can do for Cedric no more. You do for him what you can, if you willin'. He you brother and he not a bad sort, but he too much he father and that same father cause me and you grief. Now hear me 'cause it goin' soon day. The minute I shut me eye, you reach with you hand and pull out me heart. Wrap it in Tingus leaf while it still beat. If anybody want, all you could have you funeral funnery and t'ing, then throw this ol' carcass in the hole I done dig out back. Then, you and only you take me heart and bury she on Miedo Wood Island.

MEDIYAH: Miedo Wood Island? But, Granny, I can't go there. Nobody can go there alone. Since I been live on this earth, only one person me ever see go there and come back to tell it...and that is you.

GRANNY ROOT: And now, you goin' be the only one go there.

MEDIYAH: But that place have all wild animal and serpent and haunt and t'ing.

GRANNY ROOT: Mediyah! You Queen now. No place hold badness for you. You born on Miedo Wood Island like you mother before you and me. You have nothing to fear! You the Queen of Miedo Wood Island. It belong to you, now. Nothing touch you! And if you feel to take somebody there...

MEDYAH: Somebody...

GRANNY ROOT: ...nothing touch he, either.

MEDIYAH: Granny, what you talkin'?

GRANNY ROOT: Remember, you power is great. Make you no misuse it. Make you no abuse it. Make you no confuse it. Or, dear heart, you could lose it. But you could have lickle bit of fun, now and then. I always have lickle fun doin' t'ing to that Faustine Cremoney. She of the great, trifling effort. But the Gods, them, know I ain' mean she no real harm. She can sometime be lickle botheration, but she not bad a sort. Have some toleration with people like she. How-so-ever, if somebody do you a true and harsh badness, revenge yourself with all you power. Bring down rage and destruction. Don't care who it is and no mind the cost to you, so long you have honor and standin' when you see you face in you glass. Now, I goin'. I hear cock stampin' he foot and clearin' he throat to sound, "Mornin'!" Come! Let Granny caress you one next time.

MEDIYAH: I ain't want this time to come.

GRANNY ROOT: What I tell you 'bout that, eh? Granny goin' all the time be with you. When it dark. When it light. When it day. When it night. When it sun. When it storm. When it breeze. When it warm. Well, you goin' stand there and let me go to my grave without kiss?

MEDIYAH: Oh, Granny. Granny.

(From off-stage comes the lilting rhythm of Calypso music. In the distance, a dancing figure clad like a Chanticleer struts and prances.)

GRANNY ROOT: It time! Remember me! Think of me and you mother and let we have vengeance. Good-bye, Darlin'.

MEDIYAH: What?

GRANNY ROOT: 'Bye, girl. Now.

(Suddenly, there is cockcrow and the dancing figure mimics a real rooster. Simultaneously, GRANNY ROOT lifts her arms to Heaven, MEDIYAH screams and plunges her hand into GRANNY ROOT's chest and pulls out her pulsating heart. She wraps it in a large leaf as GRANNY ROOT falls back, lifeless, in her chair. MEDIYAH sinks to the ground at her grandmother's feet. The scene brightens, just a bit, and the dancing figure is revealed to be CEDRIC, twin brother to MEDIYAH. He is exuberantly tipsy and is accompanied by an entourage that consists of two overly attentive dancing ladies and some musicians.)

CEDRIC: Mediyah! Mediyah! Rouse youself and make you come out here and greet you brother, The Champion! I win again! I win again! Four time in a row I win again! I win again! King of Calypso. I vanquish all me rival and scuttle all me foe. I put them to rout with sweet word from me mout'. All I do is song out and, down, they go. Is then when they fin' this night made for me, one, to shine And I win again! I win again! Ain't I told you so? Four times in a row. One more time to go, One next time to shine and the permanent title of Mighty, Royal, Most Perfect, Grand King Calabash is mine. Yes, Girl. You shoulda see you brother. I all the time magnificent and superb, but tonight...I go past that. Tonight, I sing better than God! I win again! I win again! Me put them all to shame. I win again! I win again! Them too sorry that them came. Them Saga-boy so wilted them faint right up to the floor Them kick up them feet and can't compete no more! I win again! I win again! I lash they with me tongue. I win again! I win again! I, King of the Pecong. I bring home the medal, the cup, and the cash Higher than high is how I dos rate. Climb out you bed and celebrate. I win the title four times straight. One more time and I permanently be the great, Mighty, Royal, Most Perfect and Grand King Calabash.

(CEDRIC and his companions are dancing vigorously when MEDIYAH, now clad in mourning, comes out of the hut with the wrapped, still-beating heart in her hands. CEDRIC, on seeing her, sobers immediately.)

CEDRIC: All you, less that noise! I say, "Quiet" nu?

(Everyone goes silent, staring at MEDIYAH.)

CEDRIC: The ol' lady gone, eh?

(MEDIYAH nods.)

CEDRIC: She go peaceful?

(MEDIYAH nods.)

CEDRIC: She ain't have no pain?

MEDIYAH: No.

CEDRIC: Then, she go good. What more all we could want? She run a long and good race, so why you look so baleful. All we have to pass. Who know that better than she? No sister... We ain't have to be sad. We ain't have to feel bad. Let we take she and put she in the ground. Pronounce some pleasant word, then prance around. Let we sing and take libation then, let we make some lickle celebration. Mop up you face and let we see you smile. Granny Root goin' home...in style! *(He gestures to his musician.)* All you boy help me pick she up and tote she to she restin' place.

MEDIYAH: She hole already dig in the yard. Put she in it gentle.

CEDRIC: Where you go?

MEDIYAH: Elsewhere!

CEDRIC: What you do?

(MEDIYAH *holds the leaf-wrapped, audibly beating heart aloft. Thunder and lightning flash.* CEDRIC *is suddenly trancelike.*)

CEDRIC: I understand!

MEDIYAH: All you, be gentle with she remains!

(CEDRIC *and the men pick up the corpse and, joined by the two dancing girls, do symbolic, ritualistic movement, then exit. As* MEDIYAH *prepares to leave,* GRANNY ROOT, *now clad in black veiling and holding a large, opened black umbrella, trimmed with the same black, floor-reaching veiling, appears.* MEDIYAH *still holds the heart aloft.*)

MEDIYAH: Remember, Granny. You make me a promise to all the time be here.

GRANNY ROOT: And since when Granny Root fail to keep she promise. Granny going' all the time be with you, Girl.

MEDIYAH: I, the granddaughter of Granny Root. Let everybody know it. I, the granddaughter of Granny Root. Let everybody know it!

(MEDIYAH, *followed by the ghost of* GRANNY ROOT, *exits.*)

LIGHTS! END OF PROLOGUE

ACT ONE

Scene One
(*Some weeks later. Cock-crow on the island. In her hut,* PERSIS *sleeps on a straw pallet. Her sister,* FAUSTINA, *garbed as befits an Obeah Queen, enters with authority.*)

FAUSTINA: Persis!

PERSIS: What is it, Faustina? I just lay down me head from me revels and here you come. What you want?

FAUSTINA: Rise, Woman! Is a brand new day. You want to sleep you life away?

PERSIS: Be-shite!

FAUSTINA: The sun done rise. The cock done cry. It time for you to ope' you eye.

PERSIS: Woman, stop! I sick to death with this rhyme business. Every mornin' you wake up, you chantin' rhyme like you is some high priestess or some such. Just 'cause all of a sudden, you learn how to read lickle piece of card and t'ing.

FAUSTINA: Aha! So, that what do you of late? You jealous 'cause I get the gift. You been so ever since I get Granny Root card, them. Well, m'dear I ain't ask and I ain't make deal. I ain't beg and I sure ain't steal.

PERSIS: There she go again.

FAUSTINA: I dream Granny Root come to me just 'fore she die and she voice let out one baleful sigh. "I goin' soon," she say. "Twon't be long, but you know how I does like me rum strong. So, if you put a crock o' you best grog 'side me stone, I goin' leave you the gift of prophesy for you very own."

PERSIS: Deliver me!

FAUSTINA: When it come to brewin', you know I better than good. All the time boil up cane and t'ing better than you could. You act like is me fault that me brew up the best and make run stronger than you and the rest. 'Taint me fault when me get home and open me door, me find Granny Root tarot card sittin' on me floor.

PERSIS: I still think you does find them old, worn-out card in Granny Root trash. Why she leave them to you? She make rum better than anybody. She ain't have to seek from you.

FAUSTINA: She always did confess a secret admiration for me brew.

PERSIS: You too fool and you think me one, the same. You does march 'round here makin' utterance sound like they is pronouncement from on high. If Granny Root let you have them card, she only funnin' with you like she all the time use to do or she plannin' some special trick. She ain't leave you no book or potion or scientific power.

FAUSTINA: Well, after all, I ain't relate to she. Blood thicker than water. And all them kind of recipe, she leave to she black-face granddaughter.

PERSIS: You better hush you mouth 'fore Mediyah hear you and work goozzoo on you hindpart.

FAUSTINA: Long as I wearin' all these amulet, I ain't have the first thing to fear. 'Sides, that black, monkey-face creature ain't nowhere near.

PERSIS: Hah! The woman have ear like bat. You better watch you tongue, 'cause you ain't know what she capable of. Granny Root all the time say when that girl come into she own, she goin' be even more powerful that she. You and me, both, does know that still water does run deep, deep, deep and all that glitter far from gold!

FAUSTINA: And, pray tell, what that does mean?

PERSIS: Nothin'! I just feel to say it. You think you is the only one could make pronouncement?

FAUSTINA: Well. speak of the devil and here come she brother. All fill up with heself...and no other.

PERSIS: Hmmm. He and he entourage!

(Enter CEDRIC, quatro in hand, and his rag-tag band of followers.)

PERSIS: Mornin', Mr. Cedric.

CEDRIC: Is me you a-talk to?

PERSIS: Who else passin'?

CEDRIC: If is me you want to address, you must say, "His Mighty and Royalness."

PERSIS: Oh man, shut you face, Mr. Big Shot. The rule say you have to win Pecong and Calypse five time consecutive 'fore you can lay claim to bein' Mighty, Royal or Grand. You ain't win but four. Only ol' Creon Pandit and he daddy 'fore he win five time. And, come what you bet, if Creon did have a boy instead of he daughter, Sweet Bella, the Silent, them Pandit would still have claim to the title. Maybe you think you is a Pandit. Come to think of it...Now that I does look...you does have the look of Creon 'about you, you know. 'Specially 'round you eye, you nose, you mouth, you ear, you chin. You ain't think so, Faustina?

CEDRIC: I better than all them Pandit.

PERSIS: Is what you think. You voice like a rasp, I ain't seen how come you win four time...much less...one. I know the judge them have substance and honor, so you must be use some big magic or some such to get them pick you, Mr. Cedric.

CEDRIC: "Cedric, the Magnificent" is no more me name. I, now, the Mighty, Royal, Most Perfect, Grand King Calabash of substance and fame.

PERSIS: Oh, God. Save me from this rhyme to-do!

CEDRIC: I, one born Calypsonian. Who better to rhyme? Whomsoever come to challenge me, just waste up they precious time.

PERSIS: Shite!

CEDRIC: And what do you, Auntie? How come you so close-mout'?

FAUSTINA: Ain't none you damn "Auntie", so no call me such You can't see what I doin', Mr. Know-so-much? You can't see that I readin' card? Just use you eye. That ain't too hard.

PERSIS: Double shite! Now, the two of them rhymin'...

CEDRIC: Them card look, for all the world, like no other than them that did belong to me old grandmother.

FAUSTINA: Where them come from is my affair, 'long as I get them fair and square.

PERSIS: Stop! I say, "Stop!" It like one bad dream. If I hear one more rhyme, I goin' scream... Oh, be-Christ! Them have me doin' it!

CEDRIC: Pay she no mind. Is me you readin'?

FAUSTINA: I just readin', but it look like you in the deck.

CEDRIC: What them say 'bout me?

FAUSTINA: You ain't want to hear.

CEDRIC: You think I does frighten? You think I does scare? Nothin' does fright me. Nothin' dare!

(PERSIS, *almost silently, screams.*)

CEDRIC: I think you does forget what is the trut'. That I is the grandson of Granny Root.

FAUSTINA: That ain't mean a t'ing. All we know is only the female in you line that does have power to do science and divine.

CEDRIC: You better tell me know, you wrinkle-up, ol' cow!

PERSIS: Why you mout' so nasty? Tell he the bad news, Faustina.

FAUSTINA: I too happy to do so. These card, them say, "Some new singer comin' 'roun' and it look like Cedric goin' down!"

CEDRIC: Who? Who risin' to challenge? Where the man? Let he show he face, if him can! Find me the man so skill at rhymin'! Find me the man who have the timin' that this Mighty Calabash possess. Oh, yes. Find me the man who can beat me. If him so willin' tell the villain to step forth and try to unseat me. I raise me sweet voice, loud and clear and issue challenge to all who can hear I say to all assemble here and far and near, "In melodious combat, come and meet me and see if you is the one who can lose he life, he home, he wife, he fork, he knife, he stress, he strife. The time most rife, me son, for tryin' to defeat me. Defeat me? Hah! Never! I am the Mighty, Royal, Most Perfect, Grand King Calabash...forever!

(CEDRIC *and his "groupies" play and dance furiously. Then, at a signal from him, march off.*)

PERSIS: See how them young gal hang off he? Like them 'fraid to let go he arm. Like them 'fraid him goin' vanish into thin air. Like him so much Mr. Charm.

FAUSTINA: Eh-eh! You rhyme?

PERSIS: It contagious. Him think him the end-all and be-all, but pride does goeth before the fall.

FAUSTINA: Yes, Miss Adage. I done already read he card. Him goin' fall and him goin' hit hard.

PERSIS: You see that, eh?

FAUSTINA: Yes, man. It plain like day. And when him fall and hit the goun', is someone from he own house goin' bring he down. Hahoii! But look who crossin' now.

PERSIS: Them two! Hmmm!

(CREON PANDIT, *followed by his daughter,* SWEET BELLA, THE SILENT. *She walks seductively, giving the "eye" to every male she sees.*)

PERSIS: Mornin', Creon Pandit! Mornin', Sweet Bella Pandit!

*(*SWEET BELLA *smiles, condescendingly.)*

CREON: All you here as usual, eh? So, what's the news? For I know if there is any, all you would know it, 'cause you all the time on sentry duty like two sentinel. So, who pass durin' the night? Who doin' rudeness with who? Who deliver baby for who? Who fart?

FAUSTINA: You ol' buzzard. Me goods come in?

CREON: Them lickle piece of cloth you does order been come into me emporia long time. It there waitin' for you. You have the cash to pay for it?

FAUSTINA: I have credick. You know I always pay me bill.

CREON: Credick, shite! The last time were almost two year 'fore you pay me.

FAUSTINA: Brute! Who tell you to put me business on the road. Well, I guess you can't help yourself. Is all that Chinee, Syrian, and Indian blood mix up in you.

CREON: What you say?

FAUSTINA: As I does so often say, "Too much strain for you vein."

CREON: You ol' Zulu. I ain't have the first piece of Chinee in me.

PERSIS: How you know? You daddy keep record of he ramblin'?

FAUSTINA: And who you callin' Zulu? We ancestor come here straight from Egypt!

CREON: Strike me blue and Holy shite! Cleopatra think she white!

(He surrenders to convulsive laughter.)

PERSIS: I ain't see nothin' a bit funny. Both of us descend straight from the Nile.

CREON: Ooh-hoo! You heat that, Sweet Bella? Both of they does come from the Nile. Well, so does crocodile! Come! Let we go 'fore these two North African lift up they shift and pull two asp from 'mong them old basket of fig and sic they on we.

FAUSTINA: I readin' you card, Creon Pandit. Somethin' dire goin' befall you.

CREON: Hahoii! Somethin' dire already befall. I see you the first thing this mornin'. What more "dire" than that, eh? Come, Sweet Bella.

(SWEET BELLA, *silently laughing, obeys her father and they go off,* CREON *still convulsed with laughter.*)

CREON: She ancestor from Egypt! Is a wonder she even know Egypt. Is a wonder she know Egypt a-tall!

FAUSTINA: *(Calling after him)* The card, them say you goin' have big trouble.

PERSIS: That man still pretty, you know!

FAUSTINA: He too pretty and he still have plenty big stone for a man he age.

PERSIS: But that don't diminish with age, m'dear. Only it ability to rise up and dance 'round. I still like the way him pant fit he. You ever take he?

FAUSTINA: Is for me to know and you to mind you business. You?

PERSIS: I ain't shame to say. Yes!

FAUSTINA: You too lie!

PERSIS: 'Twas too dear and precious a moment in me life to debate with you. Who comin' next, Miss Oracle?

FAUSTINA: Yes. Change subject. Is Mediyah.

PERSIS: I does feel sorry for she sometimes. She look so sad and different since Granny Root pass. Like she ain't know life. Like she dry.

FAUSTINA: Ain't you would be dry, too, if you ain't never have man for moist you? Man don't want she. It run in the family. Creon Pandit ain't never even think 'bout marryin' she mother. Even when he find she carrying she and Cedric in she belly for he.

PERSIS: Careful, Woman! Mediyah might could hear you.

FAUSTINA: She still far off.

PERSIS: Remember she know science and t'ing. She still Granny Root granddaughter.

FAUSTINA: All we know Granny Root the Queen of Science and T'ing, but this granddaughter ain't she. We ain't have the first sign that the woman pass on she power to this one. She have yet to let we see one lickle miracle. All we know Mediyah know herb and bush for healin', but who ain't know that?

PERSIS: But Mediyah all the time know more than anybody. It come natural to she. And she still the only one can go to Miedo Wood Island for special herb and bush and root and t'ing and come back. Ain't no animal, haunt, or t'ing does ever bother she. She charm! Sometimes she does talk wild and crazy and when I peep me eye in she window, she 'lone and solitary, but I swear, and on more than one occasion, me hear she sayin', "Granny, this..." and "Granny, that..."!

PERSIS: Hup! It she, for true!

(MEDIYAH comes on, pulling a small boat on wheels in which the ghost of GRANNY ROOT sits with a small earthenware crock of rum, from which she occasionally sips. She is unseen by PERSIS, FAUSTINA, or anyone else on stage except MEDIYAH who, unnoticed by PERSIS gives FAUSTINA a casual but significant glance...at which FAUSTINA freezes.)

PERSIS: Hello, Mediyah. Where you a-go on this hot day?

MEDIYAH: Ah? The day feel hot to you? It feel cool to me.

PERSIS: Now that I does hear you say it, it do feel cool.

MEDIYAH: Yes. It cool with just a trifle too much heat.

PERSIS: I notice that. It cool, yet it hot!

MEDIYAH: You was all the time quite perceptive.

PERSIS: So, where you travellin' on this cool, hot day?

MEDIYAH: I goin' where I goin', to do what I goin' do. If you friend, the minor prophetess, could move she mouth, she might could tell you, but I had was to still she for a lickle bit 'cause I ain't care for she tone. Faustina, darlin', I only havin' lickle fun with you 'cause, number one... you no worth me energy or me true power and, number two, I in a very good mood. But you remember, I ain't never smelled fart in me life. You want know why? 'Cause no matter how silent they does come out a person's hind part, I able to hear them and move out the way. So you must figure, if I able to hear silent fart, not that I fully comparin' you to a silent fart...mind you, but if I able to hear silent fart, you know I can hear when people say vicious thing 'bout me and me family. You get that? Now, Persis, after I move on, make you count to seven and this ol' rag will regain she speech and movement. She so light in substance, all I need is me thought, alone, to send she to oblivion if me want. She could hear me, it true, but I feel you should tell she. That way, we make sure you know it, too.

(MEDIYAH, pulling the little boat, goes off. GRANNY ROOT, motionless throughout the preceding, now turns to look at the two women and laughs uproariously, but silently. As soon as they're out of sight, PERSIS bolts to FAUSTINA.)

PERSIS: Faustina? Oh, God, Faustina?

(MEDIYAH returns.)

MEDIYAH: Oh yes. Tell she to get some tanbark and weave it into a true collar for wear 'round she neck if she want some lickle protection from me. So long, darlin' Persis. So long, Creature.

(MEDIYAH *goes again.*)

PERSIS: Oh, God, God, God! You see what you and you mouth get you? One! Ain't I tell you the woman could hear a mosquito makin' pee-pee on welwet? Two! I tell you the woman have extraordinary power! Three! She know science! She have skill! Four! And you goin' bait she just 'cause you could read lickle piece of card and sign! That ain't power! Five! Is a wonder she ain't change you into a she-goat! Is a wonder she ain't make soldier-crab shew on you titty and make wart all over you face! Is a wonder she even tell me to count to seven!

(FAUSTINA *doesn't move.*)

PERSIS: I say, "Seven!" Wait! Maybe I miss. Make I recount. One, two, three, four, five, six, seven! I say it right! Seven ain't the right number. Faustina, I can't break the spell. I 'fraid you done for. I 'fraid you speechless forever. Well, at least you ain't die!

(MEDIYAH, *pulling her boat, returns.*)

MEDIYAH: Ain't I tell you I was funnin'? Now, I goin', for true.

PERSIS: But, wait, kind Mediyah. You tell me the number is seven. I count to seven and me poor sister still ain't move.

MEDIYAH: Oh, yes, I lie. I tell you I was funnin', the number is ten. For true! Better say it fast for she look, for all the world, like she goin' pass monumental gas if she don't let out some word soon.

PERSIS: One, two, three...

MEDIYAH: No! You must wait 'till I gone and I ain't in no big rush. I just going' tra-la-la at me own pace. Take me own sweet time, tra-la-la, tra-la-la, tra-la-la...

(MEDIYAH, *pulling the cart with the veiled and silently chuckling* GRANNY ROOT, *goes off. This time,* PERSIS *follows her a bit to make sure she's gone.*)

PERSIS: One, two, three, four, five, six, seven, eight, nine...and I hope she ain't havin' more hilarity with we this time. Believe me, Faustina, I ain't even seen the woman who she put on spell.

(FAUSTINA, *almost out of the spell, looks like she's about to explode. She makes muffled noises and tries to stamp her foot.*)

PERSIS: Oh, yes. Ten!

(FAUSTINA *stomps free of her enforced trance and gasps for breath.*)

FAUSTINA: Bark! Strip me some bark, Woman! The succubus try to turn me to stone. Fetch me piece bark! That damn criminal try to choke me! Bark! Bark!

PERSIS: You ain't learn? You still spoutin' insult?

FAUSTINA: *(In a more cautious whisper)* Fetch me the bark, Woman! The witch...I mean...she...that one try everything she know to take 'way me vitals. Bark, Woman! Hurry, nuh? Fetch me a big piece o' bark!

PERSIS: I fetchin'. I fetchin'.

(PERSIS *runs off-stage as* FAUSTINA *continues gasping for breath.* PERSIS *returns, carrying some strips of bark from a tree.*)

PERSIS: Here!

FAUSTINA: Why you a-hand me them for?

PERSIS: Ain't you yell and scream so 'cause you want it. Ain't you cause me to run 'round like damn wild Indian and damn near bruck up me foot lookin' for this damn shitey bark?

FAUSTINA: But, ain't you the one so "Miss Artful" with she hand and needle and thread and t'ing. Weave me a collar, nuh?

PERSIS: You hear the ingrate? "Weave me a collar, nuh?" Well you could tell me when the word "Please" dis-tappear from the English language, eh?

FAUSTINA: No time for no "Please"! I think I dyin'.

PERSIS: If wish was dream and you should live so long!

FAUSTINA: Weave, Woman. Weave!

PERSIS: Rass!

(Lights.)

Scene Two

(*Miedo Wood Island.* MEDIYAH, *pulling the boat with* GRANNY ROOT, *enters. Rocks and branches of palm trees are arranged to look like two thrones.* GRANNY ROOT *sits on one of them and seems to be listening for something or someone.*)

MEDIYAH: Okay, Granny, we here. Maybe now you could part you lip and tell me why I have to come here today. I ain't need to come here. I already have enough herb and bush and root in the house where I ain't have to forage for another fortnight or two unless is a breakout of some plague or epidemic or somesuch. Why you have such urgency for this place today?

GRANNY ROOT: Hush, Girl.

MEDIYAH: Why you have you ear on a-cock so for?

GRANNY ROOT: Aha! All in readiness. It soon time.

MEDIYAH: Soon time for what?

GRANNY ROOT: Somebody soon come.

MEDIYAH: Granny, darlin', everybody, them, know Miedo Wood Island have all sort of haunt and wild animal and t'ing. Who so fool to brave all that by comin' here.

GRANNY ROOT: Somebody brave and fool.

MEDIYAH: Well, whoever 'tis, too much fool for me. I ain't want to meet such.

GRANNY ROOT: Somebody comin'. Granny know! Granny always know! You ain't want to own it, but you does know, too.

MEDIYAH: Sometime I does forget you dead, you know.

GRANNY ROOT: Ain't I told you 'bout usin' that word?

MEDIYAH: I does forget that, too, 'cause ever since you...that word you ain't want me to say, you ain't leave me 'lone long enough to get use to the fact that you is really...that word you ain't want me to say. And, what is more, you ain't been...that word you ain't want me to say, long enough for me to get use to the fact that you really...that word you ain't want me to say. You know what I tryin' to say, Granny darlin'?

GRANNY ROOT: You know, sometime you does miss you pass. We have to be serious, Girl. I leave lickle something quite untidy on this earth when me bone get the call from yonder. I thought I could rectify in me own time, but voice greater than mine say, "All thing in they own time!" So, it fallin' to you to take care of everything for Granny. So it be! Aha! Footfall! He comin'!

MEDIYAH: He? Man comin' to defy this evil wood?

GRANNY ROOT: *(Chanting)* You Granny Root granddaughter. You be the best. You do this thing for Granny, then Granny rest. You give youself over to all them God of Greatness. Give youself over to all them old God of Greatness and Blackness. Give youself over. Let they take you. Give youself over. Let they make you Granny Root granddaughter, for true. Give youself over. I goin' be here. Give youself over and let he see, here

Granny Root granddaughter is you. Give youself over. Give youself over. Give youself over.

(There is a flash of lightening and a roll of thunder. For an instant, MEDIYAH and GRANNY ROOT seem to be frozen in time. There is another flash of lightning, more thunder, and an agonizing scream from a man somewhere in the wood. At that scream, GRANNY ROOT disappears.)

MEDIYAH: Granny, you hear that? But, wait. Where you a-go? Granny? Granny?

GRANNY ROOT: *(Off)* You ain't need to see me. Go see who scream in the wood.

(MEDIYAH obeys. Shortly after, she comes, aiding a young man, with much difficulty. His clothes are torn way to the point where, except for a piece of rag...here and there...he'd be naked. He collapses on the ground at the feet of MEDIYAH.)

MEDIYAH: Oh, God! But you is a pretty piece of flesh!

JASON: Thank you, Missy. Is so woman all the time tell me. Thank you, God for lettin'a woman be the last thing I see 'fore I pass.

MEDIYAH: Pass? But, you is too pretty to die.

JASON: Me know that, but I think I cashin' in me chips all the same.

MEDIYAH: Well you could tell me you name 'fore you make all you good-bye and t'ing.

JASON: In life I was Jason Allcock from Tougou Island. Known the entire length and breadth of Tougou as, "Jason The Ram," born Calypsonian, extraordinaire.

MEDIYAH: And tell me, Mr. Jason Allcock, you pretty ram-goat, what you doin' here in this wild, lickle piece of spit in the ocean. This would have haunt. This island death to human being. You ain't here that?

JASON: I am one born Calypso...Oh, I say that already. I come here because a ol' dead-face woman come to me in a dream and tell me to come here. She say in this wood does grow the Calabash tree. This Calabash tree does have the best wood in the entire world to make quatro. She say, too, that here it does have a cat blacker than thought... which if I could catch it and rip out she entrail, it gut does make string for the quatro. She say if I combine the Calabash wood and the cat gut, I would have Heaven for a voice and a quatro that sound like golden harp.

MEDIYAH: And why you must have such?

JASON: For the challenge!

MEDIYAH: What is this "challenge" and why it so important, you risk up you life?

JASON: I hear 'bout this pretender to the throne of Royal, Mighty, Most Perfect, Grand King Calabash. Them say him win four time and goin' for five, then him Calabash for life.

MEDIYAH: I hear such.

JASON: I here to put a stop to that, 'cause no man can match me when it come to Pecong and t'ing. But this same ol' woman tell me in the dream, qutro from this wood not only the best, but make me completely invincible. I hear this self-same, so-call champion nightingale get he wood and gut strong from here.

MEDIYAH: Is you so hear?

JASON: Is so. But this same ol' hag no tell me this forest so brutal and vicious. When I come to this place, a tempestuous storm lash out at me and overturn me craft. I had was to swim ashore fightin' and dodgin' all kind of shark, them. Then I pull meself here and all kind of wild t'ing snap and spit at me and me clothing tear off and leave me lookin' lika bare-ass pickney.

MEDIYAH: bare-ass pickney lookin' sweet to these eyes.

JASON: Thank you, sweet thing. On a regular day, I would done long time grab you and pitch you to the floor and do you a rudeness, but I ain't have the strength today. I dyin'.

MEDIYAH: Is so you think?

JASON: Well, like I say, all them wild critter does rear and tear at me, but I fight them off with me cutlass. I swingin' machete at all of them, but they too numerous and them chase me right to the Calabash tree. It like I could see golden quatro dangle from every leaf. I take me cutlass and I 'bout to fell the tree, when...yarrak! A cat, bigger and blacker than the universe, jump from the topmost branch and land 'pon top me. I tell you, we havin' some punch up before I give she a final punch. She scream like a ol' woman and fall out. I slit she open and rip out she gut. Is while I 'tendin' to this with me back turn, I feel...doop! The damn, dread Calabash tree cobra strike me a fatal blow. Look you! You see the mark? So, I ain't have long. And worse yet, I done leave me wood and me gut in the damn jungle. This the first time you could call me a fool. I believe in a dream. I guess I must be goin' now, 'cause you standin' over me and everything already lookin' dark.

MEDIYAH: What you mean by that, Mister?

JASON: I mean the blacker the berry, the sweeter the juice. Lord, it make me think...is only three thing I regret I ain't do 'fore I kick out. One! I ain't leave no son. I ain't lave son, the first, behind me!

MEDIYAH: Pretty ram like you?

JASON: I have plenty daughter all over Tougou, but that ain't no 'complishment.

MEDIYAH: No?

JASON: None of them woman, them, ever bring me boy. All man need son to carry on he name. Gal pretty, but they can't sin Calypso in the tent. The rule say, "No woman for sing in the Calypso tent!"

MEDIYAH: If you dyin' like you say, you wastin' time. What the next two regret?

JASON: I ain't goin' be here to challenge this four-year upstart for the championship. Oh, Woman, if I was not 'about to meet me creator, I would compose a lickle lilt for you. Words like honey I tell you, for I mellifluous like hell.

MEDIYAH: Ah hah!

JASON: It true, Star Apple. I open me mouth to sing and I ain't ever find woman who could resist.

MEDIYAH: I ain't say you lie. Regret three?

JASON: Well, I always did say when I check out, I want to have a woman 'neath me and me mouth all over she.

MEDIYAH: Eh-eh? But you got some brass.

JASON: I ain't suppose you could do lickle sometin' 'bout number three, eh?

MEDIYAH: Boy, you too bad. You does have some lawless mouth, you know.

JASON: Is me charm. Woman always find me so. Can't help it. I born that way. I makin' love to woman from me cradle. I think all that goin' now 'cause I don't even feel I have strength to do you one small rudeness. At least, you could bring you face down here and leave me have one kiss 'fore I pass, nuh?

(He pulls her down to him. MEDIYAH, far from resisting, is more than enthusiastic. At the moment of their kiss, GRANNY ROOT appears and gestures symbolically. Lights flash and there is thunderous sound. GRANNY ROOT, again, disappears.)

JASON: Be-Jesus! Thunder and lightning an all the element in you mouth, Woman. Me lip, me teeth, me tongue, me throat...all aflame. I comin', God. Now, ordinarily, when I say, "I comin'," I does mean just that. Howsoever, I 'fraid that this time when I say, "I comin'," I mean, "I goin'!" But this is one terrible damn time to pass, eh? Shite! I already see the face of God.

MEDIYAH: Hear me good, you altogether gorgeous thing, I listenin' while you pretty mouth spoutin' you charm and you pretty head restin' in the crook of me arm. You think I 'bout to let the smallest piece of harm come to you? I look dumb to you? You must be crazy in you head if you think I goin' let you dead.

JASON: But, who you is? How come you here in this beastly wood and no animal or haunt try for make meal out you?

MEDIYAH: You notice that at last, eh? Well I born right here and I special. I, Granny Root granddaughter. I, all herb and bush and Miedo Wood water. Is with a priestess of science and healin' you dealin'. You ain't feel, since I touch you, you fever batin'? Whoever want to claim you life, have to keep on waitin', 'cause is me, Mediyah, now holdin' you fate in she hand. Understand? Yes! Is me who snatch you from the mouth of Hell and goin' make you pretty, handsome carcass well. Close you eye and sleep, 'cause truth be to tell, I goin' 'range meself 'bout you and suck the venom out you. Oh, yes man. I goin' lift up me shift and give you the gift of new life.

JASON: I can't keep me eye open. I sorry. 'Bye, Gal.

MEDIYAH: Yes! Sleep on, me beauty! I goin' into the wood and get you wood and gut string you leave there and I goin' make you the most fine, gold quatro you did ever see. Yes! You sleep, Mr. Sugar-Tongue, I goin' keep you right here on this island with me 'till it time for you to win Pecong at the Carnival. You goin' sleep all the time I ain't here, so that when I are here, you ain't goin' have nothin' but energy...which you goin' truly ned. Oh, Man, is now life for you. In the meantime, God, I can't wait no longer.

(MEDIYAH *throws herself savagely on* JASON *who, though asleep, reacts in kind. The lights go down on them, but come up on* GRANNY ROOT *perched in a tree and laughing eerily and evilly.*)

GRANNY ROOT: No, m'dear. 'Taint for you to die of love for this man or any one of they. Love? Hah! Love does make you mind go simple. Make woman take up veil and whimple and make you face swole big with pimple. Is hate should motivate a woman fate. But, have no fear. Granny goin' always be near and she goin' steel you 'gainst foolishness and approachin' bitterness. Yes? However, 'taint no reason why you can't have lickle fun on the road to heartbreak and vengeance!

(GRANNY ROOT *cackles as the lights go out.*)

Scene Three
(CREON PANDIT's *store.* SWEET BELLA *is behind the counter.* FAUSTINA, *in a somewhat more sober-colored version of the clothes in which we last saw her, and* PERSIS *enter.*)

FAUSTINA: Where you daddy?

(SWEET BELLA *indicates the back of the store.*)

FAUSTINA: Creon Pandit, you old bandit. Come out here!

CREON: Who takin' me name in vain? (*He comes out.*) Oh, is only Cleopatra and she hand-maiden. What you want?

FAUSTINA: I come for me goods.

CREON: What goods? You ain't have no goods here. All a ol' crocodile like you could have is "bads."

FAUSTINA: Don't rag on me, Man. I come to pick up me cloth.

CREON: What cloth? You have cloth here?

FAUSTINA: Don't get me wroughted, nuh! All you know you have cloth for me here.

CREON: You mistake. Is me, one, who have cloth here. Is when you have some shillin' for show me, is then I have some cloth for you. 'Till then, the cloth mine.

FAUSTINA: You ol' pirate. Is them warrin' faction in you blood that does make you brutish so, you know. Bring me me cloth, nuh!

CREON: Show me you money, Woman!

FAUSTINA: Here! Is three Moravian coppers. Now bring me me cloth and I want me change!

CREON: Change? What change? You think you have change comin'?

FAUSTINA: Don't trifle with me, you ol' fart!

CREON: I hangin' on to this cloth so long for you, you ain't think I entitle to storage charge?

FAUSTINA: Now, the man tryin' to t'ief me money. You better bring me me cloth and me change 'fore me take a torch to you and you lickle store.

CREON: Try it, Bedlam. You seem to forget I also the magistrate. You just threaten the law. I could have you tail thrown in jail, if I want.

FAUSTINA: Is so you would treat ol' friend, eh? No wonder you house goin' soon fall. I done read you card, you know.

CREON: You can't even read English, much less piece of card.

PERSIS: You know, you two is trial. Sometimes both of you act like you don't have no brought-upsey, a-tall.

CREON: Here you damn piece of change. Next time you goin' know better. I ain't like me merchandise lay fallow on me shelf.

FAUSTINA: You talkin' chupidness. Is only two week since I order.

CREON: You too lie! The cloth have two foot dust, it there so long. I had was to wrap it so it ain't fade.

FAUSTINA: I have a good mind...

CREON: ...Since when?...

FAUSTINA:...to carry me trade elsewhere and not come in here a next time. You ain't deserve me patronage.

PERSIS: And, you would please tell me, to which next establishment you would favor with you trade, since Creon Pandit store the only one 'round here?

CREON: Maybe she know it! Even if somebody have enough craziness to try to raise emporia and want to rival with me, he ain't goin' be so fool as to sell goods to you. Bella, reach me that roll of black Bombazine from the shelf and let we get this ol' crow from out me shop.

PERSIS: Black Bombazine?

CREON: And, careful. Blow off the dust! I ain't want you to dirty you frock.

PERSIS: Black Bombazine? You order Black Bombazine?

FAUSTINA: Creon Pandit, you mouth too big. Who authorize you to put me business on you clothesline?

CREON: You ain't tell me is secret.

PERSIS: You order black Bombazine? Who you think you is? The Queen?

FAUSTINA: And what, pray tell me, causin' such hilarity?

PERSIS: Oh, forgive me, nuh! I succumb to jollity 'cause you think you quality.

FAUSTINA: I is a augurer now. I can't walk 'round here like I ordinary.

PERSIS: Oh, God! Me heart! Me heart!

FAUSTINA: Shut you fool mouth! I have to proper dress for Carnival when it come. You think I can make appearance in costume, rag and bead like common jamette? All you mere mortal can wear all them color and be the rainbow, if you so choose, but I have standin' and station. I have responsibility. Me dictate life by the card, them. They probably goin' ask me to sit on the bench and be a judge.

PERSIS: Oh, God! I goin' die and I ain't even make out me will.

FAUSTINA: As soon as you through playin' fool, you think you can run up this Bombazine into something that look dignify without makin' too much distress on the cloth?

PERSIS: Whoop! You hear that, Creon Pandit? She majesty goin' trust me to stitch up she coronation robe, underlin' that I am. I surprise she ain't want to chance needle and thread, sheself.

FAUSTINA: You the seamstress! I, the priestess.

PERSIS: But, you is too comical.

FAUSTINA: Creon Pandit, you have stranger comin'! No! Two! No! Three!

CREON: Who comin'?

FAUSTINA: You goin' see one just now. I ain't say no more.

PERSIS: Is Mediyah!

CREON: *(Shaken)* Granny Root granddaughter? What she want here?

PERSIS: I ain't know. I ain't see she for some month.

(MEDIYAH, brightly dressed, enters.)

PERSIS: Hello, Mediyah.

MEDIYAH: Hello, ladies. Faustina, you ain't have to hide in the back stall. I ain't feel for mischief today.

PERSIS: I never see you come in Creon Pandit store 'fore now.

MEDIYAH: You right! Hello, Creon Pandit!

CREON: What you want here? You come to cause ruction? *(He takes a heavy chain with a cross on it and puts it around* SWEET BELLA's *neck.)* Bella, go to the back! *(He practically pushes* SWEET BELLA *out.)* I ain't want no pass with you.

MEDIYAH: I goin' ignore all that! I need several piece of cloth and some other t'ing. You can take it from this lickle piece of coin.

CREON: That gold!

PERSIS: Gold?

MEDIYAH: Gold!

CREON: It real?

MEDIYAH: You could try it out on you tooth.

CREON: But, I ain't have change for this.

MEDIYAH: Who tell you I goin' need change? Is a whole lot of cloth and t'ing I needin'. Here me list! You could fill it?

CREON: Yes, Mistress. Sweet Bella, help me gather these items, them.

(SWEET BELLA returns and helps her father to gather items.)

PERSIS: So, Mediyah, where you was all this time? Is so long I ain't see you. I does ask you brother, Cedric, for you all the time and him, that sweet-singin' boy, say he ain't know where you is. Sometime, I does pass by you house, tryin' for a glimpse, but the shutter always shut and I ain't hear you singin' inside like I always was use to.

MEDIYAH: What do you want to get in me business?

PERSIS: I ain't mean no harm.

MEDIYAH: Persis, you does make me chuckle. Don't fret youself! I decide to stay on Miedo Wood Island.

(PERSIS and FAUSTINA *elbow each other's ribs.* CREON *and* SWEET BELLA *look aghast.)*

MEDIYAH: I decide to build me a little castilla over there.

PERSIS: But that is one angry, lickle piece of sand in the sea. How you could live there?

MEDIYAH: Careful! Is me home you talkin' 'bout. Creon Pandit, I want them thing deliver...

CREON: I ain't have nobody so fool to go to Miedo Wood Island and I, for sure, ain't goin'...

MEDIYAH: Who ask you for do suh? I ask you for do such?

CREON: But, you say...

MEDIYAH: You ain't let me finish "say." Now, I want them thing deliver to me old house. Me Granny house.

CREON: I ain't goin' there neither. Everybody know you Granny house hold badness and animosity for me and all Pandit.

MEDIYAH: How you could say such? Cedric there! The house ain't have no badness and animosity for her. Even though he ain't have the name, he a Pandit!

CREON: Ain't nobody 'live could prove that!

MEDIYAH: You right! Nobody 'live could prove it.

(PERSIS and FAUSTINA *have not stopped elbowing each other's ribs.)*

MEDIYAH: So how could the house have haunt and botheration for you if Cedric there? And you and he...relate.

CREON: I ain't claim that!

PERSIS: But, Creon, all of we does know the whole story.

CREON: Ain't nobody know no whole story...nothin'!

PERSIS: Faustina, tell the man.

FAUSTINA: Me ain't know nothin'! I does mind me business. Me lip... seal!

MEDIYAH: You grow wise since I last see you. Creon bring...

CREON: Creon don't bring! I, the owner! I, the magistrate! I don't bring nothin'. I have delivery boy for that!

MEDIYAH: Then, why you causin' such ado? Surely, me Granny house ain't have no bad spirit for you delivery boy. Unless, unbeknownst to all we, he a secret Pandit, too. Well, have them thing deliver to the porch if he ain't feel to come inside. I could, ha-ha, spirit them to me island. I got me ways, you know. Oh, and by the way, I see that fine white-cloth frock coat you have in you window. Put that in with me purchase, too.

(PERSIS *and* FAUSTINA - *elbows and ribs.*)

CREON: But that coat is for man!

MEDIYAH: You think I blind and ain't know that?

CREON: But, you can't just buy man coat, so! You have to know size and fittin' and that coat ain't look, to me experience eye, like it goin' fit Cedric, unless you goin' alterate it.

MEDIYAH: And who, in the Heaven you know, tell you I buyin' coat for Cedric. Me brother buy he own clothin'. Ain't you or nobody else have to bother you head with worriation. The coat plenty fit the one who goin' wear it. Now, fold and box it nice. While I thinkin', you could throw in two, three of them white trouser. Here! I want you wind this piece of red robbon 'round it and tie me one, big bow.

CREON: You still have change comin'.

MEDIYAH: I know that!

CREON: I ain't want you to think I cheat you.

MEDIYAH: Creon Pandit, is no way you could t'ief me. You know that. You hold on to them coin I have comin'. I establishing credick. 'Bye! 'Bye, ladies. Faustina, you could talk now and the two of you could stop "hunchin'" one another. You rib must be black and blue. I ain't coming back today. I give you me word. *(She goes and then pops her head back in the door.)* Of course, sometimes I does lie and me word ain't mean a t'ing. *(She laughs, raucously, then leaves.)*

FAUSTINA: Woman, you have me rib sore.

PERSIS: And you, me! You ever hear such?

FAUSTINA: You better hush you mout', Woman, and wait 'till she out of ear-shot!

CREON: Sweet Bella, take this coin and put it in the coffer. You two bush-rat goin' have to vacate, 'cause I closin' down. I think I goin' rum up meself, lickle bit.

FAUSTINA: Don't rush me, nuh! You think she goin' give you she patronage all the time? Hah! You got a next think comin'!

PERSIS: That gold part of Granny Root legendary fortune, come what you bet! But I wonder who them coat and pant for?

FAUSTINA: Come what you bet, them for the same mysterious person plant them two alligator pear seed in she belly.

PERSIS: What you say? What you say?

FAUSTINA: You ain't see, eh? Well, of course you ain't have the power of foresight and divination. You ain't have the gift and you ain't have the card. She carryin' two piece of something in there. Ain't I say is three stranger comin' to Creon Pandit shop?

CREON: Is so you did say!

FAUSTINA: So? She is the one stranger, for she never set she foot in here before. And she carryin' two in she oven. One and two does always come out...three...if I does know my mathematic.

PERSIS: I thought she did look sorta...different...But, no! You pickin' leaf from the wrong bush, Woman.

CREON: She look the same to me. Lickle cleaner, maybe, but...Oh, you ol' man-eater, you. How you a-know so much?

FAUSTINA: You forget me card?

CREON: Oh, yes. I does forget that you are the all-seein' Oracle. Well, you could tell me, Sybil, who she lay up with?

PERSIS: Yes! That what I want to know. Better still, who lay up with she?

FAUSTINA: How I should know?

CREON: I thought you could read so much card.

FAUSTINA: Is card tell me she carryin'.

PERSIS: Then, card should tell you who she carryin' for.

CREON: I surprise such a monumental occurrence, like who pumpin' pipe and tool to Mediyah, escape you eye. Well, it look like the two of you goin' have to trilly over to Miedo Wood Island if you want to find out. Shark won't molest you if you swim. They scare. You two is the only other two I know could go there and come back without all them haunt and animal and t'ing bother them. They know you is they relative. Get outta here now. I tell you I closin' me shop!

FAUSTINA: We goin', your brute!

PERSIS: You too rude. 'Bye, Sweet Bella. Is shame you can't speak, but is you father disposition that get the curse put on you.

CREON: *(Most angry)* Get out, you two ol' harridan!

(They go. SWEET BELLA regards her father.)

CREON: Sweet Bella, you mustn't mind what them say. Both of them is bitter, bitter woman. They soul sour with invective and vinegar. Don't look so at you daddy. You daddy love only you and you mother, rest she soul. I never play ram on she. I marry she and I stay in faith 'till she pass. Sure, I do plenty thing 'fore I marry, but I suppose to, I man and when I young, I had to run When me hair was thicker and blacker than a night without moon. I was a sheik. I could teach any damn Casanova a thing or two, believe me. Then, one day, I see this black, black girl. She hair... short and tight...like a clench fist. She lip like it 'bout to bust with too much honey and she voice like a breeze. She eye burn hole right through me. She skin? Ah, she skin. She skin was a miracle of black velet with the sun shinin' behind it. I never seen nothin' like that. I completely bewitch by she and she skin. That same skin I couldn't bring to me father table. Ah, girl. You ain't understand. I ain't make the world. T'ing is t'ing and I ain't set that rule. I was important. I was Mighty, Royal, Most Perfect, Grand King Calabash. I did win Pecong five time consecutive. Only man ever do that is me daddy. I was important. The girl was...black!

(SWEET BELLA looks at her father. The veiled figure of GRANNY ROOT passes, silently, through the room. They both shudder, as if a cold wind had passed over them.)

CREON: Still, I would rather you had all the black skin in the world, if I could just hear you voice say, "Daddy, I love you." I know that ol' woman curse me when she daughter pitch sheself off Devil Cliff. She deliver twin and then she pitch sheself into the wind. She body never find in the water. She mother swear sheself against me line from there on out. You come out without voice. I do it to you and I too, too sorry. I love you so, but you is me only regret. Oh, Sweet Bella, I was young an I ain't had better sense than to be young. Go, now. Go fetch one of them lickle black boy from the back and tell he he have delivery to make.

(SWEET BELLA starts to go.)

CREON: No! Wait! On second thought, I think I goin' take this one over meself.

(SWEET BELLA *looks, understandingly, at her father.* PERSIS *comes back in, calling to the off-stage* FAUSTINA.)

PERSIS: Just wait there! Ain't no need for you for come in. I sure I leave me purse on the counter. Creon?

CREON: I close!

PERSIS: Oh, shut up, man. Here ten shillin'. Put me 'side ten yard of them black Bombazine and I pick it up when I come in next time. And, hear me! Nobody say you have to be town-crier and put me business in the ear of all and sundry creation. You follow? (*She goes, calling to the off-stage* FAUSTINA.) I find it! I told you, ain't I?

FAUSTINA: Oh, you find it where you drop it on the floor?

PERSIS: How you know it drop on the floor, dear Sister?

FAUSTINA: I read it in the card, Poopsie! The card make me see all thing.

(CREON *and* SWEET BELLA *smile at each other as he locks the door in his shop. Lights.*)

Scene Four
(*The old hut,* CEDRIC *is sprawled, drunkenly, on the floor. Jugs, bottles, wooden wine cups, and other things indicate there have been many lengthy parties going on.* CEDRIC's *two dancing girls are sprawled, inelegantly, on either side of him.* MEDIYAH, *followed by the ever-present* GRANNY ROOT, *enters. Both are horrified at what they see.* GRANNY ROOT *picks up an old besom and starts after* CEDRIC, *but* MEDIYAH *wrests the broom from her hands before she can strike.*)

GRANNY ROOT: The place look just like ram and she-goat live here.

MEDIYAH: Don't wrought yourself. I goin' take care of this. (*Broom in hand, she stands over the sleepers. She doesn't speak loudly.*) You two courtesan, wake you worthless tail up!

(*The two girls stir, drowsily.*)

MEDIYAH: Wake up, you good-for-nothin' but good time wenches!

(*The two wake with a start and are about to scream, but a gesture from MEDIYAH silences them.*)

MEDIYAH: Not a sound. Vacate these premise 'fore I take this besom and sweep you into eternity. make haste!

(*The two quickly gather their things and, terrified and trying to scream, run from the hut.*)

GRANNY ROOT: You do good, Girl. You does bring such joy and laughter to me spirit. Come what you bet, if them have on undergarment, they soil them.

MEDIYAH: Cedric!

(MEDIYAH *pitches the contents of a water pitcher in CEDRIC's face. Sputtering, he lashes out, blindly, with his cutlass.*)

CEDRIC: Aaiieeee! I goin' kill...

MEDIYAH: get up!

CEDRIC: You brain come loose? Why for you pitch water at me for?

GRANNY ROOT: Criminal!

MEDIYAH: 'Cause you ain't wake when I call you name!

CEDRIC: Tyrant! You crazy?

MEDIYAH: Look how you does have this place. Swine does live cleaner than this.

GRANNT ROOT: Like you ain't have the first bit of brought-upsy!

CEDRIC: Who fault that? Where you was all this time?

MEDIYAH: What you say?

CEDRIC: Is well over three, four month since you set foot in here.

MEDIYAH: So?

CEDRIC: So, so don't brin you errant self in here complainin' 'bout the place look like pig sty, if you ain't here to clean it!

GRANNY ROOT: What gall!

MEDIYAH: But, you is a ol' bitch, you know that? What you think I does be? Maid servant and you the king? You too fool. You waitin' all this time for me to do you service?

CEDRIC: Who else? I, the man here!

MEDIYAH: Hear him, nuh! 'Cause he have something dangle 'tween he leg, him can't pass broom 'cross the floor. I should kick you in you vital and make you stone inoperative.

GRANNY ROOT: Blackguard!

MEDIYAH: Since you does so need a woman to pick up behind you, why ain't you make them two wilted blossom I just chase from here do such, eh? How them could lay up here cross you and you smellin' so foul? This a island with water on all side. Ain't no reason for man to smell worse than ram-goat in summer.

CEDRIC: You better hush you mouth 'fore I vex and tell me where you was all this time.

MEDIYAH: On Miedo Wood Island. Why you eye open so agape? That place ain't hold no fear for me.

CEDRIC: I know that. Is only that is 'bout this same Miedo Wood Island and you I been thinkin'. I need you to go and axe me off piece wood from the Calabash tree. I need a next quatro.

MEDIYAH: What you do old one?

CEDRIC: It mash up! Me and me company, them, saunter into Creon Pandit cantina for some merriment and libation and we sittin' there mindin' all we own business, when this bunch of bum...say them from Tougou Island...come at we to issue challenge for Pecong at Carnival. Tell me them have some dilly with voice and brain better than me and him goin' cause me to fall in the context. Of course, I accept the challenge 'cause no way me and me magic quatro could lose. Well, that devil-grog that Creon Pandit does sell in he place is the cause of it all. 'Fore you know it, one thing does lead to a next and one of them Tougou boy, full of drunk, sayin' some nastiness 'bout me ancestry.

MEDIYAH: Eh-eh?

GRANNY ROOT: I hope you kill he...

CEDRIC: ...and I had was to grab he by he collar and butt he...

GRANNY ROOT: Good!

CEDRIC: ...and before you know it, he boy, them, jump in and we havin' one grand punch-up in the place...

GRANNY ROOT: I hope you wreck Creon Pandit cantina.

CEDRIC: ...and we havin' fun, fun, fun! Then one of them devil get lucky and catch me a vicious blow back me neck and I fall quite on top me quatro. It turn serious then. I ain't utter a word. I get up. Is the first time I ever knock off me feet you know, and I evil now. I pick up what use to be me quatro and look at it. It mash flat. It like it collapse. The ruction stop and you could cut the silence, it so thick. I look at me company, them. Them lookin' at me. A look pass 'tween we that tell them is all me fight now. Them Tougou boy ain't know what happenin'! Suddenly, without warnin', I scream and spring like cat and pitch meself 'mong them. Me arm and cutless flailin' like windmill. You ain't see hurricane do more damage than me. Most of them run, but they is two who ain't goin' push nobody on quatro no more. I tell you, I was so full up, I had was to grab both them sweet, brown gal you chase 'way and wear them out at the same time. Anyway I need you to bring me some wood from Miedo and I could fathom me a next quatro in time for Carnival. Is just enough time for the wood to cure proper and I could use the same string so you ain't have to kill cat for me.

MEDIYAH: I can't do that, Cedric.

CEDRIC: What you say?

GRANNY ROOT: She say true!

MEDIYAH: I say I can't do that. Brother, is only one time I could get wood for each person from Miedo. You done have you share.

CEDRIC: You sayin' you can't get no more wood?

MEDIYAH: I could get plenty wood, but no more for you. Is one time only for each person.

CEDRIC: But, you could do it. You special. We special. We born there.

MEDIYAH: No! Is only me born there. You forget. You born in the boat on the way. Is only after we land and Granny bring mother ashore that I come out.

CEDRIC: It ain't matter. You have the power.

MEDIYAH: But if I break the law of science, I lose me power.

CEDRIC: So, brother? You desert me, eh?

MEDIYAH: You desert yourself.

CEDRIC: Okay, Sister. I ain't goin' beg! No need to worry you head. You brother still have he voice. He still have he brain. He could still sing

Callypso and shout Pecong better when he drunk and sick than any foot-jam who sober. I ain't need you or you quatro tree for help me.

MEDIYAH: Where you goin', Brother?

CEDRIC: 'Taint none you damn business, but I goin' to join me friend, them. Is one thing I did always say, "When you family ain't stand by you, you always have friend." I come into this world. I ain't ask, mind you, and ain't nobody ask me, but I come. The first thing they tell me is ain't have me Daddy name and me Mother kill sheself. Then me Granny kick out and now, I ain't even have a sister. Well, thank be to God, I have friend who love me and would buy me a cup of grog when I fellin' low. I ain't have no family would do so.

(CEDRIC goes.)

MEDIYAH: Cedric!

GRANNY ROOT: You can't stop him. T'ing is t'ing and they can't change. Everything charted and goin' 'long. It all plan by greater than we.

MEDIYAH: Granny, I ain't feel too sorry for Cedric. How come that does be so? After all, he and I is twin. I should be feel somethin' more than I does feel?

GRANNY ROOT: I already tell you. T'ing is t'ing. That is all.

MEDIYAH: Okay, Granny.

GRANNY ROOT: Now, on this particular matter, I ain't interfere before... but I think...when you get back to the island and wake Jason Allcock from he induce slumber, you better tell he that he goin' be daddy to you twin you carryin' in you belly.

MEDIYAH: You know, eh? You ain't say nothin' so I thought I had put one over on you.

GRANNY ROOT: Oh, Child, I tired tellin' you...

GRANNY ROOT and MEDIYAH: "Granny see everything! Granny know everything! Granny goin' always be here..."

MEDIYAH:...Yes, Granny, I know. I goin' tell him today. I think it time. But, first, make I clean up this place lickle bit.

GRANNY ROOT: Leave it! Cedric ain't goin' need this place a next time. You ain't goin' have no more use for it.

(From off-stage, CREON PANDIT *calls.)*

CREON: Hola! Hola! Who in there?

GRANNY ROOT: Himself!

MEDIYAH: What you want, Creon Pandit?

CREON: I bring all them thing you purchase. I transfer them to you boat already and I goin'.

MEDIYAH: Wait!

*(*MEDIYAH *goes out to* CREON, *who seems rooted to his spot.)*

CREON: What you want?

MEDIYAH: My brother and some boy, them, have a tumble and bruck up you cantina?

CREON: Yes!

MEDIYAH: Why you ain't say nothin'?

CREON: You brother sittin' there mindin' he business, when them Tougou rascal come in and start botheration. Well, I a Calabash. The only one 'live to claim such and it look like Cedric goin' soon join me in me advance state. I ain't like it the way them fellow come in and make challenge, and...

MEDIYAH: And?

CREON: Them say something they ain't have no cause to say. Cedric well within he right to knock them over.

(MEDIYAH *takes some coins from her pocket.*)

MEDIYAH: Here!

CREON: What this for?

MEDIYAH: Damage!

CREON: But...

MEDIYAH: I ain't want no child of me mother to owe a thing to you.

GRANNY ROOT: You do well, Granndaughter.

CREON: you ain't have to do this...

MEDIYAH: We get this far without you help and we ain't need it now.

(CREON *backs away, cautiously, but hides behind a tree. Of course, he can only see* MEDIYAH *as she kneels on the ground and bends her body in supplication.* GRANNY ROOT *puts her hands on* MEDIYAH's *shoulders and stops her movement.*)

GRANNY ROOT: Creon Pandit watchin'!

MEDIYAH: I know!

GRANNY ROOT: Then, let he see. 'Bye, old hut! We ain't need you no more.

(GRANNY ROOT, *her hands on* MEDIYAH's *shoulders, as if passing power into her, look upward.* MEDIYAH *thrusts her arms out and the hut "bursts into flame."* CREON PANDIT, *in terror, runs from the scene. Lights.*)

Scene Five
(*The hut of* MEDIYAH *and* JASON *on Miedo Wood Island.* JASON, *surrounded by flowers and baskets of tropical fruit, sleeps soundly and*

blissfully. MEDIYAH, *the beribboned suit-box in her arms and followed by* GRANNY ROOT, *enters.)*

MEDIYAH: Each time I does look at that man, I does want to jump he.

GRANNY ROOT: He quite pretty.

MEDIYAH: All over and all the time. In the sun or in the night, He pretty by day or candlelight.

GRANNY ROOT: And you body all a-jumble when him act all rough and tumble. Even when him claw and clutch you It still feel soft where him touch you.

MEDIYAH: I know you does always say you does live through me, but you could feel he, for true?

GRANNY ROOT: He know how make woman say, "Wuppi-wuppi!" He know he art. He a skill practitioner and if you ain't careful and hold youself...just so...you could lose you power as well as you heart. It time to wake he and tell he you news. I goin' off on some revel.

(GRANNY ROOT disappears. MEDIYAH approaches the sleeping JASON, taking a small vial from her neck and a leaf from her pocket. She puts the vial to his lips and after emptying it of its contents, passes the lead over his face. JASON stretches, yawns and wakes.)

JASON: Hi, Gal. Make you drop shift and get in this bed so I could do you. Then I want me sayuno and after I eat, I goin' do you a next time. I feelin' like a bull-ram today and I ravenous for everything in me sight. Bring you face down here and let me attack it.

MEDIYAH: Man, how come we ain't lash up 'fore this time?

JASON: Be thankful for "now", Gal. Don't have regret for the past. Is that same "past" does lead us to this same "now."

MEDIYAH: Well, Philosopher, I have lickle piece news for you. I know for long time now, but I happy with me news...so I keep it to meself.

JASON: Eh-eh? I hear this tone million time already. You knock up?

MEDIYAH: How you does know?

JASON: You think I does born yesterday? Ain't I tell you plenty gal in Tougou make baby for me?

MEDIYAH: I remember is so you say, but none of them wench give you boy like I goin' give you.

JASON: I hear that before, too.

MEDIYAH: This time, it true.

JASON: How you know?

MEDIYAH: Jason, look me in me eye! You does know me to lie? You ain't know, by now, I special? I real special! When I find you, you body all chew up and mew up and have scar and t'ing. Where them scar now? You see them? When I find you, you ain't think you goin' see the next day, you body weak and creak so. Since that time, you does feel one ache? You ain't been nothin' but young and strong and givin' me body all the pleasure with you youth and you strength. You ain't even have a memory of how tear up and sear up you was when I first see you. When I leave off from you, I does go 'bout me business here and elsewhere. With all the wild animal they does have here, any does come to give you aggravation? No! I does put up barrier that no haunt, spirit, or wild t'ing could breach. You belong to me, Jason Allcock, and nothin' goin' change that. I put charm all over you. So when I tell you, you goin' have son, believe it. And when I tell you, you goin' have two son, you better believe that too...for it too true.

JASON: You tellin' me I goin' have twin boy?

MEDIYAH: I, yet goin' convince you of me power. You feelin' young and strong?

JASON: Yes!

MEDIYAH: You feel for giving me lickle tumble?

JASON: All the time!

MEDIYAH: You feel for make me body sing with you music?

JASON: Like you the quatro and I the picker!

MEDIYAH: You feel for make you mouth run rampant all over me terrain?

JASON: Woman, you have me hotter than Satan fire! Bring youself over to me. Let me have at you.

MEDIYAH: No, Doux-doux. You come over here and get me. Come over here and let me give you all the love and fulfillment of all you dream and treasure. Come over here and take me. Come over here and make me tingle with delight. Make me fill you night with sweet scream and murmer of pleasure. Come! Come! Come, sweet man! Come! Come get me if you can!

(JASON *struggles, but can't seem to rise from the bed.*)

JASON: What happenin'? I can't move! What you do to me?

MEDIYAH: you know how you does enter me center and bury youself to you hilt while all the time you croonin' lilt and drippin' sugar in me ear? Them word does sometime cause me eye to tear. Them always cause me heart to flame. Well, try to lullaby me now! I bet all you can call is me name.

JASON: Mediyah, mediyah mediyah mediyah! Mediyah, mediyah mediyah mediyah, mediyah?

(JASON, *suddenly angry, calms himself and looks coolly at* MEDIYAH.)

MEDIYAH: So you must believe me when I tell you that I carryin' two boy for you...right here in this belly. You tell me about all them silly, flirty t'ing who make baby for you. Well, I ain't like them and them ain't like I. I, the most different woman you goin' meet. No other like me. I givin' you boy 'cause you say you want them. Jason, I give you anything you want.

GRANNY ROOT: Mediyah?

MEDIYAH: You want to be Grand King Calabash and I goin' see to it. You ain't have to ask.

GRANNY ROOT: Mediyah?

JASON: You mighty impressive, but you ain't know me. Plenty woman does love me. Why? Them know I wayward and never goin' make they legal. Them know, too, that I good to all me daughter. Every one me daughter have me love and me name and the first straight-leg rogue who even look like them come to do they badness with him stone in him hand, have me machete where him leg meet. I a rascal, but I honest and I ain't want nothin' from nobody I ain't work for meself. When you find me in this same wood, all mash up and slash up, I ask you for anything except youself for me to kiss and do a little smooch? No! And you could refuse me, you know! I ain't beg! I ask you to heal me and seal me and do all this kindness? No! I come here with me machete in hand and I prepare to do me own battle or die! Is me way! I make meown way and me own fate! is me strip wood from Calabash tree! Is me strangle wild cat and pull out she gut. Is you make up me quatro, true, but I ask you to do that? No! And, be-Christ, is me who goin' win Pecong and t'ing by meself! On me own! Now, I ain't ungrateful. I too glad you find me and mind me and sure me and cure me and love me and carryin' two boy for me. But I rather you take them two boy and yank they out you belly. I rather be all scar up and mar up. I rather you let all me blood run out and get drink up by the earth. I rather you leave me die, than deny me the right to win the contest on me own. I ain't need magic! I ain't need conjure! I ain't need sorcery! I only need me! Me! Me! Me! Now, if you want to spout incantation and work spell and do me badness and sadness and evilness, go to it. I came into this world a honest man and I go out the same. I ain't sacre of a livin' arse...excuse me language...in this world, so do you worse!

MEDIYAH: Jason, you make me love you...too much.

GRANNY ROOT: *(From afar)* Mediyah!

MEDIYAH: I ain't want to be nothin' but the only woman in you life!

GRANNY ROOT: *(From afar)* Mediyah!

MEDIYAH: I ain't care for be nothin' but she who have you all the time!

GRANNY ROOT: Mediyah!

MEDIYAH: Tell me, Jason! Say it! Tell me you ain't love nobody but you Mediyah and I do anything you tell me. Anything you say! Anything you ask! The world goin' belong to you if you say you love me the same like I love you. I use me power to give you anything! Everything!

(GRANNY ROOT appears. Lights flash. MEDIYAH and JASON freeze.)

GRANNY ROOT: Mediyah, you ain't have no power. You just give it to this man. He hold power over you, now. You surrender to he. You just a ordinary woman, now. You goin' have leave this island. Granny goin' see you out safely, but you must go. Both you and he. You can't protect he no more. You can't make he sleep with secret potion and t'ing. You goin' have to go 'fore cockcrow or you doom. Obey me!

(GRANNY ROOT gestures. MEDIYAH moves.)

MEDIYAH: Granny, what happen? I ain't know a feelin' like this before. I burnin' up. Me stomach all a-churn.

GRANNY ROOT: You fall too much in love. That is all. You lose control.

MEDIYAH: I ain't like it. It hurt. It like a million jamette dancin' Carnival and tarmpin' in me head. Me body feel like Damballah, heself, pitchin' rock and flame at me.

GRANNY ROOT: I did almost know that feelin' once. Long time ago... but I check it! I see the way of the world and I say, "No!"

MEDIYAH: Take it away, Granny! Take away this feelin'!

GRANNY ROOT: Is only you can do such.

MEDIYAH: How? Tell me how! I do it right now!

GRANNY ROOT: Remove the man!

MEDIYAH: What?

GRANNY ROOT: Banish he from you heart! Call down thunder and lightnin' to strike he from here! Cast he into the pit! Cause flame to rise up 'round he. Conflagrate! Immolate! Incinerate! Use science! Use skill! Kill! Kill! Kill!

(MEDIYAH, *aroused by* GRANNY ROOT's *fervor, gestures wildly. Nothing happens to* JASON.)

MEDIYAH: Nothin' ain't happen!

GRANNY ROOT: 'Cause you ain't want it to. In you heart, you ain't want it to.

(MEDIYAH *gestures again, falls to her knees in prayer, dances wildly, prostrates herself, does all manner of things, but nothing happens.*)

GRANNY ROOT: Is like I say, Darlin', you too much in love. A woman, too much in love, ain't have no power! Now, you have to prepare to leave here. I can give you only to cockcrow. Then you must follow me close or you mighty love goin' be you miserable death!

(MEDIYAH *sinks to the ground, sobbing.*)

GRANNY ROOT: Poor, ordinary woman!

(GRANNY ROOT *disappears as* JASON *returns to normal.*)

JASON: No! I can't say them word you want, 'cause I ain't feel to say such. I ain't lie to you or no other woman. I ain't find she yet who could make me feel and say them word. When I find she, I goin' know it. When I find she, I goin' feel it. When I find she, I goin' be proud to say it. I truly fond of you. For true, no gal ever treat me so good like you, but more than this, I can't say. Bring me boy, them, safe to this world, and I give you honor and paradise. Now on them term, you want me, still? Tell me now. We could fall down on the grass, this night, and see Heaven. We could know beauty and bliss like we never know, for I feelin' young and strong and a little extra of me juice good for them two boy you have in there! We could...eh-eh? What do you? Why you a-cry?

MEDIYAH: Jason, we have to leave this place before cockcrow!

JASON: Why? You no more happy here?

MEDIYAH: Listen!

(*Almost inaudibly, we can hear animal sounds and horrible noises. They grow louder and louder.* JASON *picks up his weapon as* MEDIYAH *clings to him for protection.*)

MEDIYAH: I scare. I can't protect we no more. We must leave this place.

JASON: Before cockcrow, you say?

MEDIYAH: Yes, Darlin'.

JASON: Then we have lickle time.

MEDIYAH: We should go now.

JASON: Before cockcrow, Doux-doux. We have time. I goin' make all them tear distappear. I goin' whisper rudeness in you ear.

MEDIYAH: We ain't have time.

JASON: Two spice bun bakin' in you oven. It take time. Just like you and me out to do some lovin' it take time. We can't go rush and reelin'. It don't pay goin' fast if you want the feelin' to last. You and me havin' lickle funnin'. It take time. Then we flee 'fore we let the sun in, but it take time. So, lay back now and I will sing you flower, cover you with kiss 'till the mornin' hour, touch you with me hand is only me hand reach you sing honey in you ear that way I will teach you the meaning of the word, a word you've only heard, "Sublime". But, it take time.

(They fall to the ground, oblivious to the once again rising sounds of animals and jungle horrors. GRANNY ROOT appears, the noise fade gradually, and JASON and MEDIYAH are in embrace. MEDIYAH, still apprehensive, tries to urge him out of the wood.)

JASON: Slow, slow, slow! I ain't use to runnin'. I take time. Time to show me cleverness and cunnin'. Take we time. So, lay back now, precious little flower. Lay back now. Only I does have the power to ease you every fear. Nothin' here goin' haunt you. Even ghost can see just how bad me want you. We can beat this jungle. Ain't no mountain we can't climb. But, it take time.

(GRANNY ROOT trails her veil over the prone pair.)

GRANNY ROOT: All thing take time, but time goin' soon done! *(She disappears.)*

JASON: Slow, Sweetness. Cockcrow a long way off. We ain't have no rush. We just go easy.

(MEDIYAH surrenders...completely.)

END OF ACT ONE

ACT TWO

Scene One
(Months later. The hut of MEDIYAH built on the site of the old one. It is overgrown with vines and weeds. Inside, MEDIYAH sits in an old rocking

chair. Very much pregnant, it's obvious she's not cleaned the place in a while. Outside, PERSIS *and* FAUSTINA *approach furtively. They wait until they are directly within hearing distance, then elbow each other in the ribs and gleefully and deliberately speak aloud.)*

FAUSTINA: Persis?

PERSIS: What is it, Faustina?

FAUSTINA: It a lovely day for Carnival, ain't it?

PERSIS: Oh, Darlin' Sister. True. It quite lovely. And this one goin' be so special, too. That drunken Cedric goin' for he number five win.

FAUSTINA: It look like he goin' take all the prize and t'ing.

PERSIS: But, wait! Sometime ago, you did tell me that you card say ain't no triumph for Cedric this time. What happen? You did read them wrong?

FAUSTINA: As mare does find new he-horse, so hart does find new hind As wind does find new chart to course, so card does change them mind.

PERSIS: You mighty prophetic and profound this mornin'. Yes, I sure goin' to this one set of Carnival. Me wouldn't miss it.

FAUSTINA: Me too, neither. I wish everybody could go, but some people can't go 'cause them too shame to show them face.

PERSIS: Oh? You could tell me why?

FAUSTINA: Plenty people have plenty reason. Some shame 'cause them belly big, big, big and them ain't have man to give them legality, properness, standin', or he name.

PERSIS: You does say true? Such people does exist? No! You ain't mean it. You can't know such sinful people. You ain't raise to know such.

FAUSTINA: Me card bring me in contact with all kind. High and low. Up and down. Fast and slow. Square and roun'.

PERSIS: You ain't say.

FAUSTINA: Oh, yes. I does know some people so shame 'cause them once so high and mighty and laud and lord theyself all over the place like peacock, but now them topple. Them drab like peahen and them hiney bare like pickney.

PERSIS: Oh, miseration. It too sad to see somebody once them think them empress and now, them ain't even have chamber pot. That how the world go. One day, you a good morsel. The next, you nothin' but somebody fecal deposit.

FAUSTINA: But, wait. We so busy chattin' and feelin' sorry for them what come low like snake, we ain't realize we passin' Mediyah hut.

PERSIS: No! You wrong, Sister, dearest. This ain't Mediayh hut. At least, it ain't the hut of the Mediyah I does know, for this place have weed all grow up on she. The Mediyah I does know does keep she place. She does trim she grass and have lovely flower all red and yellow and white and t'ing. This place does look wild like somebody what ain't have man to love they. No! You truly wrong! This place ain't belong to our Mediyah!

FAUSTINA: No! It belong to she! Oop! We ain't stop to think. Maybe she does sick and can't pick up after sheself and that shy she estate look so wild and tempest.

PERSIS: Let we go in and see after she.

(MEDIYAH, *broom in hand, comes to the door.*)

MEDIYAH: The first, 'ol, never-use, dry-up tart put she foot through me portal without me permiso, I goin' take this one besom and t'ump she into the future.

PERSIS: Oh, look, Faustina. Is Mediyah. I glad to see you on you feet. We thought you did sick. You goin' see you brother go for the crown tonight?

MEDIYAH: You two ol' fart better vacate me premise, 'fore I cleave you head.

FAUSTINA: You does have to humor she, Sister. You does get quite prickly when you carryin' baby for invisible man.

MEDIYAH: How you does know? The two of you barren like an ol' empty tortoise shell.

FAUSTINA: We does forgive you you outburst, 'cause we know it hard when woman does have to bring forth she lickle, nameless offspring and she ain't have man.

MEDIYAH: You could look at me and say I ain't have man? Is only you two ol' ghost could make baby from spirit! The first fool fellow try to fit he flaccid fiber 'neath them frowsy frock to fondle and feel you fallow, infertile, infecund, faded fruit does faint from foul and fetid fragrance of you flatulence. I should long ago turn you into the serpent you is, but I 'fraid mongoose would bite you and die from you venom. Get off me place 'fore me choke you.

FAUSTINA: Come, Persis. The woman demented. We can't help she. Them devil plant in she bely by she phantom lover done drive she insane.

(MEDIYAH *disappears into her hut.*)

PERSIS: Somethin' tell me we better haul arse.

(MEDIYAH *returns, holding something behind her back.*)

MEDIYAH: All you say I ain't have chamber pot? I not only have pochamb, but it decorate...inside and out. Here!

(MEDIYAH *flings a flowered and filled "potchamb" at them. It misses them as they flee.*)

PERSIS: *(From a safe distance)* The woman crazy and she content...foul.

FAUSTINA: Is a good thing I ain't have on me Bombazine. Yet she would soil it if she did connect. But she aim as good as she name and we all know she ain't have that.

(GRANNY ROOT *appears and gestures at the departed duo. They scream.*)

PERSIS: Oh, God. Abomination!

FAUSTINA: The bitch must have two pochamb!!!

PERSIS and FAUSTINA: Aaaiiieee!!!

(GRANNY ROOT *goes into the hut.*)

GRANNY ROOT: It do me heart good to see them two dry whore so dirty. Look this place, nuh? Everything all awry. How you could stay in such disarray?

MEDIYAH: I ain't feel to clean. I have too much burden here.

GRANNY ROOT: Other woman does carry and still keep she place. How you could expect somebody to see you house so filthy? What this in the pot?

MEDIYAH: Lanty-pea soup. Jason tell me he comin' today, 'cause it the beginnin' of Carnival. The contest, later, you know.

GRANNY ROOT: How you expect the man to eat in so filthy a confine? You soup smell good, but if I was 'live, I wouldn't eat it. You know what them always say. "Dirty kitchen, dirty pot! Dirty woman, dirty lot!"

MEDIYAH: Don't scold me, nuh! This place too much for me. This belly too much for me. I want to have these baby and done. I tired carryin'. I can't do nothin', I so tire. Me foot all swole up so, me can't take four step without I have agony. The sun shine and I weepy. It rain and I worse. Jason only does come once in a blue moon and when him come, him only stay lickle piece of time. He ain't have no talk for me. He ain't touch me and is him do this thing to me, you know. He ain't look at me. He only say him want to know how him two son comin' 'long. He come late...

when it dark...and he gone 'fore mornin'. After all this t'ing over. I goin' rip out me tube. I ain't goin' through this a next time. Never!

GRANNY ROOT: Such a much complaint.

MEDIYAH: Granny, I miserable! And, oh, God...them kick me again! How baby not even born could do they mother such cruelty?

GRANNY ROOT: You is a ordinary woman. You havin' ordinary pain. You makin' ordinary complaint. The magic gone, Child. Havin' baby is most real! Jason comin'. I goin'!

(GRANNY ROOT *disappears.* JASON *enters.)*

MEDIYAH: Hello, Darlin'.

JASON: This place filthy! I can't stay here! How you feel? Me two son all right?

MEDIYAH: They fine and kickin'. I make lanty-pea soup for you.

JASON: You ain't expect me to eat nothin' from this place? How I know you pot clean?

MEDIYAH: I make the soup for good luck!

JASON: I ain't need no soup for win!

MEDIYAH: I know, but don't rush off. Plenty time 'fore the festivities, then.

JASON: I can't find place to stretch our or sit. I goin'. After I win, I might could come back and let you peek at me trophy, but you better pick up this place...else I not settin' foot in here. Me mother ain't raise me in no dirty house. You goin' wish me "Bon Chance"?

MEDIYAH: Yes. I getting' up just now.

(MEDIYAH *rises and offers her lips for* JASON *to kiss. He offers his cheek. She kisses it.)*

JASON: Careful! Don't dirty me suit. Why you don't go to the pond beneath Yama Fall and have a dip and cleanse youself. At least, woman, you could fill a basin and drop a rag in it and then pass it over you body. I ain't like no unclean woman. I ain't like no unclean woman for the mother of me son. I have to go. 'Bye.

(JASON *leaves.* MEDIYAH, *abject and sobbing, sinks to the ground.* GRANNY ROOT *appears.*)

GRANNY ROOT: Ordinary woman! Ordinary woman! Ordinary woman! Ordinary woman, less than whole. Give 'way she brain, she heart, she soul. Now she playin' ordinary role. All because she lose control. Ordinary woman feelin' sad. Oridinary woman feelin' bad. Ordinary woman soon get mad. Then, ordinary woman once more, glad.

MEDIYAH: Granny, you did say somethin'?

GRANNY ROOT: No, Darlin'. Granny ain't say nothin' a-tall.

(Lights)

Scene *Two*

(Carnival! Music! Dancing! The townsfolk...masked and colorfully costumed! CREON PANDIT, resplendent in gold, a blue ribbon of honor across his chest, a silver and gold cape, bejeweled cane, and a crown on his head, leads the revelers. SWEET BELLA, costumed as a radiant Cleopatra, dances with some of the men. FAUSTINA, in her somber Bombazine dress, enters regally with the air of a great lady dispensing alms to the poor. Her dress is betrayed, however, by the many gauzy, fiery yellow and red petticoats that peek from beneath the hem of her dress. PERSIS enters in a more joyous manner. Her costume features more gauzy orange and red petticoats than that of her sister. Her parasol is trimmed with the same material. FAUSTINA turns her nose up at her sister and dances sedately. PERSIS, riant, is having the time of her life. As CREON passes the sisters, he uses his cane to lift their skirts.)

CREON: Mornin', Ladies. I always did think all you have secret fire 'neath you skirt, them.

(FAUSTINA *"objects", but* PERSIS *lifts her skirt even higher to show more.* CREON *laughs and whoops. Everyone swirls around a slightly elevated square festooned with gaily colored bunting, giving it the look of a boxing ring.* CEDRIC, *in his Chanticleer costume, pompously enters with his entourage. They parade, ceremoniously, as* CEDRIC *steps into the "ring". He spars, much in the manner of a boxer.*)

PERSIS: Well it look like you card finally make up them mind. Cedric done vanquish all he foe. Is only one final mystery challenger to go.

FAUSTINA: Ain't I tell you, Miss? The card, them don't lie. Them ain't like some people I does know, who when you does turn you back, does make them dress out of all me extra piece of black Bombazine.

PERSIS: Oh, hush you mouth. Is me own black Bombazine. You think you is the only one could call sheself "Lady"?

FAUSTINA: "Lady" t'ief!

(*Suddenly, there is a hush. The music and the hubbub stop. The crowd parts and* JASON, *clad in a black, figure-revealing costume topped by a close-fitting, black hood with the horns of a ram and wearing a black mask, appears...golden quatro in his hands. He walks silently around the square and then, suddenly, leaps into the "ring". Standing in the corner diagonally opposite* CEDRIC, JASON *stares, piercingly at his opponent. As the crowd comes back to normal,* CREON PANDIT *steps into the center of the "ring".*)

CREON: Ladies, and Gent, as all you does know, I win Pecong five time in a row. Is so! I, the only livin' Mighty, Royal, Most Perfect and Grand King Kalabash. Only me daddy 'fore me do what I do... and win this verbal clash. But, young Mr. Cedric, here givin' it a try and he biddin' fair. So far today, as all you does know, him done vanquish all him foe. Him only have this last to go. Is so! So, without much further ado make I present to you, Mr. Jason, the Ram from the Isle of Tougou. Yes, him come all the way from he lickle village… come all the way here to t'ief and pillage the crown quite out from Cedric han'. Yes! Jason of Tougou, the mystery man. Gentlemen, all you 'poach the center of the combat zone, if you please.

(CEDRIC and JASON *step to the center of the "ring" to receive their instructions and engage in a stare-down.*)

CREON: Yes, this Jason come to make invasion and Cedric a-boil with indignation. So, on this auspicious occasion, I goin' judge this conflagration. I tell you, nobody better qualify than me to judge and referee.

(*The crowd goes wild as* CEDRIC *prances around.*)

CREON Well, all you know the regulation. You entitle to one legal hesitation, If you does try for a double… Oh, man. Trouble, trouble, trouble on top of trouble. So, let we have the competition! No gallavantin'! Both you shake you hand and come out chantin'! Be keen like blade and sharp like pin! And may the best man win!

PERSIS: That Jason look plenty, plenty sweet in he array. He look to have plenty heavy stone. I think I goin' wager a copper or two on he leg, alone.

FAUSTINA: Fool! I tell you what the card say.

PERSIS: Um-hmm, I does hear you…but somethin' seem to catch me eye when I see that mound 'tween him thigh!

CREON: All you pay 'tention to the gong. When you hear it sound, begin Pecong!

(CREON *hits the gong. Pecong! Music plays. Raucous Calypso rhythm. The two opponents come out of their respective corners and dance around each other, feeling each other out in the manner of boxers, or if you will, fighting cocks. The Pecong is a context in which each man insults the other. When one man dos, the other will react as if he's been struck by a blow. With each verbal blow, the crowd will react, as if at a prizefight, and roar its approval.*)

CEDRIC: Come on, Mr. Challenger. Come, if you dare Come on, Mr. Big Man. Come, see how you fare. Come, come, come. Take you lickle chance. Make you lickle chant and then, me word goin' kick you right in the middle of you shitey pant.

FAUSTINA: Cedric open with wit and style...

JASON: You will pardon me if I does make so bold, but you empty t'reat does leave me cold. I does hear how you is so much "Master", but me tongue too fast and me brain too faster. So, Mr. Cedric, if you could please excuse, no way I could lose.

PERSIS: You hear that?

CEDRIC: Well, step up, Boy. If you does dare. You ain't goin' get a next opportunity so rare. I just hope you life complete if is me you goin' try to beat. Come on, Challenger, but I hope you make you peace and say you prayer, 'fore you heartbeat cease... 'Cause me word too strong and you blood too thin to ever 'low you to win!

FAUSTINA: Hahoii? Cedric have it in the bag!

JASON: T'reat, t'reat, t'reat! Is all I does hear! T'reat, t'reat, t'reat ringing in me ear But when you goin' say? When you goin' do some damage to this Jason of Tougou? It look like I goin' have to make the start and jab you straight to the heart... and say, "Cedric, you man of smallish part, you underarm have odor like ragged fart!"

FAUSTINA: Oh, God!

PERSIS: Whoop!

CEDRIC: I does hear people talk 'bout you and use bad word, you lout, you Them does see you seek you pleasure and all the time, chewin' on the treasure. I does say, "Stand aside, all you. Be calm! Don't push when Jason have he face bury in some young gal buh!"

PERSIS: Raucous!

FAUSTINA: Foul utterance!

JASON: It true! I does like them gal so young and does have them taste on the tip of me tongue. But at night, I does sleep with innocence and joy because me ain't like you. I ain't sleep with boy!

PERSIS: I, too, enjoyin' this, you know.

CEDRIC: I does see you on the make, Out there hunting female snake with you little tool in you hand doin' battle with whatever hole underneath she rattle!

FAUSTINA: A veritable blow!

JASON: And I does see what you does give to all you sundry relative. None safe from you...not even you mother, not even you brother. You would mate with you sister, copulate with a Mister. You would even rape a fever blister!

PERSIS: Cedric reelin'!

FAUSTINA: Shut up!

CEDRIC: You mother behind ain't never see tub. She mout' nasty and, here the rub, me too clean to go 'tween she hip and I ain't want that ol' haunt lip nowhere 'round me billy-club.

FAUSTINA: A good return!

JASON: I layin' in me bed. I feel this crunchin' quite at me vitals, I feel this munchin! I pull back me sheet and see you mother lunchin'... ...eh-eh...gnawin' with she rat teeth on me truncheon!

PERSIS: Riposte! Riposte!

CEDRIC: All you family ugly with wart on them face. Them not even part of the human race!

JASON: You does have the nerve to mention "face" when you ugly like a mongoose backin' out a fireplace?

CEDRIC: You mother too crazy for me part She even see it in she dream. She does run it and caress it, She does reach down and she press it, but she can't take too much, les' it make she wet she drawers and scream!

FAUSTINA: Aha! A good hit!

JASON: You mother does quite act like a crazy fool. She jaw go slack and she mout' does drool. But I think she goin' have to go back to school. She amateur when it come to nyammin' tool.

CEDRIC: It too bad it have to be this way. You not so ugly as them all does say. You know what you face does call to mind? A wilted, bare-ass, baboon behind that run into one big meat grind and lose the fight! That right!

JASON: I does give you gal friend yardstick. I fill she to she core. I tell she, "Me name not Richard!" but she screamin', "More, Dickie, more!" Then, I does have to fight she to keep she from me waist I box she, then I bite she, but she scream for lickle more taste.

PERSIS: The boy is a born composer, you hear!

CEDRIC: When last you does have woman? When last you try it out? With petite dangle 'tween you leg that always pointin' sout'. I does feel so sorry for it, layin' there for dead while mine jumpin' and mine pumpin' and you no can raise him head.

JASON: I sorry you let out we secret I woulda say you can't But now you done tell the world you familiar with inside me pant. I wouldn'ta tell nobody 'cause I ain't want you disgrace but now all does know you does bend down and could tell them how me taste. I was savin' me nether for when I get together with some gal or the other. But you nyam it all, bat and ball, and ain't leave none for you mother.

PERSIS: Jason of Tougou pullin' out all the stops!

CEDRIC: I ain't have no time to babble or hang 'round with no rabble. I goin' put an end to you once and for all. I goin' take out me fleshy cutlass and stick it up you but, lass, 'cause you cryin' out for bed on which to fall.

FAUSTINA: That ain't such a worthy rhyme, Cedric.

PERSIS: What you card say now?

FAUSTINA: Them say, "Hush you fool mouth!"

JASON: Is me you callin', "Lassie"? I ain't know you was so classy, but if you thinkin' I is woman, you is wrong. 'Cause if you thinkin' you have "slugger" and is me you try to bugger, I goin' mash you with somethin' mighty strong and long. You surely does mistake me if you think that you could take me. You confuse if you think me ass cover with lace. 'Cause I have somethin' here... You could pet it. You could pucker you lip, take you tongue and wet it, but have a care that me don't let it rear back he head and spit in you face.

CEDRIC: I...I...I...

PERSIS: Cedric falter! Cedric falter!

CREON: Yes, Cedric does falter!

CEDRIC: Hush you mouth, all you! All you, shut you yap! I still have resource me ain't begin to tap All you think that Cedric dozin'. Hah! You got a next think comin'! I still composin'! Okay! I got it! You mother swear she smart when she latch on to me part. She scream and tell, "Take me to Hell! I give you everything you think you lack!" But when me eye glance down and see what mufflin' 'round, I send she by sheself and she ain't come back.

FAUSTINA: Come on, Jason of Tougou. You have him now!

PERSIS: Traitoress!

(JASON *begins a slow, circling stalk.*)

JASON: I layin' in me bed alone. You mother jump me like dog after bone. She make a leap. Land 'top me with a crash. She does mout' me 'till I ain't know which. I wake up in the mornin' and have private itch. Is then I see I drippin' and have an ugly rash. And when I go to make wee-wee, I burn so...God! I say to she, 'may the bloody pile torment you and corn grow on you feet. May crab as big as roach crawl in you bush and eat! may the whole world turn again' you, and when you a total wreck, may you fall through you own asshole and bruck you goddamn neck!

FAUSTINA: Cedric, gone now.

PERSIS: Yes. Just like you card does say.

(CEDRIC *staggers. The crowd is silent.* CEDRIC *tries to say words, but they won't come. of course, nobody can see the veiled figure of* GRANNY ROOT *holding her umbrella over* CEDRIC's *head.* CEDRIC, *unable to speak and disgraced, runs off in spite of* JASON's *outstretched hand.* GRANNY ROOT *stays on. There is a great shout from the crowd and the scene erupts with music and dancing.* CEDRIC's *band runs after him.* PERSIS *grabs* JASON *and kisses him.)*

PERSIS: You is one beautiful and elegant lad and you cause me to win quite a few shekels. You is a born Calypsonian! You does have girlfriend?

FAUSTINA: I win some, too! Me card tell me all along you was goin' be the winner, so me wager lickle bit of penny. Move, Woman. Let the man kiss me!

(*Before this can happen, however,* JASON *is hoisted to the shoulders of some men and they parade him around.)*

CREON: Young man, I does like you attack Is through you, me title still intac'. You throw Cedric to the ground...and mash he up. You smartly earn this year Pecong Cup. You is one quite excellent fella Make I introduce you to me daughter, Sweet Bella.

(*SWEET BELLA comes forward with a wreath for* JASON's *neck. The moment she places it and their eyes meet,* GRANNY ROOT *gestures and all except* JASON *and* SWEET BELLA *seem to freeze.* GRANNY ROOT *sprinkles some dust into the Pecong Cup and gives it to them. They each drink.* GRANNY ROOT *retrieves the cup and drains it.* JASON *and* SWEET BELLA *begin a slow, sensuous, sinuous dance. There's not an half-inch of space between them. Even though the crowd is frozen, they are not unaware of* SWEET BELLA *and* JASON. *The impression should be given that the crowd is moving at a considerably slower pace than the dancing pair.*)

SWEET BELLA: Jason...

CREON: Me daughter speak!

PERSIS, FAUSTINA and CROWD: Sweet Bella, the Silent, speak!

JASON: What sound is this?

SWEET BELLA: Jason! Jason!

CREON and ALL: She speak again!

JASON: I ain't never hear a sound so. It like bird! It like bell! It like music! It like Heaven!

SWEET BELLA: Jason!

CREON and ALL: Miracle! Is a miracle!

CREON: The man make me daughter speak! He make she speak! She sin't never 'fore utter sound and she speak when he and she eye meet up. He done bruck the spell cast on she. The man, a prince! Better than a prince. Him a God!

JASON: Is feel like I can't speak. It feel like I can't make rhyme. Confusion runnin' wild in me head and elsewhere. Me breath gone! Is like I seein' woman for the first time in me life.

SWEET BELLA: Is not the same with me. I see you before Jason. I see you so many time, I can't count. I see you when I wake. I see you when I sleepin'. I see you when it sun or when the moon come creepin'. I see you in the moon very moment of me life before. I swimmin' in the sea There ain't no danger to me, I know you comin' soon Every moment of me life before. I just find word to say what I could not express. Thing people does say every day. For instance, word like "love" and "tenderness" I see you in me dream. I can't help me dreamin'. I wake up from me dream and in me heart, I screamin'. Screamin' out you name and hopin' you just outside me door. I see you in me eye In every tear I cry Each sigh I sigh, Each lie I lie. In each hello... In each good-bye, Every moment of me life before. I couldn't speak before, I save me first word for you. It take me all me life to tell how I adore you. I ragein' like typhoon tearin' up the tropic shore, Yes, I does see you every moment of me life before. Yes, I see you before, Jason.

JASON: Sweet Bella, I never say this before, I feel to say it now. I does love you. I ain't know why I say it, but I ain't scare to. It just come out. I does love you. It don't even feel strange. I does love you! Yes, that what this feelin' I does feel. Yes! I does love you, Sweet Bella Pandit I does truly love you. I ain't even have more word than that.

(All the others return to "normal speed".)

SWEET BELLA; Dad, I could speak!

CREON: Praise be! I know it was true! Praise be!

(CREON *falls to the ground in gratitude and thanks.*)

SWEET BELLA: Daddy, this man want to talk to you.

CREON: I figure so.

JASON: Mr. Creon Pandit, Mighty, Royal, Most Perfect, Grand King Calabash, all me life I ain't seen nobody like you daughter. I know you ain't know nothin' 'bout me, but I not a too bad fellow. In me life, I know a whole lot of gal and I tell you, out in the open, that quite a few does make baby for me. I know me duty to them children, them, and I does do it, but I never feel for none of they mother or any gal what I does feel for you daughter, Sweet Bella. My heart and entire soul ragin' with flame what like come from the center of the earth. I can't make no procrastination. I say to you before all assemble here. I want to marry you daughter. I want to marry she. Now!

PERSIS: Oh, God! The man fast!

FAUSTINA: The man faster than fast. Him rapid!

CREON: It true I ain't know much 'bout you, Jason of Tougou Island. But I does know this. Me daughter born without speech. You does see she for the first time...and she talk. Is a true sign. Is a supernatural occurrence. A true sign from the God, them. Sweet Bella, you want this man?

SWEET BELLA: Is more than just, "want", Daddy. I have to have him. I thinkin'...I feelin'..."If I ain't have he soon, I goin' fall down right at he foot and die and the earth could swallow me and I ain't care a t'ing. I feelin', "If you ain't let him have me and he have me, I goin' climb a scarp or Devil Cliff and pitch meself right into the wind." I feelin', "If I ain't take he soon, I could throw meself right into the flame and when I meet Satan, I would kill he."

PERSIS: Faustina, you ever know such passion was runnin' wild so, inside she?

FAUSTINA: I struck speechless.

CREON: Sweet Bella, you me only child. I ain't never hear you speak before. Even if it a miracle, I can't just throw you to the man. I does just hear you voice, sweet like a bird, for the first time. You want to deprive you daddy of that sweet sound, so soon? Everything makin' fast current, but I ain't a proper daddy if I just...let you go. Of course, this the answer to all me dream. The man have the proper look and coloration and since I ain't have son to carry on me name, I could, at least, have a grandson to carry on me blood. Andy, who know, one day this sam grandson could be Mighty, Royal, Most Perfect, Grand King Calabash. Give me three day to plan and make t'ing. Till the end of Carnival. If the two of you still does have no let-upsy, then as magistrate, I, meself, will perform the ceremony just before midnight...last day of Carnival. What does you say, Mr. Jason? If you does love she like you does say, three day is a eye-blink.

JASON: Three day is torture! A man could die in three day, but I does love this gal. So, even if it ain't fine with me, she too worth the wait. Okay!

CREON: Well-spoken! Sweet Bella?

(SWEET BELLA *thinks and, finally, nods assent.*)

CREON: Don't nod, Gal. You have voice sweeter than mornin' wind in the mountain. Don't deprive you daddy from hearin' it.

SWEET BELLA: Yes, Daddy, I could wait...but three day is all. If you ain't keep you word, I goin' run off with he, even if it Lent! I ain't care.

CREON: Then since all you willin' to wait, I give me consent. I quite happy, you know. Just think, I goin' have me some grandson, at last!

(*The crowd erupts! Music! Dancing! Whatever!*)

(*The crowd is at its frenzied peak when* GRANNY ROOT *comes out of her trance.*)

GRANNY ROOT: Now, we does begin!

(*Thunder! Lightning!* MEDIYAH *appears.*)

MEDIYAH: Jason! Jason! Jason, you son, them comin'! Come! Hold me hand! Help me! I havin' you son, them, for you, Jason, darlin'.

(*Even* PERSIS *and* FAUSTINA *are speechless.*)

CREON: Jason of Tougou, you does know this woman?

JASON: Yes! I does know she!

CREON: You know she is sister to Cedric who just fall to you in Pecong?

JASON: No! I ain't ever know that. She ain't ever tell me such!

CREON: You did lay up with she?

JASON: I did lay with she or promise youself to she?

JASON: Sweet Bella, as the God, them, me judge and witness, I ain't love nobody, but you in the whole of me life, 'side me mother and she long depart from here. This just one of them gal who I does jook up long ago when I was wicked. That, then, Sweetness! I does love you, now, with all the heart you does leave me when you take it so complete.

(MEDIYAH *lets forth a horribly agonizing scream and falls, writhing, on the ground.*)

MEDIYAH: Jason! Jason! Jason, with all you does leave of me heart, I hate you. I does curse you and before all here I swear I goin' have me vengeance. Aaaiiieee!!!

GRANNY ROOT: Aha! You Granny Root granddaughter again.

MEDIYAH: Aaaiiieee!!! Granny! Granny, call all the God, them. Attend me!

CREON: She delirious! She talkin' to the dead Granny! She talkin' to air!

PERSIS: All you hard-back man, get 'way from here. Go stand some place and hide you eye. All you woman, surround me. And one of you, tear off you petticoat and give me.

(*The men obey, as do the women, encircling* MEDIYAH, *being attended by* PERSIS *and* FAUSTINA. JASON *and* SWEET BELLA *stand off, alone.* CREON *stands apart, watching them.*)

SWEET BELLA: I does love you, Jason of Tougou. I ain't give a care what you do before I see you. I sorry for Mediyah, but you does belong to me. I sorry for she, but I ain't care. I does love you. You beling to me!

JASON: I does love you, Sweet Bella Pandit.

SWEET BELLA: Three day, Jason! Three day 'till Carnival end and then, I goin' have you.

JASON: Three day!

SWEET BELLA: Just 'fore midnight on Carnival Night! 'Fore four-Day Mornin' come in sight!

JASON: Oh, God!

(SWEET BELLA *walks off, leaving* JASON. GRANNY ROOT *passes her umbrella over the crowd. There is an audible gasp. Seconds later, there is another.* PERSIS, *after a bit, approaches* JASON *carrying two petticoat-wrapped bundles.* JASON *is allowed to see the contents of the bundles but, when he reaches for them,* PERSIS *pulls back.* JASON *walks off.* GRANNY ROOT *passes her umbrella over* CREON's *head. He starts, frightened. Looking over his shoulder,* CREON *goes.*)

GRANNY ROOT: Yes, Mediyah. You hatred make you Granny Root granddaughter, again.

(GRANNY ROOT *cackles. Lights go out.*)

Scene Three
(MEDIYAH's *hut and it's still far from neat.* MEDIYAH, *on her pallet, stares into space.* GRANNY ROOT, *eyes focused on her granddaughter, stirs something in a pot. Two rough-hewn cradles are in evidence.*)

GRANNY ROOT: You brother comin'.

MEDIYAH: I know.

(CEDRIC, *drunk and angry, enters. He surveys the condition of the hut and his sister. His eyes alight on the two candles.*)

CEDRIC: So, it true! You make tow baby. I does hear 'bout it from all who get ecstacy when the could spread ondit! And you name in everybody mouth. I now see why you say you can't help me to get wood for a next quatro. you pitch over you own brother for help some man who ain't give a fart for you. He load you up with pickney, them and then he cut out. Right now, he languishin' in the arm of Sweet Bella Pandit. Right now, he croonin' lilt in she ear...the same like he mussie done to you. Right now, he t'umpin' all we half-sister. Right now, you ain't even in he memory, 'cause he too busy addin' another notch to he count. Good for you!

(GRANNY ROOT *gestures to silent* CEDRIC , *but* MEDIYAH, *her eyes still rooted in space, raises her hand to indicate that she wants* CEDRIC *to talk on.*)

CEDRIC: You know what that man do to me? This man who you lay on you back for. You know what him do? Him shame me! Him cause me to cast me head down and not be able for lift it. Him cause everybody, who did have respect and fear for me, to laugh and stomp them foot with glee as I does pass. He does cause everybody to have only toleration for me like they does have for bug! You know how that does feel? Well I hope you know it soon. I curse you, Sister! I hope you blood and you milk does turn to ugly, hellacious green bile. I hope you body dry up and turn to black powder. You help to kill you brother, Mediyah. It like I tear up into lickle piece and throw to dog for eat. I hope both you boy know the pain you cause me. I could have be like king in this place and Creon would recognize me and call me "Son" and I could call him "Daddy," but you abdicate me. Damn you, Sister! Damn you!

(CEDRIC, *drunkenly, stumbles out.*)

GRANNY ROOT: Too bad!

MEDIYAH: Part of Cedric curse already true. Ain't nothin' runnin' through me vein but bile and bitterness.

GRANNY ROOT: You need more than bitterness.

MEDIYAH: I know.

GRANNY ROOT: I know you know, but I makin' sure. *(She tastes her concoction.)* It ready. I even put in some t'ing even you ain't know 'bout. You had long sleep. I had was to wait for you to wake. I ain't even able to talk to you in you dream.

MEDIYAH: I ain't need you in me dream. Only room in me dream for me hatred of Jason of Tougou.

GRANNY ROOT: Jason is man...and man does inspire hatred. Tell me hatred done replace love in you heart. Tell me hatred of man does replace love in you heart!

MEDIYAH: I done told you!

GRANNY ROOT: No! You tell me hatred of Jason. Tell me, now, is hatred of man you feelin'.

MEDIYAH: Yes!

GRANNY ROOT: Tell me again and swear it! *(She grabs MEDIYAH's hands and spits in the palm of each.)* Swear it!

MEDIYAH: I does swear it! By all the God, them, I does swear it!

GRANNY ROOT: Good! Aha! Right on time.

(PERSIS and FAUSTINA enter.)

PERSIS: Mediyah! Mediyah!

FAUSTINA: Mediyah, we could come in?

MEDIYAH: Yes.

PERSIS: Thank you. How the two little baby keepin'?

MEDIYAH: Them sleep!

PERSIS: And we shoutin' and keepin' noise and t'ing.

FAUSTINA: Shame on you!

MEDIYAH: Is all right. They does sleep sound. They ain't wake 'till them want to.

PERSIS: Is always such a joy to have lickle baby cryin' in the house.

MEDIYAH: Them don't cry! Baby only cry 'cause them can't tell you what do they. I know what do these two, so don't have for cry. They ain't cry when them born and tem never goin' cry.

PERSIS: As long as them have health...that what count, I suppose.

FAUSTINA: Mediyah, we could help you pick up 'round here?

PERSIS: We could do so, if you want for we to do so. I mean, we ain't want for interfere, but if you does need some help to...

MEDIYAH: Why all you does want to do this. All we ain't friend! I does thank you for deliverin' the baby, them, but we ain't waste no love or like on weself.

FAUSTINA: Mediyah, is time we does put all this ruction aside. The man do you a horrendous dirtiness. I never see such in all me life.

PERSIS: Never! You deliverin' the man baby. Two of them...as if one ain't hard enough. You twitchin' in the dirt and he rejectin' you right on the self-same spot.

FAUSTINA: It like he grab hold of all we woman and slap all we. It like he rainin' blow on all we arse!

MEDIYAH: You come to tell me this?

FAUSTINA: We come to tell you that Creon Pandit makin' big weddin' plan for he daughter and that rapscallion who did have he way with you.

PERSIS: Them goin' marry at Carnival finish tomorrow night!

FAUSTINA: Before midnight! It goin' be the highlight.

PERSIS: But even worse...

FAUSTINA: ...The man on he way here now...

PERSIS: ...Comin' to you hut for...

MEDIYAH: He comin' for take he two son 'way from here.

PERSIS: You does know this?

FAUSTINA: You ain't goin' 'low he to have he way?

PERSIS: No! You couldn't condone such action.

FAUSTINA: No! I ain't goin' believe that!

MEDIYAH: I say what I goin' do?

FAUSTINA: But you does have a certain look in you eye that does say...

MEDIYAH: You does see look in me eye? I ain't know you could see look in me eye. But you is most observant. Keep lookin' in me eye! That right! Both you keep lookin' in me eye. Closer, Ladies.

(PERSIS *and* FAUSTINA *are enchanted.*)

GRANNY ROOT: Yes, Granddaughter, you does have you power back.

MEDIYAH: Now, all you go wait just outside 'til I does call you to come in.

PERSIS and FAUSTINA: Yes, Mediyah. *(Obediently, they go.)*

MEDIYAH: You does know me mind?

GRANNY ROOT: Yes! Steel youself. He comin'.

MEDIYAH: I know!

(JASON *enters, wearing the suit* MEDIYAH *bought him.*)

JASON: Hello!

MEDIYAH: Jason.

JASON: You does feel all right?

MEDIYAH: I fine! I ain't perform no feat! I ain't do nothin' ain't ordinary. I only have twin...for you. Nothin' special.

JASON: I see them two woman outside you place dawdlin' 'round.

MEDIYAH: Them help deliver you son, them. Them came to inquire after they health. That what you a-come for?

JASON: Mediyah, you still have this place unkempt. Well, I ain't come to lash you with more word over you bad housekeepin'. I goin' be brief. You does know I fall in love with Sweet Bella Pandit and does plan to marry up with she 'fore Lent Mornin' come.

MEDIYAH: Is so I did hear. I offer me congrats.

JASON: You ain't vex?

MEDIYAH: Why I should vex? You ain't love me. I distapoint true...but I ain't vex...no more. I find you on Miedo Wood Island all hack up and wrack up. True! I heal you and comfort you. True! I give you wood and wildcat gut for fashion quatro for you to win Pecong. True! I give you two boy you say you want for so long and never have. All that true, but I ain't vex. Why I should vex?

JASON: Good! I glad you does feel so, 'cause I ain't want to make you no hurt. Well, as you does say, I always want some son. Now, I does have them and, now, I does want them.

MEDIYAH: With you!

JASON: With me! Boy belong with them daddy!

MEDIYAH: Them ain't nowhere yet wean.

JASON: If you had kick out, them two boy would have to find some other woman to give them titty. I win Pecong. I have lickle cash to buy fertile titty from woman in that business. You ain't truly want them boy, you know. You ain't need no reminder of me. I just a scalawag, you know, and it best you does forget me.

MEDIYAH: You will pardon me, Jason, but I ain't never goin' forget you.

JASON: Well, I ain't see how you could, but me charm aside, the boy, them, goin' be better off with me. I marryin' well and Creon does like me.

MEDIYAH: Of course! You make he daughter chatter after a life of silence and you does have good tint. Match it with he Sweet Bella and the two of you could make grandchild with pleasin' coloration.

JASON: True!

MEDIYAH: What about these two boy?

JASON: Them fair enough, thanks to me. Them ain't goin' get too much darker 'cause I did peek at them ear when them birth.

MEDIYAH: I see.

JASON: Anyway, them goin' be good taken care of. So, give me them, nuh!

MEDIYAH: Them goin' soon wake up and want they milk. You better leave me nurse them a next time. You could go someplace and then come back after them suck. Then you could have them.

JASON: You ain't goin' give me trouble?

MEDIYAH: Why should I do such? What you does say, true! Boy belong with them daddy. I ain't carve out to be mother. 'Specially to you children. Look how I does keep this place. Like you say, you ain't want no son from you...raise in pig sty.

JASON: True!

MEDIYAH: True! So, you go, take a trot, then, come back and...

JASON: I know you was goin' have good sense. Sweet Bella tell me you was goin' cause some aggravation 'bout this. I tell she, she wrong 'cause I does know you.

MEDIYAH: But, she ain't know me. I ain't goin' cause no excitement. I, too, glad she talkin', you know.

JASON: You ain't upset with she?

MEDIYAH: You look at she, she look at you, and she speak. That a great omen. A sign from up there. I cain't find no fault with what the God, them, does decree. What happen ain't she fault. And I no more upset with she than I upset with you. All you want is for raise up you son, them. True?

JASON: True! Give them they last milk and I goin' come back. Oh, yes. I never did thank you for the quatro. So, I do it now. Thank you!

MEDIYAH: Oh, you most welcome. Thank you for the twin!

JASON: You welcome, too.

(JASON *goes.*)

GRANNT ROOT: Worthless dog! Vile pig!

MEDIYAH: Granny, what dog and pig do to you, you does insult they so?

GRANNY ROOT: I make apology to all the animal I confuse he with. It all I could do to keep from doin' somethin' to he.

MEDIYAH: Mr. Jason of Tougou I goin' get marry, too. I sending' you a special invite to me nuptial night! Since you special, I makin' room for you, right 'tween me and me groom.

GRANNY ROOT: Hahoiii!!! Give yourself over, Girl!

MEDIYAH: Come to me, all you God from the old country and the old time. Come to me and make me harder. Steel me! God of Thunder, speak in your most angry temper! God of Lightning, wreak you havoc and illuminate the darkest hour with you blindin' power! God of Wind, be extreme in you violence and blow the path of gentility to Hell. God of Cold, plant icy river in me heart. God of Hell, attend me! Sun, Moon, Star, hide you face and let through the God of Vengeance to marry and consummate with me and spew the foul content of we marriage bed over Sweet Bella Pandit and that bastard thing she choose for sheself. Make me blood like hot oil to burn and smother all life from they and all they line! Fill me with hate and let that hate never depart! God of Vengeance, stay with me forever! God of Hate, stay with me forever! God of Screamin' Quiet and Quiet Scream, Be all my life. God of Vengeance and Hate, make me you wife! *(She goes to the cradle and regards the inhabitants.)* And for these... ...these that come from them two regrettable seed he plant in me, make me milk pure boilin', bubblin', bitter, and burnin' bane. *(She picks up the babies and places them, one at each breast. Lights swirl, flicker, and dim.)* Now, Jason, you can come for you two boy. Take they to you bride and enjoy.

GRANNY ROOT: You do well, me daughter. You please all the old God, them, and you please Granny, too!

(GRANNY ROOT laughs, malevolently. Lights.)

Scene Four
(MEDIYAH's hut. Moments later. She has nursed the babies and returned them to their cradles. She does to the doorway.)

MEDIYAH: Attend me here!

(PERSIS and FAUSTINA obediently enter and, drinking from wooden goblets offered them by MEDIYAH, sit as she directs. GRANNY ROOT indicates by gesture that JASON approaches.)

MEDIYAH: I know! Come in, Jason. These two lady help deliver you baby. They not only have plenty interest, but them does have plenty milk. They does, therefore, provide one pair titty for each one you boy. If you ain't want them, you ain't get the baby, them. Agree?

JASON: Agree!

MEDIYAH: Good!

JASON: You two ain't mind?

PERSIS: No! How we could mind?

FAUSTINA: No way we could mind.

PERSIS and FAUSTINA: In fact, we quite "enchant" to do such!

JASON: Good! I sure make two healthy-lookin' boy. I think they goin' suck you dry within the week.

MEDIYAH: Jason, if you ain't mind, I have wedding gift for you bride. Is to show you and she me heart in the right place. I guess you want know what inside. I tell you. Is a thing I purchase in Creon store. A night frock so pretty and silky, I did plan to wear it on me wedding' night...if you did ever so choose to marry up with me. But, you ain't choose to marry up with me so I think Sweet Bella should have it. At least, it still serve a bride. I put a thousand petal from flower and quite some sweet herb in the parcel to give it scent and wishes for the future.

JASON: Flower and herb?

MEDIYAH: Yes. I had mean to enchant you like any young gal on she night of night would enchant she princely groom, but since that rule out, Sweet Bella will wear it and, maybe, take you to Paradise.

JASON: On she behalf, I does thank you. Is a kind and gentle gesture. You does surprise me.

MEDIYAH: Jason, I goin' turn me back. Persis! Faustina! Take the baby and go with he. When I turn 'round, I ain't want to see none of you here. Go!

JASON: You two lady, suivez-moi! Good-bye, Mediyah! I ain't expect to see you a next time. I think you goin' have it much better if you ain't stay in this place. If you ain't think of youself, think of these two boy. Yes! It goin' go much better for you if you leave here. Remember, the magistrate goin' be me daddy-in-law! Good-bye!

(*As* GRANNY ROOT *eyes her,* MEDIYAH *arranges herself to receive the news. She stares, vacantly, humming to herself as she rocks...and waits.*)

Scene Five

(*Darkness. There are screams of utmost horror. Townspeople run to and fro in utter confusion. The lights come up to reveal* MEDIYAH *sitting impassively and* GRANNY ROOT, *anxious to swallow every word from* PERSIS *and* FAUSTINA, *who come running up, exhausted, in tears and filled with revulsion.*)

PERSIS: Oh, Mediyah...

FAUSTINA: Oh, God! Mediyah! Mediyah!

PERSIS: How could you manipulate we so? How could you do such?

FAUSTINA: How? How? How? How you could hate so much?

PERSIS: Oh, Mediyah, you is one hard -

FAUSTINA: Harsh -

PERSIS: Bitter -

FAUSTINA: Sour woman!

(MEDIYAH *sits like a stone.*)

MEDIYAH: You will relate the event.

PERSIS: Me and Faustina find weself in Creon Pandit house. We does hear some laughter and we realize, the weddin' festivity afoot.

FAUSTINA: For we part, we ain't know how we get there. It like me and Persis wakin' from some dream. We in some room. Everything sorta haze and we eye getting' 'custom to we surrounin', when we does each feel something strange.

PERSIS: Both of we scream out simultaneous. Both of we look down. Both of we does have on pitiful baby at we breast. Baby all purple and discolor. Two baby who ain't ask for this world. Two baby, Dead! Dead before they know the sorrow and joy of life!

FAUSTINA: We scream and scream and scream and scream and scream.

(In the background, under separate spotlights, JASON *and* CREON PANDIT *appear to mime out the action.)*

FAUSTINA: And Creon and Jason of Tougou come runnin' and bruck down the door and, still in them weddin' costume, cutlass in hand, whoosh in! Them see the baby in we arm.

PERSIS: The dead baby in we arm.

FAUSTINA: Jason fall down with horrible cry-out and thrash the floor. He knuckle bleed as he whimper to Heaven, "Why?" "Why?" "Why?"

PERSIS: I never hear man cry with such agony and sorriness.

FAUSTINA: Creon grab we and shake we and yell, so, at we that we does kill these two baby. When we does tell he we ain't know what happen, or how these baby does come to be dead, Jason jump up and attack we. He cutlass swingin' and flingin' and flailin' and sailin' in the air.

PERSIS: The only reason he metal ain't seriously catch we, is all the tear in he eye leave he foot unsteady and him aim faulty.

FAUSTINA: Then, we hear a sound. A scream., so high, so sharp, so pierce, more keen than blade. It halt Jason in he track When all we leg free, we run to that scream that even God would fear. It comin' from the nuptial chamber. We pitch open the portal and, oh, what we see!

FAUSTINA and PERSIS: Oh, God! What we see! What we see! What we see!

(SWEET BELLA, *her nightdress aflame, writhes and screams in excruci-ating agony.*)

FAUSTINA: Sweet Bella have on the very night frock you gift she with. Sweet Bella. It seem only a few hour since she find she voice.

PERSIS: Sweet Bella. She voice so sweet and so like a little bell that tinkle. Sweet Bella. She voice, now like a grate. Yellin' and roarin' and grindin' and raspin'.

PERSIS and FAUSTINA: And she body...aflame! Aflame! Aflame! She entire body aflame!

FAUSTINA: Creon pitch heself on he daughter.

(CREON, JASON *and* SWEET BELLA *mime the action.*)

PERSIS: Jason...pitch heself on he bride and he new in-law daddy. But the flame too hot and mighty. Creon burn too bad, but him stay clamp to he daughter in they incestuous dance to the death. Jason...fall away screamin' with no sound from he mouth. It too late.

FAUSTINA: What use to be Sweet Bella now only ash and dust and smoke and steam and burn flesh and smell that does make you sick to you bowel.

PERSIS: A stench like you never smell.

FAUSTINA: Creon, burn and disfigure, skin meltin' 'way from he carcass, run an stagger 'till he leg no longer carry he. He fall 'pon top Sweet Bella an mash she corpse to charcoal. He last breath come from he mouth like a sad whistle... and he pass into history.

PERSIS: Oh, Mediyah, what that gal do to you? What she doe to you so bad, she earn such a dispatch? What Creon do, so bad, he no longer have breath to breathe?

PERSIS and FAUSTINA: Ah, Mediyah, you is a hard, harsh, bitter, sour woman!

MEDIYAH: *(stonily)* What of Jason?

PERSIS: We comin' to that.

FAUSTINA: But we have a next bitter news.

PERSIS an FAUSTINA: tragedy 'pon tragedy. Sorrow 'pon sorrow. Bitternss 'pon bitterness. Sadness 'pon sadness.

PERSIS: And strangeness...'pon strangenss for as we runnin' here to tell you all this occurrence, we see Cedric, you brother.

(In the background, CEDRIC appears, dangling.)

FAUSTINA: Cedric, the Rhymer, now defeated. In he hand, he quatro mangle. He eye...agape and starin' straight to Heaven and he once-proud body, dangle ...dangle from a tree where there was no tree before.

PERSIS: A calabash tree that spring up overnight.

(CEDRIC disappears.)

MEDIYAH: What of Jason?

PERSIS: Woman, you can't take lickle time to mourn the dead?

FAUSTINA: You have no sorrow for none of these people?

PERSIS and FAUSTINA: Poor Mediyah. You is a hard, harsh, bitter, sour woman!

MEDIYAH: What of Jason?

PERSIS and FAUSTINA: We only have sorrow and sadness for you. Such a hard, harsh, bitter, sour woman! Pity! Pity! Pity!

MEDIYAH: What about Jason of Tougou?

FAUSTINA: Jason? That poor waste man?

PERSIS: Jason, as we say, thrash heself on the ground. He eye shed more water than Yama Waterfall.

FAUSTINA: More than the river.

PERSIS: Then it sawn on he that he should dead like Creon, 'cause he ain't nothing more to live for, but he ain't have the courage to bear the pain and grab it like Creon. And he commence to reprimand heself with blow after blow and he run 'bout the room pitchin' heself 'gainst all four wall. I never see such a pitiful madness.

FAUSTINA: Then, with brutal suddenness, him halt! Him livid and turn this dull blue and gray tint right in front of we very eye. He body and he glance grow cold. A cold like we never feel in this island. We had was to grab shawl and throw 'bout we shoulder, the man radiate such cold. Then, he walk over to them what use to have life and he look down. He come over to we, for we still have he dead, shrivel-up, baby, them in we arm. He relieve we of them and he look down. Then, he give they back to we and he look down.

PERSIS: Then, he pick up he shiny machete and say to we...

JASON: Go! Tell the witch, Mediyah, to prepare sheself! Tell she I comin' with heavy, ponderous, sorrowful, sad, and deliberate footstep to kill she! To rid this poor world of she! To send she back to the very bowel of Hell from which she spring! Go! Tell she all this! Tell she, who grind and mash and tear an break and poison and burn me heart, all this! Go!

PERSIS: Is so him say and is so we do! All we beg you leave to go. Please don't trouble youself to show further botheration for we.

FAUSTINA: If, perchance, you does see we takin' we custom, please to turn you head and treat we like people dead and gone from now on.

PERSIS and FAUSTINA: You cause we eye to be full with tear and we heart to be heavy with stone and youself forever...alone! Good-bye!

(PERSIS and FAUSTINA, *tearfully, leave.* MEDIYAH and GRANNY ROOT *sit in respective attitudes of impassiveness and waitin. In the distance, a drum beat, signaling approaching heavy footsteps. Soft, muted and measured at first, their sound gets louder and louder until, at last,* JASON *fills the doorframe with himself.* MEDIYAH, *defiant, turns to face him. He raises his weapon, grasping the hilt with both hands high over his head, as if to cleave the stone-faced* MEDIYAH *in two.)*

JASON: *(Screaming)* MEDIYAH!!!!!!!

(JASON *brings down his machete with all his might and purpose, but the blade stops inches above the head of* MEDIYAH, *whose gaze continues to "fix" him. Whimpering, he slowly crumples to the floor in an abject heap. On his knees and at the feet of* MEDIYAH, *she - slowly and disdainfully - raises a foot and, scornfully, pushes him over...leaving him prostrate and sobbing.)*

JASON: Mediyah! Mediyah! Mediyah!

(MEDIYAH *begins a slow, circular walk with* JASON *crawling, abjectly and snakelike, after her.)*

MEDIYAH: And is so you will be from now. A crawlin', grovelin', slitherin' thing that people does see and set them dog on and spit at. 'Low me, if you please, to be the first. *(She spits at him.)* You did cause me some pain and hurt! So, forever eat sand and mud and dirt! Eat dust and t'ing what does drop from dog! Eat worm and t'ing what does hide 'neath log! Yes! Know only sand and mud and dirt! Raise you head only high as the hem of me skirt! Stay down in the gravel where you does belong, Jason of Tougou, master of Pecong! Master of lilt! Master of rhyme! Master of filt'! Master of crime! As long as you does continue to be, You ain't never, never, never, ever goin' forget me! Wherever you crawlin' take you, be it far or be it near, Make you take you this name for carry forever in you ear... *(She bends down and screams in his ear...)* "MEDIYAH!!!"

(She, disdainfully, points him toward the door. Painfully, slowly, and still sobbing, JASON *crawls from the scene on his belly.)*

GRANNY ROOT: It all done now. You revenge. All man what does do you harshness...gone! My daughter, you Mother, revenge! Creon and all he line...gone! There ain't goin' never be a next Creon Pandit!

MEDIYAH: All Creon line not gone. I still here.

GRANNY ROOT: You ain't Creon seed. You different seed from Cedric. You all herb and bush and root and air and fire and smoke and earth and wild forest. You want to see you Daddy? You want to see who spew heself forth into you mother at my prayin' and incantation so she shame could be avenge? You want to see who cause you birth? Behold! Behold!

(GRANNY ROOT *gestures. Smoke! Thunder! Lightning! Fire! The awesome figure of Damballah appears and menacingly, but silently, laughs. He dances...prances...a puff of smoke, and he disappears.*)

GRANNY ROOT: When you mother come to me and say she power gone, She beg me not to damn he, for she so love he, this Creon. But Granny Root pray and Granny Root do. Spirit appear... and, out come...you! You...all Granny Root perception. You...all spiritual conception. You...all Granny Root revenge. You...all Granny Root say you was and...that all you was. Come! You and me off to Mideo Wood Island Is we home.

MEDIYAH: So! That Jason I did love and that Jason I did hate. Now, I ain't feel nothin' for he 'cause me passion 'bate. I ain't feel he a-tall! I ain't feel nothin' a-tall!

GRANNY ROOT: To Mideo Wood Island, Child. You and me goin' say we good-bye there. Me spirit tire an me can sleep...now!

(MEDIYAH *and* GRANNY ROOT *disappear.*)

EPILOGUE

(A group of revelers, stragglers from Carnival, noisily crosses the scene. Still dancing and swilling from rumpots, they're drunkenly trying to keep the spirit going. PERSIS *and* FAUSTINA *open their slatted windows.)*

PERSIS: All you...less that noise! You ain't know what time it is?

FAUSTINA: You ain't know what day it is? Carnival over! It Lent and Carnival over!

PERSIS: You ain't know that?

FAUSTINA: What do you?

PERSIS and FAUSTINA: Is time for all you 'semble here to low you eye and be austere. Go home! Go come! Until next year. Carnival over! You hear?

(The revelers reflect for a moment, wave off PERSIS *and* FAUSTINA, *and go off, still shuffling to their beat. Still drinking in the morning heat,* PERSIS *and* FAUSTINA *regard them, shrug their shoulders, regard each other, shrug their shoulders, and go off to join the merry band.)*

END OF PLAY

Interview 3

An Interview
with Steve Carter

Q: What was the impetus behind this play?

SC: It really came about as a sort of a fluke. I was doing a residency in Marin County in California, staying with my friends, the Boyces. I was in their pool with a group of people and a woman was talking about how many Medeas she'd seen. "I've never seen a black Medea," she said. I said, "I've seen one -Joe Papp's." "I think that was just Euripides's play with black people." I said, "I'll write one, then." I wrote the first scene that night. I just started having fun with it. It turned out to me the most fun I've ever had. I'd make sure the typewriter ribbon ran out on weekends so I'd have to wait until Monday to go to the stationary store, so I could prolong the writing process.

Q: What was the process of moving from fun writing to production?

SC: I was a member of New Dramatists at the time, so I had a reading there and they invited some people. People from Victory Gardens in

Chicago flew in and they said they'd do it. Dennis [Začek, then artistic director of the Victory Garden] directed it. You'll never get any black directors to do it, I told him - they're all in rehearsal for black history month. I said you should direct it and he hemmed and he hawed but he finally said okay. He said he'd do it if I came to Chicago for rehearsals. So I did.

Q: Many lines in the play make a big deal about Jason's "proper color." What is his "coloration"?

SC: This play is as much about color within the race as it is about love, magic, honor and vengeance. It's not black versus white, it's light versus dark within the black community. Jason is light-skinned, and Mediyah is dark. The first Jason we had quit the first day, just before rehearsal. Daniel Oreskes, who is white and Jewish, auditioned and I told Dennis to call him and he was at the theatre before Dennis hung up. He said, "I'll do anything. I'll go to a tanning salon. I've already got the hair." He was successful as Jason. Many women wanted to jump his bones in the dressing room. One guy asked me, "How come you got the white man in the play?" I said, "'Cause the black man quit!" The next guy to play Jason [in Newark] was even lighter skinned than the white guy. But the play is about skin color in the Caribbean. Here in America we had the "paper bag test." In the Caribbean, they look at the color of the ear lobe. Even blacks judge based on skin ton. I never had that in my family, because we're all just brown, but it exists in the islands and it's still there and it still matters. My father was American and my mother was from the Caribbean. Because I have this American blood in me, I've been called a mongrel by members of my own family, but never by white racists. It's because of blood, not color.

Q: You also added the Pecong to the story - a verbal contest between Jason and Cedric.

SC: In my bygone and much-lamented youth, I spent many happy hours "playing the dozens" with playmates. Young kids don't do that these days. They take things like that much too seriously and they all seem to have gats, shivs, or cannons. Playing that game, however, was one of my major influences in the creation of Pecong. The pecong really happens at Carnival, where guys try to outdo each other with insults. The only rule is you can't touch too close on anything that's true and you can't make fun of someone really revered, who's dead.

Q: Why did you choose to write the play in dialect?

SC: It's about the beauty of imperfect language. That's the way I talk. That's the way I was brought up. That's my natural way of speaking. When I'm not teaching, I fall into it. I'm fascinated by the natural rhythms of island language. I can usually pick out the different island accents when I talk to someone. So long as it is in English. Patois is much harder.

CHAPTER 4

THERE ARE WOMEN WAITING: THE TRAGEDY OF MEDEA JACKSON

INTRODUCTION

There Are Women Waiting: The Tragedy of Medea Jackson was part of a larger piece titled *Reality Is Just Outside the Window,* a production of the Medea Project, organized by Rhodessa Jones and written by Edris Cooper. Working with women in prison beginning in 1989 at the San Francisco County Jail, Jones and Cooper developed a modern version of the Medea story in which "Medea Jackson" lives in the slums of Oakland, California, and faces the same challenges that the women in prison faced: unfaithful husbands, poverty, drugs, and unstable family lives. The tragedy of Medea is shown to be a very modern one enacted on the streets of America every day.

The Medea Project takes its name from the tragic heroine. Jones, Cooper, and Cultural Odyssey (the producing organization) sought to use Medea as a metaphor for women in prison. These women have been wronged by the men in their lives. Like Medea they are master storytellers and "these women are seen by society as outsiders, barbarians...have committed crimes, and crimes have been committed against then. They, too, have broken taboos, transgressed laws. They are women who are ruled by their passions, who are self-destructive, and who destroy others."[1] Jones sought to stage *Medea* at the jail and named the project after the play following a meeting with an inmate who had killed her own child.

The text and the original production in 1992 were shaped by the context of the performance and reflected the reality of the lives of women in prison. If all adaptation is local, this version reflects that: It is set in San Francisco and mentions local streets and landmarks such as Haight Street, Darcy City, and so forth. The language of the play is the urban vernacular of the early nineties. Music plays a key role, and in particular the music of Aretha Franklin shapes the play with three of her songs being sung during the performance. This is partly a reflection of the soundtrack of the women's lives and partly the messages of the songs themselves.

Unlike the other plays in this collection, *There Are Women Waiting* was written to be performed by an all-female ensemble, the opposite of ancient Greek practice. The role of Medea is played by a woman (in fact, playwright Edris Cooper played Medea in the original performance), as are the chorus and the male oppressors. Every voice heard in the play is a woman's. This is a form of empowerment: Women tell Medea's story; they tell their own stories. Women are the protagonists; they have agency.

As in *Pecong*, Jason is a person of color. The difference between him and Medea is not ethnic or race but class, although Creon's daughter is "a white girl." The play is less concerned with ethnicity and more with poverty. Medea is trapped in the same cycle as the other women in her neighborhood; Jason sees his relationship with Creon's daughter as a means to improve his own life even though this means abandoning Medea and their children.

Creon is an urban king in his own kingdom: a landlord who controls whether the denizens of the building can stay or must go. He kicks Medea out because he no longer wants her in the building. Jason has hooked up with his daughter and knowing Medea is "crazy," he gives her one day to get out. Medea tells the chorus, "He done fucked with the wrong bitch now." She kills Creon and his daughter by lacing her underwear with "meth, PCP, and heroin," and tells the kids they will "celebrate with some Jim Jones Kool-Aid," a reference that carries particular weight in San Francisco, where the People's Temple (founded by Jim Jones) was located before Jonestown was established in Guyana. A large number of the cult's converts (and subsequent deaths) were lower-income African Americans.

At the end of the play, there is a major deviation from Euripides's original version. Rather than escaping, Medea is surrounded by police and told there is a warrant for her arrest. The implication of the script is that she is either shot by police or jumps off the building, although it remains ambiguous. Regardless, the end clearly states that Medea is dead. Whereas the original ends with Medea riding away in triumph to new life in Athens, no such victory can be found for this Medea developed by women in prison.

There Are Women Waiting: The Tragedy of Medea Jackson was previously published in Rena Fraden's excellent book *Imagining Medea: Rhodessa Jones and Theatre for Incarcerated Women*, which also recounts the history of the company, the project, and the play.

NOTES

1. Rena Fraden, *Imagining Medea: Rhodessa Jones and Theatre for Incarcerated Woman* (Chapel Hill: The University of North Carolina Press, 2001), 48.

PLAY 4

THERE ARE WOMEN WAITING: THE TRAGEDY OF MEDEA JACKSON

EDRIS COOPER

Music by Carol King and Carolyn Franklin

Part of *Reality is Just Outside the Window*. Conceived and directed by Rhodessa Jones. Presented by San Francisco–based Cultural Odyssey. A site theatrical collaboration of San Francisco's multicultural women's community and women inmates at San Bruno County Jail. Coproduced by Brava! for Women in the Arts and the Jail Arts Program. Premiered at Theatre Artaud, San Francisco, January 8, 1992.

CAST OF CHARACTERS (AND ORIGINAL PERFORMERS)

Singer: Jeanette Tims

Nurse/Jason: h.T. McNair

Medea: Edris Cooper

Creon: Angellette Williams

Aegus: Dorsha Brown

The Home Girls of San Francisco: Belinda Sullivan, Tanya Mayo, and
Nikki Byrd

Other roles played by Ensemble

*(Dressed in street clothes, the ensemble moves downstage in a line; music
plays; Rhodessa Jones, down in front on the floor of the theater calls out
"Work it!", "Energy!" She directs this way throughout the show. They strike
an attitude; and then break into another.)*

SINGER *sings "Natural Woman" with backup from* ENSEMBLE *who also
sing*

When my soul was in the lost and found... You came along to claim it...
Now I'm no longer doubtful, for what I'm looking for... Baby what you
done to me - - you made me feel so good inside... You made me feel like
a natural woman...

*Enter NURSE with two CHILDREN; they stand on the edge of the stage
observing the action.*

NURSE-- *(eating barbecue, all words in bold spoken by CHORUS as well)*
Chawl, why in the hell did them collegiate ass niggas have to take they
slummin' asses down to Haight Street. Like they don't got enough crack
houses in Daly City. Medea wouldn't have gotten in alla that shit. Killing
up all them people. Gave up going to **school** to be with him, where he
want. Gave up her **time** to work and spend money on him. And gave up
her **kids** because he couldn't stand the **competition** and she even gave
up her **ears** because she couldn't stand to hear the truth. And gave up
the rich black nectar of the goddess to the basest of men, **men**. Now she
down here in the Fillmore and he sleeping with a white girl! After all
she did for him. Now y'all, you know she is pissed. She just sit up in the
house crying. Girlfriend don't wanna go to the club, the movies, chawl,
she wouldn't even go get no cue-bob with me. Something's up, shit, you
know how sistah is when she gets mad. Sheeit!

MEDEA-- *(offstage)* Motherfucking bastard! *(NURSE covers kids' ears.)* You Clarence Thomas, David Duke, Wilt Chamberlain, Williams Kennedy Smith...looking ass nigger! Son of a bitch motherfucker, I hope your dick falls off!

NURSE-- There she go again!

CHORUS-- Word! *(children giggle.)*

NURSE-- All right she gone catch y'all laughing and y'all gone have a knot upside your head. *(To audience)* See, Medea's mother raised her to be too sedity. See me, myself, I don't expect nothing from nobody, just to leave me the hell alone. Don't expect no shit and you won't get no shit.

CHORUS-- *(Circle around NURSE, chanting)* Don't like, don't want, don't love.

MEDEA-- *(offstage)* Awwwww -- shit!

(SISTERS 1, 2, 3 hurry on stage.)

S1-- Girl, is that Medea hollering like that?

NURSE-- Who else?

MEDEA-- *(offstage)* I hope a bolt of lightning strikes me dead. Or the roof comes crashing on my head.

S3-- Pitiful chile.

MEDEA-- *(offstage)* Just kill me nigger, go ahead and kill me. Fuck! I hate this world and I hate niggers.

S2-- Girlfriend, please, you gone kill yoself with alla that grieving you doing. I don't know why; 'cause he slept with another bitch? Please!! That nigga ain't done nothing every other nigga done done. Shit, he wouldn't worry me. Get a grip!

MEDEA-- *(offstage)* Some support; y'all are shit. *(Loudly wailing)* Nobody understands. Jason, I'ma get you and that bitch! After all I've done for you.

NURSE-- Girl and she means that shit too, ok?

(The CHORUS *and the* NURSE *all snap together-- A* CHORUS *that snaps together caps together.)*

S1-- Girl, she need to talk to somebody. Bring her out here so we can give her the news, baby. That's what the sisters is for, girl. Laying on hands and all of that. Hurry, girl, for she hurt somebody.

NURSE-- Girl, I'll try, but you know she might cuss me out.

S1-- She ain't gonna cuss you out. Bring her on over to my house. We'll listen to some Anita Baker; that always helps me out. All she needs is to be rubbed the right way.

S2-- Girl, I don't know about you.

*(*NURSE *exits;* CHORUS *ad lib until* NURSE *returns with* MEDEA.*)*

CHORUS-- Hi, Medea.

MEDEA-- Look, I know y'all been out here just reading me to the tee. I know you think I am stuck up, but I am just tired, ok. Tired, tired, tired. Of niggas and of life. The man who was everything to me turned out to be the basest of men. Y'all women; you know how it is. Look how we're treated. First of all, we always doing everything for our men and in return, what do we get? Fucked! And most niggas feel that's payment. I did everything I was supposed to do. I cooked dinner, I cooked rocks. I even cooked in bed. But you know it's hard to find a good man with a job that won't beat you, that won't fuck around, and that'll be nice to your kids. If you get a good man all the bitches is backstabbing. And if you get a fucked up man and leave him, everybody talks about you. Shit, better just be dead or turn gay.

S1-- Word! *(Snap, approaches Medea.)*

MEDEA-- Shit, it's not fair. A man get upset and he can go out and kick it with the fellas. But a woman-- shit you ain't got nobody, you can't trust no bitch.

S2-- Girl, please, you been reading too much Shaharazad Ali. You shoulda been looking out for you.

MEDEA-- If only you coulda seen; we were really good together. We was making money, cleaning up. We could have got out of the coke business, and retired, and travelled.

CHORUS-- On the slow boat to hell.

MEDEA-- Like Bonnie and Clyde, or Donald and Ivana.

S2 -- Girl, please, they white. You are trippin'. You shoulda asked somebody and got a clue. There ain't never been shit here. People round here just like all the rest of us -- all out of work.

MEDEA-- And thank you for the news this morning, Miss Thing. Well shit, alla y'all know each other. I'm not from around here and y'all ain't really been all that charitable.

S3-- And you have?

MEDEA-- Wait, I'm sorry for that, but we got to stick together. Men always talking about how hard they got it, how hard they work. Shit, let me see one of them have a baby. Then they'll appreciate us.

CHORUS-- Ok? *(snap)*

MEDEA-- Look, y'all gotta hang with me. Just one thing I ask. If I figure out how to get this bastard, you will keep the tee for me?

CHORUS-- Girlfriend, won't no tips pass from these lips.

MEDEA-- Cools...fuck with me, shee--it. I'll show that nigga. I'll slap his ass so hard he'll wake up and his clothes will be out of style.

(MEDEA *opens her mouth to start loudtalking when S1 stops her.*)

S1-- Girl, chill, here comes Creon.

(CREON *enters.*)

CHORUS-- Hi, Creon.

CREON-- Look at you, woman, lips all poked out like you a madwoman. I think you are. And before you mess around and do something foolish, I'm kicking out outta my house. You and them damn kids.

MEDEA-- Oh great, Creon, where the hell am I supposed to go?

CREON-- Woman, that's not my problem.

MEDEA-- Why, Creon, why are you putting me out?

CREON-- Cause you crazy, woman, and quite frankly I am afraid of you. Look how you fucked up Pelias, not to mention your own brother. Now you do that to your own, what the hell's keepin' you from doing that to me? I heard you threatening me, and Jason, and my daughter.

MEDEA-- Everybody holds these deaths against me without hearing my side. If I hadn't fucked up Pelias, Jason wouldn't even be around for your daughter to enjoy. With all that shit he talked, Pelias was gonna kill his stupid ass. Here I am helping his ass and I'm the bitch. Look, Creon, I'm not crazy. I only did that shit because I love Jason. I don't have nothin' against you or your daughter. Hey, she got eyes just like me. I'm not stupid. I have nowhere to go and I have such a nice home here. It'll kill me but I'll be cool, count my blessings and keep to myself.

CREON-- You talk a good line, Medea, but I gotta watch my back. You're outta here.

MEDEA-- Creon, please. I'm on my knees.

CREON-- Well, you can just get up.

MEDEA-- Where will I go?

CREON-- Woman, that's not my problem.

MEDEA-- God don't like ugly.

CREON-- He ain't too fond of pretty neither.

MEDEA-- Creon, please, I got problems...

CREON-- You ain't never lied.

MEDEA-- Then, Creon, have a heart...(CREON *laughs)* You a cold moth-erfucker, Creon. Well, all right then, but let me ask one favor before I go. Please.

CREON--Oh lord, what now?

MEDEA-- Please, just give me a day to get my things together. I gotta get the kids together. You know Jason ain't gonna help. If not for me, think about the kids. You gone turn them out, naked and with nothing?

CREON-- I am too kindhearted, I tell you. Ok, woman, I'm gonna give you one day to get your kids and shit together, but I'm here to tell you so you'll know. If the sun rise on you and them damn kids, you'll wish it hadn't, cause I'ma play your evil game, ok?

MEDEA-- I get it.

CREON-- *(walking)* Don't try me, woman.

CHORUS-- Girlfriend, where you gonna go? You up the creek.

MEDEA-- Please, who do I look like, Sally or her sister Suzy? Girl, I ain't got time to be bumping gums with that bastard for nothing. I'ma get that crackhead bitch and that basest of baseheads Jason. That jackass gone let me stay one too many days. I'ma fuck they asses up. I just don't know whether to burn them butts up as is fitting or if I should cut off Jason's nuts, or slice a hole in her titties and stuff 'em. I got to be cool, though, cause they got lots of fire power. I ain't goin' out like that. Fuck it! He done fucked with the wrong bitch now.

CHORUS-- Jason will be back tomorrow sayin' he sorry. *(snap)*

(JASON enters.)

JASON-- See, Medea, a hard head makes a soft ass. You just had to show you ass, now you outta here like last year. You could've had everything, Medea, if you just hada acted right. I was taking good care of you. I'll give you $150 on your way out. I still care for you and the kids.

MEDEA-- $150! Just keep that shit. I don't want it. Nigga please, you never gave a flying fuck about me or the kids. Throwing me a coupla dollars pretending to be somethin'. You ain't giving me nothin' I cain't get at 170 Otis. Fuck you. I saved your life, I showed you the game. You wouldn't have nothing if it wasn't for me. Shit, I was love sick for coming here with you. And you ain't got no shame for how you treated me. Answer me this. Where in the hell am I supposed to go? I ain't got no friends left, thanks to you. You are an asshole, Jason, and you need to step off the curb with that shit. You low life bastard.

JASON-- Woman, who asked you to give it all for me? I can't help it, lady, if I got it like that, hey? And you need to clean up your motherfucking mouth. You used to be a lady. *(Exits)*

MEDEA-- *(yelling at his back)* I am a lady, bitch, I still got plenty a pussy, don't I?

(Enter AEGUS in drag.)

AEGUS-- Shake it but don't break it, wrap it up and I'll take it.

MEDEA-- Aegus, girlfriend, what's up?

AEGUS-- What's up with you announcing your goods up and shit? Gimme some.

MEDEA-- I know you can do better with it than I did.

AEGUS-- Girlfriend, tip to the tee.

MEDEA-- You know he's goin' with that other bitch.

AEGUS-- So what?

MEDEA-- She's in my bed.

AEGUS-- Oh hell no.

MEDEA-- Ok.

AEGUS-- Girl cut the nigga loose, that's all. Shit, dicks a dome a dozen.

MEDEA-- But I can't go out like a ducker sucker motherfucker.

AEGUS-- Well, then don't. I got it, girlfriend. I got a sister I know would be glad to hole up if you know what I mean.

CHORUS-- Ok! *(snap)*

MEDEA-- Thanks, baby, but I got a plan, ok?

AEGUS-- Word, girl, get him. Be slick, ok. *(Exits)*

S1-- Ok! *(snap)* Girlfriend, that queen is your friend. Now he's gonna hook you up with a lady friend. Taste the life, baby, and you'll wake up if you know what I mean.

MEDEA-- Girl, I ask you again, who do I look like, Sally or...

S1-- Ok, ok, impart the poop. Come on and listen, y'all.

(Lights dim as the CHILDREN *exit)*

MEDEA-- Now I'ma lay it out and I'm tellin you, don't sleep on this cause I am serious. I'ma get them bastards and good. Word, I'ma send for Jason and play up to him real sweet. I'll plead the case for the kids for him to let them stay.

CHORUS-- Witcha so far.

MEDEA-- Girl, please, do you really think I'm gonna leave my kids over here in this mess? For them to be treated like dirt, mistreated, and abused by her? NO! I got a wiley plan. Check this shit out. *(She pulls a vial from her pocket.)*

CHORUS-- Girl, what's that?

MEDEA-- Crystal, baby, pure and sweet as it was in '66. This will make that bitch turn her face inside out. I will send the children bearing gifts to offer to get on her good side to let them stay. A beautiful teddy and a sexy G-string, soaked in crystal.

(The CHORUS *stands there looking at her with their mouths hanging open.)*

CHORUS-- What??? Crystal???

MEDEA-- That's right, baby. And PCP and MDA and heroin and some new shit they got in 1992 most folks don't even know about yet. When they get back from delivering the deadly gifts, we are going to celebrate with some Jim Jones Kool-Aid.

(The women stop laughing and stare in horror at MEDEA.*)*

MEDEA-- They should never have fucked with me. Look, look how they treat me, a black woman doesn't have anything and no representation. Look how I'm treated, much less my kids. This world isn't for them. Maybe in another life. I know what I have to do. Nobody shall despise me or think me weak or passive. I am a good friend, but a dangerous enemy. For that is the type that the world delights to honor.

(Silence.)

S3-- Eloquently put, my sister, but you cannot kill your children.

MEDEA-- You don't see the injustice that I see. It's the only way.

S3-- Medea, this may not be much of a life, but they deserve a chance for survival.

MEDEA-- Look, this talk is tired. Now go and get Jason please and I will expect some solidarity, sisters!

(CHORUS *sings Franklin song:*)

CHORUS-- Medea, think. Think, Medea. Think about it, Medea. You gotta think, think about what you trying to do to me...Freedom...Think."

(JASON *enters.*)

JASON-- Watchu want, Medea.

(CHORUS *hums "Natural Woman" under* MEDEA's *speech.*)

MEDEA--Jason, you know, I've been thinking about how I've been acting and about how I could always count on you to put up with me when I acted like a bitch. I just get jealous, you know. It's hard for me to face that I fucked up a good thing. You have been really good to me, letting me stay here and all and I should really thank you and your wife. But you know I am what I am. I didn't know what I had. Today, no worse a woman.

JASON-- Yeah, well you a bitch, Medea, but you got some sense. It's only natural for you to miss this dick. I forgive you but you still got to go.

MEDEA-- But Jason, what about the kids? I don't feel comfortable you know, they're boys and they need a man around. You see, I'm discovering some things about myself, you know...

JASON-- Medea, I knew you was a dyke! That's why you can appreciate no man. That's ok, Medea. It's all right, Medea, it's all right. I will ask Creon if the boys can stay. No need for them to suffer and be confused.

MEDEA-- I hope it's OK with your wife. But she is a woman and she should understand. I'll send them over with a peace offering for your wife tonight. You can pick them up in the morning. I'll be gone.

JASON--1can persuade her. (*Grabs his dick.*)

MEDEA-- Just let the kids bring the gifts over. They are beautiful and expensive. She'll love them.

JASON-- Don't spend too much, Medea, you gone need the money.

MEDEA-- They say that gifts persuade even the gods, and gold is worth more than ten thousand words. And to save my children is worth it.

(JASON *exits with the* CHILDREN *bearing the gifts.* CHORUS *sings "Do right...all day woman.")*

CHORUS-- Go on, girl, eloquently put. But you are in serious trouble.

(CHILDREN *return.)*

MEDEA-- Did she like the gifts?

(They just stare at her. Sounds of hell start softly and swell throughout. MEDEA *takes the* CHILDREN *and begins to walk up some stairs with them.)*

VOICE-- *(repeats as* MEDEA *walks up ramp)* At the bottom of our news tonight there has been a new animal aimed in the direction of falling off the face of the earth. Yes, young black teenagers are reported to be the oldest and newest creature to be added to the endangered species list, to the endangered species list...

(The CHILDREN *are represented by puppets now. The real* CHILDREN *observe. When she reaches the top she bellows over the noise.)*

MEDEA-- No, by the unforgetting dead in hell, it cannot be! I shall not leave my children for enemies to insult and die if they must, I shall slay them. Who gave them birth? Happiness be yours but not in this life. Your father has stolen this world from you. I can delay no longer or my children will fall into the murderous hands of those that love them less than I do.

(She drops the puppets. A scream [the sound of glass breaking]. MEDEA *is lifted up[or given wings], and throws herself into the women's arms. She is bathed in an eerie spotlight.)*

VOICE-- Medea Jackson. We have a warrant for your arrest.

CHORUS-- Oh well! *(snap)*

WOMEN-- Oh well, Medea's dead.

ALL-- How'd she die?

WOMAN-- She died like this.

ALL-- She died like this.

(Exchange repeated four times, each time a different freeze is assumed after the last line. Blackout).

SEAN-- I work for the social work department, jail medical services. That means I work with the women inmates. Actually, this is my ID card right here. Look like I'm one of the inmates my damn self. I gotta get somebody to do something about this. I remember my first referral. It was from a woman who said she wasn't having too many problems. She just needed to talk with somebody. So I went in the day room and I found her and the thing I immediately noticed about her was that she was older than most of the inmates. I could tell by the gray hair on her head, just by the way it was set, that she was not about to take any gump from anybody. So I called her out of the day room and we went into the little interview room and sat down. I asked her, rather she told me, that she didn't have any problems, she just wanted to get out of the damn day room. Noise, clanging doors, keys rattling, youngsters, cigarette smoke. I could understand that. So I said, Miss, if you could just tell me what you're here for." And she said, "Oh, honey, it wasn't hardly nothing. I just accidentally stabbed my husband...eight times."

WOMAN--Oh well, Medea's dead.

ALL-- How'd she die?

WOMAN-- She died like this.

ALL-- She died like this.

(Exchange repeated four times, each time a different freeze is assumed after the last line.)

ALL -- *(Whisper)* Medea's dead. Medea's dead. Medea's dead. *(Cover eyes, ears, mouth, cross arms in front of chest and brush arms away. Exit.)*

End of play

CHAPTER 5

AMERICAN MEDEA

INTRODUCTION

American Medea was first written by Silas Jones in 1995 and received
workshop productions at the Mark Taper Forum in Los Angeles and the
Arena Stage in Washington D.C. in 1998. The author has since revised
the play and what is published here is the most recent version.

The title notwithstanding, Jones stated that the play is not an adaptation of Euripides's drama but rather, similar to Euripides's *Medea,* it
is a retelling of an older legend corrupted by the Greeks for their own
ends. One must be careful, then, in placing the two plays side by side,
as Jones's work is not an adaptation but an original work based on the
same source material from an Afrocentric perspective.

As the title suggests, the play is also a profound critique of America,
particularly its founding vision of itself as a new Athens—a democracy
based on the philosophy of equality and the reality of inequality and
slavery. Jason tells his sons that America "is the new Greece." For both
the United States and ancient Athens, the day-to-day reality of those not
in the privileged class exposes the hypocrisy of that society, revealing it
as a living mockery of its own ideals. Prince Whipple tells fellow slave
Delaware, "Accept your place. How do you expect democracy to work if

you don't do your part? We gota pull together girl, git this new country on its feet. One nation indivisible." The final line anachronistically references the Pledge of Allegiance. The irony, of course, is that slaves are not free, are not a part of the democracy, and therefore are not one nation indivisible—Americans are actually still fairly divided, especially in the understanding of history, race, and power. Jones's play indicts a nation whose very ideals were completely undermined by its behavior toward Africans from the beginning. It also accuses members of the African American community who sided with and worked for the European Americans. Prince Whipple is "the original oreo," meaning a black man who behaves and thinks like a white man, failing to understand that to those in whose name he actively oppresses his fellow African Americans, he is nothing more than another slave. He claims to be a "servant," not a slave; a volunteer who serves and who looks down on other Africans. Prince Whipple even masquerades as Washington at one point, clearly wishing he were his white master. As Jones himself argued, everything in the drama is a play on opposites, exposing the contradictions of America.

Jones also advocated an Afrocentric mode of thinking about African American history and heritage. Medea herself is a strong black woman who knows that the history of African accomplishment exceeds and is older than that of Europeans. The Choral leader introduces Medea in a manner that echoes the arguments of Martin Bernal in his book *Black Athena*. Here, Jones's concept is in agreement with Herodotus, who wrote, "For the people of Colchis are evidently Egyptian... and the Colchians had remembrance of the Egyptians more than the Egyptians of the Colchians; but the Egyptians said they believed that the Colchians were a portion of the army of Sesostris" (2.104). Medea, in short, is of African descent.

The reader/audience is given a complex backstory demonstrating Medea's ancestral wisdom and her origins. Medea is the child of the dark goddesses, born with power and knowledge. Most importantly, Medea names herself at birth. As the play repeatedly demonstrates, names are powerful and the one who gives names has the power to define or redefine. One need only look at the practice of renaming Africans brought to the New World with European (often Biblical) "slave names" (perhaps dramatized most memorably in Alex Haley's *Roots*) and the embrace of African names by African American artists beginning in the sixties (e.g., LeRoi Jones renaming himself Amiri Baraka) to see the power of being able to name one's self. Silas Jones's play, in a few lines, captures this power and demonstrates Medea as a woman of cultural power and self-knowledge.

Unlike in Euripides's version, the children are much more of a presence in Jones's. The two sons of Medea and Jason are named Alexander and Imhotep, the former light skinned and the latter with a darker complexion. The former is also named after the Hellenistic conqueror (colonizer?) of Egypt (one of the first instances of Europe invading, conquering, and colonizing Africa). The latter is named after the twenty-seventh–century BCE Egyptian polymath—the first architect, engineer, and physician, highly respected by all (Africa as source of knowledge, freely shared). The sons are named after emblematic individuals who manifest their cultural desires: conquest and domination versus knowledge and free collaboration. Alexander admires and emulates Jason, Athens, and America; he values power, conquest, stolen accomplishments (like slavery—one's comforts come from the labors of others). Imhotep is his mother's (or motherland's) son; he admires and emulates Egypt, finds kinship with the African slaves, and values knowledge and culture.

While Euripides has a Creon figure to stand for the power of the state and an Aegeus, a benevolent ruler of Athens who welcomes Medea, Jones has an absent–yet-present George Washington the President King, frequently mentioned, though never seen, embodied only in the pronouncements of his comic slave Prince Whipple. Washington, "Father of the Country," war hero, "Founding Father," moral teacher, and first President, is mostly referred to as "Master," removing the heroic sheen and replacing it with the identity of "slave owner." Anachronistic language and malapropisms transform the man into a figure of comic derision and employ the legend of Medea to make the familiar unfamiliar. This play is not Euripides's and the iconic Washington hides the reality of a slave owner.

Medea seeks to return home. Return is impossible in Euripides's version because Medea has murdered her brother and this is why she seeks sanctuary in Athens. Jones has no Aegeus to offer Medea sanctuary, primarily because there is no need for one. Some scholars believe Euripides may have added the element of child murder to the Medea story. Jones's Medea is not a killer. She is a healer. No brother was killed for Jason's sake and Medea does not kill her children. Unlike the slave-owning Europeans, Africa is civilized and the cradle of civilization and nobility. Medea wishes to leave the United States and return to Africa. Instead, tragedy falls upon her and her sons because of the violent realities of America. Medea does not seek revenge; she seeks justice and home but is denied both.

Excerpts from *American Medea* were originally published in Smith and Kraus's *The Best Stage Scenes*. The play is published here in its entirety for the first time.

NOTE: *American Medea* is an extrapolation based on Herodotus's declaration that Colchis was conquered by the Egyptian Pharaoh Sesostris and its people were descendants of Egyptians.

PLAY 5

AMERICAN MEDEA

SILAS JONES

TIME: Late 1700s

PLACE: The Mt. Vernon, VA estate of President George Washington

CAST OF CHARACTERS

MEDEA, elderly, Ethiopian

JASON, 28, Greek, a California Golden Boy

ALEXANDER, 14, Medea's White son

IMHOTEP, 15, Medea's black son

HELEN, 60ish, Greek, Medea's attendant/nurse

DELAWARE, 16, African American slave

PRINCE WHIPPLE, 25, Washington's personal slave (our 1st Oreo)

SET (Satan), murderer of his god-brother Osiris

EUROPEAN GENTLEMEN (4)

WOMEN'S CHORUS

WOMEN'S CHORUS LEADER

TRIO OF SLAVE BOYS

ZEKE

INDIAN

OVERSEER

SET 1: Back Yard of Mansion. Yard gate, bottomless black hole representing Slave Quarters.

Set 2: Front lawn of Mansion.

PROLOGUE

HELEN *in traditional white tunic and sandals stands on the steps of the Mt. Vernon mansion, which is reconfigured and lit to suggest ancient Greek architecture.* ALEXANDER *and* IMHOTEP *in white chlamys broached at the shoulder sit at the foot of the steps.*

HELEN Imhotep, Alexander, good morning. Our History lesson today will be taken from the writings of Homer and Herodotus, our Father of History. So far our studies have focused on the glories of Greece, your father's culture. Today we will touch upon the glories of Ethiopia, your mother's culture. Imhotep, you were named after the world's first universal genius. He was an Egyptian scribe, chancellor, poet, vizier, chief priest and physician to King Djoser, and the architect who designed the first step pyramid. Long before Hippocrates, we Greeks regarded Imhotep as the Father of Medicine.

ALEXANDER *(Jumps up an jabs his finger at* HELEN.*)* You lie! *(He storms OFF up the steps past* HELEN.*)*

IMHOTEP Ignore him, Helen. He's a Gemini. Go on please.

HELEN No, I'd better not. It's just history, but I might get us into trouble. Besides, only your mother knows the truth, and she has trouble explaining such things.

IMHOTEP Please, Helen. Father doesn't know, and Mother says it's ancient history. What is it I'm not supposed to know?

(WOMEN'S CHORUS *enters at the top of the steps. They are dressed in black choir robes.* HELEN *sits, listening.*)

LEADER Rest, good Helen. We will give this boy a history lesson before his enemies record their version. Listen well, Imhotep. You are a citizen of Greece but a child of Africa. Your name means, "He who cometh in peace." Some of the wisest Greek citizens: Socrates, Plato, Solon, Dioderus, all travelled to Egypt, an African country, to become initiates in the School of Great Mysteries. Much of Egyptian culture is rooted in your mother's culture, Ethiopia. Herodotus said they, the burnt faces, the Ethiopians, were the most just of men, the favorite of the gods. Homer reported they were the most beautiful and long-lived of the human races. The Delphi from which the Greeks got their most sacred oracles was in fact founded in Egypt by the Ethiopian dynasty. Long ago some African societies were matriarchal. Herodotus said the women went into the marketplace and engaged in trade while their husbands stayed home and sat at the loom. The marriage agreement stipulated that the husband must obey the wife in all things. This was the world into which your mother was born. A world in which to be both black and female was doubly auspicious. Know these things Imhotep, for they will not be recorded in history books. Your mother, Imhotep, was born no ordinary woman. She is the daughter of Aeetes, King of Colchis, of pure Ethiopian blood. When the physicians, priests and teachers gathered to bless and circumcise the royal infant, they saw the third eye pulsating in her forehead and beheld her androgyny, the marks of a divine sorceress. They fell down on their knees and covered their faces. For they knew that only one such creature was born every one thousand years, and that this child's future would be in the hands of the dark goddesses of the underworld.

The gorgon Medusa, Hecate, the goddess of witches, Magna Hepta, the Nubian shape-shifter, all gathered round her crib, fighting to claim her spirit. Well, the King, asked his royal attendants, What shall I name my daughter? But they dared not speak. Then Isis, the mother of Heaven, appeared and laid her hand on the infant's forehead. Your infant mother herself spoke: "Medea," she said, "my name shall be Medea."

END OF PROLOGUE

SCENE I

An old INDIAN sits on the front lawn facing the steps. An Englishman comes down the steps of the mansion.

INDIAN George?

ENGLISHMAN Lovely weather we're having.

(A Frenchman comes down the steps.)

INDIAN George?

FRENCHMAN *(In French)* Lovely weather we're having.

(German comes down the steps.)

INDIAN George?

GERMAN *(In German)* Lovely weather we're having.

(Russian man comes down the steps.)

INDIAN George?

RUSSIAN *(In Russian)* Lovely weather we're having.

(PAUSE. INDIAN waits. Nobody appears. He stands up and yells up the steps.)

INDIAN Hello King George / Maybe Martha too / This Indian's in a pickle / And That's a redskin fact / barbecue the goddam buffalo / Invest my Indian head nickel / But I want my country back.

LIGHTS FADE OUT

SCENE II

THE BACK YARD. LIGHTS RISE on ALEXANDER *and* IMHOTEP. *Both boys now wear contemporary American clothes.* ALEXANDER *paces about with great authority;* IMHOTEP *waits near a tub Center Stage.*

ALEXANDER I tell you men, this will be a history-making voyage. We'll all be Greek heroes. Any more volunteers?

IMHOTEP I, Hercules.

ALEXANDER Mighty Hercules, the strongest of men. By-god Zeus smiles on us today! Come on men, the Argo waits.

IMHOTEP Captain, what about Atalanta? She wants to go too.

ALEXANDER Atalanta? Why she's a woman. All aboard men. We're off to fetch the Golden Fleece!

(They squat at the tub. ALEXANDER *captains the Argo.* TRIO OF SLAVE BOYS *enters through the yard gate and stare at the action. They ease forward cautiously.)*

TRIO LEADER Can we play?

ALEXANDER Are you Greek?

(The TRIO *stare at one another then hurriedly exit.)*

ALEXANDER It's smooth sailing mates. We've caught a great west wind.

IMHOTEP Beware the dreaded Whirlpool Captain.

ALEXANDER I see it Hercules. I'm veering north east. Tell me when you see the Crashing Rocks. Yipes. What's that ungodly sound?

(OVERSEER *enters through gate with whip in hand.*)

OVERSEER Heh boy! Yeah yo. What you doin' ovah yah?

IMHOTEP Sorry. I don't believe we've met.

OVERSEER What?

ALEXANDER Oh look, a whip. Is this a new American game?

OVERSEER It's the little darkie, young master, he can't be ovah yah. I'm Master Washington's overseer. I'm responsible for—

IMHOTEP *(laughs)* I'm a darkie? What's a darkie?

OVERSEER Young master, you been teaching this boy? It's agin the law.

ALEXANDER Well overseer, it appears we must teach this little darkie proper respect for our law. Your whip please.

(ALEXANDER *takes the whip and immediately begins to whip* OVERSEER. *Too surprised to speak* OVERSEER *runs out through the gate. The boys laugh.*)

IMHOTEP What's a darkie?

ALEXANDER You're a darkie and I'm a whitey. But we're still Greeks.

IMHOTEP How quaint. Captain, we're nearing the isle of the Sirens. Their singing will drive us crazy. Tell the men to put wax in their ears.

(JASON, *unseen by the boys, comes down the steps. He wears traditional Greek garb. He removes one of his sandals and sneaks up on the boys.*)

ALEXANDER Men, put wax in your ears. Ahoy mates, dry land dead ahead! Prepare to drop anchor.

IMHOTEP It's Iolcos. We've landed on the Isle of Iolcos.

ALEXANDER Iolcos. That name rings a bell. Look. A man is wading ashore? He's lost his sandal.

(IMHOTEP *points at Jason.*)

IMHOTEP Captain! Beware of the stranger with one sandal, remember?

ALEXANDER Of course. He's come to overthrow the king! By Zeus we'll send him straight to Hades!

(*The boys attack and wrestle laughing* JASON *to the ground.*)

JASON Zeus. Help. It's the dreaded harpies! No. It's Atlas and Hercules! All right men, I surrender. You're too strong for Jason. (beat) What a fine pair of gladiators your two turned out to be. Helen tells me she saw you two wrestling with the slave boys.

ALEXANDER Imhotep took them on two at a time and never once went down. Look Father, his garments are spotless.

JASON Excellent. And you Alexander, I see no dirt on you.

(*Beat*)

IMHOTEP That's because they won't touch him. When he tries to play they just let him do whatever he wants. It's no fun. I'm sorry Alexander.

JASON They sense the heroic Greek in him. That's why.

IMHOTEP Father, except for a handful of indentured servants, all the slaves are African.

ALEXANDER Yes, poor devils. In Greece we fed our slaves well. But here it's cornmeal and fatback. They even eat the guts of pigs. A delicacy. Chitlins they call them. Someday they'll want what King George eats.

JASON President, you must address our king as president. Or General. He fancies being called general.

IMHOTEP But Father--

JASON Imhotep, for the past three months we've been guests here, honored guests. During that time I've come to understand that this thing called Democracy isn't always democratic. We Greeks invented the word you know. Sometimes it's aristocratic, sometimes plutocratic, even pseudocratic. So to speak. Here it's Americratic. Separate but apropos. OK? *(Beat)* It's a new world concept. Greece wasn't built overnight you know.

IMHOTEP Father that's sophistry.

JASON Didn't Helen teach you that to be a master is no honor, and to be a slave is no disgrace.

ALEXANDER She mentioned the example of Aesop, the African Greek slave who rose to prominence as the most respected fabulist of all time. But Dad, most of our slaves were white.

JASON Yes yes yes. Boys, understand this: the old Greece is dead. America, this is the new Greece. OK?

ALEXANDER That's blasphemy. Greece will never die! Never.

IMHOTEP But Ammon, Osiris, Isis, Horus-- Have all the gods of Africa abandoned their people Father?

JASON It certainly looks that way, doesn't it Son.

ALEXANDER But they were gods. Where could they all have gone?

JASON To Greece. Some of them. The rest died out because people stopped worshipping them.

IMHOTEP Poor savages. Who will look after them now?

JASON We will Son. We will look after the Africans.

IMHOTEP And Mother, what will happen to Mother?

JASON Nothing will happen to Mother if she keeps her promise to behave. The President didn't appreciate her powers.

IMHOTEP Well he'd better no challenge her. She's dangerous. Father, do you think someday we'll all be together, like one big happy family. Without all this drama.

ALEXANDER Like Africans, huh Im.

IMHOTEP Like normal people. Our mother is African. To an African woman all life flows from family.

ALEXANDER He's sentimental Father. Im, all life flows from Greece, right Father?

IMHOTEP Father make him stop calling me Im.

JASON Don't tease your brother Alexander. Is there a problem between you two? You can tell me.

ALEXANDER No Father. Im knows how I feel about him. It's just that... Well, in Greece he looked like a Greek. Here, when I see him playing with the slave boys...

JASON You play with the slave boys a lot Imhotep.

ALEXANDER Yes, and then I see only slaves. I don't mean to. It's not my fault.

JASON Imhotep, your brother's being honest. Unfortunately seeing is believing. Personally, I rather like the sound of Im.

IMHOTEP Father why did you bring Mother here? Didn't you know about the racism?

JASON I suppose I can't imagine her without me. I came for the adventure, the challenge. This is the new Greece boys. Your mother can be difficult.

ALEXANDER Difficult? She turned my pet dog into a pussy cat. Just because he barked a lot. And my lover--

IMHOTEP She was a famous slut.

ALEXANDER That was no reason to make her a snaggle-toothed lesbian.

JASON Looked just like Socrates. *(JASON, IMHOTEP then ALEXANDER laugh.)* No Imhotep, you're Greek. You must learn to suppress your African instincts. You'll never get anywhere in this world unless you do. *(Beat)* Me, well domestic life is not in Jason's nature. He was born to honor the gods of History. I have a higher responsibility. You see Son, Zeus captured the beautiful Europa, took her to Crete where she created a line of incredibly beautiful offspring. I'm a descendant of Europa. And Zeus of course.

IMHOTEP That's not what Helen says. Hadn't we better tell her?

JASON Let her believe the myth. It's all exciting. Only Medea knows the whole story. People get bored with the truth.

ALEXANDER That's why Zeus made him a party animal.

IMHOTEP But I miss you when you're gone all the time.

ALEXANDER A hero's gota do what a hero's gota do. I have a question for you Father. Just curious...

JASON Yes my little Alexander the Great. Then I have to go.

ALEXANDER We Greeks already had more gods than I could remember. What the hell did we do with all those African gods?

JASON Do? Well we adopted some and sacrificed the rest.

IMHOTEP Sacrificed? To what god did we sacrifice them?

JASON To History Im. *(Beat)* So to speak.

ALEXANDER History? That's another one I don't remember.

IMHOTEP You were speaking metaphorically, weren't you Father? About the gods?

JASON Don't blame Greece. History buried them. I must go now boys. The President wants to see me.

IMHOTEP Warn him about the slave's diet.

ALEXANDER And don't mention the fact that Im steals food from the kitchen to feed the slave boys.

(HELEN *enters through the gate.*)

HELEN Master Jason. Oh Master--

JASON Not now Helen. Talk to the boys.

HELEN But I must tell you--

JASON *(Exits up the stairs singing.)* Jason sailed the oceans blue Eureka fourteen ninety two!

ALEXANDER Yes Helen, what is it?

HELEN It's your father I must speak to-- *(Points to tub)* Oh boys, not the water. You know how it upsets your mother.

IMHOTEP Where is Mother? I haven't seen her in weeks.

HELEN Please boys, remove the water.

ALEXANDER You see Im, water is a spiritual conductor. Helen is afraid if mother sees it she'll be tempted to perform her black magic.

HELEN Your mother's special gift is neither black nor white. Please take this away.

ALEXANDER You're the servant Helen. Earn your keep.

IMHOTEP Here Helen, I'll help you. I'm very strong you know.

ALEXANDER You're no Hercules. *(Beat)* Would you help her if she were black? You're spoiling her you know.

(ALEXANDER *follows them OFF through the gate.*)

SCENE III
THE BACK YARD, SUNDAY AFTERNOON

The TRIO OF SLAVE BOYS *are having fun trying to teach* IMHOTEP *the "hambone." (ad lib) They laugh at* IMHOTEP, *who has no rhythm. Their loud fun attracts* ALEXANDER, *who Enters the yard.*

ALEXANDER Im! What the hell are you doing? Boys, go play with your own kind. You're trespassing.

(TRIO *Exits.*)

IMHOTEP Now why did you do that? They weren't harming anyone.

ALEXANDER You looked ridiculous. I'm going to teach you how to be American. I brought you some books to read. I'll teach you what they teach me. OK? We're going to change this country. Two Greek boys!

IMHOTEP I want to ride the milk white steed.

ALEXANDER You want too much. I'll find you a horse to ride. Now every day when I return from my studies I'll teach you what they taught me. OK?

IMHOTEP I don't like the way you've been acting lately Alexander. I don't want to be American. I'm going home to Colchis with Mother. I just want to be myself.

ALEXANDER Im you can't. I don't mean to sound indifferent, but Mother is history. She can't be in this world. Her age, her time has expired. Mother is the past and her past is not prologue. This is our world to have and to hold.

IMHOTEP It suddenly occurs to me that nobody loves Medea.

ALEXANDER Imhotep, how do you love a legend as a mother? There's a lot of history to be made here. It's too late for Mother Im. Let her go home. Stay here. Stay here with me Im. We'll become Americans. Greek Americans. OK? Before you know it we'll run this country. We'll ride around all day on our milk white steeds. And we'll free the slaves. What do you think of that?

IMHOTEP Well...there goes the neighborhood.

(They laugh and Exit through the gate.)

SCENE IV
BACK YARD. EARLY EVENING

(4 EUROPEAN GENTLEMEN Enter with folding chairs)

GENTLEMEN It's very pleasant out here this time of day/Soon it'll be dark and they'll be dragging their sweaty black asses in from the fields./ Stinking to high heaven/ *(They unfold their chairs and sit.)* Are you going to the dance tonight?/When I left London for this paradise of milk and honey I swore I'd never dance another French Minuet/Let's go watch the slaves dance/Too physical. They make me perspire/You're sick of the French Minuet, I'm sick of niggers, flies and foreigners/Don't look now. Here comes crazy old Zeke/What does he do back there in the slave quarters/He makes them pray with him. He assures them that one day they'll be free and their great great great great grandson might even become our president/That's going too far/Don't they have their own religion?/The less we know about them the better/Pretend you're sleeping/Clearly the gourd is cracked/ *(ZEKE Exits through the gate.)* Wake up, he's gone/ That Zeke, I'd swear he's Jewish/How can you tell?/I can tell, I'm a Jew/ Careful, you're illegal you know/How did you manage to immigrate?/I was rejected the first time. Then I learned French, became a Protestant and practiced rolling my ass when I walked. Worked like a charm/ Splendid. But how's your ass now?/It was just an act fellows/It's hours before the dance. Let's go watch the slave auction/I'd have to change clothes/I'll never get used to seeing naked men, women and children being paraded on the block/The men have horse dicks/They exude lust, uncontrollable lust/I wish I could exude uncontrollable lust/Frankly I'm getting sick of this whole race/class thing/Back home in London they're singing that new ballad/"The World Turned upside down";/I haven't heard it. How does it go. Speak it Your singing voice is amazing/ "Our Lords and Knights and Gentry too, doe mean old fashions to forgoe/They set a porter at the gate, that none may enter in thereat/They count it a sin, when poor people come in/Hospitality itself drown'd/Yet let's be content, and the times lament, you see the world turn'd upside down"/

SCENE V
BACKYARD. OFFSTAGE we hear PRINCE WHIPPLE *yelling at* DELAWARE.

*(*PRINCE WHIPPLE*– a pompous, powdered white, periwigged Paul Revere in tights – Enters with a kind of hip-hop flamboyance. With his stick cane he chases in* DELAWARE, *a beautiful barefoot slave of 16. She runs round and round in circles.)*

PRINCE WHIPPLE Stop right tair! I say Whoa gal!

*(*DELAWARE *stops and turns on him.)*

DELAWARE I don't cur if the Good Lord Hisself say so, I aint going nowhere near that evil black witch. She got the evil eye, Prince Whipple. Old folks say that aint no ordinary home-grown conjure woman down 'ere, that African bitch can turn me into a hyena in heat. Naw sir, you can beat me beat me beat me all you want to. But you tell Georgie Porgie if he make Delaware serve that spooky old hant, his midnight bed gon git colder than Valley Forge.

PRINCE WHIPPLE Every time you open that pickaninny mouth of yours your tongue does a breakdance. You verbose little pickaninny, you contraptious factotum, you will do what Prince Whipple command. And I shan't deign to vulgarize my class by taking off the gloves, as it were. Overseer just dying to scarify your backside, debitchify that insubordinating tongue. And as far as the master's pleasyre do go, he don't give one iota bout your dilapidated booty gal. I got two more ready willing and able to conjugate his desire. Chile, sometimes you stupefy my prerogatives. You surely do.

DELAWARE Oh Prince Whipple, hab mercy on Delaware. She too pretty to suffer. I'm tryna be American too.

PRINCE WHIPPLE Chile, your monistrations gainst that dried up old negress are totally unfounded, totally. Who ever heard of an African with power? Heavens to Caucasoids, you superstitious darkies with bill the death of Prince Whipple. The Master said as much. Now stop that moaning and a-groaning. Accept your place. How do you expect democracy to work if you don't do your part? We gota pull together girl, git this new country on its feet. One nation indivisible. You don't hear Prince Whipple complaining do you?

DELAWARE At's cause you the Master's personal slave.

PRINCE WHIPPLE *(Canes her.)* Slave!? Servant child, servant. I servant, you slave. You all physical. I, niggertheless, am required to be contemplative, speculative, perspicacious. Ever since Master George and I crossed the Delaware he made me responsible for more chores than you can shake a stick at. The Master don't call me Ambassador to the Slaves in jest. I can warrant and indemnify that. Why every hour of the day and night I'm called to adjudicate some pickaninny's picayune. And what about my privy to white folks? I've got to tow the line, straddle their dichotomy. I'd like to see you intercoursing with Caucasoids. And now with Master Jason -- aint he beautiful! – I'm prob'ly gona hafta polyglot my tongue. (Snorts) Me, Prince Whipple, talking Greek. Prince Whipple, you surreptitious little devil, you're unspeakable! Niggertheless, I shall persevere.

DELAWARE Why can't Helen be no nurse no more?

PRINCE WHIPPLE *(Canes her.)* Miss gal, Miss Helen. You stubborn little pervert. A white woman serving a black? Oh the scandal of it, the scandal. Chile, you discomfit my consternation. You been sleeping with every Tom, Dick and Harry on this plantation. How come you can't get pregnant chile? What, you tryna put the master out of business.

DELAWARE You want some of Delaware, Prince Whipple? I'll give you some.

PRINCE WHIPPLE Girl don't you raise your dress to me! I'll beat your funky boody flat!

JASON *(entering)* You girl, fetch Mistress Medea.

(DELAWARE runs off flirtatiously into slave quarters)

PRINCE WHIPPLE *(Totally flustered.)* Oh Master Jason, Prince Whipple just can't tell you how dastardly your presence perturbs him. El pulchritude, is all he can say. El pulchri--

JASON So you're the prince they speak of. I see. The old man's belly warmer, eh?

PRINCE WHIPPLE *(confused)* Oooooow?

JASON How decadent, how Roman.

PRINCE WHIPPLE Huh? Oh...Roman...indeed.

JASON *O fairies, O buggers, O eunuchs exotic! Come running, come running You anal-erotic! With soft little hands, With flexible buns Come, O castrati Effeminate ones!* I thought you'd appreciate a little Roman ditty.

(PRINCE WHIPPLE, frightened beyond words, drops his cane and runs off. Jason roars. DELAWARE re-Enters from slave quarters.)

JASON Well, girl? Where is she?

DELAWARE *(Hysterical, panting)* She say -- she say naw, she aint coming. When I say your name she-- she clapped her hands and -- Delaware's eyes crossed! I swear fo' god, Master Jason!

JASON You're lucky you escaped with your tits. Go back down there and tell her her ship has arrived. Just don't mention my name.

(DELAWARE, cupping her breasts, gawks at Jason, lets out a groan and drops to her knees)

DELAWARE Kill me, Master Jason. You can just go on and kill me know cause Delaware aint going nowhere near that black thing down there.

(JASON lifts and shakes her.)

JASON Be still Girl!

(JASON removes his hands from her breasts then feels her breasts.)

DELAWARE Oh, Master Jason, you one pretty dog. I spec I wouldn't mind you crossing my Delaware.

JASON *(considers it)* You women, you're all alike. Off with you. Hie, hie.

(DELAWARE runs off through the gate. JASON stares at the entrance to the slave quarters but decides not to enter. He turns to leave just as HELEN enters through the gate.)

HELEN Master Jason. Here you are. Do you know what they've done to Mistress Medea?

JASON Done, Helen?

HELEN They've put her in the slave quarters! And they won't let me see her. The slave quarters!

JASON Helen, your mistress volunteered to live in the slave quarters until her ship arrives. You know, while in Rome. She's keeping her promise to the President to behave herself. As long as she stays in her place and casts no spells--

HELEN Stays in her place? My little dragon? The slave quarters? But I -- The overseer said I can't go down there. I told him I'm her servant and he laughed at me. She needs me. I have to see her. What shall I do, Master Jason?

JASON Do, Helen? Thank Zeus you're Greek at the right time in the right place. You're free, white, twenty-one, and too old to marry. Enjoy yourself. You're free now. It's called life, liberty and the pursuit of happiness. You'll get used to it. *(Beat)* The slave quarters. Pity...That woman. She could save us all a lot of trouble if she'd simply turn herself into a white woman. She could do that, you know. False African pride. Don't tell her I said that. Never a dull moment...

(JASON exits up the steps. HELEN starts to follow, stops starts toward the entrance to the slave quarters, stops, then just stands there, facing the audience, lost in time and space.)

HELEN In Greece I knew my place. Here the whites take their freedom for granted and the blacks take their enslavement for granted. They belong. Now they tell me I'm free. Neither black slave nor white mistress, what a terrible freedom this would be if I did not belong to Medea. She is my freedom, my destiny. She educated me to be the boys' tutor. I felt as if I were a member of the family. But this family is no more. Medea isolated, Jason off somewhere scheming, and they boys, those unsung little Greeks, are being drawn deeper and deeper into this foreign black/white reality. It breaks my heart. It all began a couple of weeks ago when I explained to the boys that much of our Greek culture was actually based on North African philosophy. In the beginning even the Greek historians acknowledged the fact that when Alexander the Great and Aristotle conquered Egypt they looted the Egyptian Royal Library and overnight Greece became the intellectual light of the world. In Egypt scholars did not put their names on their discoveries. Knowledge belonged to everyone. Alexander reacted violently to this fact and told the President, who insisted that Jason put Alexander in one of those private academies where they teach young white boys to become proper masters. Every morning now I watch Alexander ride the milk white steed. The boy rides like a master. Sometimes Imhotep manages to join him riding an old black work horse that refuses to run. Otherwise he reads books Alexander slips him. Except on Sundays, the only day slave boys are free to play. They all go down to the creek and stare at themselves reflected in a pool of still water. They stand there, buck naked, lined up in a row like little black Buddhas, then suddenly, without a word, they all rear back and piss on their reflections. It's mass suicide. It frightened Imhotep. He didn't realize the slave boys aren't allowed to own mirrors.

(Enter WOMEN'S CHORUS.*)*

LEADER Faithful Helen.

HELEN I've been with her since I was a young girl. She treats me like a sister. *(Beat)* Without her, I'm afraid I've lost my bearing...

CHORUS Be still, Helen.

HELEN Medea is the only home I've ever known. When she and they boys sail for Colchis she'll take me with her.

CHORUS Rest.

LEADER Tonight go to Medea. She'll instruct you. Go now.

*(*HELEN *exits through the gate.)*

CHORUS Do you smell it? / A chill just ran up my spine / Someone just stepped on my grave. / What is it? Something black and terrible is headed this way, and nothing

can stop it. / It's from the old country. / What is it?

LEADER The bloom of death.

CHORUS Lord have mercy.

*(*CHORUS *exits. In the distance the soft reverberating grunt of a pig. Presently,* IMHOTEP *chases* ALEXANDER *in through the gate.* HELEN *follows them in.* ALEXANDER *is laughing.* IMHOTEP *is not.)*

HELEN Boys! Boys! What's wrong?

IMHOTEP Liar! Admit it!

ALEXANDER Bastard! Bastard bastard bastard.

HELEN No! No no no. You can't fight. You're blood brothers.

ALEXANDER Nonsense. That is not my brother.

HELEN (Gasps) Alexander! Shame on you! This can't be happening.

IMHOTEP He swears we have different fathers. He called our mother a slut. He says my name is too African. He calls me Im. I don't like it. He says I'm not—

ALEXANDER Look at him. Now look at me. How can we possibly be brothers? Momma's baby. Poppa's maybe. But I doubt it.

HELEN Stop it now! Boys, listen to me. A true sorceress comes along once in a thousand years. A royal sorceress like your mother is even more rare. She has god blood in her veins. An ancient African legend warns that the spiritual bond between the offspring of a royal sorceress is fixed. The spirit is in your blood. No power in heaven or earth can change that. You are rare--

IMHOTEP He insulted our mother. I will not have it.

ALEXANDER You are a stain on my father's legacy.

IMHOTEP He's my father, too.

ALEXANDER Oh don't you wish! You're the son of a Greek slave. We adopted you boy.

HELEN That's not true. Listen, in a few days we're going home. No more running and hiding from your mother's enemies. Things will be right again. We're going home, home to Colchis.

ALEXANDER Colchis is not my home!

IMHOTEP You're half African.

ALEXANDER Greek! Greek until I die!

HELEN Stop it now! You are the very special children of a royal sorceress. You cannot--

ALEXANDER Silence woman! It is not your place to lecture the son of Jason the Argonaut. You are a mere servant who crude notion of ethics was learned from the antics of an African witch! We Greeks have our own legends, Helen.

(Enter CHORUS OF WOMEN.*)*

HELEN Please go to your mother. She'll know what to do.

ALEXANDER Stop calling that witch my mother!

IMHOTEP That's it! I demand the Rite of Outcast!

HELEN No! Forswear the thought! Hurry!

ALEXANDER Granted! Helen, you will be my witness.

CHORUS LEADER Do not witness this, Helen! They will open the gates of Hell.

HELEN *(Backing away)* Medea! Medea!

ALEXANDER Helen, stay! You will be my witness.

HELEN No! I will not! Medea!

IMHOTEP Helen, I accept you as my witness.

HELEN No! This is a curse. I will not witness this. Medea!

ALEXANDER You are bound to honor the designation. You have no choice. You're still Greek. You must obey. It is the right of every kinsman. Say it!

IMHOTEP Do you know it, Helen?

(HELEN turns and faces the boys and kneels.)

LEADER Run away, Helen! Don't listen to them. They're just children.

HELEN It is the right of every kinsman. I'm Greek. I must obey. I, Helen of Corinth, servant of Princess Medea, sweep away all earthly persuasions and purify my intentions. *(With open palms, she brushes her arms.)*

LEADER You will curse a thousand generations. Run away!

HELEN Come together, hold hands, close your eyes in prayer. *(They comply.)* Swear to your gods.

ALEXANDER By Zeus I solemnly swear devotion to and compliance with this Rite of Outcast.

LEADER Do not do this!

IMHOTEP By Osiris I solemnly swear devotion to and compliance with this Rite of Outcast.

(Each places his palm over the other's naked heart.)

LEADER We shall not witness this tragedy.

(CHORUS exits.)

HELEN Do you, Alexander, son of Jason and Medea, wish to release all blood ties to him whose heart you hold in your hand? Swear it.

ALEXANDER I swear.

HELEN Do you, Imhotep, son of Jason and Medea, wish to release all blood ties to him whose heart you hold in your hand? Swear it.

IMHOTEP I swear.

HELEN I, Helen of Greece, do bear witness to this Rite of Outcast. Boys, reclaim your blood.

(Simultaneously the boys claw each other's chest.)

ALEXANDER & IMHOTEP With this blood I do cast out my brother.

(They lean forward, kiss each other's bloody heart, then rear back and spit the blood into each other's face.)

HELEN I, Helen of Greece, have borne witness to this: Alexander and Imhotep, sons of Jason and Medea, have duly performed the Rite of Outcast. From this day forward, under penalty of Purgatory, neither shall claim the other as brother. It is done. Your blood is brotherless. May you find peace. And may the gods have mercy on your little souls. Forgive them Medea!

(ALEXANDER exits up the steps, Imhotep exits through the gate, both hesitating several times to consider what just happened. HELEN weeps.)

LIGHTS FADE OUT

SCENE VI
JASON, *dressed now as a proper American gentleman, paces about at the Entrance to the slave quarters, rehearsing his lines.*

JASON Medea. Sweetheart. It's me. I thought we could have a pleasant little chat...I've lost my Greek accent...How are you? Will you miss me when you're gone?...I appreciate your sacrifice, Medea. America --

(TRIO OF SLAVE BOYS enter singing and dancing. One does the "hambone," one dances a spirited jig. Jason hides. Their performances frighten him and he doesn't know why.)

TRIO LEADER When I was young I used to wait On Master and hand him his plate Pass him the bottle when he got dry

And brush away the blue-tail fly.

TRIO **Jimmy crack corn, and I don't care Jimmy crack corn, and I don't care Jimmy crack corn, and I don't care My master's gone away**

LEADER When he would ride in the afternoon I'd follow him with my hickory broom The pony being rather shy When bitten by the blue-tail fly.

TRIO One day he rode around the farm Flies so numerous that they did swarm One chanced to bite him on the thigh The devil take the blue-tail fly. When the pony jumped, he start, he pitch He threw my mast in the ditch He died and the jury wondered why The verdict was the blue-tail fly.

LEADER Now he lies 'neath the old oak tree His epitaph is there to see\ Beneath this stone I'm forced to lie The victim of the blue-tail fly.

TRIO **Jimmy crack corn, and I don't care Jimmy crack corn, and I don't care Jimmy crack corn, and I don't care The master's gone away**

JASON Boys, wait. Tell me, why are you so happy?

TRIO It Sunday, master.

JASON The three of you, you're always together. Are you court jesters or what? Who are you?

TRIO LEADER He bound Irish, but he don't speak no Irish. He West African, but he come from Montserrat where the Irish and slaves speak that talk called Gaelic. Nobody understands him so he stopped talking. Me, I'm a native boy, bred and born in America.

JASON This Gaelic, can you say something? I'm a citizen of the world. Speak Gaelic, boy.

SLAVE BOY *(in Gaelic)* I dreamed of becoming a citizen of the world before you gentlemen snatched me from my happy home. By the way, you look like a pussy in that outfit.

(WOMEN'S CHORUS appears at the top of the steps. As they descend, the frightened TRIO runs off through the yard gate.)

TRIO Spooks!

WOMEN'S CHORUS Jason.

(JASON *watches the* WOMEN'S CHORUS *descend and block the entrance to the slave quarters.*)

JASON You're not from around here, are you?

WOMEN'S CHORUS Why did you bring her here?

JASON Truthfully, she followed...

LEADER Even now he masturbates the lie. She's weaning her powers. Let her be, Jason. End this farce.

JASON It's not my fault she's in the slave quarters. As a matter of fact--

CHORUS Another lie...

JASON I plan to ask the President to make her a special citizen.

LEADER Have you no shame? How can you stand there, dressed like a cockadoodle dandy eunuch, and profess sympathy for the woman whose life you made your own?

CHORUS Pray for forgiveness.

JASON Wait a minute! It's not my fault. Can I help it if the gods made me beautiful? They gave me diplomatic immunity from reality. No one expects me to be ordinary. In Greece--

LEADER This is America. For conversational purposes, fuck Greece. The President brought you here as a symbol of Democracy, hoping you might contribute to America's cultural and political development. Instead, you've done nothing but organize parties and bed every female blinded by your unearthly beauty.

JASON They seduce me. I swear to god they seduce me.

CHORUS Of all the strange worlds we have visited, none can compare with this America./ Its ideals rival those of the most wondrous civilizations / yet it breeds slaves to build its world / Every nation has its original sin.

LEADER This one, with the most noble ideals of them all, has slavery.

JASON Look, I tried to reason with the President. I told him that Medea was of royal blood, that she had special powers that we could use to defend our nation.

LEADER But he could not imagine a royal black princess with god-blood in her veins, right? He only saw a dried up old black woman who bears the mark of a slave. You, Jason, have turned her world upside down. You have found refuge in a young, godless land where cruel men breed human beings for slaves. What about Medea? She is in there now trying to wean her powers so that when she and the children return to Colchis she will be as powerless as a sacrificial lamb. Jason, Medea is dying.

JASON *(Stunned as he then enters the slave quarters calling desperately like a little boy.)* She can't die! Medea! Medea!

LEADER Come, sit. Let us observe. He does not recognize us. Wait for Medea.

(The CHORUS OF WOMEN *sits on the steps.* JASON *backs out of the slave quarters. Presently* MEDEA *appears dressed in slave burlap. The* CHORUS *stands.)*

CHORUS Oh Child / Look what they've done to you / She looks like a dying creature irritated by life's remains / Oh, why did she give him her eternal youth?

MEDEA *(laughs)* What gorgeous hunk summons Medea? Wow, it's Jason, that eternally youthful little love machine. Speak you slut. Lie to your haggard has-been.

CHORUS You should have let his beauty fade / like all vain men's.

JASON Medea! You look downright scary. Why are you dressed in slave burlap?

MEDEA The children, Jason. Are they safe?

JASON Of course they're safe. They have the protection of the President himself. I'll have Helen fetch new clothes for you.

MEDEA While in Rome these will do. I'm weaning my powers.

JASON Oh. Good, very good. I appreciate your sacrifice Medea. I really do. The President will be pleased. He's grown very fond of Alexander, you know.

LEADER That's goddam white of him. Like father, like son. Oh, I've seen him, that petty-perfect gentlemen, prancing about his plantation of his milk-white steed.

JASON Generals do that, Ladies. Prance about on their steeds.

LEADER A homespun me-lord, surveying his heaven-on-earth.

JASON I'm tickled pink, Medea, that he's letting you and the boys go home. I convinced him it was the decent thing to do, all things considered.

LEADER Jason, America's patron saint pinup. You'll go far. Too bad he's sold his half breed daughters to the highest bidders. but then, he didn't know that Jason the Greek prefers dark meat.

JASON Ignore them. Won't you be happy for me, Medea?

MEDEA Go away, Jason. I don't want to look at you.

CHORUS Happy? Did you hear that? / Be happy for Jason? / The slave should be happy for the master / Yes indeed.

LEADER This place is pregnant with paradox. Irony rocks its cradle. The slave women suckle their master's children. The slaves grow their own masters. The milk of Africa flows in the masters' veins, yet they pay homage to Greece.

JASON Be happy, Medea. It's Spring. "Spring sucks at the breasts of Summer."

LEADER But Winter's white milk is cold as hell.

MEDEA Leave me alone, Jason. I'm empty. I have nothing left to give.

LEADER Don't despair, Medea. You have god-blood in your veins. Listen to the maleness of your spirit. We're here Medea.

MEDEA I'm weaning my powers…The slave cabins have dirt floors.

JASON You sound…normal. I've never seen this like you before. You're changing…

MEDEA Yes, I have been feeling a little African lately.

JASON And I American. Please, Medea, don't spoil it for me. I have roots again. He's made me Commander of the Navy. It's ceremonial for now of course. But I belong again. Oh, don't look at me like that, Medea. Let's face it, you could never belong here. Your past, your heritage, your culture. The old black gods are dead, Medea. The golden age of Ethiopia has ended. Accept the new world order. Let Africa drown in her own tears.

LEADER Believe it or not, Jason, Africa shall rise again. So long as there is the Golden Fleece, Africa shall rise.

JASON I'm sorry you still love me, Medea.

MEDEA I've laid my love to rest. My well-licked wounds have healed. This place has made me realize that throughout our lives, Jason, we too were alone in our togetherness, our yours-and-mine togetherness. Jason, let's not quarrel. Our historic drama has ended. It's time to take our final bows. Let me go savoring the illusion that at least in bed you loved me.

Promise me that when Medea is no more you'll mend your ways for the sake of the boys. Will you do that for me, Jason?

LEADER When did he ever do anything for you? Don't let him sweet talk you again, Child.

JASON Would it help if I told you that every time I made love to a stranger it was in the dark? It was you I made love to, Medea, only you. You never once cast a spell on my philandering. That's how I knew you loved me. Admit you still love me. It's all right. Admit it.

LEADER He doesn't know / To a royal sorceress / Hate is the eyes the back of Love's head / Before this night is over, he'll wake her dragons.

MEDEA Our drama has closed, Jason. There'll be no further performances. I go home to die. Let me be real, Jason. No more Greek fantasy. I've accepted my fate.

JASON America is Jason's fate and loving Jason is Medea's.

LEADER That's your version, Jason, the theatrical Greek release. You've had your little sailor boy melodrama. Now it's time for Medea the African to perform. Medea is here, dressed like a common slave because she is a slave so long as she resides here. Say farewell to this sacrificial lamb, Jason.

MEDEA Someone is trying to usurp my powers.

JASON Careful, Medea. That's witch talk.

LEADER Be still, man. Listen...A powerful god dwells here. I can feel him...scheming. He's determined to create a new world order. American destinies will be color-coded. It's Set, Medea. Be very careful...

JASON You know, Medea, in my own way I loved you, too.

LEADER The gods warned you, Medea: beware of gifts bearing Greeks. The womb of a royal sorceress is sacred. You opened your legs to love and the rest is myth.

(Soft grunts of a pig: Unh unh unh.)

MEDEA There! Did you hear him? He's eyeing me...He's both male and female. Of royal birth. *Medea*! He knows my name!

JASON Medea, stop this witch talk. You promised to behave yourself. The end has come. Memories are all you have left. Remember when you first met me? You couldn't take your eyes off me. You cast a spell on me, remember? You cried out to heaven when I took you in the forest. Remember that?

(MEDEA trembles and slumps.)

LEADER Go to her. The memory is too strong.

(Two women from the WOMEN'S CHORUS *rush to hold up Medea.)*

LEADER She remembers...She remembers an arrogant, over-weaning little sailor boy whose knowledge of life began and ended with Greece. But he had an insatiable lust for the dark wonders of woman. He was the first white man she had ever seen. The virgin Medea prayed at long last she had found her spiritual mate. So she fucked him until he became addicted to the pollen of her powers. And then she loved him beyond belief. Loving Jason became her life. For Jason she slew dragons, betrayed family, defied gods; even give to this this laughter-loving lecher the gift of her own eternal youth. She was both black and beautiful. Had she been Greek would he have screwed her so royally?

MEDEA It was my fault. I was weak with loneliness. I never wanted to be Greek. He loved me before we came to Greece. His people hated me.

JASON She loved me. I was her Greek god. The very passion of my presence fired her soul. She swooned to my Greek rhetoric. Her skin was like black marble yet soft as a god's goose down. Her eyes, radiant black pools of lust no living thing could resist. And when she smiled the air grew fresh with innocence. She was dangerously beautiful, but Jason tamed her. She brought out the poetry in me. Night and day she begged him to caress that curly mound of Venus, to kiss those unsuckled breasts, whose wine-purple nipples tasted like dawn-sweet dew. God, she was beautiful!

LEADER His whiteness blinded her.

JASON How she loved the light of Isis, queen of heaven.

MEDEA He and she used to ravage each other on moist warm moonlight nights along the banks of the Blue Nile in Ethiopia. Oh yes she remembers After his ship sailed around all of her wet tributaries they bathed in the Nile and sucked pomegranates as Ra rose.

LEADER Oh, Medea, try to forget! That's all he remembers, the conquest of your love. He's still blissfully ignorant. You spolit the dear boy. All Greece spolit him. Super heroic sailor boy with a satyr's appetite for mating. Look at him now, Medea -- eternally youthful, vain, full of wonder and expectation, convinced he's god's gift to everything big, bad and beautiful.

MEDEA It's not entirely his fault. I should have taught him his place in the web of life. For Greece he sailed the oceans blue and they made him a myth. Perhaps I could have saved myself.

LEADER Instead you went to bed with the myth and got fucked by a metaphor.

JASON It can't have been as bad as all that Medea. I loved you. I must have loved you. Look, I couldn't help it if all women loved me. Was that a crime? You love me even now. That's no crime.

MEDEA Medea's unforgivable crime is not that she loved Jason, or betrayed her family, her people. Medea's unforgivable sin was...

LEADER Silence, Medea!

MEDEA ...to use her sacred powers to help you steal the Golden Fleece-- the Cloak of Knowledge.

CHORUS Oh bloom of death!

JASON *(stunned)* The Cloak of Knowledge! The Cloak of Knowledge? Medea? The Fleece? The Fleece. It's real? There really is a Cloak of Knowledge? My god. "The one who shoulders the Cloak..."

LEADER "...shall own the right to mind the world."

JASON My god. No wonder they demand your head. We must find it.

MEDEA I have it. I have the Fleece.

JASON You have it? But you said you lost it in Corinth.

MEDEA For once I lied to you.

JASON But why didn't you use its powers? All those years of running, escaping one enemy after another. We could have--

MEDEA Jason never ran. The evil black savage and her babies ran, remember?

JASON Now I know why you insisted on returning home to Colchis. You're going to return the Fleece, aren't you!

LEADER He's never looked into the eyes of a slave. The light is not more. All of Europe swallowed the body of Africa; you and Medea stole its spirit.

JASON I killed the hydra. I stole the Fleece! The Fleece is mine.

MEDEA The Fleece cannot be owned. Our drama will end when I have returned the Fleece to its proper place. Leave me know. Let me go finish packing my humility.

JASON Where is it, Medea? Your black trunk? Your black trunk? Medea, the Fleece belongs to me!

LEADER Savage! The Fleece belongs to Ra! The Golden Fleece is the sacred ram of Ra.

JASON The sun god RA? My god...

(JASON *runs off into the slave quarter.* MEDEA *yells after him.*)

MEDEA Stop, Jason! The Fleece is cursed. No mortal can ever touch the Fleece again until I have paid for my crime. My atonement shall be public. In exchange for my death my children shall become honored citizens of Colchis. This born-again African will no longer play the villain in your Greek melodrama. Stop, Jason!

JASON *(OFF)* Africa will never forgive you!

MEDEA Oh how I must have loved you Jason...

CHORUS God knows she did.

LIGHTS FADE OUT

SCENE VII
NIGHT, THE SAME DAY

(HELEN *comes through the gate and stops at the entrance to the slave quarters.*)

HELEN Medea, please come out. I'm not allowed to enter. Please, I must tell you about the boys. Your boys. Medea, I must--

(MEDEA *appears.*)

MEDEA Lend me your shoulder, Helen. (HELEN *does.*) The boys...Do they miss their mother?

HELEN Oh Medea, Medea, Medea. What have they done to you?

MEDEA My powers, Helen, they won't leave me. Set wants my powers. I asked Isis for help but she refused.

HELEN Set. He's here?

MEDEA He calls himself Satan now. He's a tricky old devil. But something in me won't let go. I miss my boys. They're all I have left. Jason came to visit me. He's looking for the Golden Fleece. He'll never learn.

HELEN The boys need you, Medea. You must come with me.

MEDEA The boys are safe, Helen. Jason promised.

HELEN No, Medea, no.

MEDEA Hush, Helen. Soon it will all be finished. Did I tell you last night I remembered loving Jason. I no longer hate him, Helen. I simply despise his kind. I'm feeling weak but good. Look up at the heavens, Helen. See the black holes? That means all the gods are sleeping. Now see how the stars blanket the sky? That means Isis is up, tending her garden of light, singing to her lover Osiris. Helen, I'm ready to atone for my foolish life. I want you to promise me that you will tell my story. For the boys' sake. Tell them that I lost my soul to love and deserve no pity. But remind them that once I was a good girl. Before the Greeks got hold of me I was a good girl. Helen, my babes and I are going home soon. Come with us. Be my friend. Look after the boys when I'm gone. They'll be honored cit--

HELEN This morning the children performed the Rite of Outcast!

(MEDEA *flies away, transformed.*)

MEDEA The Rite of Outcast? Impossible. Who witnessed this?

HELEN The forced me to, Medea.

MEDEA They performed it properly? The blood and--

HELEN Yes, Medea, yes. It was done properly, according to Greek protocol. Didn't they tell you? Your ship has arrived but the boys have run away. Imhotep stole the shite steed and raced away. Alexander is out searching for him. We can't find them.

CHORUS LEADER The boy ran away when he learned that Jason had struck a deal with the president. Both boys are now free to stay in America. As master and slave. It's all right now, Medea. The other half of your spirit is back. You're free to be your old self again.

HELEN Oh, Medea, our world's turned upside down. Last night I dreamed you killed the boys. Medea, you won't--

MEDEA You've been reading those Greeks again. African mothers do not kill their children. God-blood flows in these veins. The Greeks have their rituals and I have mine. Men fill their heavens with gods to meddle in every human endeavor but they're powerless against the mother instinct. It is off-limits to myth and magic. Now I know why my powers will not leave me. Jason. He let this happen. He thinks his gods will protect him. I dare any god to interfere with Medea's revenge! My drama requires no *deus ex machine*. Set, you want my powers? I'll make you an offer you can't refuse. Helen, fetch my robe. Medea has one last ritual to perform. Fly, Helen!

(HELEN *runs back into the slave quarters.*)

LIGHTS FADE OUT

STROBE LIGHT

MEDEA'S MUSICAL/DANCE TRANSFORMATION. IN WHICH MEDEA CHANGES OUT OF HER SLAVE RAGS INTO THE RITUAL WHITE ROBE. DIDGERIDOO SOUNDS INTRODUCE THE PRIMEVAL YODELING OF LEON THOMAS.

STROBE LIGHT OFF.

SPOTLIGHT OFF.

SPOTLIGHT MEDEA IN RITUAL COSTUME.

SPOT OFF.

SCENE VIII
IN THE DARK. FRONT LAWN

MEDEA *(OFF)* Jaaaa-son!

LIGHT RISE

(MEDEA *stands at the bottom of the steps calling up. Her face is painted white, her eyes red with the Egyptian hieroglyphic symbol for weep. MAN appears in the shadows at the top of the steps in full military uniform wearing a George Washington mask.*)

MAN Stop that yelling, old woman!

MEDEA Jason! Jason, Jason, Jason. Send me Jason.

MAN Silence! Return to your quarters. Now!

MEDEA Fetch Jason, boy.

MAN Woman, do you know to whom you are speaking? You are in the presence of the Father of this country.

MEDEA Be still. You are in the presence of Medea, Supreme Princess of Colchis, divine sorceress. Be careful what you wish for, boy. Jason, your absence fondles my wrath.

MAN Good Lord, woman, don't you know when to retreat? Do not test my patience. Because of Jason, and against my better judgment, I granted you safe passage to your native land. But I will no longer tolerate your special circumstance. Go before I change my mind and put you in your place. Go and pack your belongings, your ship has arrived.

MEDEA Medea needs no ship. Treachery has awakened her dragons. Imhotep! Alexander! Fine me. Come to your mother.

MAN Stop that! This morning Alexander became an American citizen like his father. You can't touch him. The colored boy is free to go with you. Take him and go!

MEDEA I've kept my promise. I've behaved. now my babes and I will go as soon as I do something I should have done long ago. Now bring me my vengeance. You can't protect him. He's mind now.

MAN Didn't you hear me, woman? Jason and Alex--

MEDEA Boy, I can gut you with a grunt.

MAN Heathen Child, your invectives are impotent here. This is not the African jungle. This is Christian land.

MEDEA Christians? Savages! You breed human beings.

MAN One cannot expect an African to appreciate the power and glory of a democracy at work. Slavery is God's curse upon your race, not ours. It is the charge of Christianity to save your souls.

MEDEA Medea did not come here to debate reality or myth with the surrogate of a wayward Englishman. Your ignorance is obscene. Save yourself, little man.

MAN One more effrontery and by god I'll have your hide.

MEDEA Fear me, little man, fear me.

MAN Fear you, a black witch? You're ancient history, Medea.

MEDEA So, you're dying to be a master. So be it. I'll make you king for a day. You and your ilk call Medea evil, yet you profane the very ground Life walks on. Name this madness which compels you to god about creation recreating. Civilization? You're second class savages. God? Headhunters for Christ. Manifest Destiny? Tell Medea, oh Great White Father, who gave you the right to mind the world?

(MEDEA claps her hands. MAN freezes.)

MEDEA Stay, and behold your Manifest Destiny.

(She turns to face the audience.) Sisters, natives, alas, They've defleeced us all. A congress of old white men in wigs with rouged cheeks ruled all white men are equal. And so they are sisters. Beware lest you fall prey to this perverse equality spawned by frail males in opportune times. This once virgin paradise now pregnant with Greed's lust Medea might have loved more dearly than her Africa. O fey pimps, how could you make your mother a whore? Your seed has built a house for every nation's

homeless, a home to none. A cauldron where foreigners breed, enemies mate and veiled offspring speak in tongues. Twins Apathy and Indifference will rape your son and daughters. Sweet milk will flow in hairy breasts and fair ladies lust for self. From now till nigger eunuchs crow at midnight, Like Medea's lips this land's off-limits to love. Set, Set, Set. Come now, sweeten Medea's revenge.

(SOUND OF SET APPROACHING. MEDEA claps her hands. MAN falls. MAN is PRINCE WHIPPLE. MEDEA backs off into the stage entrance as squealing grunting Set approaches.)

PRINCE WHIPPLE Medea. Whoaaaa!

(SET enters an stands at the top of the steps breathing noisily. He is a monstrous creation, an enormous deconstructed symbol of evil ancient an prophetic. He is a decadent, androgynous, obese boar with ear and nose rings, red fishnet stockings, platform shoes, a steel cup bra and miniskirt. His snout is lipsticked red, his mane set in curlers. Standing erect, he is vulgarity incarnate.)

PRINCE WHIPPLE Oh God!

SET Gooood? Ages before your counterfeit Christ, Horus, the first Christ, Son of my brother Osiris, buried my beneath that sweet dark continent because I killed my brother Osiris, God of Life and Death. Kiss me.

PRINCE WHIPPLE Unholy beast. Go back to Africa. This is Christian land.

SET Ah yes, Christians, of thee let me sing. From Buccaneers to missionaries corseted in grace, you came, you saw, you coffled till my tombstone rolled away and I, Set, in the body of a blue-eyed slave was christened chained to your cross aboard the Good Ship Jesus. A pilgrim god found home you see across the Middle Passage. I love it. Say Amen and kiss me.

PRINCE WHIPPLE Thing, crawl back into your hole!

SET Oh yes, holes, Set loves holes. While in holes below the souls of Africa screamed on deck Christians scribbled Negro spirituals and I, Set was sanctified. A slaver crown's my pride and joy. I love you dearly dear. Kiss kiss.

PRINCE WHIPPLE Get thee behind me Satan. Our Father, who--

SET Iiiiiii am your father, and Iiiiii am your son. And Iiiii am your holy ghost. And by-god I am everlasting. Kiss me boy!

PRINCE WHIPPLE But I'm the king, the king. Dare you kill a king?

SET *(Sardonic curtsy)* Ah yes, a king. Your kingdom will be done me-lord. Picture you, and the Eye of Horus atop the pyramid. The dollar bill's my promise. You shall rule until the long night, the upside down day, when Sun and moon return in their proper order. Until Liberty's torch radiates ten thousand points of light for man to see his Hell on Earth, and I my Heaven. And when there are no tongues left to mouth forth light, I shall sit upon your throne in broad daylight, and you will whisper my name, Set, Set, Set. Say Amen goddamnit!

PRINCE WHIPPLE *(SET mouths)* Amen.

(SET seizes and kisses PRINCE WHIPPLE)

LIGHTS OUT

SCENE IX
LIGHTS RISE as JASON runs in through the gate and stops at the entrance to the slave cabins.

JASON Medea! Get out here! Let me see your evil--

(MEDEA appears at the top of the steps)

MEDEA Medea is here, Jason, you heroic fishmonger. Have you prayed today.

JASON You bitch! You evil black bitch. What did you do to Prince Whipple? He's running through the meadow babbling something about the book of Revelations. He says the Devil made him president.

MEDEA May he boil in Satan's vomit.

JASON You're in ritual costume. Medea, you promised.

MEDEA You promised to protect my babies! This morning the children performed the Rite of Outcast.

JASON The Rite? Impossible. You mean they're no longer brothers?...

MEDEA Oh Jason, I have tolerated your transgressions for years, but this time you have seriously miscalculated. Fetch my lambs and your death shall not be without mercy.

JASON They ran away, Medea. We can't find them. Oh Medea, what is it you want of me?

MEDEA Eat my anguish.

JASON Oh fuck you, Medea. You're headed for history.

MEDEA Tremble, white boy. You forget your place. You sliver of a mortal, you're talking to Medea, divine sorceress of the sun god's race.

JASON I didn't know about the Rite of Outcast. I swear. The boys -- Look, you can leave Imhotep here with Alexander. He'll be a free black African American.

MEDEA His own master or his own slave. Better they should perish than live segregated lives. This is the new Greece, Jason, and your kind are its chosen people. Until the fire comes. Beware the wrath of Ra, Jason. Ra is coming soon. And none shall hide from the hole in the sky.

JASON Medea, your ship has arrived. Go, please take Imhotep or leave him, but just go. Go now. The troops are coming. They have orders to kill you on sight.

MEDEA You have earned a special place in American history, Jason. I have decided to make you a metaphor. You'll be the talk of the town.

JASON You demented black bitch. I will be rid of you! Go before these hands forget they once loved you.

MEDEA *(Roars)* My gut is full, I carry in my witch's craw bile enough to poison a thousand generations. Yet you have the gall to wag your mock heroic tail. Vengeance abide!

(JASON *snatches the necklace from* MEDEA's *neck)*

JASON We'll see who trembles now!

MEDEA So you remember...The curse...

JASON The double pointed wisdom tooth of the Colchis hydra that guarded the Golden Fleece. This, in the hands of a loved one--

MEDEA Murder me, Jason! With Medea dead all her curses will be lifted, you'll have the Golden Fleece, you'll rule the world. If I still love you, kill your beloved has-been. Hurry, Jason, kill me before I curse you. Slay your royal slave.

JASON Scream, savage woman. Pray to your dead black gods. Let me hear your wail echo across that empty dark continent. Medea, you're history!

(JASON's *thrust is suspended in mid-air.)*

MEDEA You damned Greeks have rhetoric for every occasion. I warned you, Jason. Now it's too late. Vengeance, your tongue is mine. Oooooh Evil, you love me still. Jason, tonight you will stand before your mirror and howl. From this day forward your name shall be "boy." Generation after generation will pity you your curse. Your race will forget its noble spirit because History will turn a blind eye to the day Europe raped your mother and left behind a bleeding Dark hole. Not now, not tomorrow, but Africa shall rise again, Jason. Look for the sign. When East meets West and North is South again (*ancient map with reverse polarity*) When the Prince of Smarm (*picture of Reagan*) saddles the throne and left-handed vice routs reason (*left-handed V.P. Bush*) when liberty's torch radiates ten thousand points of light, then The ghost of each and every chatteled soul Christianized today will plague your streets tomorrow. The brotherless blood of suicidal black boys masturbating murder will baptize your streets. Love-sterile bitch virgins gang-banging Indifference will cuckold chaos and husband the homeless, for there shall be no wedding rites in America. Kneel, Jason!

(JASON *kneels, entranced. The approaching SOUND OF GALLOPING HORSE distracts* MEDEA. JASON *jumps up and plunges the weapon into Her heart. She falls.*)

JASON (*with pride and regret*) By-god. She loved me still...

(JASON *runs off into the slave quarters. Presently* MEDEA *stands and removes the weapon.*)

MEDEA Alas, I'm free of Love, of Life. Set, I've kept my promise. My jinx is yours. Jason will be your metaphor. Hurry, Set. I ache for home, the final voyage. Deliver my babies to their mother's arms!

(*The galloping horse pulls up.* IMHOTEP *rushes in through the gate.*)

MEDEA Imhotep! Find your brother! We're going home. Hurry. Soldiers are coming. Hurry!

(ALEXANDER *runs in from the slave cabins.*)

ALEXANDER Mother! Father's found the Golden -- Imhotep, no!

(IMHOTEP *has picked up the weapon. As* MEDEA *turns to face him he plunges the weapon into her heart.*)

MEDEA (*Smiles*) Alas, I love you still.

(MEDEA collapses. IMHOTEP drops the weapon. ALEXANDER runs in, seizes the weapon and draws back to stab IMHOTEP who, suddenly child-like, is too stunned to react.)

MEDEA No! Not your brother! You'll curse us all!

(Too late. IMHOTEP falls face-up beside MEDEA, the weapon protruding.)

MEDEA Oh my little hearts. Set, you traitor. I have dear friends in Hell!

ALEXANDER *(Embraces MEDEA, weeping.)* Momma, I thought you were immortal.

MEDEA Immortal? I'm a mother, Alexander.

ALEXANDER Yes, Momma.

MEDEA Your mother is damned, your father is doomed to live in the Hellfire of Reality. Your brother, the other half of you is gone. Your family is no more. Do you love your family, Alexander?

ALEXANDER Yes, oh yes.

MEDEA An your brother Imhotep, do you love him?

ALEXANDER With all my heart!

MEDEA Be strong, be brave. Your brother Imhotep, call him, call him by his blood name. Give him back his blood.

(ALEXANDER kneels before IMHOTEP.)

ALEXANDER I'm very strong. I'm very brave. Brother!

(ALEXANDER falls on IMHOTEP, heart to heart. MEDEA slaps her heart.)

MEDEA Oooooooh Bloom of Death! How sweet thy fragrance now. Isis, Mother of Heaven, welcome my babes into your loving arms. Africa, forgive me. Patience, the Fleece will come to you. Osiris, lord of Life and Death, Medea is ready. Bring my boat. Take us home. Let your oars strike the water gently. Don't wake the children. Row us cross the Night Divine in silence.

(MEDEA *dies. In mourning garb* HELEN *enters through the yard gate with suitcase in hand. She kneels beside the pile of bodies.*)

HELEN Alas, the tragedy has begun. Farewell, my mistress, my sister. I've lived my life attending your love, your hate, your fear. Yet only now, in the end, have I been proud of you. I'll tell your story as best I can, Medea. *(stands)* I don't know where I'm going but wherever, whenever I hear talk of that evil black woman they call Medea who killed her babies, I'll tell them the truth. And in the end even Africa must forgive you. For did not my little dragon live and die for Love, the deed most honorable of all? Farewell, Medea. I'd better go now before I turn this tragedy into a Greek melodrama. You'd hate that.

(HELEN *exits.*)

(JASON *charges out of the slave entrance. Cloaked in contradiction, radiating madness, he shoulders the Golden Fleece, and he is physically Black. Slowly he spreads his arms and proclaims:*)

JASON EuuuuuReeeeeKaaaaaa!

END OF PLAY

AN INTERVIEW WITH SILAS JONES

Q: What was the impetus behind adapting Medea?

SJ: The play is not intended as an adaptation but rather a dramatic rejoinder. Frankly speaking, as a student of ancient African myths, I thought the Greek Euripides pimped and abandoned Medea, i.e. her race, her culture; and I was outraged by the suggestion that Medea would kill her babies to spite the man she has given her very life to. I wanted to write a response to an outrageous proposition. Euripides wrote a play for Greeks: I wanted to write a version for everybody else.

Q: The play combines two major aspects: a satirical deconstruction of post-revolutionary America, in which the ideals espoused in the founding documents are indicted by the reality of slavery, and an Afrocentric approach to ancient history, displaying the primacy of North Africa over Greece. What made you link these two ideas/approaches to the material?

SJ: Euripides loved Jason (Greece); I admired Medea (Africa). I attempted to connect both contradictions to arrive at a purposely flawed quasi-Greek style, as it were.

Q: Given that much of what is taught in universities is still a Eurocentric approach to understanding ancient history, are there any texts you'd recommend as a starting point to understand the true context of the play (both yours and Euripides)?

SJ: The one book I recommend as a reference source is *Introduction to African Civilizations* by John G. Jackson (Citadel Press). Wonderful reading!

Q: In Euripides' original the children do not even have names, but Alexander and Imhotep are not only older than their Greek counterparts, they are the central figures of the first half of the play. What was the impetus behind focusing on the children? Is there a Cain-and-Abel element here as well. The most famous aspect of the original is the child murder, but here you have made it brother-on-brother murder, both metaphoric and literal. Is there also a comment here on Black-on-Black crime, or is Alexander's identification with only Greece and America ensure that this is a form of racial violence?

SJ: The children are the racial hope for America. Let me caution you: You are very perceptive, but you will prevaricate from the original meaning of the play when you compare it with the Greek version, even though I use Jason as a metaphor.

Q: Set is also a new presence. He is not quite the Egyptian god of antiquity, nor is he the Christian Satan. What is Set's role in all this and is he a trickster figure for you?

SJ: Careful that some of your assumptions aren't based on Eurocentric distortions! In my use of Set, he is the jealous brother of Osiris, who is brother/husband of Isis. All of this is explained in the play. He is not a trickster. Set is the evil that must hide his face, like Washington. It would be more accurate to say that the entire play is a trickster!

Q: Washington is a major presence in the play, despite never appearing on stage. Prince Whipple, on the other hand, serves as a Creon figure without being a Creon. He is, instead, "the first Oreo," which links him on some levels with Medea. (He is also hilarious.) What should the audience take away from the absent Creon (Washington) and his present tragically comic, self important slave Creon?

SJ: If the audience comes to see my play thinking it is a "version" of the Greek construction, they will miss my play entirely. My play is as original as Euripides'. Listen to Medea. It's her play, her version.

Q. Fair enough. I know one of your favorite lines is "You went to bed with a myth and got fucked by a metaphor." Does that also apply, in this sense, to America, or African-America?

SJ: Yes. Absolutely. Everything in this play is a contradiction or a play on opposites.

Q: Lastly, the first version of this play premiered in 1995. Has the election of a biracial/African American president in 2008 changed how we understand this play at all?

SJ: No, but it is ironic, isn't it. We have a black president but racially little has changed socially. Obama is the American prospect of Alexander and Imhotep conjoined.

CHAPTER 6

MEDEA, QUEEN OF COLCHESTER

INTRODUCTION

The first play in this volume depicts characters in Africa planning to travel to the New World; the last play depicts characters in the New World that have traveled from Africa, bookending four Western Hemisphere-set dramas. *Medea, Queen of Colchester* by Marianne McDonald begins with a recounting of life in Cape Town, South Africa, but is set in present day Las Vegas. Medea is played as a gay, black drag queen from South Africa who has brought his white, drug-dealing boyfriend James (and James's two sons) to the United States. James leaves Medea for the daughter of a casino owner, driving the drag queen to madness and infanticide. The play, which premiered in San Diego in 2003, was called "a compelling and provocative work" by the *Los Angeles Times*.

Maryanne McDonald, currently a professor of classics at the University of California, San Diego, has also written and worked in Ireland and South Africa. Her background results in perhaps the only classically aware Medea: "Her mother worked as a housekeeper for a Greek professor and she heard him talk about a woman in a play who was a very smart survivor and always ended up on top." Therefore McDonald's

Medea is named after the Greek (or rather Colchian) original and knows the story of her namesake.

The title is a play on the word "Queen," meaning both female ruler and flamboyant gay man. Medea, in this play, is a gay man, a drag queen, and a cabaret performer whose nurse-character, here called Nuria, is a transvestite from South Africa. She is also a Cape Coloured—someone of mixed race descent. In other words, Medea is a liminal, hybrid figure, between man and woman; between black and white; between Africa and America. And like her namesake, she is unwelcome in both her homeland and her new home.

Thus far in this volume Medea has been presented as African priestess, voodoo queen, and without magic in the streets of San Francisco. Here, the drag queen comes from a line of *sangoma*, traditional South African healers who have power and a connection to the divine realm. When Edward Jameson (who, like Aegeus, needs help in having children) arrives to visit Medea, McDonald's play changes its narrative implications from the original. In *Medea*, Aegeus offers a home to Medea in Athens, yet another Greek polis, whereas Edward offers this Medea an opportunity to go home: His club is in Cape Town. Medea will return to South Africa and be kept safe in this play.

This Medea also provides a transformation in the horror. Although Medea kills the children, they are not, biologically speaking, her children. Since "she" is a man in drag, she is the children's stepmother. While child murder is still horrific, the idea of a mother killing her children in revenge for the father's wrongs is missing from this version. Having said that, however, one should note that the update provides for commentary on more modern concerns: families with stepparents, parental rights, gay marriage, and Western exploitation of Africa. This Medea, like others in this volume, is an African who has been used and discarded by Westerners and who then insists that they pay for their actions.

This is also a Medea aware of the theatrical nature of her crimes. Euripides's Medea understood performance and staging. McDonald's Medea is literally a star of the stage who uses her own sense of showmanship to craft a devastating revenge. The pleasure of the play is that the audience is allowed to watch that revenge unfold.

PLAY 6

MEDEA, QUEEN OF COLCHESTER

MARIANNE McDONALD

Cast (All male):

Nuria, Friend of Medea, a transvestite, a Cape Coloured (mulatto) from Cape Town, South Africa.

Nick, Gay Manager, white, American.

Medea, "Queen of Colchester," a Cape Coloured transvestite and cabaret artiste.

Michael Creon, Greek-American, Owner of the Parthenon, a large gambling house in Las Vegas

James Eliot, Medea's lover, WASP American.

Edward Jameson, Irish, Owner of the Phoenix theatre in Cape Town, South Africa (has other businesses).

Two boys (James' children) about nine or ten years old.

Two "Bodyguards" (silent parts). Can be used throughout.

First Reading: Fall 2002, Sledgehammer Theatre, San Diego

Directed by Kirsten Brandt

Cast:

Nuria: Walter Murray

Nick: Tristan Poje

Medea: Hiroshi McDonald Mori

Michael Creon: Ruff Yeager

James Eliot: Michael Severance

Edward Jameson: David Tierney

The children (played by one actor): Anton Swain-Gil

First Performance: August-September 2003, Sledgehammer Theatre, San Diego

Directed by Kirsten Brandt

Cast:

Nuria: Warren G. Nolan, Jr.

Nick: Chris Hatcher

Medea: George Alphonso Walker

Michael Creon: Ruff Yeager

James Elliot: Robert MacAulay

Edward Jameson: Greg Tankersly

Two Children: Alternating between Nathan August, Michael Cullen and Kevin Koppman

Two Medea Divas: Kim Strassburger and Jessa Watson

Enter MEDEA's *friend,* NURIA, *busying "herself" around the house as she speaks. The house should suggest Las Vegas modern, a tawdry chic. Perhaps a carpet, table and a few chairs. A door center back.*

[Optional: as NURIA *speaks we see* MEDEA *in full splendid "show" dress singing a song, but only quietly as either video background or miming. Every word* NURIA *speaks should be heard.]*

NURIA Out of chaos comes chaos. How I wish Medea had stayed in Colchester, that township outside of Cape Town where she was born and grew up, and not come here to Vegas. She loved James so much she murdered for him; I'm not exaggerating. She did it to help James in his career. Until he came along, she was doing fine playing the international theatres: beauties like her pulled in big audiences. They loved her in Salzburg, in Prague, then invitations came from Paris, London, New York. I'm getting ahead of myself. Let me fill in some of the bits. When Medea was born, and his mother saw how beautiful her new baby son was, she dressed him like a girl. Somehow she thought that way not only could she have the daughter she always wanted, but her child had a better chance to grow up. Boys in South African townships die young. Macho games, murder, prison, gang wars. None of these for Medea. Her mother had another boy who she let stay a boy. This way she had both a daughter and a son. As for her name, Medea? Her mother worked as a housekeeper for a Greek professor and she heard him talk about a woman in a play who was a very smart survivor and always ended up on top. She wanted that for her child. Medea went to school like all the rest, but her beauty and wit singled her out. Early on, she decided she would have a life on the stage. Her real start came from leading the annual Cape Coloured Coon parade. This was a street carnival like the one in Brazil, and traditionally a transvestite led the various groups. Anyway, a director, who ran a theatre there, spotted her talent as a performer and gave her work. Medea's troubles began when she was working in London and hooked up with an American named James Eliot. He was married to an alcoholic who gave him two little boys. The boys were with her one night when she was drunk and she drove into a tree. *She* died instantly, but *they* lived. So then Medea became their mother, and she's been a good one. They moved to Cape Town, and James supported himself by running drugs, with Medea helping. They got into some serious trouble when a drug gang tried to cheat James; Medea's brother was part of the gang. She managed to get James back his money, but ended up killing the drug king and handing her own brother over to the police to save James. Her brother went to prison where he was killed in a gang fight. Medea and James went back to London. Her mother now has lost both her children: she will never forgive Medea. For many years everything was fine. Medea and James lived together happily, and Medea raised their sons. She supported them all with her shows as "Medea, Queen of Colchester," the drag queen comedienne; she has a store of comic material, and is as inventive as the headlines, a trick she learned from her first director who taught her the ropes. She is a star, and one of the best. Read the raves if you don't believe me. But James got restless. It's hard having the woman be the breadwinner of the family, especially if she's a man. Eight years went by, and Medea got a lucrative invitation from Las Vegas: this house is one of the perks. James thought it would be good for them both to move. He felt he could regain his own life, with the protection of some of the bigger kingpins in the gambling world. When they moved here, I came with them from London, just as I had gone there with Medea from Colchester, years ago. It was better than James' wildest dreams. Michael Creon, owner of the Parthenon, largest casino in Vegas, took a fancy to James. Michael just learned he has cancer, and he's been training James to be his successor. Michael has a daughter, Athena, and he came up with the idea that James should marry his daughter, and leave his "Queen." You should hear what Medea says about Michael now, cursing him...I just hope he doesn't hear anything. News travels fast in Vegas. Word of mouth beats the internet. Did I say Medea's show is at the Parthenon? James had been flirting with Athena for a while now, but Medea didn't take it seriously. She was used to his little flings. Sometimes she had to threaten him: "I'll cut your balls off if you ever see the bitch again!"

James knew what she was capable of if he pushed his luck too far. Medea never dreamed he would leave her for good. WRONG. James dropped the bombshell on Medea last night after the show. He told her he was leaving her and has married Athena. So that is where we are. My friend Medea has been abandoned, and she's sick. She hasn't slept all night, and now she's locked herself in the bathroom. She won't eat, and she keeps blaming James for ruining her life. She won't listen to anyone. It's like talking to a stone. She can't stop crying and she's going to miss her show; she's already missed rehearsal. They'll sack her for sure. And their children? She hates to see them now. They only remind her of James. I'm really afraid. Wild thoughts are running through her head. She's dangerous, and anyone who fights with her will get hurt. Badly hurt. She has special arts; things she brought with her from Africa. Even a few tricks from the witchdoctors. One took a particular fancy to her, and she spent a lot of time with him. Some even say he was her grandfather. He taught her all about drugs. Deadly drugs. *(Children's voices from offstage. They run into the house shivering and wrapped in towels. They play around in the background.)* Here come the children now. James conveniently left them with their "mother." At least they don't know what's going on. They don't have a care in the world; children are children.

(NICK, MEDEA's *manager knocks and* NURIA *lets him in.)*

NICK Where's Medea. I've been waiting for her back at the casino. Is anything wrong? Is she sick? She's supposed to be rehearsing her new routine. A busload of Japanese businessmen is due in tonight. I need Medea. Now.

NURIA You don't know what's happened? You haven't heard the news?

NICK No. What news?

NURIA James told her last night he's married Athena. I know you need Medea, and she should be rehearsing but her whole world has collapsed. Nowadays people don't take love seriously. It's just a game like everything else. People around here change partners as easily as they do slot machines. Quicky marriages and quicky divorces are Vegas specialties: another way to make money from misery. Medea's life until now has been on a winning streak, and she's a bad loser. She's different. I'm doing what I can for her, but I'm glad you're here too, maybe you can talk some sense into her.

NICK I'd suspected something was up, but I never realized it had gone this far. What is she going to do?

NURIA You don't want to know. The pain has just begun.

NICK I've got a little something to add to the pot.

NURIA What are you talking about.

NICK No. Forget it. I'd be out of line if I say anything.

NURIA Tell me. I can keep a secret, if I have to.

NICK Well... I was doing my rounds at the Parthenon, just checking the game tables before going to the theatre, and I heard people talking. Big people with hired guns. They say that Medea should leave if she knows what's good for her. I suspect they know something that we don't. I didn't think too much about it at the time. Now it adds up.

NURIA But what about the kids? Will James let them go with her? They would be lost without her, and she without them.

NICK I suppose he'll do anything for this marriage. Medea's hours here in Vegas are numbered.

NURIA That's it. That's the last straw.

NICK Now you be quiet about all this. You could get us both in trouble... deep trouble.

NURIA And his boys? What a father they have. Damn him. You'd think he would have some loyalty after all she's done for him.

NICK Who's loyal? Are you really that naïve? Self-love is the only game going. This marriage glitters with gold, and it outshines the past. I'm sure James has decided to forget the good times he had with Medea. He's hot for his new bride and all she brings with it.

(One hears the occasional screech from the children playing computer games nearby.)

NURIA Boys, you had better be quiet. Keep out of your mother's sight. She's not feeling well, and I don't know what she might do if she sees you. O God, I hope she won't hurt anyone close to her. I don't care about her harming the scumbags responsible for this.

(Offstage, screaming. The sound of things being smashed.)

MEDEA Damn him! Fucking shit heel. I want to die!

NURIA Boys, get out of here now. Your mother is upset, so stay out of her way. Keep quiet. Don't let her know you're here. *(Boys leave.)* Nick, you'd better try to get someone else for tonight. Medea can't go on in this state. Make some calls from here and hang around a while. I might need your help. There's a hell of a day shaping up. A fire is raging inside Medea. It's growing.

MEDEA *(Still offstage.)* Filthy bastard. Asshole. Insensitive cock-sucking, ass-licking prick! *She screams.* And the bastards from the bastard. Those boys that I raised: shit father along with shit sons!

NURIA What do your children have to do with anything? What have they done? They aren't to blame. I'm terrified for all of us. I know Medea. I know her only too well, and all that she is capable of. She is proud, and if she is crossed... No!...I don't even want to think about it. For myself, Nick, I take it easy. Accept what comes. Don't ask for too much. I meditate and put my money on the sure thing. I just want to grow old in peace. I've learned that enough is enough. Too much spells trouble. The higher you fly the harder you fall. The gods get jealous easily, and they can topple you with their little finger. They'll even do it just for fun. No! Never catch the eye of a god.

NICK What do you think she will do?

NURIA She's had it. There's no hope. James left her for greener pastures, greener bucks more likely. And she's inconsolable. Nothing we can say will help.

(Offstage, screaming.)

MEDEA *(Rap style.)* O for a bolt of lightning now To kill myself: I'll never bow To sorrows and this fucking life. I'll forget through death I'm James's wife.

NICK O you god of the lucky sevens, God that lands you in gambling heaven, O you spirit of the bouncing ball, Won't you listen to this poor woman's call? She's screaming for that dark lover death, But all too soon she'll draw her last breath. That's a prayer better left unsaid: We all know how we'll end up dead. Why cry that your man has left your bed, That man you kept warm and saw well fed? He's gone and left you for that filthy bitch: Leave them alone to scratch their itch. Why shed a tear for that bastard gone. Start a new life and sing a new song.

Still offstage.

MEDEA O great gods of the land of my birth Great spirits of this sanctified earth. Do you see how I suffer all these wrongs At the hand of a man who's upped and gone. No good the promises from this shit Who's made me weep in this fucking pit. May I see his slut for whom he lusts Along with his home all ground to dust. O mother and country that I left in shame, And betrayed my brother while I sought fame. Forgive me now that I ever left, You see I'm punished: I'm now bereft.

NURIA Hear the cries of this poor woman lost, Just for vengeance no matter the cost. She's strong and wise, and she has her craft; She wants justice but that's just a laugh. Broken promises are a way of life In Las

Vegas where the gambling's rife. There'll be a payback that won't be small: Medea'll win, if you know her at all.

NICK Let's get Medea to speak to us. Perhaps we can talk some sense into her. Even if it doesn't change anything, talking does sometimes ease the pain. Gives us a chance to say something too. Go now, and get her out here. Hurry before she does something we'll all regret.

NURIA I'll do it, but I wonder if she'll listen to me. She scowls at her friends like a wounded hungry lioness. No one dares speak to her. Her grief is growing: the whirlwind has started spinning. I understand Medea, both her sorrow and pain, the cry that comes from lying in a bed alone at night with broken promises. That is a special sorrow. She did so much for her man's sake, and came from a land far, far away. Now she's homeless.

(*Wild and distraught,* MEDEA *suddenly enters from the back room, every inch a queen, statuesque and commanding. Dressed as she does for her show.*)

NICK Medea! Nuria's told me about James. What a lowlife shithouse.

MEDEA (*A brittle laugh.*) Darling Nick, so I don't need to fill you in. Didn't Nuria offer you something to drink? Vegas hospitality after all. I'm sorry about not showing up. I can't go on today. There's no justice in the world, Nick, darling, and that's a fact. And the moment you're seen as different, people judge you on appearances. No one tries to find out who you really are. I learned this lesson the hard way. All Las Vegas loved Medea, Queen of Colchester, but Medea the human being with feelings like everyone else? The one who weeps? Hardly. At least I thought James knew me for who I really am. But now he's walked out on me. That man has destroyed my life and I let him do it. I made him my king, my lord and master, my one and only love. I wasn't a bad wife. I raised his kids, and kept his bed warm. I learned every need James ever had, and I satisfied every one. No cunt was my equal. I even didn't mind him playing around a bit. I always knew how to get him back. Until now. Women have it bad enough, but we queens have it worst of all. My mother dealt me a bad hand when she made me half a woman. Stupid bitch. A freak? James seems to think so now. Leaving me for *poes*! He prefers that boring fuck to what I can offer him. Does he think she's hot stuff? He'll learn. You're different, Nicky. You're born here in the states. I only have a green card. This is your home. I gave everything up for James, and now I can't go back. I have no mother, no father, no brother or sister to help me when I need help. And what am I? That *moffie* from Cape Town? But I know you're my friend, and I ask you just this one favor. If I find some way of making this shit pay for what he has done to me, you know nothing about it. That's all I ask. Who says a woman is afraid of taking up a gun, or a knife, or fighting back? If she loses the man for whom she sacrificed her life, there is no one more capable of making him pay – and it's payback time now.

NICK Your secret is safe with me, Medea.

(*A knock is heard.* MICHAEL CREON *is at the door.* NICK *goes into another room to make more phone calls.* NURIA *opens the door.*)

MICHAEL Medea, Medea, my friend. May I come in and speak with you? I won't stay long. (*She waves him in. He settles into the couch. He looks ill and weak and breathes with difficulty.* Is Nuria around? Could she get me a glass of water?

I'm exhausted. (*Looking around the room.*) You have a new carpet, my darling! And such a match with the curtains...you always had a touch for those things. Ah, yah! (*He looks at Medea and coughs for a while until he catches his breath.*) Here I am, an old man. Did you know I have cancer? Pancreatic. They say I've only got a year at most. We all get surprises in this life. You and I know how tough it can be. And *this* is how it all ends (*gestures to himself, indicating his infirmity*)! I'd thought I'd earned more. I wonder if you know how hard it was. But, you do. You're an immigrant too. I came over during the Greek civil war. My family scraped together a little money to send me to some relatives in Boston. I struggled with all the jobs, serving tables, cleaning after others, I'm sure you know what I'm talking about. I ran numbers on the side, and did errands for "people." Then I got my break. Yes, you're from Colchester and I, Michalis Creon-topoulos, I am from Granitseka, two places only the locals know about. And now I want to help you, Medea. You shouldn't let this business with James and Athena get you down. James is a good boy; he's like my son, the son I never had. I'd never seen eye to eye with anyone until he came along. I've taught him how to run the place, and he's learned everything. He's a good learner, really sharp. I won't be missed. As for Athena, she'll be looked after. I want a family, and with any luck I'll see a grandchild before the end. You don't begrudge me that, do you? Those things people tell me you're saying about me. They make me very sad. Have you been badmouthing me? I thought we were friends? We could all have lived here and helped each other, but I was wrong, and so you leave me no choice. Everything comes to an end, and now that goes for your time here in Vegas, don't you think? It's time for you to leave. It's better for all of us. So stupid of me to think that you and my daughter Athena could live in the same place. You'd be like two randy leopards tearing each other apart, going at each other's throats ... and Athena would lose. She's no match for you. (MEDEA *stands silently listening to him. Not yielding an inch.*) You know you can't stay here, but a great star like you won't have any problem relocating! I've come to help with that too. (*Pulls out a fat envelope, obviously filled with cash and puts it gently on the table. There's an airline ticket with it.* MEDEA *is still quiet. Deadly quiet.*)Come on Medea. Say something. I want to help you.

MEDEA Do you really care what I have to say?

MICHAEL But of course! Medea, Medea, I'm afraid for Athena. I'm afraid of what you might do to her, to us, to James. Compared with you, they're children. They don't know how to protect themselves against you. I know your reputation. I know you have contacts, and people whisper about the strange powers you've brought from Africa: I'm afraid you may use them. We need a surgical cut here. Then the healing can begin.

So, now I have no choice but to ask you to go. You're lucky I'm asking you to leave, because you know I could make you leave quickly and quietly, very quietly. In fact, you wouldn't make a sound.

MEDEA *(Speaking softly now. Surprising everyone.)* You judge me too harshly, Michael. Harshly and unfairly. My reputation has been my own worst enemy. Other people just resent me for being different, and God forbid I should be clever as well. As for being artistic, that's the worst of all. I have other "specialities" that set me apart. Straight women hate me. They can't understand what their husbands or boyfriends see in me. They should come backstage to see their drooling faithful "mates" undressing me with their eyes, looking at my crotch, to see what I've really got under my costume. And you're afraid of me? Michael Creon, owner of the Parthenon, the Caesar of Las Vegas, afraid of "Medea of Colchester"? But don't you see you have nothing to fear? I would be out of my mind to try anything against anyone as powerful as you. I'm not insane. You chose the husband you wanted for your daughter. My quarrel is with James, not Athena. Good luck to her! And you're blame- less. Actually now that I know what James is like, and that he would leave me after all I've done for him, I see I'm better off. No one can keep a man against his will. Force love? Impossible! So I have nothing against you or your family, or even him, now that I've thought it out. As for those "strange powers from Africa," you and your daughter can't believe that sort of rubbish. What are you talking about? Let's just work some- thing out like two civilized human beings.

MICHAEL *(He claps slowly.)* Very good! You almost convinced me! But why not? You're a good actress. Come now, Medea, in your heart of hearts, did you really think you could get me to trust you? I'd have preferred you call me a son-of-a-bitch right up front. Your gentle words are as disarming as the rattle of a snake. No. You have to leave now. I'm taking no chances with you. No more talking. I don't want to keep a rattlesnake as a house pet.

(Medea falls down before him and begs him.)

MEDEA Michael, Michael, try to have some human feeling for me. Balance the huge weight of your daughter's happiness against a little sympathy for someone down and out. You know, the tables turn.

MICHAEL You're wasting your breath.

MEDEA I need time. Just a little time. You should know that.

MICHAEL I've got to protect myself and my daughter.

MEDEA So where can I go? I can hardly return home. The police are waiting for me with open arms. They like to make examples so they can keep their pet criminals in power. There's the choice of a dozen endings waiting for me back there.

MICHAEL That's your problem. Yes. My home and my children are *my* problem.

MEDEA Love is a losing hand.

MICHAEL Not for everyone. Sometimes we're dealt a good one.

MEDEA Who shuffled the deck this time? Satan?

MICHAEL You're wasting my time Medea. Just leave.

MEDEA Trouble. I'm drowning in it.

MICHAEL Do you want my men to help you pack?

(He stands up to leave.)

MEDEA No, don't ! Please listen to me!

MICHAEL Why am I still here speaking with you? I have other things to do.

MEDEA I'll leave. You don't have to worry about that.

MICHAEL Well, what are you waiting for?

MEDEA I need some time to sort a few things out for myself and my children. There's all my costumes, and eight years of my life here. How do you pack a life? Do you think I can put it on my head like in Africa and walk off? Hardly. By rights I should have a month to organize and make arrangements, to say nothing of packing. As a father, surely you understand that. I'm asking you for just one day.

MICHAEL Michalis, Michalis, you're going to regret this. You've been burned often enough in the past. Damn it, I know I'm making a mistake, but I'll give you your day. God help you, if you are still here tomorrow morning. Don't underestimate me, Medea. So I give you what you want. After all, what can you do in a day? But that's all you get.

(Exit Michael.)

NICK Now Medea, for God's sake don't try to be smart. Go while the goings good. There must be someplace you can go, someone who will take you in.

MEDEA Do you think I would have spoken to that pile of stinking shit that way if I didn't have a plan? That I would flatter him, and wag my tail like I did? The fool. He gave me my day. We'll see who's laughing at the end of it. Now. I just have to figure out what I'm going to do. I don't want to be caught, and the last thing I want to do is serve time in some filthy jail. My grandfather taught me a few things and he taught me well. Then what? Where can I go? There's extradition. But if someone hears about me they would hardly welcome me with open arms. I know there are fools in the world, but trying to find that type of trust is asking for the impossible. I'll wait and see. But I don't have much time. I'll have to do something in secret. I still have friends, and means for pulling this off. If I'm forced out into the open, I'm not afraid to die. The thought of paying back my dearly beloved James, his happy father-in-law, and his blushing bride will set me up for life. I'm not going to let them laugh at me. That marriage will be a marriage made in hell. Did they really think I would just walk away? My honor is at stake. Medea, be true to yourself.

A woman can give life, but she also knows how to take it away. And this is my specialty.

NURIA *(Delivered in rap style.)* Rivers flow back to the source, The normal order reversed. Medea's honor's Medea's curse. Men are criminals, never believed. Now women, praised, instead of deceived.

All those songs that listed their sins Will find their way into time's dustbin. It's time for women to sing their own songs. The real dope on men - it's been far too long. We'll answer the slander, Sauce for the gander, And mud now slung against men. Medea's been a victim of love: Time to enlist the powers above. She left her home for a worthless man, And traded her nest for this corrupt land. Now he's left her for a bitch's bed; Little does he know how it will fall on his head. Medea's dishonored and told to leave, But I know that she has some tricks up her sleeve. What good were promises? No regrets in Vegas. We all play the cards the Gods once gave us. A Vegas princess now lies in the bed That should be yours: she'll soon be dead.

(JAMES opens the front door and walks in confidently. Although age is beginning to show, he is still blond, handsome and self-assured. He walks over to the liquor cabinet and pours himself a drink, mixes one for MEDEA and hands it to her.)

JAMES Medea, Medea, will you never learn? Your temper will be the death of you yet. All you had to do was to keep quiet and give me some time to plead your case. Michael heard what you said about him. What did you imagine he would do? A casino boss like him? Do you think he's going to listen to things like that and do nothing? I don't care about myself. You can call me the biggest shit in the world, but your forked tongue is your own worst enemy. You're really lucky you're still alive. I had him agreeing that you could stay here with the kids. We could all have lived here safe and sound, one big happy family. But you really have made it impossible for me. You've been stupid, when you could have gone on living in luxury. Now you have to leave. But I've come to help you. You know how I care about you, and I know what the kids mean to you. As much as I love them, I think they should stay with you. But don't ever forget they're still my boys. I'll give you whatever you need, addresses, money. I'll never let you starve. You helped me once. I welcome the chance to pay you back. You can take whatever you want from me. You may hate me now, but I'll always love you. And one day you may understand I have done this to put us both on easy street.

MEDEA How can you dare to stand here in front of me and talk to me about that slut? A dog would have more shame. But I'm glad you came because it gives me a chance to tell you just what I think of you. Sit down. First off, shall I count the times I saved your ass? The first drug deal you made in my country and you'd fucked up? I bailed you out then. And the last one, when I handed my brother over to the drug squad just for your sake? You know what happened to him. My mother now lives alone without any help from anyone. She hates me. How many years did I support you? And the hours I spent waiting for you at home alone. Professional commitments you said. Bull shit! Cock commitments more likely. To boost your fucking philandering ego. You could never get enough, could you... I was a good "wife" James, and now I'm inconvenient. Someone else can help your career better now. And the kids. Does all this count for nothing? What I gave up for you? What I did for you? The promises you made to me? So where do I go now? Home to my adoring mother? Or maybe I should just give myself up to the police. Simpler for everyone that way. Free board and lodging for Medea. What about our children then? Your new bride won't exactly be a loving mother. Our past is an inconvenience for you in your new career. You don't think that I'm going to accept your help, do you? Oh God, if only I could have known what sort of a bastard you would turn out to be. Certainly not someone to trust with your life.

JAMES You always had a way with words, Medea. You know how to bend the truth to get out of tight spots. But this time you've really gone too far. Now, you blame me. But didn't you fall in love with me? If that

hadn't been the case, you would not have lifted a finger to help me, but
help me you did. You did something good there, and I know I owe you
bigtime. But you got as much as you gave. Sure you had to support me for
a while, but even then you exchanged your backward country for a civilized one. What's South Africa now? AIDS and rape capital of the world?
Now you live in a society governed by just laws, not the law of the jungle.
You're famous too. Medea is known all over the world, and here in Las
Vegas you've had your greatest success. Everyone talks about you and
your reviews have been stellar. Every performance is sold out. Your wit
and humor are legendary. That sort of fame doesn't come to everyone.
Is that no reward? I can't imagine why you would throw it all away just
because you're angry. So you ask, why did I leave you to get married? I'll
tell you and if you listen to what I say, you will praise my foresight and
see how well I have provided for you and our children. What the fuck
does getting married mean? That shouldn't change anything between
us. You know I'll come to see you as often as I can. I want you in bed –
that should be clear by now. You talk about me as if I've never had to
struggle. I grew up in the same poverty you did. Yes, I know you helped
me, and I'm grateful. But it was my own good work that made Michael
Creontos respect me, and I hoped that by marrying his daughter and
taking over the business I could make all our lives easier. If they made
background checks on us, we could be deported, or worse. I *had* to do
something for you and our children. Do you know how lucky we are
that Michael Creon, probably the most powerful man in Vegas, took us
under his wing? You seem to think this means I was tired of you. Hardly.
I just wanted to secure our future. Can't you understand that I did this
for both of us? And the children. "Our" children. Was this so bad? But no.
You had to spoil it all. You're just angry because you think I'm leaving
you for a cunt. I know you. All you think about is sex, and believe me,
I've never regretted anything there. But don't you realize that sometimes
you have to look at the larger picture?

MEDEA You and your excuses. You've never thought of anyone but
yourself. If you think you can talk your way out of this one, think again.

Do you really imagine you're making sense? If you had such a good plan, why didn't you tell me about it in the first place?

JAMES And you would have agreed? Fat chance. Look at you now! Raging away, making all kinds of threats. Don't you think that I could have guessed your reaction? I had to go it alone.

MEDEA Crap. You wanted it all sewn up before I found out.

JAMES Medea. Listen to me. I don't care about Athena. She's nothing compared to you. I did this only to get an insurance policy for us all...a marriage to set us up for life.

MEDEA You can keep your shit wealth. My heart is what matters to me.

JAMES What can I say to bring you to your senses? Can't you see that this could have been our biggest payoff?

MEDEA It's easy for you. You have a home, but I'm kicked out.

JAMES That was your own choice. If you'd kept your mouth shut you would still be in clover. Blame yourself.

MEDEA Really, Jimmy baby? Did I go off and marry someone else? Did I abandon you?

JAMES It was your threats to Michael that ruined everything.

MEDEA Yes. Don't think they don't apply to you too!

JAMES I'm tired of arguing. Just remember you're in Vegas - America now. You need me for help: just say the word and I'll give you whatever you want. There are lots of cities with great clubs where you'll be more than welcome. You would be a fool to refuse my offer, Medea. Forget the past. Don't be angry. Just be a good girl and realize that you still have friends who will help you.

MEDEA You patronizing bastard. I won't take any help from you or your friends. Gifts from a man like you are no gifts at all. They're poison.

JAMES God knows I've tried to help you and the kids. This is not the first time that your stubbornness harmed you more than anyone else. You don't know what is good for you, and you're just going to suffer for it.

MEDEA Piss off, James. Go fuck your bride. What a bridegroom you're going to make! Wait until she sees what you're like in bed. You say I'll be sorry? Wait a while. Soon it will be your turn to learn what it is to suffer.

(Exit James.)

NURIA *(Rap style.)* Love. A losing streak and you want to die. Every throw turns up snake eyes. You lose your name, and then your fame, And now your fortune. It's all the same. A winning streak, and you're up high, But soon you'll lose: it's your time to sigh! A life without love's a surer thing, Never gamble and you'll continue to sing! Cupid may shoot his poisoned arrow, But I'd rather walk the straight and narrow! I only want what I can get. A lover sure, and a house to let. No quarrels for me or constant fights, Then I'll sleep in peace throughout the night. No lusting after a stranger's bed, Stuff like that, and you'll end up dead. I want a home that I call mine, With a love that's stable, that's just fine! Never an exile in the cold cruel world, But a lover safe in my arms curled. I want friends, and the world I know, No strange land filled only with foe. Medea's fucked and her man is fled, So just remember the words I've said!

(Noise of car. Enter EDWARD JAMESON, heavy brogue, in a good humor, oblivious to MEDEA's mood.)

EDWARD *(He kisses her.)* Medea, may the saints protect ye, an' sorrow neglect ye, an' bad luck to the one that doesn't respect ye. It's been a while since I've seen you. Nice pad you have here.

MEDEA I wish the same to you, Edward. I heard you were settled in Cape Town, Phoenix theatre isn't it? I heard it's really taking off. And that now you have people you can trust. Vegas tells us all the stories. Is it true? What are you doing out here?

EDWARD I'm a respectable man now, not the Irish bum you knew in London. I've been able to make a home in Cape Town, thanks be to God. Mbeki's been good to me. The new constitution finally lets me do just what I've wanted! But I've missed you Medea. You know I have everything now, friends I can trust, wealth, but one little thing is missing: a wee bairn. A child of my own. Actually I came out here to see you. I remember all that talk about how you had those special powers. You know how to help me get what I want.

MEDEA Are you married now?

EDWARD Yes. But I'm still childless.

MEDEA Have you seen doctors? You and your wife?

EDWARD Done all that. Useless.

MEDEA So you've come for alternative medicine. You have definitely come to the right place. It's not for nothing that I spent years studying with the Sangoma from my country. With my help, you'll soon have the children you want. All your heart desires!

EDWARD Medea, we've been friends too long, so I can read you like an open book. What's wrong? We're talking about my problems, but I can see you have some of your own. A friend's eye is a good mirror.

MEDEA You always did have a good eye, Edward. And this time you've seen it again. Things have gone sour for me.

EDWARD But I hear you're a great success! What is it?

MEDEA It's James. He's left me to get married.

EDWARD Jesus, Mary, Joseph. I can't believe it. After all these years? You've raised his kids. You made him what he is. I wouldn't want to count how many times you saved his lily-white protestant ass.

MEDEA I know, and look what I get in return.

EDWARD But come on, tell me more. Remembering my times with you, I can't imagine he grew tired of you in bed. No one can do what you do. It has to be something else.

MEDEA He's found the love of his life. So he betrays his family.

EDWARD Good riddance. Believe me, it's best to be free of a man like that. But I still can't understand it.

MEDEA You will. Let me go on. He married Michael Creon's daughter. He wants that hot young cunt, and the inheritance that goes with it: money and power.

EDWARD What a shite!

MEDEA Creon gave me twenty-four hours to get out of Vegas.

EDWARD And has James gone along with that? Surely he'd try to get Michael to change his mind.

MEDEA He gave lip service, but he goes along with it. Edward, are you really my friend? We go a long way back, and I can help you get the child you want.

EDWARD If you could do that for me...I'd do anything for you.

MEDEA Will you take my act at the Phoenix in Cape Town, and protect me if they follow me? I've been looking into this; under Mbeki I'd be pardoned. But I'll be settling a few scores before I leave here.

EDWARD Of course, Medea, you know how I feel about you. Yes. I want your help, and I'll put you on stage, and protect you...Nuria too. I'll protect both of you. So, we have a deal, yes?

(*After a moment's hesitation.*)

MEDEA Can I really trust you, Edward?

EDWARD We know there's no loss like the loss of a friend, but I'm there for you and I always will be. By all the years we've been friends, and

even the years we were lovers. Medea, my name is Jameson, not James.
I have honor. I'll leave a car with you and a couple of the lads. Tickets
and passport will be waiting at the airport...an airport I use for special
occasions. Friends will be waiting to take care of any unfinished business.
My boys'll park around back...we'll be real discreet. You can leave when
you like.

MEDEA Thank you. I'll be with you soon and you won't regret it. I have
a few things to see to, then I'll be off.

(EDWARD *kisses her goodbye.*)

EDWARD You're a wild one, darlin' – so be careful. For God's sake don't
do anything you'll regret. If you do not sow in spring you will not reap
in autumn...for what you're planning that harvest would be tears.

(*Exit* EDWARD. *Sound of car driving off.*)

NURIA May the god of chance speed you on your way, Edward. You have
proven that there are still generous and good men in the world. You'll
see us soon. Vegas is for losers. Cape Town, here we come!

(*Reenter Nick.*)

NICK What's going on? That guy who just left was in a real hurry. I
know his face from someplace.

MEDEA Just an old friend, who showed up when he was needed. Gods of
my forefathers, you still love Medea. I feel my powers returning. Medea
has not lost her African roots and her country makes her powerful.
(*Chanting an unintelligible prayer.*) The wheel has stopped spinning and
the ball is in the sweet slot. Now you're going to see what real payback
is. Just when everything looked hopeless, I'm raking in the chips. Nick,
please get a message to James. Tell him I want to say goodbye. I'm going
to sweet-talk him and tell him he's perfectly right. Any man's a sucker
for that. I'll say that he made the right decision, and I can see how he
only has my good at heart. I'll ask him to keep the kids. I'll add that our

boys are better off with him, because it's a tough life on the road. Then I'll send some gifts with them for the new bride.

NICK That's more like it. We need some peace around here.

MEDEA I've wised up. Nick, go and bring James here to me. (*Nick exits.*) (*Gloating to Nuria.*) That dress is woven from the finest gold thread, still soft to the touch, but drenched in poison. Wait until you see what happens when she puts it on. I'll send a necklace too: a real choker. The gifts have to stay in the box, and no one else is to touch them. Athena, the happy bride, will soon pray to die. This poison is very painful, both for the victim and anyone who touches her. Next. I'll deal with our two little ones; I saw them grow from babies to young boys. I love them, no denying that, but I'm going to kill them. Everyone loves his children, and James is no exception. I'll get at him the way he got at me, even if I have to pay with my own pain. What does my life mean, without a home, or a country, without friends or family? I should never have left my mother, won over by the lying words of an American. James will suffer for what he did. He will never see his children again. And with Athena dead, no hope there. He thought I was weak. Mistake. Once you're a killer, always a killer - but I'm loyal to my friends. It's my enemies that have to be afraid.

NURIA Medea, I want to help you. But murder? How can you think of killing your own children?

MEDEA Nothing you say now means anything to me.

NURIA You can't kill your children.

MEDEA Watch me. I want to stab James' heart. I want to see him bleed for the rest of his life.

NURIA Then find something else. For God's sake, whatever you do to your children you'll be doing to yourself!

MEDEA Wasted words. I've made up my mind.

(MEDEA *leaves to prepare the gifts.*)

NURIA *(Rap Style.)* Cape Town, Cape Town, always been my dream, Of all swinging wishes, by far the queen, Bright constellation of Africa, There's all new sights in that sky far. Cape Town's light warms up the coldest sky, That's the place to live, until I die. Your theatres dazzle, their marquees above, All men dreaming of their wild new loves. Pockets bulging as big as their crotches, Eager eyes as they look at their watches, Just biding their time for a girl like me, To show them the sights that *they* want to see. But you Medea, what will life be there? Don't you know the pigs are everywhere? Jails tailor-made for someone like you? There you won't find your room with a view. Childkillers are fucked worse than a thief It's not in Cape Town you'll find relief. Mbeki's a leader who welcomes the free But not criminals as you'll soon see. In our country we knew the ropes well But there you'll find your personal hell. So you get away and escape the law, How do you escape your guilt's giant paw? What monstrous courage will be in your heart When from your children you see you must part? What will you say when they kiss your cheek? Stab them to death: you'll be a freak! You can't live with their blood on your hands, You won't wash it out, try as you can.

(NICK *returns with* JAMES.)

JAMES You wanted to say goodbye, so here I am. I know you hate me, Medea, but I still want to help you.

MEDEA James, James, I'm so sorry. I really don't know what to say. You have had to put up with a lot from me. Please forgive me. After all the love we shared, you would think I would have known better. I realize now you only had our best interests at heart. I was mad to rant at Michael Creon who only wants to help us too. He certainly has a right to a family of his own. I can see how this family can benefit our boys also. It is a lucky dream come true. Here we blow in from abroad, with only a few pennies to our name, and you find this jackpot for us! I'm really sorry James. Second thoughts are best. I've finally come to my senses. And it's not as if you're abandoning me! I know you'll see me whenever you can. Love like ours can never die. Thank God you didn't act like me...you've been the soul of patience. Do you forgive me?

JAMES Of course I do. Anything for you.

(MEDEA *speaks to the children who were playing in the other room.*)

MEDEA Boys, boys, come here and hug your mother and father. No need to worry anymore. We have made up. (*The boys run in into her welcoming arms. She hugs and caresses them. One drops a ball he was carrying.* MEDEA *picks it up and tosses it to him gently. They run and kiss their father. Tears come to* MEDEA's *eyes, which she tries to hide.*) Oh children...Oh God, I don't know why I'm crying... See. See. It's just because I've stopped quarreling with your father, and I'm so happy. I'm weeping for joy.

NICK It's good to see an end to your quarrel.

JAMES Thank God you've come to your senses. Of course I forgive you. You just acted like a typical woman: you were jealous. But you know I'll never abandon you. You finally sorted it out and see how I'm acting in everyone's best interest. Come here boys! (*They run to him. He strokes their hair.*) Boys, I've been busy thinking about how I can help you. After you've grown up, then you can work with your old dad and we'll be one big happy family. You won't have a worry in the world, because your father has provided for you. And your mother and I agree about everything. (MEDEA *continues silently to weep.*) Here, here, what's this nonsense? You should be laughing with us.

MEDEA It's nothing, really. I was just thinking about our children.

JAMES So then, why the tears?

MEDEA Oh, nothing. You know how I raised them over the years. And when they were sick, how worried we were. Oh well, they survived everything God threw at them. I was just worried about what's to come. What their future will be.

JAMES You don't have to worry any more. You know I'll provide for them.

MEDEA I believe you. But you know how we women cry over nothing. But there are a few things to sort out. As you know, I have to leave. Now I see that it is for the good of all of us, and I agree. You have to start a new life without me, but I think it is best if our children stay with you. I wouldn't like them to be on the road. It will be difficult enough for me to find a job and get settled. This way they could stay at the school that they are used to. Will you ask Michael? I'm sure he will understand.

JAMES I'm not so sure. But I'll try.

MEDEA Why not ask Athena to help. Her father will listen to her.

JAMES You're right. And she'll do what I say.

MEDEA She'll follow you just as I did. I have something to sweeten the ante: a priceless gift I brought from back home. A dress, woven with fine gold thread. Nuria, you know that box I prepared with the gifts. Would you please bring it out here for my boys to take to Athena? *(NURIA goes into the next room and returns with an intricately carved wooden box.)* *(MEDEA turns to JAMES.)* Athena will be thrilled; you know how women like presents. It's finery to match a fine husband!

JAMES Medea, don't be silly. You shouldn't be giving this away. Athena doesn't need anything of yours. No. Her father showers her with gifts. As he will our sons. Keep what you have – you'll need it in the future.

MEDEA No! Gold counts more than a thousand words. We have to convince Athena, and I would do anything to save my children from a life on the road. I'd give my life, not just gold. *(MEDEA turns to the children and hands them the box.)* Here boys. Take this box to the nice lady who lives in the big house with your father now. See that she takes it into her own hands. It is important that she opens it herself. So, off with you now. Nick, darling, will you go with them? Later you can give me the good news I'm waiting for. (MEDEA *kisses the boys affectionately. They leave with* JAMES *and* NICK. *They are carrying the box.* MEDEA *goes inside a room.*)

NURIA (*Rap style.*) The children are walking to their death; No turning back now from that bloody path. The bride takes up her glittering dress: If she puts it on, there'll be one bride less. That gift will deliver her final kiss, Fatal embrace, whose poison won't miss. The dress will flash and its beam will beckon, The last light she'll see, that's what I reckon. No Vegas neon to light her way To the world of the dead on *her* final day. All that glitters is not gold, I've heard: But shining proof Medea's kept her word. And you, cool James, chasing happiness, Never a thought of this present mess. But death will dull your lust's evil gleam, Killing the bride you burdened with dreams. Your gift will kill both bride and hopes; So now you've lost, how will you cope? How wrong you were to gamble your wife, Now you see how it's cost you her life. Never trust the throw of the fickle dice; If you gamble with love, you'll lose twice. I weep for Medea, the mother of sorrows, For once she kills, there'll be no tomorrow. Don't kill your children, because of your man! Changing partner's old as time's span, Hardly worth this pain 'til the end of time, The pain that burns a hole in your mind, But madness comes from searing hate: Medea's Medea, and that's her fate.

(NICK returns with the boys.)

NICK Athena couldn't take her eyes off the gifts you sent. She agreed to everything. All your wishes are about to come true.

(*Tears come to* MEDEA's *eyes.*)

NURIA Oh do cry! That's really going to help. How about changing your mind?

NICK I'll go and keep an eye on what's happening and I'll report back to you.

(NICK *exits.*)

MEDEA Oh Nuria. It's finished.

NURIA Yes. For you as a human being. Medeamachine is taking over.

MEDEA There's worse to come.

NURIA You've lost it. Medea, you're mad.

MEDEA Aren't you on my side?

NURIA Yes, I am. That's *my* problem.

MEDEA Don't you understand how important honor is to me? I'm not going to give up what I struggled for all my life: my honor makes me who I am.

NURIA You're better off without James, but your boys? You love them. They are part of you.

MEDEA

Sometimes a wound needs to be cauterized. My pride is sick and I'm aching for a cure. I call it justice.

NURIA Justice? Justice? Killing innocent children? Nothing justifies that. Play the hand you've been dealt. That's life. You'll win more if you accept what is.

MEDEA Fine. Just leave me alone. (NURIA *shakes her head in disgust and goes inside.* MEDEA *speaks to the boys, playing with them, putting her arms around them.*) Children. There's a new home you'll be going to soon, without me. I'll be off now too. How I wish I could see you grow up. I would have dressed you for your weddings, or seen you happy in some other way. I remember all these years I fed you, stayed up all night when you were sick, and made sure you had everything you wanted, even when your father was too tired to take care of you. I wanted you to take care of me when I grew old. What a sweet thought that was. I can't imagine my life without you. I won't touch you again, feel your soft skin, or smell all the sweetness of your fragrant youth. You will be somewhere else, somewhere entirely new. Oh darlings. Why do you look at me that way? Smiling that smile? Oh, I can't. Your bright eyes are stabbing me. No. Change of plan. Forget what I said. I'll take you with me. But what am I saying? Do I want that bastard to laugh at me? Get away with what he's done? I've got to punish him. I know how to hurt him so he will never recover. What am I? A coward? Am I the victim of a bully? No more words. It's time for action. James has forgotten who I am. OK boys, it's time for lunch now. Go into the dining room and tell cook you're there. I'll be in shortly. (*Boys run off.* MEDEA *speaks to herself.*) Medea. Don't do this. You're mad. Let them go, they're only kids. You love them, and they're innocent too. What did they ever do to harm you? They will be your joy and delight in Cape Town. Do you think you can live without them. You can't leave them here. Well, James is hardly the ideal father, or Athena, the devoted mother. My thoughts are racing. I don't know what to do. Yes. I won't let that bastard go free. His children must die, and it has to be me who does it. My choice is clear: Medea will be Medea. (*She calls out to the boys.*) Boys, my darlings, come here, back to your mother. (*The children run to her. She showers kisses on them.*) What soft hands. Your lips, and handsome faces, so dear to me. How I want you to be happy...but now it will be there, not here. Your father took "here" away from you. Oh, sweet kisses, your soft skin...your mother's joy. Go now, leave me, leave me quickly. I can't look at you. *Children go out again. They are a bit frightened.* This is too much. I give in. Passion rolls the dice now. It's payback time.

(MEDEA *goes into the back room with the children.* NURIA *returns.*)

NURIA (*Rap Style.*) Nothing can hold a good woman back The toughest course she can easily hack. She'll solve life's riddles, a piece of cake, And bring home the bacon for her mate's sake. Her wit is endless and her muse on hand To make her famous throughout the land. If she can't make it, there's always a reason, Every woman will have her season. But kids hold you back from this great path, Living without them, you don't feel the lack. You may miss the joys, but also grief Happiness with them is all too brief. Those who have children have only worry How to feed them, it's an old story. Bring them up after years of struggle, Only to find they're not worth the trouble. You'll see that I've saved the worst for last: After all the years, and tests you've passed, You love your child more than yourself, With his trophies lining every shelf. Then comes grim death to carry him off, And sorrow follows on footsteps soft To haunt your life forever more; Your mind is only a bleeding sore. Peace a stranger to a heart that beats In tune with pain and endless defeat.

(MEDEA *comes into the room.*)

(NICK *calls from offstage.*)

NICK Medea! Medea!

(NICK *bursts in through the door.*)

MEDEA My angel of glad tidings! I've been waiting for you. Any news?

NICK You had better leave, and quickly. They're right behind me.

MEDEA First, tell me everything, all the details – slowly too so I can savor them.

NICK They're dead. Athena and her father are dead.

MEDEA What a delightful tale.

NICK You're mad. How can you stand there and say that! Don't you know what the police will do to you when they get their hands on you?

MEDEA Oh, I have friends, Nicky, Darling. Tell me the story and don't leave a thing out.

NICK When everyone saw your children come into Michael's house, bringing presents to Athena, they were happy. They thought you had made peace with James, and that you were now willing to leave: you'd accepted the inevitable. The boys were fussed over, and then they asked to see Athena. We were escorted into another room where she was sitting on James' lap, and she was playing with his hair. She was smiling until she saw the boys. It's hard to like someone else's kids. James calmed her down. He said, "Please honey, they're my children. If you care for me at all, learn to get along with them. You know, we'll have plenty of our own kids soon too. Here, they are bringing you presents. For my sake, please let them live with us." She sat there silently listening to James, but when the boys gave her the gifts, she couldn't say no. As soon as James left the room with the boys, and she immediately tried on the dress and then put on the necklace. She went to a long mirror, and admired herself. She danced around the room in the glittering gold, pleased to see her bright image in the mirror. Suddenly she stopped and gasped for breath, then stumbled, weaving this way and that, barely able to grab a chair to prevent herself from falling. I don't know what poison you used, but my God, it worked fast! One of the servants thought she was having a seizure and went to get a doctor. Her eyes started from their sockets; she gagged, grew very pale, and began to scream. Then she vomited. Blood started oozing from every pore. No one knew what to do. Someone ran to get her father, another to get James. She screamed again, and again, then we heard a weird cry that stuck in her throat. We could see she was suffering from the necklace that was strangling her. She fell to the floor and the clothing seemed to be eating into her skin like acid. Her flesh melted, and her blood and skin dripped off her body like sap from a tree. The poison was devouring her. It was awful to see and we were all afraid to touch her. But her father didn't hold back. He rushed into the room and took her in his arms. He groaned and kissed her, "Athena, my darling daughter. For God's sake, don't leave me. I can't live without you." He got his wish, sooner than he thought. He tried to get up but his body stuck to hers. The more he tried to get away, the more skin he pulled off himself. Soon he was bleeding from every pore. We continued to watch this grim wrestling match. Whenever he tried to free himself, she pulled him back: more flesh ripped off him and more blood flooded the floor. Finally he gave up and collapsed on her body. It was as if he knew there was no escape for him. Now the daughter lies there dead, with her old father, both of them blackened corpses. What did you smear on the dress, Medea? Those bodies were a sight for tears and terror.

NURIA Awesome, Medea. You really got back at James, and made him pay. Fuck the daughter and fuck the father!

MEDEA That was just the first act. Now for the second. I must deal with my children, and not leave them for others to harm. They'll be the first target when it's seen what I've done, and they're my only vulnerable place: so I'll hurt my enemies, before they hurt me, and it will be my hand that does it. That way I'll also punish James in a way that he's never been punished before. Steel yourself Medea. Arm your heart. Take up your knife, and go to your destiny. Don't be a coward. Forget you loved them. Remember that you were betrayed. You will make him pay, with his heart's blood. Forget your children for this one brief day, then you can mourn them for the rest of your life.

(MEDEA *pulls out a knife, and holds it up high over her head, as if enacting some unholy ritual. Her face is beautiful, and demonic. She exits.*)

NURIA Oh where can we turn? The dice are thrown and those who lost must pay. I don't see any escape. Poor children. Poor mother. The blood of murder is like a plague. Medea may escape jail, but not the memory of what she has done. It will end up destroying her. (*The children scream.*) Did you hear the children cry? I'm helpless. How can she do this?

FIRST CHILD Mommy, Mommy, what are you doing?

SECOND CHILD No, Mommy, don't kill us.

NICK I've got to try something. (*He runs to the door, but it's locked.*) I can't open the door.

CHILDREN Help us! Help us!

NURIA (*Shouting to the children.*) I'm trying, but the door's locked. Medea, stop. You're mad. Totally mad. Stop it! I know what you've suffered, but this is not the way to get revenge when you suffer more than your victims.

JAMES runs in.

JAMES Where's Medea. I'll kill her. I've come for my boys. I want them safe.

NICK James, you may think you have suffered, but wait...

JAMES What is it? Does she want to kill me now?

NICK Medea killed your boys.

(*He groans and gropes for words. He cries out.*)

JAMES God! No. That's impossible.

NICK It's true. Yes. She's done it. I heard them screaming. They're dead, James.

JAMES (*Screaming.*) She killed my boys! They're innocent! I know she once loved them and they did nothing but return that love. Now she's paid them back with death! Where are they?

NICK In there.

(*He points at the middle door that opens suddenly. MEDEA is standing there all bloody with a knife in one hand and a gun in the other. The gun is pointed very steadily at JAMES. MEDEA has never been more regal than at this moment. The bodies of the children can be seen next to her. NICK and NURIA flee in horror.*)

MEDEA Hello, James, darling. Are you looking for your boys? Here they are. I'll let you see them for one last time, but I won't keep you long.

I just want to gloat a little. The dice James came up all sevens for me! They were loaded, of course.

JAMES You fucking cocksucking whore! Is there nothing you would not do? How could you kill my children? I finally see you for what you are. A savage animal from a savage continent. I must have been mad to think I could civilize you. You murdered before, and sold out your own brother. How could I think you could change? Killing our children, just because I left your bed? No sane person would have done a thing like that. It took a bitch like you. I've learned the hardest lesson of all. I don't have words to describe you. You wouldn't understand them anyway. Well, fuck you! Go to hell, you murderess! You've destroyed me. But wait. You have feelings too, and they will burn such a hole in your heart, you'll pray to die.

MEDEA Did you really think you could leave Medea as easily as that? Throw me away like a used rag? Laugh at me from the safety of your bed in a petty drug-king's house? You can call me anything you like, but you are also my victim, and I've poisoned the rest of your life. Now you can live with the memory of all you have lost.

JAMES Do you think you will escape the memory of what you have done? Our two little boys?

MEDEA I'm prepared for that. Honor, James, honor. But you don't know what that means, do you? At least I've taught you what pain means. I can see it in your eyes now. That will last. How could you leave me after all I had done for you?

JAMES That's your reason for killing my children?

MEDEA You really think that means nothing? You still don't understand anything. I'll spell it out for you. I hope you know I didn't do this out of spite or petty jealousy. Hardly! I knew that when I put the knife in our boys' bodies I was putting it in my own also. This was the sacrifice I made so that you would be punished. And there is nothing worse for me.

I loved those boys as much as you did, and probably more. But I had to pay you back. What you have done to me, you and your kind have done to Africa for centuries...you and your slave ships on which millions died and millions more on the plantations they were forced to work. Well, James, I have broken the shackles of your western greed! You killed me on your own private plantation. Medea the mother is dead. You sucked the life out of me, and now I have drunk your blood in return. You know I thought this out very carefully. I wanted to make you feel pain like you have never felt before. I could have killed you, but that was too easy. That pain doesn't last. But the pain that comes from seeing your children's bloody bodies in your mind day after day will. You killed them as surely as if you held this knife in your own hands and thrust it yourself into their bodies. The memory of this pain won't grow old and fade like the memory of Athena, whom you've already started to forget. So you lost your white bitch, your power fuck. You can always find another one of them, but your children are something else.

JAMES The murder of these innocent children will be a waking nightmare for you as much as me. No escape. Aren't you afraid of their ghosts? They will haunt you for the rest of your life.

MEDEA They know who hurt them first. We'll see who's haunted by ghosts.

JAMES Bullshit! Their only memory of me is of a father who gave them love and did all he could to protect them. The memory of you will be of their murderer.

MEDEA I hate the sound of your voice.

JAMES And I hate yours. I never want to hear it again.

MEDEA And you won't. So what are we waiting for?

JAMES Just one thing. Leave me my boys' bodies. Let me touch them, kiss them for the last time and then bury them.

MEDEA Hardly. And use them as evidence against me? (*Sweetly.*) Why I didn't do a thing, darling. (*Sharply.*) You will never see them again. (MEDEA *shouts into the room behind her.*) You back there! It's time for us to leave! (*The two men that* EDWARD *left her appear from the back. They pick up the bodies and carry them off. One hears the sound of a car warming up in the background. One might do something with the lighting, and also have faint drums in the background as* MEDEA *goes into supernatural mode with her predictions which are curses.*) I think we've done enough talking now. I'm off. You really underestimated the powers I have. You're a groundless drifter, but I'm rooted in an ancient land: Africa has gods who have taught me lessons I'll never forget. I have one more present for you. I see your future James. You will go from job to job. People will think you unlucky, and that's death in Vegas. You start to drink...and drink...and drink. And one day...but that's a story for another day. I can only say, you will never be able to drink enough to forget. You think you suffer now. But wait until you are old.

JAMES Goddamn you, Medea!

MEDEA The gods are on my side, James. At least some gods. Gods you laughed at and whose powers you always underestimated. You and your "civilized" world.

JAMES Unclean murderous whore. Child-killer!

MEDEA I think you should go home and scrape your wife off the floor now. It's time for you to bury what's left of your bride.

JAMES Yes. Without my sons. O boys, where are you now?

MEDEA Loved by me, not you.

JAMES Yet you killed them?

MEDEA Yes. To make you suffer.

JAMES How I long to hold them in my arms.

MEDEA Too late. Bye darling.

(MEDEA *leaves. Sound of car driving off: a really neat souped-up car reving up (as for a drag race) followed by the sound of a chopper taking off...then silence for a little ...slightly unbearable....then:*)

JAMES Fuck you, you bitch from hell. I want to erase you from my life and memory. (*Something cracks inside* JAMES. *He wanders around the room.*) Boys, Boys? Can you hear me? Daddy's home.

Silence.

THE END

AN INTERVIEW WITH
MARIANNE MCDONALD

Q: What was the impetus behind adapting "Medea"?

MM: It's one of my favorite plays because it empowers women. It shows the strength of Greek tragedy where the female characters have never been surpassed in complexity and power, not even in Shakespeare. I also knew that Greek tragedy was performed by men (as many Japanese classical dramas). I wanted to investigate the complex sexuality in every human being, of the men and women in each. Jung certainly recognized that. By switching gender, it also forces the viewer to think about these questions.

Q: The play links South Africa and Vegas, reimagining Medea's journey from Colchis to Athens. What made you use those as modern equivalencies?

MM: I didn't have that mythical journey in mind. I wanted a new myth. I wanted to have Medea escape to a new glitzy place, where she could shine as the showgirl she was. Both Las Vegas and Cape Town are tourist places also riddled with crime. Medea gets away with her crime and goes free. She is the first terrorist, murdering innocents. Oddly enough, we cheer "her" on. When I teach Medea, most women are on her side; many men on Jason's. Athol Fugard and I wrote two works called Medea: The Beginning and Jason: The End. We performed them as linked readings in Dublin, in Cape Town and in England. I win the audience over in the first part, Jason seduces them in the second. The children only appear to him as ghosts; Medea lost that privilege by murdering them.

Q: Some critics asked if a man in drag could "possess the maternal feelings that make the female Medea's crime so appalling?" Could he?

MM: Any man or any woman can love an adopted child; some adopted children are preferable to one's genetic children and can be loved even more. As Orestes said, "Relatives are a given, but we choose our friends."

Q: And how do you think making Medea, arguably the most "feminist" character in Athenian drama, a man, transform the character and the play?

MM: I don't think it changed the character or the play at all. In both plays the Jasons are upwardly mobile, simply interested in success and money that endorses success, as well as the outward trappings. Medea, here and in the original speaks a different language...The language of the loving heart versus Jason's language of the calculating mind. Many men still cannot fathom this difference (Men are from Mars, Women are from Venus). Many women support a man for years, only for him to abandon her for a young trophy wife. It is a cliché.

Q: The play received very good reviews in its Southern California production (one critic calling it near perfect). How has it been received in South Africa, where three years after the play premiered, the government became the fifth in the world to legalize same-sex marriage but also where there has been a very conflicted history of acceptance of homosexuality?

MM: Neville Englebrecht who co-authored Happy Endings Are Extra with Ashraf Johaardien, a South African reworking of the Oedipus myth in a gay context, wants to bring Medea, Queen of Colchester to South Africa. So I shall tell you after those performances what the reaction is. As you point out, same-sex marriage is legal there, but there are still hate crimes; I suspect many of them are committed by some conservatively raised self-hating gays. My heart goes out to both of them. (That's my Buddhist reaction).

Q: Given that the play is ten years old this year, if you were to reimagine it today, would there be any changes as a result of new realities in South Africa (or, for that matter, in Las Vegas)?

MM: Perhaps now since in the new South Africa you can't be black enough, whereas under apartheid you couldn't be white enough, I can only say much of the same abuse is the same. Wealth is concentrated in the hands of a few at the top. Is this different from many places in the world? I think the problems between the "wife" that sacrificed herself for her husband, who is then abandoned because that "successful" husband needs a new status symbol, hasn't changed at all. Personally, I wouldn't kill my kids. I, like Medea, love my children to the point that I would then be killing part of myself instead of simply punishing my husband. I don't think a husband who abandons his wife this way is worth it, and the best punishment for him is living with the twit he's chosen as his trophy wife.

BIBLIOGRAPHY

Allan, William. *Euripides: Medea*. London: Duckworth, 2002.

Apollonius. Rhodius. *Argonautica*. Trans. William H. Race. Cambridge: Harvard University Press, 2008.

Aristotle. *Poetics*. Trans. Kenneth McLeish. New York: Theatre Communications Group, 1999.

Bernal, Martin. *Black Athena*. London: Free Association, 1987.

Butler, Guy. *Demea*. Capetown: David Philip, 1990.

Clauss, James L. and Sarah Iles Johnson, eds. *Medea*. Princeton: Princeton University Press, 1997.

Cullen, Countee. *The Medea and Some Poems*. New York: Harper and Brothers, 1935.

Euripides. *Medea*. Trans Rex Warner. In *Euripides I*. Eds. David Grene and Richmond Lattimore. Chicago: University of Chicago Press, 1955.

---. *Medea*. Translated by Ruby Blondell. In *Women on the Edge: Four Plays*. New York: Routledge, 1998.

Ferris, Lesley. *Acting Women: Images of Women in Theatre*. New York: New York University Press, 1989.

Foley, Helene P. *Reimagining Greek Tragedy on the American Stage*. Berkeley: University of California Press, 2012.

Fraden, Rena. *Imagining Medea: Rhodessa Jones and Theatre for Incarcerated Woman*. Chapel Hill: The University of North Carolina Press, 2001.

Gordon, Lewis R., T. Denean Sharpley-Whiting, and Renée T. White, eds. *Fanon: A Critical Reader*. Cambridge: Blackwell, 1996.

Hall, Edith, Oliver Taplin, and Fiona Macintosh, eds. *Medea in Performance, 1500–2000*. Oxford : Legenda/European Humanities Research Centre, University of Oxford, 2000.

Herodotus. *The Histories.* Trans. Robin Waterfield. Ed. Caroline Dewald. Oxford: Oxford University Press, 2008.

Jones, Jennifer. *Medea's Daughters.* Columbus: Ohio University Press, 2003.

McDonald, Marianne. *The Living Art of Greek Tragedy.* Bloomington and Indianapolis: Indiana University Press, 2003.

Pindar. *The Complete Odes.* Trans. Anthony Verity. Oxford; New York: Oxford University Press, 2007.

Pinn, Anthony B. *Varieties of African-American Religious Experience.* Minneapolis: Fortress, 1998.

Ramsay, F. Jeffress. *Africa.* 6th ed. Guilford: Dushkin, 1995.

Wallace-Sanders, Kimberly, ed. *Skin Deep, Spirit Strong: The Black Female Body in American Culture.* Ann Arbor: University of Michigan Press, 2002.

Walton, J. Michael. *Living Greek Theatre.* Westport, CT: Greenwood Press, 1987.

Wetmore, Jr. Kevin J. *Black Dionysus: Greek Tragedy and African-American Theatre.* Jefferson, NC: McFarland and Company, 2003.

---. *The Athenian Sun in an African Sky.* Jefferson, NC: McFarland and Company, 2002.

Wren, Celia. "In Medea Res." *American Theatre* 19.4 (April 2002): 22–25, 60–61.

INDEX

8 Mile, 128

Aegeus, 1, 3, 10, 243–244, 294

African, 4–8, 11, 13–16, 19–20, 23, 25, 45–47, 59, 67–69, 72, 74, 123–124, 145, 225, 242–243, 245, 247, 251–254, 258–259, 262, 264–265, 268, 272–273, 277, 279, 281, 284, 289–291, 294, 299, 318, 337

agrioi, 3

American Conservatory Theatre, 127

American Negro Theatre, 7

American Theatre, 4, 13, 74

Angola, 7, 15

Antigone, 3–4, 11

apolis, 3

Arena Stage, 241

Aristotle, 1, 13, 262

assimilation, 9–10, 16

Ateca, Dorothy, 7

Athens, 1–4, 10, 13, 225, 241, 243–244, 294, 335

Atlantic University, 7

barbaroi, 3

Beloved, 5

Bernal, Martin, 242

Black Athena, 242

Borden, Lizzie, 8

Butler, Guy, 8, 14

California, 13, 17, 219, 223, 245, 293, 337

Cape Town, 293–294, 297, 299–300, 306, 315–318, 320, 325, 336

Caribbean, 7–8, 72, 127–128, 130,

Caribbean (*continued*), 132, 220

Carter, Steve, 127, 130–131, 219

Circe, 10

Civil Rights Movement, 16

Civil War, 5, 7, 306

Clauss, James J, 4, 13, 74

Clytemnestra, 3, 11

Colchis, 3, 5, 71, 129, 242, 244, 247, 256, 263–264, 270, 276–277, 280, 285, 335

Cooper, Edris, 223–224, 227

Cullen, Countee, 6, 14

Damballah, 72, 76–78, 81, 83–85, 87, 90–92, 94, 100–104, 108–109, 112–114, 116–117, 124, 129, 131, 179, 217

dark complexion, 4, 220

Deafman Glance, 5

Demea, 8, 14

Diary of a Mad Black Woman, 10

Dodson, Owen, 7, 67

drag queen, 6, 8, 293–294, 300

drugs, 223, 293, 300–301

East River Players, 15, 17, 67

Egypt, 4, 107, 144–145, 242–244, 246–247, 262, 280, 290

Elektra, 3, 11

Elia, Nadia, 9, 14

ethnicity, 4, 6, 8, 224

Euripides, 1, 4, 6, 8, 10–11, 13, 15–16, 69, 71, 123, 128, 219, 225, 241, 243–244, 289–291, 295

European American, 8, 11, 242

Ferlita, Ernest, 71, 75, 123

Foley, Helene, 6, 9, 13

Fraden, Rena, 225–226
Franklin, Aretha, 224
Garden of Time, 7
Garner, Margaret, 5–6, 8
gay, 230, 293–294, 297, 337
Haley, Alex, 243
Harlem Renaissance, 6–7
Helios, 10
Herodotus, 4, 13, 242, 244, 246–247
Howard University, 7, 15, 67
hybrid, 294
I Can Do Bad All By Myself, 10
*Imagining Medea: Rhodessa Jones
    and Theatre for Incarcerated
    Women*, 225
Jahnn, Hans Henny, 8
Johnson, Sarah Iles, 4, 13, 74
Jones, Jennifer, 8, 14
Jones, Jim, 225, 236
Jones, LeRoi (Amiri Baraka), 243
Jones, Rhodessa, 223, 225–228
Jones, Silas, 8, 241, 243, 245, 289
Jonestown, 225
King, Martin Luther, Jr., 16, 69
Kool-Aid, 225, 236
LaChiusa, John, 7
Las Vegas, 11, 293, 297, 299–300,
    305, 308, 313, 336–337
Ludlam, Charles, 5
Machinal, 8
Madea, 10–11
Magnuson, Jim, 15, 19, 67
male dominance, 9, 128
male oppression, 2, 9, 224
Marie Christine, 7
Mark Taper Forum, 241
McClendon, Rose, 6
McDonald, Marianne, 5, 13, 293,
    297, 335
Medea in Africa, 7

Medea in Performance, 1500–2000, 4,
    13
Medea: A Noh Cycle, 5
*Medea's Daughters: Forming and
    Performing the Woman Who
    Kills*, 8
Medeamaterial, 5
mixed race, 294
Morraga, Cherrie, 5
Morrison, Toni, 5
Müller, Heiner, 5
New World, 16, 39, 45, 72, 121, 243,
    252, 272–273, 293
Ninagawa, Yukio, 5
No Snakes in this Grass, 15, 67, 69
Noble, Thomas Satterwhite, 6
People's Temple, 225
Perry, Tyler, 10
poverty, 223–224, 313
*Reimagining Greek Tragedy on the
    American Stage*, 6, 13
revenge, 2–3, 16, 31, 53, 71, 78, 86,
    127–129, 135, 217, 244, 279, 282,
    294–295, 329
Roots, 243
San Diego Black Ensemble Theatre
    Company, 17
San Francisco, 8, 127, 223–225,
    227–228, 294
San Francisco, 8, 127, 223–225,
    227–228, 294
San Francisco County Jail, 223
Sesostris, 242, 244
sexuality, 9–10, 335
Smith, Susan, 8
Snyder, Ruth, 8
Sorgenfrei, Carol, 5
Staub, Agnes, 8
supernatural, 10, 71–72, 198, 332
Suppliants, 3

Suzuki, Tadashi, 5
The Hungry Woman: The Mexican Medea, 5
The Medea of Euripides: A New Version, 6
Treadwell, Sophie, 8
Tricycle Theatre, 127
urban, 224–225
Victory Gardens Theatre, 127

voodoo, 7, 10, 71–72, 80–81, 86, 90, 97, 124, 127, 129, 294
Wallace-Sanders, Kimberly, 9, 14
Washington, George, 7, 243, 245, 280
Whitaker, Mikal, 15
Wilson, Robert, 5
xenon, 3
Yates, Andrea, 8

CPSIA information can be obtained
at www.ICGtesting.com
Printed in the USA
LVHW090906260821
695894LV00020B/73